Adeline Dutton Train Whitney

Sights and Insights

Vol. II

Adeline Dutton Train Whitney

Sights and Insights
Vol. II

ISBN/EAN: 9783744748360

Printed in Europe, USA, Canada, Australia, Japan

Cover: Foto ©Andreas Hilbeck / pixelio.de

More available books at **www.hansebooks.com**

SIGHTS AND INSIGHTS:

PATIENCE STRONG'S STORY OF OVER THE WAY.

BY

MRS. A. D. T. WHITNEY,

AUTHOR OF "THE OTHER GIRLS," "WE GIRLS," "REAL FOLKS,"
"LESLIE GOLDTHWAITE," ETC.

VOL. II.

BOSTON:
JAMES R. OSGOOD AND COMPANY.
(LATE TICKNOR & FIELDS, AND FIELDS, OSGOOD, & CO.)
1876.

RIVERSIDE, CAMBRIDGE:
STEREOTYPED AND PRINTED BY
H. O. HOUGHTON AND COMPANY

CONTENTS.

SIGHTS AND INSIGHTS.

CHAPTER I.

BEAU SÉJOUR.

. . . .

. . . . We had to change our rooms the next day after. The hotel was crowded, — it was high season at Lugano; and we had only been put in "*tempery*," like dear Aunt Hetty Maria's teeth. Numbers 90 and 92 were engaged for an English family, that was coming in a couple of days.

Mrs. Regis could keep her apartments, and she was well satisfied. They were high, corner rooms, overlooking the lake and garden. We must see what could be done in the "dependance."

Edith and Margaret were sorry to be in different houses; "but *some* of us must stay in the fascinating old monastery," they said. "We mean to explore it all over."

The dépendance was directly upon the lake; its pretty little balconies overhung the water; but it was a damp old building, actually falling into decay in the rear, unused part; and those rooms over the water were more romantic than salubrious, I feared; though they say there is never any fever at Lugano.

Stephen Holabird interested himself for us. He ran up and down, interpreted, reported, suggested. At last he came knocking at my door, hat in hand, late in the afternoon.

"Miss Strong," he said, hurriedly, "if you just want rooms in Paradise, come and see! It's opened to-day; Monsieur B—— is just going over now with a German countess.

We picked up our parasols. We walked through the garden and round a turn of the road, over here to "Beau Séjour." It is a palace-dépendance of the monastery hotel.

Recently bought, and the repairs just finishing, there had been question about opening it quite at present. They had told us nothing of the possibility when they showed us rooms in the lakeside "Belvidere." But the German countess brought it to decision. She and we, and others that would be coming, might "spill over" into it, since the convent was brimful and running over at this very moment.

It is up behind the "Parc,"—set against the hill; a magnificent house, the home and heritage of an old Italian family, dwindled to a last survivor, who gives it up as if to Death and Fate, and wanders away into a world, that has for him no more home in it, since the last life he cared for went out of this.

The enormous saloons, cut up into spacious suites of beautiful lodging rooms. They run round the four sides with doors between them all the way. They look out in every direction, upon some new loveliness. In front, the garden entrance, through which we came to it, slopes away beneath the great stone terrace — an esplanade some eighty feet long and eighteen wide, where stand vases with orange, and lemon, and pomegranate trees. There are two approaches from the high, double iron-and-gilded gateway, over which a big lantern burns at night. The one, straight to the door, is a broad avenue of horse-chestnuts, grown into a solid hedge of twenty feet in height. The other turns away to the right and comes up by the wall; it is an arcade of laurels, trained over trellises, till the huge stems make their own strong, twisted frame-work; it is thick with glossy heavy leafage. Over the tops of all these trees you see, from the upper windows, out upon the lake, that lies, clear blue, at the feet of a ring of mountains. But upon this you must look with me presently; when I get settled, and take you with me to my very own window.

One side stands upon the street; but across it you still rest your eyes upon the water and the hills. The perfect green cone of St. Salvador is right before you. The other side runs up along the edge of the park and ravine, and looks above them toward a grand height, where another palace stands. At the back is a lovely garden, all flowers and radiance near the house, — a fountain playing into a pond with little fish in it, — statues, and lanterns, and flower-pots of tilework along the walls and up the balustrade of the long flight of steps leading to the wilderness; at the upper end the garden loses itself in a little wood.

The large doors at front and back stand open; across the polished inlaid floors, and between the marble-wainscoted walls of hall and saloon, you look through, and see the flowers, and the fountain playing, and the dimness of the little forest shade beyond all. We went up the grand staircases, their sides ceiled with colored stone work, into upper corridors, from which open dining and drawing-rooms, and which lead around to the apartments among which we came to choose. Think of our having "our pick," — next to the German countess, who entered and moved on just before us, — of all these rooms, delightful in height and aspect, in finishing and furnishing; curtained and frescoed, — with new, luxurious-looking beds and pillows piled up on the pretty bedsteads, — sofas drawn to the windows, easy-chairs rolled into the cosy corners; Venetian blinds outside the windows, and straw blinds in, — a smell of newness and freshness about everything, and the soft balm of summer air rushing in as soon as we set back a sash! Of the glory that disclosed itself to sight, I must tell you separately.

It was two francs more a day to live here, and we should have to go down to the hotel for meals. But should n't we get our forty cents worth? Edith demanded. And was n't it just a delight to go to and fro under those laurel and chestnut shades? There was only the bit bend of sunny road, and a little dust, perhaps, as we went, — And if it rained? It would n't, for weeks yet, they told us, and when it did, there would be voitures sent over.

I have dwelt on the description because it was to be our home for perhaps-two months. Here we would really settle down. Edith would have a piano; they were to be readily procured in the town, Monsieur assured us. And for singing lessons, if we desired, there was the Cathedral organist, a professor from Milan, and a trainer of voices for the stage. Emery Ann and I would sew, knit, paint, write; sit in the garden, walk in the park; we would all sail on the lake in the twilights and moonlights. We would drink in fragrance, and color, — we would rest in the peace of the shadowed waters. Mountain excursions? All at once we were willing to give them up. The "sweet do nothing" of Italy took gently hold of us. In

Switzerland there is a keen excitement, an eager passion; its stimulating air, its tumultuous grandeurs make you restless, hurry you on. Here you are content to be still yourself, and look up to that which lifts itself above you.

Emery Ann said: "The mountains are *there;* let 'em mount!"

At first when they found how beautiful it was, Mrs. Regis and Margaret were inclined to change their own quarters. But their quaint old convent rooms held their own special charm; the cool windows, deep set in the thick stone walls and balconies outside, looked into the bright lower garden, and the band played exquisite music every evening underneath; they would have access here by our being here, and they would not need to traverse the distance when they did not feel like it; we could mutually accommodate each other. The young folks would investigate all the captivating mazes of the ancient church and cloister, — all the sweet recesses of the glens and gardens. We were at the delicious beginning of an idyl, — a romance.

Who knows?

I said "young folks," for Stephen Holabird seemed to belong to us right off. It was enough, almost, that he came from Massachusetts; he was from the dear, little, old door-yard. He sat with Emery Ann and me that very afternoon, among the oleanders by the fountain; and he told us about himself, and his home, and his people. His sister Barbara, wife of Lieutenant Goldthwaite of the Katahdin, is in Nice with her husband; the ship is stationed there for the winter. Harry had had leave, he said, and they had been traveling with him in Switzerland. He himself had just finished at the Sillig Institute, and now they had written him from home — amongst them — to stay abroad a while and see something more. He was to spend most of the winter, he supposed, in Italy. I came to understand the "amongst them," gradually.

Stephen was the youngest of them at home, growing up through hobbledehoyhood, he says, while his three sisters were turning into women all at once, and dropping away out of the Westover nest. He missed them, awfully. I could not think how jolly it was to him to be with a girl again. He had fancied, when Barbara married into the navy, that the navy was the

finest thing in the world for anybody — man or woman —
to be in; and he talked Annapolis and the Academy till the
rest of the family began to think it was serious, and he —
began in his own mind to have misgivings that it was n't.
So he told his father one day that he wished he could find out
whether he was most sailor or doctor, and whether his sea-
notion was anything more than a notion of getting a sea-look
at the world. And his father, if you will believe it, Rose, had
the sense to respect him for not quite knowing his own mind,
and for knowing that he did n't. So "amongst them," and that
meant, chiefly, at that time, amongst his Uncle Roderick and
Aunt Jane, who are the rich heads of the family and have n't
any children, and who did n't always — (this is an insight,
partly) make much allowance for there being any human growing, and so wanting, in the world, and particularly over at
brother Stephen's, but who had come to it beautifully by means ·
of " Ruth and Revelation " in time for him; — amongst them
they sent him over here to see the world and learn French and
German at Vevay. " Ruth " is his youngest " sister-in-love ; "
cousin, really, but always one of them, and especially of him ;
married to a rich young Mr. Thayne; *he* did n't say rich, exactly, but it was a corollary from things he did say, and I have
heard of Mr. Thayne elsewhere. So Ruth, I fancy, has come
into the amongstness this time (that is n't a very bad word,
Rose, is it ?) and a birthday happened to him a month ago, and
a nice letter of credit was a family gift that came to his hands
the very day, and here he is. I thought I might as well run
off the whole string while I was about it. Of course he did n't
say it all at once and at first ; especially that about Edith.

And — just a little more, and you will know Stephen as well
as I did, when he had said most of these things; that is when I
had known him in the greatest intimacy — the intimacy of a
boy with an elderly woman he takes to, — for a fortnight, after
which other things began to happen, that I must take hold of
presently.

I suppose he must know he is bright; he has been born and
brought up in a brightness, — of a family who have had some
rubs to bring the sparks out; but I wonder if he knows how

deep he is? Think of his telling me that he found out there was a fascination *behind* the fascination that was in a ship and the sea; that its coming so near being a live thing in a live element was what did it, so far as it was anything beyond the glory of the flag, and the bewitchment of novelty and adventure; that *life* — and its secrets, and the helps and management of it — in plants and trees and animals and human creatures, — had been the centre and solution of all his bents and proclivities ever since he began to have any. That he could always make things grow; he could graft trees, and bud roses, and nurse up difficult cuttings; he could raise late chickens and young canaries; he could cure sick puppies, and prescribe for horses; natual history, organic chemistry, anatomy, the microscope, — they were his older delights; yes, he grew surer and surer, that as some people had an instinct for justice and the reasons why, — and some for faith and inward illuminations, and some for mechanical forces and the works coöperative alongside, — and some for the multiplication table and trade and rolling up percentages and interest, — and some for government and political economy, — his gifts and affinities all have hold among lifes, breaths, growths; there was where his work must be. And a physician could serve his country too, in the navy or the army, if he had a mind, or upon occasion; that would come after. But a physician was what he was going to be. He was satisfied when he had got to the root of the matter. Think of a boy going so deep as that.

He and Edith are friends outright, and most open allies. It was n't in regard to them and their seventeen and eighteen years, — except the simple life and joy of them — that I talked about an idyl and said, " Who knows? " as I find I did a few pages ago.

Who knows — what Mrs. Regis wrote to General Rushleigh, for instance, and what will come of it? For she had a letter from Ragatz, — I suppose she expected it, — and she sent an answer.

You can "put yourself in her place," — and guess, doubtless, as well as I can. Maybe, better. For you have John, and I have never had — yes — the telegraph lines run through some little " uncalled " heart-battery in my woman nature, and I *can* count the clicks.

Something like this perhaps, — " We find it charming at Lugano. An old monastery, — a waterside dépendance, — a modern palace; these make our hotel-world, and an excellently delightful one. We are resting upon our Alpine experience, — taking it in and living it over. Miss Strong and her friend are very tired, and we shall all remain here several weeks. I hope your way down into Italy will lie our way. You can find nothing more exquisite." — And then, at the very last, run across one corner, perhaps, one line; — " Do you know I half fancy you had some little mistake in your mind when I talked last with you ? "

Yes ; I think she would leave it something like that. Nothing for *her*, necessarily, to take up again, if he did not ask ; but something, if her guess, her hope, — yes, and mine equally, — were true, might bring him swiftly and certainly to her side again.

We have got our trunks from Geneva. It is nice to see the girls in their pretty summer muslins, after the weeks of whisk brooms and traveling dresses. And even I, with my best black silk and fresh white ruffles and modest lace coiffure and a little lavender bow at my throat, because it was the color mother-dic loved, — feel a much daintier self again. Emery Ann still wears the brown satin braid and the " half-piece." But she got a new one in Paris, and somehow they have come to be a part of her, though underneath I think something is shining toward a more beautiful revelation, one of these days, that she will, one way or another, be persuaded to. The braid is sturdy honesty ; " not that she could cheat anybody with ropes of hair," she says ; " but that it owns right out she knows she has no business to have ropes of hair." The half-piece is thin and possible; what she might have a right to ; " sober and decent," twisted up plainly behind. " You know I have n't a particle of knack with caps," she says, " and I could n't fuss with 'em. That *would* be vanity and vexation of spirit." But she wears a black lace barbe when I put it on for her.

Mrs. Regis, in her white morning dresses, and her black vel-

vet polonaise for the cool evenings, — is — just exactly Mrs.
Regis, — royal-beautiful. She is very much looked at; no young
girl at the dinner table, or in the drawing-room is followed with
half so many eyes.

Margaret and Edith sing together with Signor ——; we all
have French conversations, three times a week, in my room,
with a nice, funny little elderly Mademoiselle. She "racontes"
us something, — and she tells a story to admiration, — and then
we try how much of it we can "raconter" back. In the midst
of it usually arrives the old woman with hot chestnuts, that are
boiled for us every day; great things, the size of horse-chestnuts
with us, and plump to the shining skins with rich, sweet nut-
meal. These are what the poor peasants live on, — and we
should think they might. We always have a Swiss fruit basket,
a straw satchel with two handles, hanging in our coolest window,
full of white grapes.

We go down, early in the morning, especially on the Tues-
day market-day, — into the arcaded streets, to lay in our sup-
plies. Such heaps of white and purple grapes, and white and
purple figs, and yellow lemons lying among their stems and
leaves, and pomegranates, and apricots, and plums, and such
fabulous cheapness; we think seventy centimes a pound for
such grapes as we never saw in our dreams before, quite an
imposition; we know that ninety is insufferable; and we choose
out our bunches.

Coming back we are apt to stray into the cool, dingy old
church, where there are almost always a few peasants kneeling,
and an artist or two with easels, near the door, making copies
of the queer old fresco above the altar by Luini; I say queer,
honestly, for it was the first impression to our untrained eyes,
though it is said to have been one of his finest works. It is the
Crucifixion.

The meanings and the beauty dawn upon you, as you look,
from the old dimming colors. It came to be more to me at
last, than many a greater painting afterward, that I had no
chance to see day after day, and live into.

There are seven distinct subjects — or scenes — blended into
one picture by different groupings. Foremost and central, the

scene on Calvary. The Roman centurions, on splendid horses, soldiers bearing spears and banners, Jewish dignitaries, cruel and solemn, watching their work; common people, who had "heard him gladly," — some who may have been healed by him; there is one figure, thin and mournful, perhaps recently restored, perhaps come too late for healing, sitting close by the base of the cross; — disciples worshiping and weeping; the Virgin fainting in the arms of the other Maries; women of Jerusalem, with little children, turning their faces away with their babies clinging and shrinking as if they knew of the weeping that was to be for the children; even animals crouching, howling, down among the feet of the crowd.

Above all the three crosses; the tall banners floating in the air between; the central Figure, white, pure, — meek and sweet in every outline; — the others, more or less contorted, and more or less darkened with the life stain that is in them; the impenitent malefactor nearly black, his face hopelessly turned away; the repentant and believing one with his head bowed toward Jesus, and a rest stealing over the upper limbs and muscles, his very flesh whitening under the new pardon and cleansing, while over his head kneels an angel, withdrawing the escaping soul in the figure of a naked, spotless child. Over the left hand cross, a horrible devil, with skinny wings and horned head, and forked and twisted tail, *squirms* exultingly, grasping a black, writhing, ghastly little shape that is the new-born infernal.

These are the grotesque elements in the representation, as you see it first, at mere outside. And I give you, in all, rather the inward than the outward picture; for in line and detail I cannot see in these old works, what I do see behind line and detail, — the strong suggestion, and intent, and insight of the painter.

The upper grouping fills the gable angle of the church. It is of white-winged angels and cherub heads gathered close above and about the head of the Crucified; two are leaning on the cross-arms, a hand of each resting on the nailed hand of Jesus; lower, around him, even to his knees, and to the spear points, and the uplifted sponge, and between the banners of proud authority, float others, reaching and bending towards Him, the hands almost touching the flesh in which

23

yet He suffers. Highest of all, a lovely face in the very apex, white wings and tenderly drooping arms following the roof outline, and soft-robed knees resting upon a cloud, from which a cherub head leans over the lettering of Pilate.

Back of all this, in the middle distance, are seen, right and left, the Bearing of the Cross, and the Burial in Joseph's Tomb. Right and left again of these, in sections of pillared architecture, the Crowning and Mocking, and the "Neither do I condemn thee," to the Woman in the Temple. Above these last two, as in the distance again, the Agony in the Garden and the Ascension.

Out of the first confusion grows the gradual thought of how those old artists knew, or said unconsciously, that all things of Life are one, and all are present. That already the Lifting-up and the Agony, — the toilsome Cross-bearing and the peace of the new Tomb, — the gibing crowd and the near-breathing angels, are over against and counterpoising. That there is a correlation even, between the Christ of the thorns and the scourge and the mocking suffered for sin, — and the human soul under its sin-caused shame and pain, yet franchised inwardly by the word of Him only that condemneth; the "Christ that died," since the Christ in us was dead; but is "risen again, and maketh intercession for us!" That raiseth up Himself in us, even at the last day!

Our letters have not come. A small packet only, of old dates, was forwarded from Geneva with the luggage. There is some miscarriage or mistake. The delays on this side are so hard to us who are the exiles, while we know how straight all our own letters go back to you! Another illustration of the rolling stones. You, quiet at Dearwood, get all that is meant for you; we are continually running away from and dodging what should come to us.

Margaret writes to her sister; I think she lets those other letters wait. Because hers are always replies; in her conditional understanding with Harry Mackenzie, it is quite natural that she should wait for him, not ever taking the lead. I wish we could know what *are* lost, and what may never have been written.

CHAPTER II.

THE CLOISTERS: A PROWL.

. . . .

. . . . WE had just got through the pleasant, long dinner.

The dining-room is the ancient refectory in the old convent. It is a queer old hall, high vaulted, with windows above windows. I wonder if it was always so, or if the lower ones have been let in. Emery Ann wonders how they ever washed the upper ones. The sills are six feet, I should think, above the head of a man. There is a gallery in one of the long sides, and there are doors that open into parts of the building apparently not in use by the hotel.

Between the courses I often sit and fancy how it was here twenty years ago, when the monks in their gowns and cowls filed in, and crossed themselves, and said their prayers before they ate; and I got lost in a dream, from which Gasparo, — our handsome Gasparo, with the scar across his cheek and lip, that he got fighting under Garibaldi, — wakes me, touching my shoulder, as he puts two fruit baskets in between Edith and me; and I come suddenly into the scene of the moment; — the long tables, flashing with lights and flowers and wine, the closely-seated "Messieurs et mesdames les voyageurs," in handsome, if not elaborate, dinner dress, — the grim-looking, but charming-to-talk-to, old Russian count at the head of our board, nodding or scowling imperiously at the waiters over the dishes they serve him with, — the German Professorin opposite, with certainly a "whole piece" if Emery Ann's is "half," and eating in her spectacles, who also, at this instant, is sweeping a whole basketful of grapes upon her plate, and even into her lap, while the man who holds it struggles with amusement, and we find it hard not to let our glances meet his, — the nice Prussians from Leipsic, mother and three daughters, all so fair and sonsy and merry together ; — and, close by, our own elegant Mrs. Regis, speaking French with an Italian army-officer, — Margaret, with bits of scarlet and white verbenas, and a dropping ivy spray in her hair, — and Edith and Stephen Holabird laughing together as they pick out their walnuts, and plan something eagerly with which they turn to me presently.

"Miss Patience, — there's just one corner left that we have n't gone into. We want to find out how the old friars got into the church from here, and we have never been able to discover. You 'll go with us to-night, won't you ? "

They had got into a way, after dinner, of striking off " on a prowl," through the long corridors and by-turns of the building; they had enticed Emery Ann into it, who said she went " because it was proper," but really, I 'm sure because she was " proper " pleased. She has a turn under her primitiveness and sober sense for mystery and wild romance, and is secretly looking out for the Castle of Udolpho, and wants to stop at Modena to see the Orsini palace and the old oaken chest Ginevra hid in. It is a capital thing for some of the unconfessed nonsense in our own natures that we elderly folks have the young ones to " see after."

" Do, auntie," says Edith, " we 'll take it all in review, if you will ; and you won't know, in the very least, where you are."

Which was a state of blessedness to make some effort for.

The orchestra in the garden was playing lovely airs from Strauss as we came to the broad recessed window at the intersection of the main passage on our way from the dining-room. We sat there on the sofas for a few minutes, breathing the fragrant air, and listening. The crowd was passing down the staircase, and pouring into the drawing-rooms and out upon the walks and terraces. Some men were fixing pieces of fire-works among the shrubbery, to be let off by and by.

Mrs. Regis went to her room for a shawl, — that exquisite white Shetland thing, so large and light and fleecy, that she flings over head and dress and shoulders, and makes a vision of herself in.

" We will meet you in the drawing-room, mamma, or find

you in the garden," said Margaret. "You won't mind for a little while? We are going to explore."

Mrs. Regis was sure enough not to be alone, unless she chose. She had her own circle here of English and Americans, already ; and the Russian count, and the Italian colonel, and the English clergyman, who played chess, were always at her service. So she only said, with a little gracious surprise, " You, too, Miss Patience ? " and left us at the head of the stairs.

" First," said Stephen Holabird, " we go up. That heightens the effect."

" Naturellement," said Edith, laughing.

We went up till we came to the life-size picture upon the stair-way wall, however it happened there, — of the Emperor Nicholas on horseback at a review of troops ; then we turned to the left and walked away down the wide, vaulted passage, past the closely ranged doors of the old cells, remaining here unal-- tered, — into the gloom of the far unlighted end. A window looked out upon the roof and towers of the old church, solemn in the faint young moonlight. The bell swung and sounded. The trees of the park and the woods of the mountain behind it, rose dark and still at the left.

" Have you shaken off the gay dinner-world and got the clatter of the dishes out of your ears? Have you forgotten the people and the fire-works, and the coffee-tables on the terrace ? Do you feel eerie ? " said Stephen.

One might easily forget and shake off. We were in utter stillness. There was a pause, even, in the far-off music.

Edith turned to a dark opening on the right. It was the head of a staircase that plunged into perfect blackness.

" You are not going down there ? " I said. " You cannot see your way. And how do you know — how *did* you know where it might take you ? "

" What fun would there be, auntie, if it were all lighted up, and we knew just where it went to ? "

I saw I must not object to the very mystery I came for. We felt our way, stepping cautiously, one after another, down, down, ever so far, till I felt lost in the depths between the walls. At last we came to the foot and found a turn. We groped along a chill, stone passage to a place where the dense darkness was broken as by an aperture. We came to an open door-way, and passed into a second subterranean passage, — as I fancied, — where we could just discern each other's figures. Light stole in feebly from somewhere. We followed towards it retracing the direction of our descent, turned to the left, and came into the beginning of a dim arcade. Emery Ann stopped me.

"Where do you presume you are?" she said, with the tone of a Grand Master, or something, initiating an under craftsman.

"I am past presuming," I answered. "I humbly wish to know."

"The very mood of mind which immediately precedes knowledge," said Stephen Holabird, and gave me his arm. Ten steps more and we were quietly promenading the north cloister. Before us was the glass door and the inner hall, through which the lights and the moving groups in the garden were visible beyond. The moonlight was reflected in the high court-yard beside us, and along the opposite arcade was the usual passing to and fro of servants and visitors about the bureau and the entrance halls and staircases.

We walked across the paved court, and Stephen turned us toward the great stairs. I felt pretty sure by this time that wherever we were going he knew the way already, and that he had not gone blundering about those dark places with the two girls and Emery Ann, without some previous reconnoitring. So I went merrily and confidingly along with him, pleased with the play.

We climbed four flights of the broad stone stairs, and turned from the high landing into the sarcophagus passages. Along these to the far eastern angle we made our way.

"Somewhere in this wall," Stephen said, "must have been the church communication; though I fancy it was more likely to be farther toward the chancel. This, you see, is just at the front. *That* is a bedroom; there's a perfect net-work of little rooms here, leading every way, if you could only go through them to the opposite doors. But we'll try this stair-way, and see where it will bring us out."

It was a corner flight, winding down and down. Doors opened from each little landing, on the end nearest the church, but they were all closed. A light iron rail ran all the way, at the edge of the solid granite steps. The lamps far back in the galleries we had passed gave us just light and just dimness enough to be exciting. We knew, of course, that nothing in the world would come of our investigations; that the mystery and the marvel had been all swept out long ago; that the old religious and romantic life had been, not scattered suddenly, but let die out in years; until two old men, of all the ancient brotherhood, had gone out from these vast walls to leave them to secular uses, and themselves to die elsewhere. But we made our own marvel as we went along. We imagined more, perhaps, than had ever been there.

We came down into an enchanting depth and blindness again. We seemed to be in a sort of square cellar. We moved cautiously, straight on, feeling our steps and holding our arms before our faces. Pits and pools might be there; did it never seem so in your own room, if you got up or groped about at midnight?

At last, — and Stephen let us make it as much "at long and at last" as we liked, — a dimness was just visible again upon our right. It was up a little, above us. We felt and found some steps. We went up through a door-way, and down again on the other side. Now we were in an outer room or cavern, apparently; we could discern walls, and another door-way. Crossing to this, we came into a square recess, open wholly on one side, to which we advanced, and lo! the paved archway under the front, — the court-yard lanterns, — a large voiture landing passengers and luggage at the stair foot, and behind it, just driven in, and stopping our own egress, a lighter, single carriage, in which sat a traveler, busy with picking up his books and sticks and wraps.

"Wait a minute," I said, softly, and drew back. The gentleman looked round.

The light from the porter's room opposite fell, as I did so, upon Margaret's white dress as she stood beside me, and made the blossoms in her hair gleam bright.

A voice said, "Miss Margaret!" And Paul Rushleigh, one

arm piled full, sprang from the vehicle, and with his other hand grasped hers.

He did not even look surprised to see us there.

It seemed suddenly to me as if he had found just what he had expected ; the *where* never occurred to him.

We all began to explain. I don't think he listened to us much. There had surely come a change over his manner. He let himself seem very glad; gladder than he had ever openly showed himself before.

Of course we did not stop there. He had the voiturier to attend to, — the porters were coming round him, — Monsieur himself, released from the first party, advanced to listen to his requirements. All we said was very common words ; we were delighted to meet him ; it was very odd ; we should see him again later; we would tell Mrs. Regis he had come. And then we slid round into the arcade again, and passed by the open salle à manger, and went in at the far end of the full drawing-room.

Edith told Mrs. Regis. "Just think," she announced, as we came up to her among a group of people, outside upon the terrace, where they were watching the inflating of a fire-balloon, — "General Rushleigh has just come. We explored right upon him in the porte-cochère. And we have been losing ourselves delightfully !"

"In very safe company," said Mrs. Regis, smiling ; "I imagine Miss Strong and Mr. Holabird were not exactly lost. I think, Mrs. Ashknowe," she continued, speaking to the English lady beside her, "I must decide after all, if you will excuse me, to give up the boating for *this* evening. General Rushleigh is a particular friend whom we were expecting."

She received it very quietly. She was coolly heedful of our American propriety in those English eyes. And she had expected him, as I supposed. But there was a fresh lighting in her face, a quickened glow in her superb beauty. Her lips took the curve which has a live joy in its repose.

Margaret stood a little aside, and watched the fire-works, silently. A splendid rocket shot into the air, arched itself over our heads, and broke in green and golden stars. In the blaze of it I saw her clear, uplifted look that followed it.   And there were stars in her eyes also.

But General Rushleigh had been very long in coming.   This was our third week at Lugano.

He told us he had left Ragatz upon the thirtieth.   He had come down to Como, and had been staying at Cadenabbia.

He must have received Mrs. Regis's letter before he left Ragatz.

CHAPTER III.

GRAVEN IMAGES.

. . . .

. . . . EVERYTHING was certainly very different from what it had been a month before. General Rushleigh was allowing himself a frank pleasure with Margaret; as frank as hers with him. It was easier perhaps here, among all these people. It was more as it had been on shipboard, where all were thrown together in such freedom of intercourse, that there was no particularity with any. It was not an alternative, as it had been in those Alpine journeys, between one *tête-à-tête* or another. General Rushleigh was not less with Mrs. Regis; only more with all the rest of us. When he turned from her, he did not leave her alone. We were in the midst of society. The charming society of a quiet, unceremonious place, where people came to be at ease, and felt the sort of fellowship that grows out of the relaxation of rule and formality.

I think it was only I — and Margaret herself — who detected the difference; a difference as of some curb-rein let go with which he had been continually checking himself. He fell into pleasant drifts of talk with her now, and resigned himself to their flow, as he would with anybody; not catching himself up at every little, special access of interest, or approach of personality, and changing or dropping the subject. He did not keep aloof from her side, and carefully join himself to some other, when we all walked together. He did nothing, as yet, which was really the reverse; he did not make her his evident object, — it seems to me that this is always a high and delicate test of gentlemanhood, — and yet, to me, who felt an underpulse in all these things, there was a plain perception, that as it had been she from whom he went away, it was to her now that he was come back.

Could it have been Mrs. Regis's letter? Had he understood more, or differently, from it than she meant? Or had she meant that he might understand either way? Had she put it to thoroughly brave and honest proof? Yet Mrs. Regis herself seemed so very content. I thought she had a surer look than ever, in those few first days.

There will be some things, here and henceforth, in my story, Rose, — for I admit now that I do find myself dropping into a story in the light of a friend, though I by no means set out to do so, — which will get in where I think they belong, though I may have come to the knowledge and understanding of them afterwards. There may even be bits of pure insight — of links I could not give as literal fact — but which in that which supplements facts and feels how they must have joined, is just as real with us all as the things we are direct eye or ear witnesses of. For witness is larger than eye or ear can make it; and we wit well of many things that we would never prove.

For example, that very first morning after breakfast, when General Rushleigh and Mrs. Regis paced up and down the garden path together, from the terrace where we were sitting over to the gate at the foot of the cliff walk; I know they talked of his coming, and touched vaguely, doubtless, upon the immediate why. I knew he thanked her for writing as she had done, and he said something, — for I heard that as they came back once to the end of the flags where my chair was, — of waiting at Ragatz and afterwards at Cadenabbia for letters from home, which he was expecting, and had telegraphed for to the Lucerne bankers. This explained something of the why not, at which I had wondered.

I am sure she could not volunteer any fuller explanation of her own written words. Unless he asked, how could she say anything more about that mistake? And yet it was in both their minds.

Some day he would ask; was it not what he had come back for? He would begin again, — " If I could have felt that I had a right, — if I could have replaced what you would lose; " and then, on some such word as this, might not hers be, — " But this is what you have misunderstood; I should *not* lose, — I could not lose by anything you would tell me "?

It was this that waited between them, — waited only for a little while, — in Mrs. Regis's apprehension; as she walked back and forth with him under the magnolia-trees, that were coming into their late, white splendor. For at Lugano there are two blossom-seasons.

Whatever she might have resolved to face as possible when she sent that letter, whatever she felt she risked in her own disabusal by taking a course that should " make all plain," and disabuse certainly either herself or me, — even though she had, out of honest courage or just for " thorough comfortableness," shaped her expressions that they might bear either way, — his presence or his manner had replaced her in her first confident belief; that which she thought he had given her a right to believe, when he stood with her upon the top of Rhigi. He was thanking her for letting him come back; for understanding, — trusting him; and she was putting in most reticent, womanly phrases, her entire reliance, her faith in his friendship, whatever might seem or not seem. " But, — or only, — or perhaps, — " and her pause there, which he met with no question, would be the nearest she would venture toward that which was still unexplained, unless he so divined it that he required no more.

But — only — perhaps. In his mind any word like one of these, would link itself, possibly, quite differently. Perhaps, — he himself, I think, was certain of it, — he was quite wise to wait yet longer. There was quite a new attitude for him to take. There were other things for him to make sure of, now that he had been assured his own chief hesitation had been needless.

So, as I said, Mrs. Regis read all one way, and was very content. Content to wait his way, and time, and reasons. It touched me, — this trust and sweetness in her. Yet I could only wait also, and hope but for the truth : since the truth alone and always, is the one best thing for all.

As for Margaret, she had her friend again. I think she would have resented, if any one had so much as *looked* a thought that he was more. She would have angrily contemned herself, if she had suspected in the least the happy calm of her own feeling, that asked nothing, resting only in the present.

She looked up to him. He was older, wiser; he was just her friend. Girls do not always know the deepest thing when it first comes. They who are capable of the deepest are not watching and sounding for it. I believe there is a time with every such affection, — the heavenliest time, perhaps, — when it has absolutely nothing yet to do with passion, when it does not even covet jealously to itself, but joys and glories simply in what is.

I dare say you recollect, as I do in writing these sentences, that first little careful, scrupulous act of Margaret, when General Rushleigh had just become her friend; that letter she put uppermost in the pile when we gave him our ship-mail for Queenstown.

Yes; but a girl will often be shy and scrupulous of those little outside beginnings of intimacy, concerning which she has imbibed her technical, traditional notions of delicate honor, when there is yet not the least question with her of anything but very general and remote contingencies. If there is anything to make known, a sincere woman will want it made known then, — beforehand. After that, she is not afraid to make friends; and I insist that a girl who is not poisoned by bad romance, will rest for a long time in a friendship, before she finds out at some unlooked-for crisis, that it has got to be either a great deal more, or drift away from her and leave her to a desolation. That lives, in this world, must often either make one or part utterly.

We used to get up early at Beau Séjour.

It was so beautiful to wake when the first light touched the dark top of St. Salvadore, and spread along Generoso and Caprino, and slid down softly upon the still lake. I got in the way of waking for it, even when I slept again.

The Lord walked abroad in the cool of His day. Did you ever remember that there are *two* " cools of the day?"

Mrs. Regis was usually late. Margaret often came up through the chestnut avenue, and met me on the stone esplanade, where we walked together, before we went down and gathered our party at the hotel for breakfast. General Rushleigh, an early riser also, would sometimes join her in these days, when she came out through the garden, and we three had many a lovely morning time together. In all such ways as these, but never singling and separating her, he fell more and more into companionship with her. I could see that some delicate feeling still kept him partly back, but that gently, gradually, and as of a purpose, he made himself more known to her, and let her make herself more simply, unrestrainedly, manifest to him.

Then there were rambles through the town. Our forenoon market-stroll often extended beyond the streets, up the long, steep, paved way, perhaps, to the Cathedral, and thence around and down again behind the town, till we came into the walled lane-way, that ran between our garden and the ravine, and brought us to the long terrace steps behind the fountain. Mrs. Regis did not walk much for mere walking. She was a good traveler, by rail, or horseback, or carriage ; she held out well in shopping or in sightseeing ; but her habit was, otherwise, to make few excursions. She was almost always to be found on our return, in charming toilet, with unruffled hair, and cool, pure complexion, in the garden, or by a drawing-room window, occupied with some delicate needle-work or a book, either of which was easily laid aside. I noticed that she played fewer games of chess with the English clergyman ; at any rate, that they were apt to be over before we came. After that, General Rushleigh quite devoted himself to her, in the same friendly, intimate way they had always had together.

Then there were the evenings, after we had been listening to the orchestra, under the shadows of the ilexes and magnolias ; when he would, of a natural courtesy, accompany us out-lodgers up the little hill and through the stately, lovely avenue to Beau Séjour, where we said our good-nights on the esplanade, with the lights shining behind us through the wide, high halls, and the fountain gleaming and tinkling in the garden back of all.

One day we had just filled our baskets with grapes and apricots at the old woman's stand at the far end of the street arcade, when General Rushleigh and Stephen came across the public square beyond, from the Post-office. "No letters yet ?" we asked Stephen, as he held up empty hands. "No answer from Geneva even?"

"Perhaps that will come to-morrow. They are looking them up, I suppose."

We had had no letters from Geneva for almost a month. Nothing from home of later date than August 15. General Rushleigh knew that we had been wondering and expecting, but he did not know how long.

At this moment he turned rather suddenly to Margaret.

"When did your last letter come?" he asked.

"We had a large packet the week after our arrival," answered Margaret quietly, "and mamma has had letters by the way of England, within a fortnight. But Miss Strong and Edith have had nothing for ever so long. I am sure there must be some at Geneva."

Now Mrs. Regis's letters were from Louisville and San Francisco, and one business communication from her bankers in New York.

I understood Margaret's quiet tone, and partial explanation. She was always quiet about anything that troubled or perplexed her. And she had been troubled, not only because of the delayed letters, but about letters that ought to have been written before, and to have reached her in that first large packet. Yet somehow I had noticed that the trouble did not rest with, and weigh upon her, as such things had used to do. When she was reminded, she looked sober; a seriousness fell upon her face, — a disquiet even, — as if she discussed something solicitously with herself; but she did not settle into her old moods. Neither did she reach impulsively to an extreme. There was a thoughtful waiting, mingled with a real present peace, which nothing seemed to stir quite from its foundation.

General Rushleigh's face cleared of some sudden slight anxiety that had seemed to cross it. He looked as if a doubt were answered. And then, — I thought because he saw the shadow upon Margaret's, and it occurred to me that he appeared to comprehend it in some way, at which I wondered a little, — he said, putting his own letters into his pocket, — "Would you not like to walk as far as Villa Cigni this morning? Or; if you like, we might row across. There is a lovely air upon the Lake,"

We chose the walk because we had thought of making a boat-party in the evening. The moon was rising late now, and we should see it come up over Monte Brè. We would go after the music, as late as ten o'clock, perhaps. The night stillness was so beautiful upon the water.

We had never been to the Villa Ciani. It was quite a mile around the upper end of the town, and along the bend of the lake. We left our baskets with the old grape-woman, and set off, — Edith and Emery Ann, Stephen and I, Margaret and General Rushleigh.

Margaret wore a little white straw hat which became her charmingly. She had twisted a stem of ivy round it, and tucked a pink rose in at the side. Its only permanent trimming was a narrow band of black velvet and a black lace edge inside the rim; but she and Edith improvised fresh adornments from the glen or garden every day.

The peasant people looked after these two young girls, always; and said pretty things about them in Italian. The woman who kept the gate at the Villa, and let us in, whispered something to her daughter, with her eyes fast upon Margaret's face; and then, as she and General Rushleigh moved on together, I caught in the soft Tuscan sibillation, the sound of " bellissimi sposi ! "

I thought General Rushleigh caught it also, though Margaret did not; for I saw a quick look flash down from his eyes upon her quietly unconscious face beside him, and then a smile light in them just a little, which he did not allow to reach his lips.

The young Italian girl guided us into the grounds. We walked a long way through sweet, shady avenues of old trees, between which we saw the green expanses of the park and the young deer feeding. We crossed low glades, where the thick turf was full of wild blossoms; we came out upon a still little beach, to the clear shining of the Lake bay, where tiny waves purled up with a lisp as if they had learned a baby-talk from the old roars of Ocean.

General Rushleigh and Margaret stood there, by the water. The thoughtfulness was still in the sweet lines of Margaret's face. She had been quiet, all through the walk, since the meeting in the fruit-market,

"You are grave," General Rushleigh said to her. "You are troubled about your letters. I am sorry."

"I am grave at myself, I think," said Margaret. "I am more troubled — at not troubling — very much. But you can't know quite what I mean. If you did know, I would tell you. I mean — I like to speak truly, — and seem true."

"Perhaps I know," said Paul Rushleigh, "some things you have not told me. I knew *that* at any rate, before you said it."

There was a ring in his tone, low and gentle as it was, as if it sounded out of some gladness her words had given him.

"You know what?" asked Margaret.

"Your truth," he said.

But the shadow dropped deeper over her face. Her mouth took a little downward curve of pain.

"I am afraid — oh, what *is* truth?"

Pilate's question came strangely from those pure girl lips. But it was such a different asking.

"It is not always telling all," said Paul Rushleigh.

"No," Margaret answered, "the truer you try to be, the more perhaps you do not know what you might tell. I do not think I ought to stand talking here."

She ended it suddenly, with that. It was the one certain thing at the moment. I do not believe she knew or questioned why. She did what was whispered to her, below all self-questioning. And that was wherein the child was strong.

Paul Rushleigh moved instantly away with her. He made some inquiry of the little guide, with whom Stephen Holabird was talking.

"She must take us round to see the statues," Stephen said. "That is the most curious thing of all. I wonder what Miss Strong will say to it. Are you very tired?" he asked, turning to me. And when I assured him not, he said, "Are you, Miss Emery Ann?" How droll that sounded! Droller than "Miss Tudor," even. Miss Emery Ann walked on with him. They were growing intimate in these days. She made him think of "Aunt Trixie," he said, only Aunt Trixie was older.

The statues were four figures, seated in an alcove. Four marble likenesses: father, mother, two sons. In front of them,

24

under the shade, was a garden-table. The whole was in a deep, lovely garden recess, shut in with pleasant gloom of trees, whence rich scents of flowers, wandering from their beds beyond, crept, and lingered in the still air. Beneath the trees that faced the arbor, drooping their boughs to meet it over the carpet-sward, were rustic benches and chairs. One could see, in an instant, what the place was ; a home haunt, — home-haunted. A nook where all had used to come and sit together ; where the living came now, and the stone shapes sat in the places of the dead. They were memorial sculptures, put here, where the presences had been, instead of away among the tombs.

There was something in that which at first seemed beautiful to me.

And then, as I looked and thought, it grew stiff, hard, unreal. And the more I looked, the more I felt as if the dead forms ought to be buried away. Stephen asked me what I thought, and I did not answer. Emery Ann said sternly, — " Graven images ! "

" You say graven images to so many things, Emery Ann," said Edith, " and they are sometimes so different."

" Yes, graven images ain't always stone," Emery Ann answered, " except — it 's a kind of stony way of holding on to things, or having 'em second hand, or makin' a cold sham of what ought to be live fresh. That 's graven images. And it 's in everything, mostly, as the world goes."

" I wanted to know what you would all say to it," said Stephen. " I 've been here before, and I could n't make it out. I liked it, — and I did n't like it. I thought at first the making it real, was good ; and then the very realness seemed to take away all it tried for. Miss Emery Ann has put it ; it is a thing that ought to be live fresh."

" That is the heart of the Commandment," said General Rushleigh.

" Graven, — cut in hard form and substance. That is not what we ought to try to make our worship, or our faith, or our life. I never saw it before," said I, " but it is there."

" But life is images, after all," said Margaret. " Everything is in an image. When these people were alive, their bodies were images ; their looks and their motions were signs. You can have nothing in any other way. A thought is a sign ; for it must come in a sign shape, or else, as we say, we do not 'get hold of it.'"

" But they are the *instant* signs," said General Rushleigh. " You cannot stop, or harden them ; think what an 'expression' is in a photograph ! A thought put into words even, is a dead thing, except as the words touch back upon the life out of which they came, or that which is quick to receive it."

" And stone is the very hardest, most literal thing ; the deadest, the lowest ; so I suppose it stands for all the rest," said Stephen.

. " That is just it," said General Rushleigh. " It stands for that all through the Scriptures. The stones of the Temple that should not be left one upon another, because the Lord had come to make a living Temple ; the stones that He Himself would not make bread of, because a man shall live by the gift of God ; the *promise* about the giving, — that if a man asks bread the Father will not give him a stone ; and the forbidding ; — ' Ye shall not make to *yourselves* graven images ; ' — don't they all mean one thing, — that life is not dead, but living ? Fluent in beautiful change ; coming down and out, always ; fed to us, not held and stored away; pulsed into us, not set outside of us to grasp and define. The moment you look *at* any reality, it is gone from you. You cannot look at, and analyze, your human affection, or your heavenly hope. The wind bloweth where it listeth. Miss Emery Ann, you have preached us all a sermon."

" You know better," said Emery Ann, concisely.

But how nicely he took up that calling of her. I think they will all come to it; I like it, — " Miss Emery Ann." It seems to put her more among us ; more in the gracious middle, instead of at the bare ends of ceremony or unceremony.

I said to General Rushleigh as we walked away, — " You have given me fresh comfort this morning. I have a new sight now, of how we ought to believe *more* in life because the body of it dies away. It is because our friends are *real*, that they cannot stay in the flesh. God does not make graven images of his souls that He gives to each other."

" He did not make a graven image — an undying body — for his own coming in the flesh. He went away — that He might come again — always."

" The grass withereth, the flower fadeth ; but the Word of our God endureth forever."

I only said it to myself. It came new and living to me.

The form of our life, motherdie ! That faded ; and the flower fell ; but the love, — the secret of it, — the thing that showed because it was, — that we remember *together* because it *is*, — that is in the inner heaven, that never passes away.

We went out on the Lake, that night, after the music, just before the moonrise.

What a hush it was, of air and water ! They seemed *very* stillness in themselves. Not a ripple upon the clear depth — the dark pureness ; not a stir in the delicious fullness of the atmosphere that rested above, in which the life of vineyards and olive-yards and cypress-covered hillsides touched subtilely the charmed sense ! Only our oars made soft-parting lines in the flood that closed calm after them ; only our own motion, — as we slipped beneath the frescoed water-walls of villa-gardens, — along under arcaded terraces, hung beautiful with vines, — into the black shadows of Monte Brè, and the mysterious opening channel of the long lake-reach, — only our own motion made change in all the tranquil, starlit picture.

St. Salvadore changed slowly, without motion, as we moved ; his great shape unfolded behind us, from the vast dark cone we always saw it from the shore, and showed his southward-stretching battlements ; it was so dim and dreamy that I cannot tell you whether we crossed eastward, and followed new bends along the Caprino shore, or kept on north, beneath Castagnola. We had the shore at our left part way, and part way we floated over a wide, open water ; — the turns and winds and little bays are an exquisite bewilderment, and the midnight gloom and beauty were all I knew. Not midnight by the clock ; but by the dusk and stillness, that could be no deeper sweet at any hour.

Nobody feels like talking much at such an hour, under such influences ; after we were settled, we grew very quiet. Mrs.

Regis and I sat in the stern of the boat; Margaret was at my left, and General Rushleigh opposite her, at Mrs. Regis's right.

Away out, or across, — when we lay drifting where a water aisle and winding bay, near us, strange in the night mystery, seemed to be dimly before us, and the steep shores lifted their barriers to inclose us all around, and when over our right, if we turned our faces, the solemn mass of Salvadore stood black among the broken clouds and gleaming stars, with its wide base losing itself in black waters, — the boatmen, with their oars drawn in across their knees, rested, and sang an Italian hymn.

All at once, some tender dawn trembled into a half-light in the east. The tops of the hills and the rims of the cloud-drifts took a faint edge of silver. The darkness widened out from us; the water-gloom softened from its blackness. There was a glint upon the rocky crest and bosom of St. Salvadore, around which the deep forests wrapped themselves below. The mountain shapes in the lake answered to the forms above, separating themselves from the including dusks.

And the moon's crescent, rounded and golden toward the morning, sailed, up into clear space.

The rowers turned the boat and headed homeward.

Then Edith and Margaret began to sing, — the Angelus; in which Edith's pure, bell-like soprano and Margaret's rich, soft contralto are so beautiful together. The boatmen lifted their oars out of the water, and held them still in the row-locks, to listen.

After that Margaret's voice, alone, rose, gently at first, and then full and glorious, in the Prayer from " Der Freischütz." She sang the German words. The soft " adoring and imploring " breathed itself through the opening strains, and gradually lifted and swelled to the fervent beseeching of the last notes; till the last line, with its clear, highest reach, and its sweetly-dropping cadence, seemed to touch and bring down with it its own spirit-answer. " Sende deine Engel-Schaaren ! " It was like the descending footsteps upon the angel-ladder.

We were coming swiftly into our own little bay. The town lay sleeping in the moonlight, and Salvadore towered up silent beside it. No one spoke to say, " It is almost over," or, " How beautiful it has been!" The music and the moonlight and the tender shadows were stealing far away within us, a beauty and a memory to be kept; we withdrew with them into our deeper selves.

But, once, there came an echo, gentle, yet strong, as if it finished, involuntarily, an inward repetition. It was General Rushleigh's voice, that sung the last lines of the Angelus: —

> " From out the years, —
> From out the years;
> With thee are waking from out the years! "

" I am going up with Edith to-night, mamma, may I?" said Margaret looking back, from between Edith and Stephen, to her mother, leaning on General Rushleigh's arm. We were at the street gate of the hotel-garden. Our way to Beau Séjour lay on around the curve of the outer wall. Naturally Mrs. Regis would enter here, and naturally General Rushleigh would continue with her. Stephen was quite escort enough for us.

I left them *tête-à-tête;* and the good-night would be all their own. It was a little awkward, perhaps, entering at that hour without the rest of the party. It was with an instinct of it, I thought, that Mrs. Regis turned to call some little word back to us from half way, and get our answer. The boatmen, however, were hotel porters also, and passed in at the same moment, under the porte-cochère. It was all quite well, and I am sure Mrs. Regis was not annoyed.

Margaret often came up and shared Edith's room. They enjoyed so much their early morning rising, and the garden or terrace walk together. Besides, Margaret seldom failed to want some little particular word with me; and I was pleased to think it was at least partly what she came for.

I was in my wrapper, just ready for bed, except the little window-lingering, that even to-night, after all, I could not resist; when Margaret, in the soft blue dressing-gown she keeps up here for these improvised visits, half turned the latch between the rooms.

" May I come in, Miss Patience?" she said.

" Come; I guess I was partly waiting for you," I answered.

She came and knelt beside me, upon a hassock, as I sat there;

leaning one arm on the sill of the open window, and laying the other hand upon my lap.

It is the first time I have brought you to my window, Rose, that I told you in the beginning you would come and look out at with me. Look now and see this: —

The Lake Chalice among the encircling hills trembled full of broken beauty. A fair confusion of moonlight and shadow, — of mountain reflections, — of white cloud-images, — all tossed down into the perfect stillness that showed by no faintest sweep or quiver the line between the upper and under world. Peaks below; peaks above; soft vapor-masses and intense purple depths overhead and underneath; shafts of pale light streaming down, and down; or up and up; the earth and the heavens all afloat together. I hardly think you will believe me; but it was simply impossible to divide and realize them.

We ourselves looked forth into its midst, — for we could hardly say whether we looked most up or down, — from over the tops of densely-foliaged trees.

" Miss Patience ! "

Margaret spoke softly, hesitatingly, as if to a person sleeping.

" Are we both in a dream together ? It almost made me forget what I came to say."

" I think the world is in a dream."

" And that makes me remember again. The graven images. You see nothing in the world is a graven image, — hard, finished. Not even the mountains. The very peaks of ice are flowing down to the sea. And the rocks crumble and wear down into the fields and valleys. And they are made soft and changing, even while they stand, with clouds and shadows and colors. The world is what he said, — " fluent." And we try to make for ourselves graven images; instead of just taking the beauty as it is born to us."

I listened to the child in wonder. She spoke so simply, straight on, just as the thought that had lain in her mind unfolded itself. She did not stop to think that her thought was high; that poetry was speaking in her.

" Miss Patience, I feel as if I had been making a graven image of my life. — And now there it is, hardened into its shape;

and I don't know whether it is a true shape; or whether a true shape can ever come of it."

"The children of Israel made for themselves a foolish image in Horeb; in the early beginning of their journey. And they made it out of their gold, — their very precious things; and it was but a foolish image after all.

"And God was angry."

"Moses was angry; and heard God as if He was angry. That is all I feel sure of. Moses was angry with his brethren, for their ignorance and impatience, and in his impatience he broke *both whole tables* of the law he had just received. God had patience with them after all. . He gave them his own sign of Himself, all the way. He came down to them in the glory upon the tabernacle; between the cherubim over his own ark that they builded after his *word*, when they had given up their idols. He led them on and He promised them — right after their great mistake and sin — the land flowing with milk and honey."

."After forty years," said Margaret.

"Forty years of his own close companying," I answered. "Forty years of kind undoing for them."

"If I knew which my graven image was!" she began once more, leaving Israel and the forty years. "If I knew what I had made, — or what *was*, and I ought to be true to! Sometimes it seems as if the idol was just my own hasty, uncertain will; and as if I ought to go straight on — with what is — in spite of it; and sometimes as if I had been in a silly hurry long ago, to shape everything for myself, and had hardened up something that — I could n't *let* be my life!"

"It will be shown you." That was all I could say.

"I have tried to take the 'certain true steps,' — and to wait for them. And I partly see — once in a while — how the very best might be coming out of what I have been doubtful of; and then again, it is as if everything stood still, and there *were* no steps; only I was drifting — to some plunge that would come before I could see my way. I *want* to be true, Miss Patience! I want to *belong* among the true people!" They were the words she had said to me once before.

She put her other hand with the one upon my lap, and leaned

down her cheek upon them. There was no excitement, — no passion in her voice. It was low, earnest; it told of strong searching, impelled by the stirring of strong deeps in her; a tide moved in her that swelled forth and up after some unseen drawing. The whole kingdom of heaven was beyond the .attraction of one life that had come near to hers from toward it.

She was no common girl to be taken possession of by a personal fancy. It was righteousness itself that she was coming to be in love with.

And I told her so.

"It is God's right, I said, that you want. And it is that He is coming to. And no graven image can stand in his way, unless we persist to hold it in his way. The minute we give life up into his hands, no matter how we have hardened it, it turns plastic again, — to Him. What we cannot do in that we are weak through the mere flesh, God, giving his Son, his own divine Humanity, that is both fellowship and power, — his *wish* to our wish, — his might that *can* for our might that cannot, — condemns — destroys — the wrong in the flesh; the sin, the mistake in our life that we have made. It cannot do anything more against us. It cannot *be* any more."

I said all that, because I could not help it; because these are thoughts that have grown very strong and real in me, and are the only hope to me for all the wrong and trouble I know, in myself, and in the world; and because here was a child in want of it.

"But yet, there may be the forty years," she answered. "We have got that to bear; we must have the doubt and the wandering; though He may know all the time."

"No, not since the Son of Man was lifted up. He can hold us up above .it all, and let us see. And so — it can be taken away the sooner. The minute we *see*, it is taken away."

"The worst of it. But the *things* remain, as we made them, long ago."

"They do not remain," I said, earnestly. "They begin at once to change to his own will for us. He takes them all upon Himself, and subdues them to his own truth. He delivers us from the evil, because his is the kingdom and the power, for *ever* and ever. What are those two evers, but the two that reach *back* and forward?"

She stayed still, her face upon my lap, for five minutes, I think.

Then she lifted her head, and said again, —

"Miss Patience!" She began each distinct asking, of the different askings she had come to me with in her heart, with that calling upon my name. "Miss Patience, what was it Miss Euphrasia told you about Mrs. Armstrong when *she* was a girl? When she was — engaged, — was n't she, to General Rushleigh?"

"My darling," I said, "it is too late for me to begin to tell you that to-night. Do you know that it is nearly one o'clock? You should say your "Now I lay me," and leave all this now — where things can always be left, while He giveth his beloved sleep!"

She answered me as submissively as a little child. I think those words soothed her, and made her feel as if she could. They have soothed me often.

"Well, I will. And you will tell me to-morrow?"

"Yes, I will tell you to-morrow."

She was standing, now, ready to go. But she paused an instant, before she kissed me, and said, —

"Miss Patience, I think I like those old words better than almost any other prayer. I remember saying them to my mother."

"'Now I lay me?'" Yes, they are dear old words. I will tell you my grown-up Now I lay me, if you like. There is a night and a morning to it; —

"Now I lay me down to sleep
I pray the Lord my soul to keep:
And when in death I sleep — to wake,
I pray the Lord my soul to take.

"Now that I wake I pray the Lord
This day to keep me by his word:
In all my life Himself to live,
And daily bread my soul to give:"

She just kissed me, and went straight away.

CHAPTER IV.

THE NEXT WORD.

. . . . I LAY awake a long time after I had sent her away. I had put her off, — as a teacher has to put off a scholar sometimes who comes with a hard question that he himself must study into his books for. As a physician goes away to call again before night or in the morning, and shuts himself up to search out all he can for the difficult symptoms. I wanted time to think it over.

She was coming very close to the thing I was always thinking of for her, and dared not hastily to touch. Her whole fate seemed to hang poised, as a great boulder hangs, which no human power can lift or manage, but which a child, with the laying on of a finger, could swing from its ticklish balance, and urge, with all its own fearful might of gravity, to some destruction, perhaps.

It may seem strange to you, that, persuaded as I was of the *present* unfitness of her half relations and ties, — of the perfect answer to all her needs and questions that *might* be waiting for her, — I did not say right out, plainly, —

" Write to Harry Mackenzie and free yourself from this unspoken pledge. Tell him it can never be ; that you have outgrown it ; that it *is* not. Hold yourself free from the moment you have done so."

Oh, Rose, I have told you that I can always see two sides. Margaret is another who sees double, in this way, also. It was why she said, " she could not help being inconsistent."

I could think of that other life as well as hers. She had been made to be something to it. She had thought she was able to be everything. Only through her own deep certainty, her own clear, true seeing, must the word come that should bid her declare herself utterly changed from that old intent — that implied promise. Harry Mackenzie could not be flung away into the air, to be nothing anywhere, because he was to be nothing any more to her. His life would go on with this twist in it. And his life is just as truly something to the Lord as hers is. How could I tell what might be growing in him, — what might have been teaching him, — in this very same time?

I could not help remembering the half-boyish, half-earnest — or ready to be earnest — way in which he had written, — " I'm glad you find it, if I *am* only a dog under the table. You need n't think I despise it. You must take it in nonsense, Madge — I shall never put it in sermons. If I do any growing it will have to be along with you, as it began."

There was the making of a man in him too. And it was not even as if we could know that there had been no letters written since that. We knew that letters had been lost, or left, somewhere. There had been many that we had been sure were on the way.

I feel so certain of the Divine showings. And yet — as Emery Ann had said — one may " leave straws unput ! " I had come into the story. That was for something. Was it only to help her wait, — or to prompt her action?

Things were getting so tangled. If all had only come straight, as it ought : if she had been writing often, telling her own story, showing her own self, as she had meant to do ! Yet this, also, was of the happenings that are ruled outside of us.

General Rushleigh puzzled me. I had thought, with his knowledge, that he would have waited. That no crisis would come yet. That they would all be at home together again, perhaps, and all would grow quite clear, one way or another, before Margaret would have to ask herself these last questions. That life and meaning would be proving themselves, in a sure, gentle order, if only each did, from step to step, from word to word, the one certain thing.

And now, in some way I could not understand, Paul Rushleigh was — not hurrying, — no; he carefully kept from that, as if he felt that there was something to which time and test must still be given; — but steadily pursuing an intent, — a hope. I thought he was. I thought his measured self-control had given way to a happy freedom. That he permitted himself, though he did not urge Margaret. And before she was ready, the need for some decisiveness might come.

Would things miss by a hair's breadth of circumstance?

I could do nothing but trust all circumstance in the Hands that are round about that.

What should be *my* next word or doing?

She had come to me for that story of Paul Rushleigh and Faith. And the story had come to me. I could tell her just what it was. I need not be in a hurry to plan more, or to rush into more. When you think of a thing you will say or do, in some very important matter, you need not feel that there is to be no *other* saying or doing; that you have got to shoulder all, and carry it through to its result. Somebody else will speak; your next word will come to you with the next attitude of the affair. You are not to play the whole play; you have only your own cues to mind.

And with that, and my " Now I lay me," I went to sleep.

Margaret and I were up early; earlier than usual, even, after our short night. I think, after an excitement, and a brief, deep sleep, it is apt to be so.

Edith was sleepy; we were quite willing to let her rest, and to go down together upon the terrace. Gasparo was in· the great saloon as we passed out. " Mesdemoiselles sont toujours de bonne heure," he said, as he answered our good-morning. The gouvernante was in the little side office; she and Gasparo had morning business to and fro; otherwise we had the great terrace and the early morning to ourselves.

And so I told her that old story that Miss Euphrasia had told me.

The tears came into her eyes as she heard how Faith Gartney had given up Paul Rushleigh.

" It was a shame," she said, not condemnatorily, but pitifully.

" Would n't it have been a greater shame if she had married Paul after she had found out she loved another man better ? "

"I don't believe — hardly — she ought to have found it out! Suppose she had been married already, instead of only promised? The world is full of people. We cannot meet them all and then choose!"

"I suppose we can only act from what does happen. It came to her and found itself. It did *not* come afterwards."

We had paced up and down the flags in our talk. Gasparo had gone in and out, dusting garden seats, arranging chairs. His step was following just behind us, I thought, as we came up to the south balustrade, and so I stopped there for a minute, as I said those last words.

"I can't help it," said Margaret, impetuously; "I think she was wrong, if she *is* Mrs. Armstrong. And see what he has come to now!"

"God has led them both," I answered.

The step had gone away again. Margaret had noticed nothing. She stopped as I stopped. We turned presently to walk back.

Quite at the other end, at the head of the laurel avenue, stood Paul Rushleigh. His face was toward us, and he came to meet us as we approached. He had some letters in his hand. Gasparo had not been near us. He passed into the house from the chestnut avenue with a tray upon his shoulder as we crossed the entrance.

"I did not really expect to see you yet," General Rushleigh said; as we joined each other. "I walked up to send these to your room, Miss Patience; and to leave word for Miss Margaret that there is a large packet from Geneva for Mrs. Regis. They came late last night."

Margaret's face had flushed all over when she saw him. I felt her arm tremble in mine. I do not think it occurred to her that he had heard her words. It was not that. It was the feeling in the words; the feeling of this man that the rejected Paul Rushleigh had become. And the man himself stood so suddenly before her. Differently at that moment than he had ever stood before.

Was she going to find out now?

He saw the beautiful color come; he could not help it. And

he saw what she could not be conscious of, though one may feel a color come. He saw the look in her eyes, that had just a little before been full of tears. And he must have heard those words, — "See what he has come to now!" There was a shining in his face, too, touched with a soft stir of feeling, though he did so quietly just what he had come to do. Did it impel him sooner to what he did next, or had he come for that also?

For the next thing that I knew, he was saying to Margaret, — "I have had letters, too, this morning. May I tell you something?" And he offered her his arm as any gentleman does, to lead away a lady.

He did not mind me at all. He left me with my letters. He knew very well when mere politeness is a miserable sham, and when people — who are anything — can understand each other.

There was nothing for me to do but to sit down there on the garden bench, and open my packet. And a minute after, when I looked up, he had walked along with her through the little gate beside the laurels, and up the side path toward the long steps that led to the ravine.

There had been no time for her own thought, or for her escape, if she had wished it. She must just listen, now, to what he had to say.

"See," I said to myself, "how it is all taken out of your hands, just when you did n't know what to do with it."

And it always is so.

Yes; notwithstanding that which came after, I felt that still.

CHAPTER V.

PURE INSIGHT : A PARENTHESIS.

[THE steps came up on a high ridge-path under the tall ancient cypresses which are the remarkable feature of the place. These black-green spires shoot up, solemn and straight, above the surrounding foliage, to a height of a hundred feet. Beneath are bosky woods, and beautiful shrubbery, rich with shining leafage of evergreen. The footway runs over the crest, and then beneath it along the cliff-side, up·the glen, through which, low down, a lovely, rambling stream, with little breaks and cascades, finds its way toward the Lake. Against the crags hang the luxuriant ferns and clasping ivies that make every nook and rock face beautiful in this region of green, brimming life.

Paul Rushleigh and Margaret Regis had often walked here before. Everybody walked here ; it was the most charming part of the Pleasance. But not everybody in the fresh, quiet, early morning. Only the birds and the water had it now, except for themselves.

After she had let him lead her away, Margaret could not turn and run from him. She could not take a fright at what he might be going to say. She had to wait and hear ; and he did not speak for some moments after they had gone up the steps, and crossed the brow to the ravine. She walked beside him, her arm dropped from his ; she withdrew naturally from that brief courtesy of invitation and acquiesence, when they had reached the stairs.

It may be that Paul Rushleigh willingly prolonged the few lovely moments that were his, let what might come after ; they would be among the " living moments " henceforth in his life.

No girl approaches so near the awaiting revelation as this without a prescience of it. There was no time for her to think distinctly; there was a rushing consciousness of something close upon her that began to make it seem almost equally impossible for her to keep on, unhesitatingly, at his side, or to turn and leave him. Her breath came in half breaths, that she thought he would notice; her steps lingered; she stopped, and gathered a fern leaf from the rock. Something in her movement said, "I must not let you take me farther." Her eyes began to lift themselves toward his face, as if their pure simpleness would say, "What is it for? I must have one word, that I may answer something."

Then he stopped also, facing her.

"I have had letters this morning, that I cannot answer, unless you tell me how."

"General Rushleigh!"

Her voice was timid, troubled; but her clear eye still lifted itself to his.

"I must either go at once; or I must stay here — because I belong to you. I *do* belong to you, already; whether you will have me or no, — Margaret?"

Then her look dropped; a martyr-pain passed over her face.

Her hands sought each other, as if they must hold to something; the fingers clasped themselves together, with the little fern-leaf in them; her head drooped.

"I ought not to have come up here with you," she said, slowly. "I did not know."

"But now you know, Margaret. I love you. Can you not love me back?"

"Oh!" she cried, with a faint sharpness in her voice. "I had counted you for my friend!"

The same words that she had said before. But so different! There were loss and woe in them. The giving of more was the taking away of all that she had.

"Is that all that you can tell me, Margaret? Is the rest" —

She interrupted him. "I must not let you say it again. The *rest* is impossible."

She was pale as death. "Will you forgive me? Will you let me go?"

25

" Are you *sure*, Margaret?"   He held out both his hands and took hers in them.

"I could not say it, if I were not sure."   The simple sylla-bles dropped, truth-clear and strong, though very low.   So had those syllables of that other word, " Impossible."

As if a tremble ran all through her limbs, her fingers quivered out of his grasp.

" You will leave me?   But I think I shall never let you go ! "

She did not answer that.   She only turned and walked slowly down, into the thick shadow.

Paul Rushleigh picked up the little broken fern-leaf from the path.]

CHAPTER VI.

BY THE SUN-DIAL.

. . . . NOBODY came back to me from the glen-walk. I sat on the terrace till Emery Ann came down, and said that Edith was just dressing, and wished we would not wait for her. She would come before we should have finished breakfast. So Emery Ann and I walked over to the hotel garden. By the great stone sun-dial, we met Stephen Holabird, and he went up on the drawing-room terrace with Emery Ann, asking some question about Miss Edith. I stopped a minute, as I was fond of doing, to see what hour the sun pointed by the shadow of the large brazen gnomon, and what time it was at other places whose names were carven under their own meridians upon the face, and where the line would touch that would make it just that hour of night instead of morning.

While I stood there General Rushleigh came out at the garden entrance of the hotel, and walked straight over to my side.

He took out his watch. I doubt if he did it for much except the apparent and habitual errand that people made there. I think his real errand was to me.

As he put it back without setting it, he said, — "Miss Patience, I shall have to set my watch by other meridians soon. I am going to Egypt and the East." He knew he might be abrupt with me, and I should allow for any blank he left. His face was different from his face of half an hour ago.

" I am obliged to go to the bank and the telegraph office this morning. I must beg you to excuse me to Mrs. Regis at breakfast ; and perhaps you will tell her what I have said to you. I have had a letter from an old army comrade, who wants me, — needs me, if I can come. I am to join him at once at Naples. Ten days from now, we shall be either in Syria, or on the Nile.

— Don't look shocked and sorry, dear Miss Patience; it is all right; I could not have expected to be *more* wanted here."

I could only say two words: " My friend!" and he answered me in two: " Thank you."

" But I am afraid it is *not* all right." His words, and the face of the man, twice so bitterly pained and denied, — as if life had nothing that he, so noble, so grand a man, might reach out his hand and take, as common small creatures find so easily ready for them every day, — made me bold.

"It is a conscience answer, not a heart answer. It is only *part* right. The last right may come yet."

I almost wondered if he understood me, or whether, after all, he had known just how things had been. He answered me so strangely at the moment.

" No, dear friend, it is not that. I knew that she would be very exacting, very searching with herself. I have waited. I should have waited longer but for this coming. — She says she is *sure*. She says it is impossible. And now I shall only have to go."

Our few sentences had been exchanged in less than two minutes, doubtless, by that slow shadow on the dial, that we could not see had moved. But round the dial that counts what the sun-minutes stand for, how swift the shadow had wheeled!

There was chance only for a few words there; in that open garden, with the gay people moving all about. General Rush-leigh lifted his hat to me, and went away. I think he had come to me there for that very reason; because he wanted to speak to me, but not to say many words. Because, you see, he could so easily have come back to me on the terrace at Beau Séjour.

I stood where he left me, till I suddenly remembered that there was nothing to account for my still.standing there.

Why must there always be something outside of you, to account for you to outside eyes?

Why can't you stop still, anywhere, if your thought stops you? Why must you be always bound to do something or to move on? Why, with a soul inside of you, can't you cry, or laugh, or muse, as the need comes, without other people seeing the pain, or the fun, or the absorption? You can, if you like, in just one place on earth: in a lunatic asylum. Sane people keep their souls in their safety-pockets. I suppose, taking all together, it is a more comfortable plan.

So I went in to breakfast, — that of me which could break-fast, or pretend to. That which could not, still stood out there, — stayed there, for the most part, all the day, I think, — at the sun-dial; lingering in what had come to me beside it; wondering and reading a mystery; how this way, that way, the shadow is always falling across some human creature's noon.

If I had not stayed there, thinking of a sure thing, that had the sun behind it, I should have found hard work not to say to myself: "Just at the wrong minute; why must it happen so?"

But the dial kept telling me: "There never is a wrong min-ute, but the minute in which we do some known sin."

But why must it have happened that I should have that story to tell just then? To waken all her jealous nobleness; her feeling of the shame it was to cast aside a trust, — to snatch back a hope, a motion that has been given; to make her say of Faith Gartney, — "She ought *not* to have found it out!" Of Paul Rushleigh: "See what he has come to now." It was as if I had set her on some pinnacle of her own future, from which she could see things as they might prove; as she ought now to have faith they would prove; as she must not by any act, or recognized thought of hers, hinder them from proving.

"We cannot meet all, and then choose." We cannot have the best for ourselves and leave the rest to take care of it-self. Even a mistake — a wrong — for others' sake, may be truer than a goodness for our own. Here and there, making friends of the Kingdom, we may find and learn and love the best; but we are commanded also to make friends with — yes, to *serve* — in one way — the mammon of unrighteousness.

Now "Mammon" is something hidden in the earth.

And the "earth" perhaps is the "unrighteousness." There is treasure hidden away in that which is not yet righteous. And if it come to us, — if its help lies in us, — some such meaning as this, though we cannot see it all clear, may be the meaning in the parable. Christ sent the woman of Samaria back after even him who was "not her husband."

Out of some high, self-judging mood like this, — his very power over her a power of uncompromising right, — his very presence a reminder and an influence to "belong to such people," though she had to turn away that she might belong, — she had answered what he had, so suddenly, come and asked of her.

But why must that letter have come to him just then? Why must he be going away — so far? To Syria, *or* Egypt, — nobody was to know which first? Why must that question have come just between his letters and hers; hers in which all the old claim would be renewing itself, so that the consciousness of its waiting in them was prepossessing her at the very instant when he took her arm in his and led her away to put all his purposes to her decision?

With all my whys, I rested in the belief that the *happenings* must be right; but I could not quite understand Paul Rushleigh.

These things passed through my mind and repassed, while I sat and ordered my breakfast with the rest; while I was telling Mrs. Regis that General Rushleigh had been obliged to go down early into the town; while she was telling me that Margaret had had too little sleep, and had gone to her own room with a headache. I just attended enough to wonder if she had really seen her, or if Margaret, as most likely, had spoken half a dozen words at the door between their rooms, and then had shut herself in to be let alone. And immediately — and all the while — I went on and over again with those perplexing "whys."

I did not tell Mrs. Regis all the message, there in the public breakfast-room. I waited till we got away, at the lower door, near which we sat that morning, and found ourselves apart for a moment in the cloister passage to the farther drawing-room.

There I stopped her. "Mrs. Regis," I said, "I have something more, — one minute! General Rushleigh met me; he told me, — he asked me to tell you, — that he found himself obliged to go away."

She stopped then; she had only half stopped at the first word. I felt it was a shock to her.

"He is going" — I did hesitate; it was hard to tell her how utterly he was going away.

At that moment Mrs. Regis gave a shock to me. A shock of absolute surprise. I have seen many people in what Emery Ann, in her homely way, calls " hard spots ; " but I never saw a woman stand right up in one, and defy your perception of its being one, as Mrs. Regis did then. " Is there anything *more*, in this, Miss Strong, than just the fact that General Rushleigh thinks of going away ? You almost speak as people do when they have to *break* something to one."

She put me quite down. It was not my business — then, certainly, before he or Margaret had had chance to speak, if they would — to "break" anything else to her. I had not thought of doing so.

I only said, very meekly, — for I do feel meek, and I cannot help it, when people fling a light full upon something in my consciousness that I shrink from *their* consciousness that anybody else can be conscious of : —

"That is all. Only it is such a pity ; and I am so very sorry. It was a message."

"Yes ; thank you. I will be in the way when General Rushleigh returns. That was what he meant, no doubt."

She opened the door as she spoke, and passed into the inner drawing-room, which was always quiet of a morning. She took a French newspaper from the middle table, and went with it to another table in the corner, behind which she often intrenched herself when she did not care to put herself at the disposal of the first chance comer. I went on and stepped out of the long open window.

Edith and Stephen had begun a game of croquet. Emery Ann sat near with her strip of knitting.

I turned back into the room, — for I would not go the outside way, and by the south staircase, which was quite as near, because that did not feel exactly outside, but a little bit covert, to me, — and crossed again by the glass door into the cloister, and walked along to the great front stair-way and went up.

As I passed through, I had noticed that Mrs. Regis had put the newspaper aside, and was busy with her many letters, which she had doubtless brought down to read, but in the instant of hearing my news, and taking her consummate action upon it, she had forgotten.

CHAPTER VII.

"JUST GONE."

. . . .

. . . . I MET the sommelier in the upper corridor. "Bring me, if you please, a glass of milk and some sticks of pulled bread, — crisp," — I said. "I will wait here, at Number 85. It is for Mademoiselle, who does not find herself very well this morning." He knew all our party, and Mrs. Regis fees this sommelier generously. So I had hoped the crisp sticks would not be "tout-à-fait finis."

I had spoken at the door, so that Margaret should hear my voice. When he had gone I knocked softly, and said, "Don't let me in, dear, if you would rather not; but let me give you the little tray when it comes, and please eat and drink something."

I had hardly finished when the key turned in the lock. I was standing between the double doors that these cell bedrooms have, and had drawn the outer one toward me. The inside leaf was gently swung back, and Margaret stood before me, perfectly quiet, but very, very pale.

She put her hand out and drew me in; then, but still quietly, she put her arms up round me, and laid her face against my neck. She did not say a word, and she did not cry or cling to me. She just did that, as if she needed me, and was glad of me, and then she stood up again, and turned back into the room. She walked over to the little sofa by the window, where the blinds were drawn down, and the soft air stole through. She stood there and waited, — her face toward the window, — while I remained beside the door. It seemed as if she asserted her strong intent in her attitude. I have heard of men who died upon their feet. Margaret Regis was giving up a ghost in that way. I do not believe she had been sitting or lying down.

Her hair and dress were unruffled. She was just a beautiful, calm figure of resolve and sacrifice. But no sculptor could have put that white, pure pain of her face into the marble.

"It has all come in a moment," she said to me, after I had made her sit, and eat and drink a little, and had put the cushion behind her, and persuaded her at last to rest her head. "And I cannot talk about it, — but I have done it. It has put everything out for a time, but presently the rest will come back. But, *twice*, Miss Patience! And that the second time it should be me!"

One drops like a child into that little objective "me," when the "I" stands over against it and regards it in any struggle or sorrow.

Not a syllable to tell me what it really was to her. Her thought was of him. Ah, but that told me! I could not help one little question of three words.

"Are you *sure* — Margaret?"

"That was what *he* asked me!" The words came like a low cry. "Yes, sure," she said, then, gathering up that strange quiet strength. "It is only one of the might have beens. I could just see that, — and that I could *not* take it and leave Harry behind. For I had not even quite found out, you see. I was waiting — promised to wait. I feel as if I should be nearer knowing now. When I can think. When the rest comes back again. I may find out that the other will not be right; but this — *now* — would have been wrong. It would have been as if I had been married — and promised myself again — before the other died! It would have been a shame!"

"And there is his letter. Flora's and his," — she turned her face to a scattered pile upon her bureau beside her, of which one, in a large envelope much crossed and post-marked, lay open upon the top, — "that has been wandering round and round after me, all these weeks that I have been wandering — into this! — Please put them all away, Miss Patience. I cannot read them yet. It wouldn't be *fair* to read them yet!"

She had opened one letter only. It was in the peculiar, strong, Regis family-hand; from Mrs. Vanderhuysen. She had tried to read her sister's letter, even in the very stress of her trouble.

"Won't it be good, Miss Patience, when we get into the kingdom of heaven?"

I laid the letters by in her bureau drawer.

Oh dear me! Why did I not know better? And why, if I had known better, could there not have been just one hour more? But there was neither the hour nor the knowledge.

Half an hour later Mrs. Regis came into the room.

"General Rushleigh is just gone," she said, calmly. "He had to hurry to reach the train at Camerlata. He left good-byes for you."

People have to walk away from death-beds. They have to say, perhaps, to somebody, that sentence, — "He is just gone." They do these things, and then the years begin in which the moment's meaning rolls slowly back upon their hearts. Trouble is a glacier, not an avalanche.

Mrs. Regis came up to Margaret's sofa.

"Have you read your letters?" she said, kindly. Her voice was tender, subdued with some sympathy it had never had in it before. That, also, comes away with people who have stood by death-beds.

I said once that Mrs. Regis had never stood by any that was dear. I think now she had seen some life go out that her own life had watched for ; that some dear hope was dead, and she had shut its eyes. General Rushleigh had been with her, and was gone. She had questioned him, doubtless, with all the privilege of friendship ; she had spoken with the tact and generous frankness that a woman of her age and grace can use. There were a thousand words that she could say, any one of which would bring the word from his lips, if it were waiting. She knew well enough, that it was not time nor opportunity that lacked. She knew, well enough, as I knew, that a man like Paul Rushleigh can make time and opportunity.

She had risen and met him, there, at that door, into the cloister as he returned. She had left Emery Ann and Edith sitting just within the window where they had come back out of the sun, to wait for me. He might easily have let her pass into the dim, quiet arcade, where we all walked up and down so often ; he might have spoken with her there — or led her away, as he had

Margaret — if he had pleased; but he came forward with un-slackened step and she almost had to turn back with him as he stopped.

"Dear Mrs. Regis," he had said, "Miss Strong has told you? — I am obliged to be very abrupt. I leave at once for Camer-lata." And a voiture drove into the quadrangle at that moment from the stable court-yard.

"But why? What *must* is there?" she said, not disguising the pained remonstrance in her voice.

"What has happened? Has anything — ?"

"It has happened that it is my duty — and necessity — to go. I had a letter from a friend last night. He begs me, if I can, to accompany him to the East. He is an army comrade, disabled by a wound, and broken in health; and I — there is nothing to prevent me." He spoke sadly. "I am quite free and alone, you know, except for the pleasant link you have let me make with your party. Now I must say good-bye."

"To go so far away?"

I do not suppose she stopped to really take it in, as she heard or said it. Women — like Mrs. Regis — do not shriek or faint their surprises that are like this; they behave themselves, and take things in afterward. "To go so far away? Are you quite sure about the duty? Forgive me, — but you said once, — I thought you would tell me if there were anything," — she spoke low, hurriedly.

Emery Ann, wise woman, got up, and went out across the terrace to a garden seat, Edith getting a little admonitory pinch upon the shoulder as she passed, followed.

"He's a man that can find his own way round," said Emery Ann. "We need n't make guideboards of ourselves."

"You are far too kind," General Rushleigh was saying gravely a moment or two after, as he moved with Mrs. Regis toward the window, and paused to finish the words before he came out to them. He held her hand in his. "I have always felt sure of your kindness, and your friendship is very dear to me; but, indeed, there is nothing that I have to ask of it, beyond itself."

She had stayed, and had shaken hands with him again, and

had stood with the others, — Stephen came back, just in time from the fruit-market, — to see him step into his carriage in the quadrangle, and drive out under the old archway. She received his messages, — he would not have us called, since he had said good-bye to us once already, — and watched him off as any friend would do. Stephen, sorry, and perplexed with all the suddenness, wanting to do something for him at parting, — had put a basket of grapes upon the forward seat, just as the carriage moved; he never thought, he said, till afterward, what basket it was. It was one of the little straw satchels, and had " Margaret: Glion ;" worked in scarlet on the side.

General Rushleigh lifted his hat, as he went; the porters took their caps off, Monsieur politely wished him "bon voyage," the old paved court was dim and still again, and Mrs. Regis came up-stairs.

"You have read your letters?" she said to Margaret, with that strange softness.

" Only a little — of one," said Margaret in the tone of a person tired with pain, but touched with a kindness. And then Mrs. Regis had stooped and kissed her step-daughter upon the forehead.

How could either of us guess what paragraph in one of her own letters that she had been unfolding and looking over mechanically whilst she waited there below, had arrested suddenly her full surprised attention, just before General Rushleigh had come in? How could we know what accounted simply enough to her for Margaret's sadness and pain? What set her at rest, perhaps, seeing that pain, concerning any other thought of Margaret which she would be sure now was only my mistake? What might even be a shadowy compensation, — a comfort of worse spared, — in the parting in which her own half hope had been let go?

It still remained to her that General Rushleigh was her friend.

A woman can bear to be only a friend, while nobody else in the whole world is anything dearer or more.

CHAPTER VIII.

THE HAIR'S-BREADTH OF CIRCUMSTANCE.

. . . .

. . . . MRS. REGIS went away into her own room.

Margaret still lay upon the sofa; her hand had gone up and covered her eyes; there was a tender, tremulous curve in her lip, sometimes so proud and determined; her step-mother's kiss had dropped upon her heart.

That pride and self-reliance, which seem to keep some natures cold and separate, are truly, often, but the defense of feeling too deep for daily, careless stirring. Margaret's was stirred now; a new kindness had come like a new pain.

Had she mistaken everything? Had she flung everything away?

For a few minutes, — for many, — she lay so, and said nothing; when she did speak, it was in that quiet undertone which passionate earnestness takes with her.

"I thing I have never understood anything. If she cares for me like that, I have been hateful. Miss Patience, what do you think made her kiss me so?"

"I do not know. Unless" — but I did not think General Rushleigh would have told her. If he had, I did not believe she could have come to Margaret like that. Truly I did not know.

"She is sorry, I think, and that makes her tender to you," I said.

"Sorry! Oh, yes; he is her friend. And I have sent him away. And she can be tender to me! I have spoiled everything. I begin to think, Miss Patience, that I have misunderstood the very truth in my life. I have been fierce and proud, instead of honest. And I can never go back of it. I can never make it right again. There is no help, now."

It was coming fast upon her, as it does come with every great, searching experience. The spirit that reproves — reminds — of all things. It had been gathering, before; it swept down now, like a storm from the mountains.

"The help is always in the present moment. The Lord is not asleep in the hinder part of the ship."

I had not meant the literal instant, or any literal thing for her to do. But she took it so.

She sat up. "I will go to my mother," she said. It was the word of the prodigal. The heart of the prodigal was in her, accusing herself. Would the other heart be there to meet her?

She rose and went to the door between the rooms. She opened it, and left it open as she passed in. She walked quickly to her step-mother's side. Mrs. Regis was sitting in a large chair in the window, with her back toward us; she looked steadily out upon the lake and mountain; she did not notice the opening of the door.

Margaret slipped down upon a cushion at her side. She laid her forehead down upon her knee. "Mother," she said, "I did not know you cared, or I would have come to you long ago. I have made it all go wrong. I have hurt everybody. I have sent him away — and I did not know what was right!" It was very confused. No wonder Mrs. Regis's first feeling was utter surprise and confounding.

"You, Margaret! Sent whom away? How?"

"I told him that what he was thinking of could not possibly be so. He spoke to me of it — this morning."

I do not know what strange, absurd idea swept for an instant — vaguely without reasoning, it must have been — across Mrs. Regis's mind, occupied with only one perception and relation in all that had so swiftly happened. Margaret had never been used to come to her with her own things.

She started to her feet. She let Margaret's head drop away from its support, and left it to raise itself sadly, wonderingly, to her as she stood above her, tall and angry. I had never seen Mrs. Regis angry before. I almost doubt if she had ever been so, since, perhaps, she was angry as a child. "Margaret!" she said, vehemently. "Do you mean that you have taken upon yourself —? If you have sent away my friend from me, I can *not* forgive you!"

"Mrs. Regis!" I hurried toward her, and stopped in the door-way. I did not belong there except for that one minute. But I could not let her go on like that, in her first bewilderment. "You do not know, — you do not see what it is. Margaret" —

Margaret passed me as I spoke, and gently closed her door behind me. She left it all to me. She gave it up in pain, rebuked, repulsed. I finished my sentence.

"She sent him from *herself*. She came to you with her trouble. She came to you — you were so kind, — with a new feeling that she ought to have come to you before. You do not understand Margaret."

I had at least given her time. She gathered back her self-command. Her clear perception came with it.

"Margaret has refused Paul Rushleigh?" she said, slowly. It seemed, even, as if she saw more in it than I did. "And now — when it is too late — she comes to me with it? I cannot take it *back* for her, Miss Strong!"

"She does not want you to take it back," I said, indignantly. "She means — so far, at least — to keep her own faith. She has let him go. But she wants *you* — her mother!"

"I think we are all at some strange cross-purposes," said Mrs. Regis. "Do you not know — does she not know that Harry Mackenzie is married by this time to that Southern heiress, — that Nellie FitzEustace?"

That was what was in the letters; the long-belated letters, crossed and stamped, that had gone "wandering round." The letters that had come this morning, and that I had put by for her, because she did not feel it "fair to read them now!" There had been a "diamond wedding" going forward there in Boston, while Margaret Regis had been keeping the heart-diamond of her truth shining and pure with sacrifice!

And General Rushleigh had been gone an hour, and was to travel to Naples. And two steamers for the Levant would sail on Friday. I looked at Bradshaw and I found that out. But what did it signify? Even if it were not so? Even if he were here?

Could anybody go to him and say, — This news is just come ; she is free for you, and she will take you ?

It would not be seemly. It would be as if — Margaret's own words suggested it — the other had just died.

There must be time. Time had been put between. Yes, I looked at it in that way at last, and rested so.

CHAPTER IX.

THE OTHER FERN LEAF.

. . . .

. . . . Something had come to me to test that belief of mine in the nice, and intimate, and dear ordering that I do believe in. Something had come very early to test that faith and the young creature who had just begun to rest her thought in it. Could she rest her life in it, — now, just in its missing, and tangling, and breaking? When it seemed as if some main spring had either never been, or had flown apart, and the wheels were running wildly, and round and round on the dial swept an aimless index that knew not any poise or purpose, and presently would stop helpless, and in the wreck of one little beating life that had been meant to measure it so blithely, all great time itself would stand a blank?

At first, the hard thing was, that in her very beginning to be most true, most careful of the moment's right, — the one sure step at a time by which she had hope to be led safely, she had gone right off the brink.

"It seems," she said, "I know it cannot be so, — but it *seems* — as if I could have taken care of *myself* better. As if I had given myself to be held, and had that minute been let drop. For I know I meant to do so rightly!"

"You do not know *all* that has to be taken care of for you. This one thing you might have grasped and saved to yourself. But you are not meant, at last, — to miss *anything*. All your life is to come right. It is like a child taking something it had tried to make and spoiled, to mother or teacher. All the mixed-up snarl, — all the broken pieces, — all the confused mistakes, — are just brought and given into the hands of the stronger wisdom ; and perhaps the very first thing we see that wisdom do, is to *un*make and separate, and seem to break and mix yet more.

26

But the child — the scholar — stands patient and sure, until the perfect knowledge, the unerring touch, begins to put together again."

" But the pieces are lost. I cannot bring them all. It is n't my *own* things only. Think of *his* life ! "

" The Lord is in all lives. And there are always the twelve legions of angels. We are in such a hurry to think that out of our reach is out of all reach."

" If we even knew where he was, or was going to be! But it is almost as if he had gone away out of the world. We may not meet again for years."

That was just what I had kept thinking. If I had only known where he was, or would be! If anybody could only write. I think I would have dared to write to him. I think Mrs. Regis ought to have dared.

But when Margaret said it to me, I answered her and myself, both.

" 'The Lord knows. He has got hold of us all. If *I* knew, you would have some faith in something I might do, maybe. And I would do, anything that I knew. And the would, and the might, and the knowing, are all in One. How much better that is ! "

That was the way I tried to talk to her, and, as I say, to myself at the same time.

I had also Emery Ann to talk to, who without knowing or asking to know, precisely anything that had come about, could see very well that things had happened, or, as she said, " had taken place," and that " something ought to take place again."

" 'Taking place' is a good phrase for happenings," I told her. " When the place is ready, something *will* take it."

She and Stephen Holabird were great comrades. Emery Ann had determinedly matronized Edith, until she had matronized herself into a sort of elderly relative, and at the same time a kind of compeer of the youth. When everybody else had disappeared that miserable day, — when I myself, leaving Mrs. Regis, had betaken myself to my own room; when Edith having a real, simple headache, had given up and gone to bed again, — Stephen found Emery Ann up in the garden, all alone in her favorite seat.

"Things have taken an awful turn-over," he said to her.
How could anybody have supposed that to-day could have
come after yesterday? I don't pretend to know, but there
must have been some terrible scrimmage or other, when everybody is either wounded or missing. What can it possibly all
mean, Miss Emery Ann?"

"It means a pretty spot of work!" said Miss Emery Ann,
knitting very fast, to make up for shutting up her lips very tight,
after just those syllables had escaped, as if there she meant to
wind up the conversational yarn and put the needles into the
heath. But she went on again in spite of herself. "Don't
ask me about it! And don't tell *me!* I believe in Providence,
and I believe in Patience, but if ever I felt clear meddlesome in
my life, I feel meddlesome now! If only I knew where to take
hold and meddle!"

"I wonder," said Stephen, speculatively, "if it isn't a sort of
case for a kitten — or something; if one only knew, as you say,
where it would be a good plan to lose it."

"I presume you know what you mean, Mr. Holabird!"

"I presume I do, Miss Tudor. We lost a kitten once at our
house, Ruth and I, when there was something else — very important to our family — that wanted hunting up, and we had
a dim guess where to look for it. We looked for the kitten
you see; we shot another arrow that self way, and we found
Shakespeare's idea a very good one. I wish we had a kitten
to shoot now; I wouldn't mind being a kitten myself, and being
shot: if I could only put on a few more clawses; on to my letter
of credit for instance; and a letter of instructions!"

"What a jumble you do talk! I can't make head nor tail to
it!"

"If you could, you could pretty nearly make the kitten!"

"We're too old — between us — to talk nonsense over this,
ain't we?" said Emery Ann.

"Yes 'm," said Stephen. "I don't know but it would be good
sense in me to go and see the Pyramids. Or Jerusalem, or
something. But I don't know which. And perhaps I could n't,
either. My sister is in Nice, you see, and she might want me,
if the Katahdin should cruise off anywhere. — Miss Emery

Ann!" He spoke in strong italics. "Do j
eral Rushleigh's banker is, — in Boston?
Banca Svizzera here, of course ; but you s(
the correspondents — and anybody should h
respond ?"

" What makes you think they should have
Ann asked, with a certain indefinite dignity
haps ought to be assumed by somebody.

" Now, Miss Emery Ann, we certainly a
tween us, to have picked up a little general (
think that people go off like that, and leav
an epidemic of headaches and things, unl(
some kind of a buzz, you know. And ther
something that they ought to have waited fo
up after they 're gone, as it might perhs
somebody's business, — and that 's where the
on the how-not-to-do-it principle, — to cii
them. I 've three sisters married, you see
three older sisters gets a good deal of ready-
bara had a buzz, and came near enough ne\
the Katahdin. And — well, General Rushl
a fellow !"

" And Margaret is too splendid a girl," b
Ann before she thought.

" It was certain enough about him," remai
bird quietly, "but I should n't have dared
from all the rest of you."

In due order of things, since everything
not for several days, — that talk worked rou
idea in it.

I knew that General Rushleigh's bankers
our own, — Kidder, Peabody, & Co. And
over my letter of credit, and found that the c
in Alexandria was ——, and in Beyrout —

One day I just told that to Mrs. Regis.
that she did not expect to have any occasi
Rushleigh's address. If he wrote to her, h(

aid nothing more about it. I just left it in her mind. Because knew it would have to adjust itself there, and that she would ot be comfortable until it did. There would be a door a-creak.)ne has at last to go and attend to a creaky door, either to shut r open it; one cannot sit or lie quietly for it. If, I mean, it is recisely one's own concern.

Somebody else's door, quite out of your reach, may creak or am all night; it does not slam into the ears of conscience; it as no pull upon any little creaking nerve of your reluctant ill. I tried to discriminate carefully, and I made up my mind iat this was Mrs. Regis's door. I felt that I had no right to · pen or shut for her.

We were in Lugano two weeks longer. We all had to get ver our headaches, and come down to dinners, and appear mong the other visitors as usual. I wondered if any other istories were living out around us, just beneath the every-day, nalterable surface that no heart-gasp must make a ripple in, — ; ours was.

It was a comfort that the rains set in early. That we could c dull and listless, if we liked, about the weather. How kind ie moods of earth and atmosphere are, that make such excuse nd shelter for our own! An east wind, — a fog, — a drizzle, – something outside of us to complain of, to be hindered by, — ·hat should we do without the " correspondence" of them now nd then, when the inward barometer stands at the line of heavi- ess and tears?

I did not know when Margaret read those letters. It was vo days after that morning in her room that she said to me — You know what has happened at home?" She might have felt in my manner, or guessed it from some things I did not say. t might have appeared in what Mrs. Regis would have natu- illy said. For that impetuous word spoken in my presence did ot end words between them. They had been two days to- ether, as usual; and usualness is a great power.

Mrs. Regis is not a woman to be silent and separate and dis- grecable. She believes in comfortableness. Let what will be- ll, I think she will always arrange the resulting position of things so as to sit down amongst them with such ease as may be, if she must sit down. She would never cry without a pocket handkerchief; she would never fling in lesser miserableness to the bargain of a big trouble. She would find a way to go down with a sinking ship without needless knocking among the timbers. Here she was with Margaret; she was not going to quarrel, in literal, every-day, vulgar fashion, with her step-daughter, though she had said she could not forgive her.

"That was what mamma was sorry for," said Margaret. "It was good of her to be sorry for that, when she never wished it. And it was no wonder that the other vexed her."

She did not blame her step-mother; she had only failed to come near to her, as she had been just ready to do. She was ready now, rather than further and finally estranged; she had grown very tender with self-blame, — very meek with judgment of her own old pride. She felt she had held willfully to that in which her step-mother had known better for her; she had rejected that of which her step-mother had recognized the rare behoof. She had sent away her mother's friend. And Mrs. Regis was very ready to leave her hasty utterance where it was. I do not think they had much talk about it; it was not likely, on either side.

It was to me that Margaret came with the strange hardness of the happening; with the lost and mismatched pieces that pained and puzzled her; with that doubt about the bestness of things that even to such as have never found out that faith was dear to them, is the secret central ache and vital hurt of trouble.

We had no long talks, or deliberate beginnings; I think it was only once or twice, that we spoke directly of it, that first week afterward; then some instant feeling broke in words, — few, and taking much for granted; and I said the things to her that I would by all means insist on to myself. But I think she said most to herself, — or received it most within her, — after all. Day by day, even then, her look began to grow serener; a comfort, that was a real quiet, replaced the quiet she had had to wear before that little outside world of people; it came *up* into her eyes; it was not set there carefully as a coin weight is set to hold the eyelids of the dead.

One night she said to me,— it was out in the cloister, where she went with me to look if the voiture was ready to take us up to Beau Séjour through the pouring rain, — "It makes it easier, Miss Patience. It makes the real thing right, even if it never comes right."

There was where she rested, as only a high, young faith — a love very pure from passion — could have rested.

Her life was clear to her, let the outward living go on as it might. Its beautiful secret was her honest and unalienable own.

In what Mrs. Regis rested, or if she did rest, — how could I know? I am sure only that it would be upon the least thorny side of her pain, if she could find one. I think she was still far from understanding Margaret in the depth and height of her nature, and so- of this experience. I think she was far from perceiving where the point of her trial had been in it, or what had been her relinquishment. Margaret's quietness and calmness now might easily continue to prevent her. I think she even pitied her still that she had given her best and sole enthusiasm where it had been trampled upon and flung back to rend her. And that underneath and correlative to this perception of the matter was still, the compensation to herself that it had been so ; Margaret might have done a harder thing for her to bear, than to have *sent away* her friend.

For Paul Rushleigh had told Mrs. Regis that her friendship was very dear to him.

And Mrs. Regis's womanhood, with all its failure and its fettering to mere easy going commonplace, has, because it is a pure bred' womanhood and not coarse sexhood, a possible height in it which I believe real, delicate womanhood does have as its very essence ; a height which lifts it above mere passion until passion itself is glorified by being lifted into that which is divine. A possibility of pure loving and pure satisfying ; making its only selfishness that it asks and longs to be *first ;* to be put beneath and displaced by no other and no different loving. It marries with and gives itself in marriage just that it may sit upon this throne, of which the marriage choice is highest sign ; that it may be owned as type and fulfillment of ideal woman-nature by the man-nature in which it finds ideal manly glory.

If Paul Rushleigh were never to marry, now, but were to hold Virginia Regis as his woman-friend of all the world to whom he would come for counsel, for understanding, for feminine insight, for the grace with which a woman, having it in herself, touches and invests the world around her, — I think it would have fulfilled her dream.

But that, I think, is the woman's side of it, and where she may most bitterly delude herself. When a man does feel all that for a woman, I think he does go and ask her to become his wife.

What had been in those letters, also, was left without any sort of mention. It was quite easy to fancy. Persuasions that had been growing for much time past, that it would be very indifferent to Margaret how things ended; a boy's justification mixed with some shade of a man's honorable scruple and shame; a girl-friend's reproach that it was all her own fault; that she had been half-way and disappointing, always; and now, how could Harry help loving such a dear, fascinating little thing; that had fallen in love with him without all those weighings and measurings? Passing from this, quite likely, to touch upon the brilliant plans, and the congratulations, and Colonel FitzEustace's munificence, and the exquisite trousseau; with hopes at the last that they should all be good friends always, after all?

The Mackenzies had had Nellie with them, visiting, in a cottage they had taken at the sea-shore; the little stunner had been got away from the crowd, and brought right home to Harry, as it were, on approbation; there was no jostling, no rushing to be gone through with; no trouble to take, no uncertainty to bear. In short, here was something ready-made, and for immediate possession; and he had taken it.

Those last rainy days at the lake, had been snow upon the mountains. There was a white glitter outlining the peaks that had been shadowy blue beyond the Caprino hills; and when that last afternoon, as the sun came out and made again a few hours' summer softness, we walked up the park terraces to where we stood above the red roof levels, we saw away off in the north and east the great heads of the nearer Alps, splendid in their winter crowns.

Margaret and I left Edith and Stephen in the upper walk, where the great aviary is, and where the little rabbits scud about in the hillside underwood, behind the tall, close palings that end the promenades, and went down together into the ravine.

"I should like to walk up here just once more," she said; and I knew that she had not been here since that day.

She is different from most girls. She would not go off sentimentalizing alone. There was something far more real and living and noble to her in what had happened to her here, than any mere sentimental romancing, or brooding forlornness would have made it. I am sure she took me with her that she might not fall into any lesser mood.

We did not walk all the way up, to where the rustic seats are, and the pretty view. She stopped in the shadow of a great rock, beautiful with ferns and ivies; and she pulled a little fern leaf, as she might have pulled one then.

I think now, — I write this a good while after, — that I have little by little entered into what that walk and talk were; that little by little, in thought and act, it was given almost all to me, as things and words came round. It would not be hard to tell anybody's story, that you had ever been very close to, pretty much as it must have come.

She held the little fern leaf tenderly; as if, perhaps, it had grown there since; had got into its life, somehow, some breath of life that had been lived there then.

She told me one thing, as we stood there; she holding the little leaf, and bending her eyes soberly upon it (do you know soberly means purely, — calmly?) as if that way it returned to her.

"When I asked him to let me go," she said, "he told me that I might leave him; but he thought he could never *let me go*. I may take that now and keep it. If only he had anything."

"He has the other part of that," I said. "The old broken sixpence was only a sign of truth. There is an each half to every true thing and word."

And so we came away.

CHAPTER X.

MARIÆ NASCENTI.

. . . .

. . . . We were in Milan. We were going to see the Cathe
dral. We had caught a glimpse of its great mass looming i
the distant Piazza across the head of our street, — the Cors
Vittorio Emanuele, — as we were driven to the Hotel de Ville
We went to sleep under its shadow. For all Milan sleeps an
wakes beneath it, — the beautiful Alp of Architecture.

Can you pass from life-story to marble-story? We had to d
it. We have had to be thankful for some of the great thing
that have been put into the waiting-time. And there is reall
no waiting-time, since all things are continually passing into th
life and making part of it, making place for that which shal
take place.

I shrink, Rose, before the beginning of the things that
ought to be able to tell you, — of what I ought to be able t
take to myself out of this great, rich Italy. It needs a grea
rich knowledge of all Art and History, — which you know
have not got, — to come into this treasury of things and signs
and choose, and understand, and interpret, and make the mosl
Anybody can chatter and cant, picking up phrases and statistic
— you get all that, till you are sick of it, at every table d'hôte
where tourists meet, and air their little connaissances of to-day
but, you know, I won't do that, even to myself. There ar
many things I do not even go to look at, because I am bus
trying to take the last thing in. As Emery Ann says, "I can
do it so rapid; lookin' is n't seein'." I find that even in th
midst of the dead centuries, this little three-score and ten, —
more or less, — of my own, Patience Strong's, has to be give
place to; that I am living a piece of my own little life here

even in Italy ; that day unto day of it uttereth its own speech, and that after all it is only by the very key of that small speech that I can catch any syllable out of the vast, echoing Past.

I doubt very much, — notwithstanding the kind of factitious traveler's-conscience one seems to get put upon one about it, — whether it is, after all, a bounden duty to get all those old centuries into the three fourths of one for which apprehension and meaning are especially and individually given ; whether one needs to recognize and assimilate particle by particle all this dust of them that is garnered up in these ancient magazines; whether in art or history, or even science, the best thing is to be a sort of Golden Dustman, living among the mounds; whether Italy herself might not have a grander Present, if she had not cumbered herself so with accumulation of mere *things* of Time Gone By. For, after all, they are things and signs solely ; grand and beautiful and full of token as they are. And signs are coming, and should be making, all the time.

Emery Ann goes back, very often, to the " graven images."

" They 've always been breakin' it, — the second command-ment; and they 've got the curse of it, I verily believe. Why have n't they turned to and *done* something, instead of *painting* their Virgin Maries and Saint Sebastians and Saint Georges and things ? Men ain't to set up likenesses to look at — not even in their own minds — and think it 's done ! "

But here is the Cathedral at Milan; the Church Mariæ Nascenti ; an inner world-history built up to sight in fretted marble.

If one stopped to read it through, — to read it *up*, from sculpt-ured base, along slow-rising walls of rich reliefs, through forest-pinnacles and crowding imaged niches, and from height to height of roof, and circle to circle of its statue-types, one might give up, not the rest of Italy only, but the rest of life before it. And then one should die and only have begun. As men have died, generation after generation, passing down from each to each the unfinished sentences. For it has been all read but once ; and that has been the long reading of the five hundred years in which it has been builded. It has been the slow spelling of the chisel.

Yes, spelling is the better word — no doubt; for I think many

of these old architects and workers were more like children
spelling letters and syllables carefully along, not knowing, really,
the story they were making, in its wholeness.

"To Mary, being born." Is that it, the translation of its
dedication of two words? Or is the beautiful metonymy of it,
— "To the Virgin that ariseth?"

To the pure humanity toward which all this labor and struggle through the ages, climbs? To the humanity that can receive the Holy Ghost, — of whom the Christ — the Divine —
can at last be born in the world? For it begins away down in
its foundations, with the beginning of it all. And it goes up, —
I can only tell you here and there, what it goes up into, as we
climbed and saw it.

"Have you made up your mind what it is?" Stephen asked,
when we had slowly paced, twice round, the great square, gazing up at the wonderful, delicate, many-hued body of it, pile of
solid stone and masonry as we knew it, — breath, almost of a
dream made visible, as it seemed in its lightness to become, —
rising into thin fine traceries and needle spires, that stood with
their hundreds of white points glittering against the pure, blue
sky; when we had stopped before pillar after pillar with their
great bas-reliefs — each an epoch and a history in its theme, — a
thing of years in its patient carving; when we had wondered at
the monstrous gargoyles, — figures of fierce evil things, leaping
as if driven from under every sacred eave and cornice; — when
we had noted how the statues of heroes and saints, each in his
niche, filled all the window arches and the pilaster angles, line
after line, to height after height of the attaining; when we had
lost trace and order in lovely confusion among the exquisite
pointings and surmountings of buttresses and parapets and cupolas
and thousand clustering slender pillars of turret and steeple;
until it seemed as if the whole vision were born out of the blue
deep up there in which it ended, and could only have gathered
itself together, drop by drop, as jewels gather. "Have you
made up your mind what it is?"

"Yes."

"Is it a crystallization? Frostwork? Did it grow? Is it
growing? Was it enchantment? Will it melt?

"It was lived. It is being lived."

That was all one could think or say.

For it began away down there in its foundations; and you could see it was just human life, — the world's life, in legend, type, and story.

There is the Creation of Adam sculptured over the great door; the calling of man into his natural life; the Lord lifting him as if out of a birth-sleep, to stand up and look around him in his Eden. Forms of brute life are gathered about him; it is the first man Adam, just a living soul among the other first, simplest consciousnesses. There are the First Man and the First Woman under the condemnation of the first sin. There is Abel, who gave up *life* to the Lord, slain by Cain, who labored in the things of the ground only, and hated his brother for his higher sacrifice. There is the Tower of Babel; there is Noah on Ararat; there is Abraham; — there is Hagar, mother of all the wanderers; there is the fiery perishing of Sodom; there is Esau buying pottage with his birthright; there is Jacob wrestling with the angel. There is Moses by the Nile, — before the bush, — at the Rock that pours forth water at his smiting. There are Gideon and Samson and Saul and David; there are Daniel and Job; there is the Queen of Sheba listening to Solomon; there is Elias awakened himself by the angel, and Elias again, restoring the dead; there are Jael and Judith, and Deborah and Esther. And above all these, as the building rises, stand John the Baptist, — greater than all the prophets, — and Apostles and Evangelists of the Kingdom, of whom the least even, was greater yet than he.

Tier above tier, niche above niche, as the solemn strength lifts upward, gleam forth the forms of saints and seers, heroes and servers, whose lives and deaths have been in the building of the world. They front the grand pilasters; they stand right and left in the tall window-arches where the light streams in; above their heads, where the cleansing rains come down, under hallowed eave and cornice, spring out, exorcised, the fierce, horrible shapes that may not abide in the House of the Ages as it rears to its final height and its roofing in with beauty.

Not all seers and saints; not all conscious and purposeful

servers; yet there they are, kings and leaders, and men whose •lives were powers; and their glory is brought into it, whethe they know it or not.

Napoleon the First stands upon a pinnacle over the roof o the great nave. Napoleon the First, at the height of his impe rial command, ordered the final completion of the Cathedral, — the laying of these stones one upon another. He comes in, ii his turn, to the world-building; he stirs a great impulse in it It will sweep, not his way, but God's way, at the last. His own age and kind put him on a pinnacle; let him stand there Samson and Saul are down below and the builders of Babel; and Cain, the slayer, also.

But far within, in the deep, central shine, where the light are always burning, and the prayers are always said, is the sign of something holier. Carlo Borromeo sleeps there in a crysta sarcophagus, with gold and marble and jewels about him that he recks not of, and sculptures in silver of the deeds he did, along the walls. Sign, only. The life went out among the poor and the plague stricken. It was at the Heart of the Building; as the body it wrought by lies here in the inmost of the Temple. As the Son of Man lay also in the Heart of the Earth.

But we went up on those great, high roofs. Another time we came and lingered in the solemn, beautiful interior. To-day the sun shone, and we were to climb among the towers and spires.

Round and round, up the long stair-way that threads a turret in one of the transept corners, we toiled giddily and breathlessly. "An easy staircase," they tell you, "of one hundred and fifty-eight steps;" and this is only the beginning. But by the time we emerged through a queer little labyrinth of pillars and raft-ers upon the first outer foot-hold, Emery Ann and I, at least felt ourselves come pretty nearly to an end. For, think; one hundred and fifty-eight stairs is nine or ten common staircases and we could n't stop for more than a single breath, for we were getting out of sight of one another all the time, round and round and other people were pressing up behind.

We found ourselves beside a long parapet, — within which a kind of passage ran along the transept to the main roof.

" It's a dreadful — hard — world — to do — your duty in,"
observed Emery Ann, sitting down upon the nearest projection,
and gasping fearfully.

Margaret was not gasping, but she stood beside her, and her
just-recovered breath came forth at the moment with a slow,
weary sigh ; and Emery Ann recalled herself.

" But then — we shall all — get — our second wind — presently ! " she added. " It's only — the first strain — that we
lose breath with. I wish — they had — Shezzerpoterzes —
though ! " She had got it out of its " finicky French twists "
into a single solemn and respectable word, with something of an
Old Hebrew consonantal solidity to it, which she was more
familiar with. It sounded as if it had something to do with
Belshazzar and Mesopotamia, and she pluralized it to her own
liking. Emery Ann has no objection to French when it is 'nt
crimped and curled, she says ; or " if you could only boil it
down and skim the froth off." Italian, she thinks is better ;
" there's some-sense to begin with in it, if they'd only stop
when they get through, and not stick an oso, or an ino, or an
etto, or an ebbero, on to everything."

But this is only under the parapet, while you take breath.

We were where the marble gave itself off, as it were, into the
intangible air, with thousands of last, fine, beautiful frettings and
taperings ; rushed up into lofty slender piercings ; crowned itself, — but that comes after and higher, — with holier presences.

We were up above the heavy walls and portals ; the carven
pedestals and pillars ; the sculptures of wrestlings and visions
and battle-storms and victories and miracles, — stories of that in
which the everlasting struggles in the earthly, or the one leans
down to touch the other with a sign and help ; up above the
typical adornings of pediment and ceiling ; above the ash-trees
and the plane-trees and the cedars, and the mystic " Glories of
angels," graven over doors ; up above the statued consoles ; up
above the horrid gargoyles.

We stood where we could look across the vast slope of the
southerly roof. These were " The Gardens," our guide told us.
The lovely creeping arches ran down in rows from centre to

eaves ; the graceful buttresses sprang across the angles ; and
everywhere, along the parapet lines and over the trefoiled
mouldings, in light, exquisite finials, flowers and fruits blos-
somed and rounded from the marble.   In pairs, — a fruit and a
flower, — like the knops and the flowers of the candlestick in the
tabernacle, made after the pattern shewed Moses in the mount.
Thousands of them ; making the Housetop a wilderness of
beauty ; sloping up over side roofs from the basis of the eave-
pinnacles through central spires again to the upper wall of the
nave with its innumerable fine pointed archings, its windows
glorious with color, its groovings and flutings of close pilaster
work, frosty white in the sun.

Saints and preachers, and I know not who, standing on the
first pyramids, look down into the busy world of every day :
warriors with spears, martyrs with palms, are above and above,
a multitude we could not count.   We were led up into the great
bell tower, and we stood among the first forest of them ; we
climbed again into the first balcony of the great dedicatory spire,
and a higher crown of pinnacles, a higher circle of saints,
prophets, evangelists were round us, face to face ; we ascended
again, and looked forth among winged angels ; once more, away
up in the narrowing circle, and golden stars shone upon the
tops of the minarets, like the stars of the seven churches that
John saw in the heavens ; last of all we leaned against the marble rail, carved still to minutest beauty in quatrefoil and fret-
work, three hundred feet above the city, and seated archangels
drooped their wings above our heads from over the gallery-
arches.   Beyond these, the slender line of the last and upmost
shaft runs into the air, and bearing the Cross and wearing the
Crown, the golden figure of Our Lady rises in light, — emblem
that the world uprears as the knight binds a woman's colors
to his lance, and takes God and my lady ! for his valor cry.

Our Lady !   It is the sweet, pure, high apotheosis that kings
and prophets waited for ; that men dream of and long for in our
humanity, and press toward, knowing or unknowing, through all
the climb and turmoil of History.

" Mariæ Nascenti ! "   The storied pile, with struggle and
triumph, faith and vision, written upon its marvelous stones, is

raised to tell of the birth of the holy ; of the human that the Divine shall meet. She stands there, not the Mary of Galilee, but the Mother Soul that shall be born ; the purged and blessed nature of the race, out of which and unto which the Lord Himself and his Kingdom Cometh !

In this Cathedral of Milan, I think I have seen, once and first, all Cathedrals. I am glad that it is in the world.

Over against it — with only the blue air between Church spire and peaks of Ice, — away across the Lombardy plain stand the white Alps. I think you are not surprised to see them. You have come up out of the world of hindrances that crowds the sight with little meannesses, and holds the feet to heavy miles, to where great things and pure spring to each other's presence. The little city underneath, — the little distance that it took you days to come, — are nothing with their walls and leagues, to the outshining of these mighty, beautiful births, the one upon the other, face to face.

All the heights of life find each other, and are near, in the heavens.

We ourselves, when we are raised up, shall even meet the Lord in the air.

27

CHAPTER XI.

IN THE BRERA.

. . . . THE next day we went to the Brera.

I was plunged in among old masters. I was suffocated and confused. I floundered and caught at straws, like a drowning creature. The sea rose up over my head; it was a great deal too deep and wonderful for me. Should I ever learn how to open my eyes and see, — how to dive for the pearls among the weeds and sponges? How to come up to the light, and to common breathing; and bring treasures with me?

Do you remember how we used to sit and turn over the portfolio of old engravings that John brought home from Munich? Do you remember how we studied Corregio's grand faces of Saints and Evangelists, from the frescoes at Parma? How they looked forth with calm grandeur from the spandrils between the great arches, and we wondered if these were the groupings for the lesser spaces, what the wide walls could be covered with, and what vision could fill the wonderful Dome, of "Christ in his Glory?"

Do you remember the pictures from the Chamber of St. Paul, in the Convent, where the dear little child-faces and the heads of gentle animals lean through the medallion openings framed in with vines and flowers?

Do you remember the few Madrid Raphaels in the gallery of engravings of the Boston Library, before which we used to sit for hours, until Mary and Elizabeth in the Visitation, — the sweet girl's head of the Virgin in the separate picture, — Mary and the Christ and the dear old St. Ann and little John the Baptist, — Joseph, from the Nativity, — the mighty manhood of Simon the Cyrenian and the pain of horror and interrogation in all the

strong lines of his face as he grasps the beams of the heavy cross
and lifts it from the sacred shoulders; more than all, the holy,
beautiful countenance of the Son of Man beneath the burden
that he bore for all the world, — took living possession of us,
and we came away at last, as if we had been glad with the
women in the hill country and at Bethlehem, and weeping
among the daughters of Jerusalem in those very far-off, yet
near-forever days?

Do you know the Holbein that dear Mrs. H. has, and of
which she gave me the great beautiful photograph; the sick
child brought to the Mary's child, — the Healer? Where the
human baby is just standing on his little feet as the new life
flows into him and lifts him up, and the Divine One lies back
against the Mother's shoulder, his tiny hand held out with the
gift in it that going forth from his own vitality leaves him
"bearing the infirmity?" The faint, tender little face, the
sweet mouth, the resignful eyes?

I have had years to know these few in; they have come to
me one by one, — little by little in the meanings of each. How
much can I carry away in thought and memory from the *too-
much* of Italy, to make real and my own by and by, slowly, at
home? How much of it all is real, and anybody's own?
Blessed be the sun-pictures! They will tell it all over to me,
and put me in mind.

Raphael's Espousals is here, which we all know so well,
with its marriage group in the low foreground, — the beautiful
slope of the long, ascending steps rising behind, — the open
temple, and the sweet, soft distance of clouds, and hills, and
palms ending and crowning it all beyond. These are what
make it Mary's marriage; not just Mary and Joseph standing
there, like any other twain, the robed High Priest, or the lovers
of her girlhood, breaking the rods as they turn aside. Raphael
knew how to put that wide, upward, stately-fair and heavenly-
gracious distance beyond the moment; there is something in it
that one feels, but cannot say. It could only be said by a picture; a part of speech of the celestial tongue; the first and final
language.

Guido Reni's Rebuke of Peter by Paul, seemed nobly

awful to me. The genuineness of the thing that was between these two, — the unselfing in the earnest looking for truth itself, whether it lay for the moment more with the one or the other, — the gentle, yet mighty " withstanding" in Paul's face, as with calm, raised hand, and direct, grave eye, he bends toward Peter, — the upward, equal directness in Peter's face, — the waiting patience of the impetuous-natured man, that shows in every line of limb and figure, as, seated on the rock, with the mighty keys beside him, and the pillar and the vine behind, he yet receives chiding like a child, who is simple-willing to be put right, who wants to be good and learn ; — the listening of the whole countenance in which no muscle grows restless with reply, and the mouth behind the grand, white beard is shut before a Word that is not his nor Paul's, but of the Spirit of truth that testifies in both : the meeting of the two men's eyes, between which one seems to feel the electric line thrill live and straight ; — it all speaks of something that had got into the world and forth into men's souls that made them absolutely real to each other with the realness of God's own meanings. How many men this day, — yes, of Christ's own very apostles that receive the succession, — would look into each other's faces so ?

Edith stopped before a charming Holy Family by Girolamo Genga, of the School of Perugino. " Our Lady with the Baby and Saint John the Baptist ; besides her four Doctors of the Church, and certain Saints, men and women ; God the Father above, surrounded by many little Angels who scatter down flowers." That is the English of the Italian note in the catalogue.

It was such a lovely Baby ! It was such a moment of joy ! There was that quiver of quick, glad life, that is in nothing whatever but little baby-limbs ; that in this Baby was the very quickening of God anew in his world ; there was the Holy Mother-blessedness ; there was the presence and gathering of all that was to be of that Life, now that it was born ; the saints that were to be sanctified with it ; the Teachers that were to receive and give its word ; there was the joy in heaven of heavenly childhood and the watching of the well-pleased Eternal Fatherhood. And the little child-souls that were close within the glory, the first loving, creative thoughts of souls, were fling-ing down a rain of blossoms upon the earth whose wilderness-places should flush into rose-splendor before the feet of the gen-erations that were to be.

It began to come to me at that moment; and writing of the picture brings to mind what came to me more and more after-wards, as I saw so often in sacred paintings the representation of Apostles, Saints, Bishops, not contemporary, grouped around some central act or scene. Often there is a John the Baptist, where John the Baptist never was in body; often there are Church Fathers made present at that which happened before they were born; dead and living, — past, present, future, come around that which belongs, and is of the same life, as the Son of Man said it should be, when the disciples asked Him concerning the Coming and the Taking, — "Where, Lord?" "Whereso-ever the body is, thither shall the eagles be gathered together."

It is another showing of the eternal moments; that are for always, and for every soul. We shall none of us miss of any-thing. John the Baptist in his wilderness or his prison, while the Christ is talking and healing in Galilee; the simplest soul hidden away from opportunity to-day in its obscure and stead-fast living, while its kindred are out in the light, doing and be-holding and partaking larger.

When we get into the eternity we shall see how it is and has been; that there is no backward or forward, — past and gone, or far on and uncertain; when we awake in his likeness to be satisfied, it will be all there in which He manifests Himself, from before Abraham was, to the Omega of the worlds. Only the pain and the evil shall be gone out of it, or be all transfigured with the overcoming that was in them; and we shall stand pres-ent to every grand living and meaning, every high, good, beauti-ful and precious instant that has ever been or can be, for our perceiving and our full-filling. We shall not even miss, I do be-lieve, any dear bits of our own loving and living that were set apart in this time; the years that we and our darlings were on different faces of the round world; the doings in which we missed each other and did not know each other's deed. It is all safe with Him to whom it is committed to the last Day, — the Day that holds all days, and upon which no night goes down.

The continued representation of the Divine Child and his Mother are a part of this same word.

In the Church of Santa Croce, in Florence, there is a picture of the Assumption of Mary, before which I stood seeing that glorification of her Motherhood, and how the painters always made it so, with the Baby of Bethlehem in her arms. "Blessed art thou among women," was not a short, mocking blessing, to be replaced and ended with the sword-piercing. No, nor even with the glorification of the humanity that was born from her, held in her heart, and in her arms; though moments must come afterward, when for the world's sake He must say, "What have I to do with thee? I must be about my Father's business."

I remember how my own mother used to have sad yearnings over the little children she had lost into their manhood and womanhood, as much as ever the babies that were buried in little graves. "If I could just go back into the dear days, and have them in my arms and round my knees!" she said. You have had them since, motherdie! I have felt my own self, in my own babyhood, with you again, since you went away, leaving me with the gray in my hair!

And Mary — though her Son is raised up to be both Lord and Christ — has Him always, also, in that first dear love. He is always her first-born Son, that she brought forth and laid in the manger!

It was good to see how Margaret Regis could take these things; could see that they were really there, and put her own word and her own event together. I could read that in her face when we spoke of them; I could see how high she reached above her trouble; how she reached her *trouble* up and held it in the light; how love and faith had been born together to her, and her comfort sprang up straightway beside her pain.

"You are *glad* in it," I said to her. She knew what I meant, though I never said it plainer. "What would it be good for, if I could not be glad in it?" she answered. "Why should one thing be real to me and the other not?"

Truly they were both of the spirit; and whoso soweth to the spirit reapeth life, while the sowing to the flesh is only harvest of destruction.

We who are old and learn late, as so many of us do, have to bring our dead things to the resurrection of new hope ; we can bring them, and they will live again ; for " whosoever believeth, though he were dead, yet shall he live ; " but " whoso *liveth* and believeth shall never die." The old have separated life and promise so often, they can only set the one against the other ; it is the *children* who take right hold of the inheritance and begin upon the Kingdom now.

There was no death in this young, clear soul ; she had moments of ache in her waiting; but she had moments, also, in which the waiting was a blessedness.

CHAPTER XII.

TWILIGHT IN THE CATHEDRAL.

. . . .

. . . . Our last day in Milan was a rainy day. We drove to Santa Maria delle Grazie, and went into the old refectory, which is now a barrack, to see the fresco of Leonardo's Last Supper.

Fading out upon the dingy wall, — vanishing away into blankness, — is the faint shadow of what was once, glorious in fresh color, the very life of a great thought; around which little easels stand in a crowd, hurrying now to catch some likeness of it before it quite goes out.

I had to look at the copies to help me in making out the original picture ; and from one and another I could catch, now here, now there, what must have been in Leonardo's work, and which these copies had got in bits, — each having his own success, each marring it with his own failures ; so that when I tried to think which painting, if I could have it, I would choose out of all that were there, there was not one I would have been content with, — there was not one that held not something I could not be content without.

I had no least intent or anticipation of the "everlasting moral," Rose, when I began to write that sentence. It is not my fault — nor my credit — that the everlasting moral is so surely there.

In the twilight, that same day — the rainy twilight — Margaret and I walked up to the Place of the Dome, and went into the Cathedral.

It was like the solemn solitude of a great forest at dusk.

For the few human figures — so little beneath the far height and in the wide distances — only made it seem more hushed and separate for every one. They were hidden in vastness. It was like the separateness and the hiding that we have in the vastness of God's thought. Kneeling down there must have been something like creeping into the Saviour's heart that holds so many, but makes a quietness round every one.

Two large funeral processions were passing out at different doors, and were but as small groups in the great place, as the events were but bits of happening in the great world. One was of a man; a long line of gentlemen with uncovered heads followed. The pall was black; the cloaks were black; it went out gloomily into the rain.

The other was of some young girl; little maidens dressed in white and carrying flowers walked after the white bier, each of them holding the ends of the long satin ribbons of the snow-pure pall. They tripped along to overtake each other; they whispered and smiled, they were gay and sweet as if it were a May day queening.

We passed these close as we went on into the shadows of the aisles.

It is made like a forest solitude, here in the cramp of the city. Out from the narrow, noisome streets the poorest that never dreamed otherwise of any hush or loftiness, — that know nothing of mountain-hearts or forest depths, — can come and kneel down and feel the depth and beauty over-arching them; the majesty of trees, the vaulted silence; the bending about them of mighty power and shelter.

Margaret said, "If there must be cities, I think it is a good thing to have Cathedrals."

"And yet," I answered her, for her word brought up the word of promise to me, — neither in this mountain, nor yet at Jerusalem shall men always need to be, to worship the Father."

"Because there will be the Temple of the Revelations."

"Yes, the *Revelation*," I repeated. "But the hour cometh, and now is. The New Jerusalem is built already, and men stand in it, and the light of it is on their heads and they will not know it — while their deeds are evil."

The pillars of stone rear up their carven and clustered columns, capitaled, far overhead, with surrounding niches in which white statues stand. Beyond and higher, they tower again and

break and sweep away into arches and groinings between which
the richly foliated frescoes of the ceiling continue the curious
frettings of the stone, across whose lovely openings only the
dimness seems to shut, beyond. Chapels open up and down
on either distant side; the transepts are full of sculptures;
Saint Bartholomew, the flayed saint, stands before the sacristy
in his martyrdom, the very marble quivering — and your own
flesh creeps — with the keen fidelity of the chiseling. The
choir, with its pulpits, its tabernacle, its organs, its great in-
closure at the back, — a wall of statues and bas-reliefs at whose
base low broad arches, railed across, open down into the splendid crypt of San Carlo Borromeo, — is just a pile of gorgeous
workmanship in marble and gold, and wood and bronze. The
carvings around the choir wall are a series of presentations of
the Divine Story, from the Nativity of the Virgin to her Assumption and Incoronation. A troop of angels fills the spaces
between these and the lesser tablets of symbols ; the palm-tree
and the plane-tree, the cedar, the vine, the lemon-tree.

But we went in for the great, tender quiet of the whole ; as
we sit under the stars, knowing the heaven is full of wonder,
but letting it say its single, sweetly awful word to us.

We found our way around behind the altar ; we sat down on
some projecting marble heads in the face of the sculptured wall,
and looked across, at the three painted windows that fill the
eastern end ; each pane of glass of the three hundred and fifty a
scriptural story, from some old picture, vivid in clearest blue
and crimson, and purple, and green, and gold, — with soft rich
shadowings of brown and gray, — with clear flesh tints of faces ;
luminous, splendid, even in the decreasing light.

We were all alone here for many minutes, with those Old
and New Testimonies, through which the light came. What
else has ever been kept in the world like those parables of the
kingdom, those chronicles of the dwelling of God in the earth
among men ?

We forgot about the time. The place grew dim ; but still
the colors shone. All the day there was, gathered and streamed
through them. The starlight and the moonlight would find
them in the long nights. The storm might make an absolute

darkness, but there would not be storm always, and as the stars and the moon waited above, and the sun wheeled round to a new, splendid rising, the blue and the crimson and the emerald and the gold of the pictured years and their mighty meanings would wait for new readings in the window set toward the East.

An old priest came round from the sacristy, and said something to us in Italian. We had risen and were standing together, and we bowed respectfully, but very ignorantly, as he addressed us, and continued as we were. He came back again across the great pavement, and repeated his words, of which we now caught enough to understand. They were shutting up the Cathedral.

We hurried down through thickening gloom, along the solemn aisles. We came out upon the wide front pavement, and the long, shelving steps. We were in the rain again, and we gathered up our garments, spread our umbrellas, and picked our steps between the pools in the worn hollows of the stones, across the square and down the Corso.

On the way, Margaret said to me, —

" Mamma wants to go to Venice. I would rather go straight down with you to Florence. If I were to ask her, — but I do not mean to ask her, Miss Patience. I have kept from her long enough. I mean to try to be something to her now. Only there is no particular good in it — as there might have been, — because now there is n't anything for me to gain."

She said it just as simply as some people might have said the opposite thing. " There is no good in it, for it is all in the way of bettering myself."

I do not think any final, far-off, second benefit ever shaped itself into a calculation with her, even enough to make her pride refract. The condition put upon her action in the present years was what had chafed ; there was nothing now to rebel or acquiesce in. She knew her pride had been the real thing to sacrifice ; in her true repentance she would fain have sacrificed it now. She would have made herself sweet and humble enough to do something by which even some advantage might come to her again. But there was nothing of that sort to do. Therefore, there was no particular good in being good. Mrs. Regis had been talking vaguely of Venice, for some days past, but nothing had been settled. It was not even settled then that any of us were to leave as we did. But we decided that night to go from Milan the next morning. Margaret and her mother to Venice; we others to Florence. It was to be many weeks before we should all be together as we had been.

Just as we had been — and no more — we should not ever be. Because something had begun in our relations to each other that would still be going on; and this piece of our lives must go on also. So much the more of each other, and not so much the less, we should have when the weeks were over.

It was not a gap; I have learned very well, long before now, that a place or a time in which I may feel concern is not a gap just because I may not be bodily in it.

It did not turn out to be a gap in my knowledge and joining of things even; I can put some of them together in the telling, as well, now, as if I had been there.

CHAPTER XIII.

"ALL THROUGH THE WORLD."

. . . . MRS. REGIS rested in that. General Rushleigh was still her friend. He was said to care little for women in a society way, and to have been a man of few friendships in these last dozen years that he had been fully and seriously a man in a full and serious life. Margaret had refused him. It was not likely that he would think of marriage any more. When that fever is over, other things take first, strong place. With some men, money; with some, name and power; with some friendship and beneficence. And he had told her, at that last moment, — that very *first* moment of disappointment, which was more, — that her friendship was very dear to him.

Mrs. Regis must rest in something. She did not know how to be miserable. Days must be smooth, — nights must be restful. Some people can give their lives for a love. And that does not mean always the mere easy thing of dying. It means facing a fact, — taking up a cross; healing live flesh over a ball that cannot be probed for or extracted, — bearing it on into the years that remain, and living them through with keen, conscious pain at the undermost of everything; at best with a strong hand always held down upon something that *would* spring and palpitate into an agony if it were let go.

Mrs. Regis must find an alternative to this, to live at all.

He would come back to her. Friendships last when loves have to be got over. Margaret would marry. With herself nothing would change. She, and Paul Rushleigh now, were beyond that beginning of things in which people must marry or go away into separate lives. All the rest of her days might be rich with his regard, that might grow, — that *should* grow, for how much she might prove herself to him with her free, queenly womanhood and her large power, — to a something that was neither son's love, nor brother's love, nor lover's love, but the chivalry of a whole manhood that might, in differing circumstances have been the very passion of either. She would yet be the woman of women to him. To be representative, — of charm, exquisiteness, loftiness, tenderness, possible companionship, — to make a man think what it *would* be for her to have been sister, wife, mother, to anybody; what it was that she should be dear and sure friend to himself, — to a certain temper of woman this is possession and satisfying.

That it could not be if there were bond or bar against utmost and exclusive relation is the subtle test of nature in it.

They were both free, she and Paul Rushleigh. She could care for him so, she could so draw him to herself, without misgiving or overlooking. Let the years take care of the rest of it. The years and the forever; for it all widens out before her, and she is young in it. The birth of an affection is always the birth of a life, and the beginning of a forever.

But how of Margaret, at her side? How of easy chairs for everybody? How was it in this with the woman who could not help herself to a favorite dish at table, till she had distributed to others even with careful exceeding, that she might be free to appropriate and enjoy her own part; who gave away generously that conscience might not trouble her comfort in the things that were left?

How of something that she might do for these other two lives before she rested in that alternative for her own?

It had been put into her mind how a word of explanation might be made to reach Paul Rushleigh. A word that might bring him back; or to which his answer would be an eager renewal of what had been spoken just an hour too soon; a new asking for a hope to wait in, to come back to, by and by?

She could have been equal to it; that curious nobility of hers that made conditions for her selfishness, and paid taxes for it in every little daily thing, would not have let her be easy now until she had paid this. Only for Margaret; for her quietness and peace; for her having come to her one day and said, "Mamma,

you were right, and I was mistaken; it has ended for the best."
And grown more cheerful afterward, as if, with the end of the
old story, she put away, finally, the trouble of it.

More cheerful and more friendly; as if she would make
amends in kindness, in dutifulness. As if all were open now,
between them, for a better confidence, a truer intimacy. No
word or sign about Paul Rushleigh, no seeking, in this new confidence, of counsels or comfort that way. That too, had ended
for the best. It had been a part of the other ending. She had
refused him because she had not loved him ; had not thought of
loving anybody but the poor Harry Mackenzie, who took life as
he would not take tailor's work ; who must be served to order
with his coats and trousers, but to whom the world was a slop-
shop for vital concerns, in which he looked for circumstance and
providing " ready-made."

She was a girl, as her step-mother had said ; she could give
only a girl's fancy. And she had not known how to fancy Paul
Rushleigh !

What was there to call Paul Rushleigh back for? She
watched Margaret, and she thought this honestly of her. She
did not question her. Own motherhood would have done that.
Own motherhood would have watched the child's heart as a
deeper heart of its self. There is own motherhood that is not
born motherhood ; and there is that of the flesh which is never
completed in the spirit. But a real mother would have asked
Margaret Regis questions. And a real 'child would have run
straight to its mother's arms. There was where it dropped between them and was, for a while, a lost end, that might have
been unraveled.

So two and three weeks went by, and Paul Rushleigh was
sailing up the Nile, or slowly traversing the hills of Benjamin
and Judah, or the deep ravines of the Jordan and the Dead Sea.
It was little use to send letters after him now. The door shut
itself to, and the creak of it did not trouble Mrs. Regis any
more.

Until at last, one day, Margaret laid her hand upon the
latch.

They had been to the Church of Santa Maria della Salute,

and afterwards to Salviati's for mosaics ; and late in the afternoon were rowing round the Punta to see the sunset from the
Guidecca.   In the church they had found themselves suddenly
side by side with the English clergyman they had played chess
with at Lugano; and in the Fabriccia they had fallen in with
a whole party of American ladies who had been on board the
Nova Zembla, and whom they had encountered afterward at
Lucerne.

"How curiously people turn up, when one has once met
them," Mrs. Regis had remarked.   "You absolutely cannot lose
anybody in Europe."

"Or anywhere, I think, mamma," Margaret replied.   "That
is, people of the same order, who will be sure to come, sooner or
later, to the same things.   We are of the traveler-order now,
bound to see the churches and the pictures, and being of the
woman-order too, to buy jewelry; so of course we come across
the rest of them.   Switzerland — where we met everybody two
months ago — is all poured down into Italy now.   In the spring
they 'll all drift back to Paris and London and the steamers.

"There 's a comfort in it," she went on, I can think with what
a slightly different tone, like a trace of effort, too, in the speaking ; as if she said out what her impulse would have been to
keep to herself, but which something different admonished her
not to hide away covetously or shyly in the old reserve.
"There 's a comfort in it.   If you can't drift away out of the
current, from the travelers, you surely won't drift far away,
very long, from the friends ; in the world, — or out of the world.
If we are after the same things, the things will bring us together.
I 'm sure Miss Patience would say that."

"You have got a good deal from Miss Patience."

"Yes, mamma.   How different this water-world is from the
world of the mountains.   And we have come so quickly from
one into the other !   And how good it is that the *whole* world
is round, and does n't go on and on, over a great stretch, with no
end either way.   I 'm sure, — Miss Patience would be sure, —
that it means the same thing again."   Margaret spoke slow, and
softly.   She could not be glib in giving up real thoughts, as she
had never been used to give them to her step-mother.   But she

wanted if she could, to give her something now. "To be something to her," as she had said. She had come away with her, detaching herself from readier companionship, to try if there might some readiness come up between them; to see if some of the old distrust and reserve that she had been sorry for might not be flung away. And of things she found a "comfort in," did she not owe a part, if she could render it, to the same want that her own act had made for them both? For had she not sent away her mother's friend?

So she spoke of driftings, and meetings, and seekings of the same, — of the round world that east or west brings home again, — when she could not by any means have pronounced Paul Rushleigh's name.

The sun was lowering behind the palaces of Venice, behind the far-off hills; the water and the sky were rosy, — the oars dipped into light, and domes and towers stood up in it; the day dropped close and lovingly upon the earth in pouring itself on around its rim.

"Miss Patience and you seem very sure of things," said Mrs. Regis. "The world is a large round; and there is a great up and down in it."

"In thirteen hours there will be a sunrise; and in a year the light goes everywhere; — does n't it?"

Margaret added the last two words lightly, girlishly; making the question offset the graveness of the enunciation. "Yes, Miss Patience *is* sure; and she has made me feel sure. She has been the best of all this time to me; except" —

She might have stopped or she might have said "almost" instead of "except;" but her truth had its own way; it did not search about to pick safe words

"Except what, Margaret?" said Mrs. Regis. And with an instant instinct, would have caught back her question. But she could only catch back the breath upon which it had been spoken.

"Except, mamma," said Margaret, with a brave, sweet clearness, "what I sent away from me. What will come back again, some day, and I shall wait for; if I have to wait for it all through the world."

28

Perhaps Margaret would not have said it, but that she thought also she was promising back her mother's friend.

Some day it should be all right for both. Some day, when the light that goes everywhere, came round. She could wait her year, though the year should be all her life.

And now her mother knew. It was clear between them. She knew that in the might and reality of something that asserted itself above all possible baser motive, Margaret was no longer afraid to please her, — to " be good; " lest it should seem to be "for what she could get."

They had come back, along the rosy water, and rounded the " Punta." They had glided across the wide entrance of the Grand Canal again, and their gondola lay at the foot of the stairs of the Hotel Barbesi.

·CHAPTER XIV.

BUILDED WORDS.

. . . .

. . . . WHAT do you think was the first thing we did in Florence ? What do you think were the first works of art we went to see?

Patterns and wools of every lovely device and color in a little French shop on the Via Tornabuoni. And we each bought materials, — Edith and I, — for a fascinating piece of needlework.

Because we wanted something, as Emery Ann said, to calm down over. Something to sit down with and make it seem like home in the big salon we had taken at the " Alleanza." When we had opened out our books, and put our pictures and little Swiss things round on the tables, and hired in a piano, and got roses and carnations in the vases and a pyramidal fire in the triangular fire-place at one end, and the window open to the air and sunshine at the other, — had " made the room *chirpy*," Edith said, — and had each chosen a chair and a corner and only wanted some work to cuddle down and chirp over. For we were quite determined always to have home, in the first place. We were determined to take the breath between things that no thinking creature can live without. Or rather, we were determined, since the soul-lungs are like the body-lungs, to take our inspirations in breaths and not in whole atmospheres at once, which can't be done.

We would get up and· go to bed a whole week perhaps here in Florence, thinking to ourselves every now and then, " Just a little way off — we can walk out any morning˙ to any one of them — are the Duomo and Giotto's Tower, and Ghiberti's great Bronze Gates ; there is the old Old Palace of the Lords of Florence ; there are the galleries full of Raphael's and An-

gelico's and Titian's and Corregio's, and everybody's pictures;
there are Michael Angelo's sculptures; there are Galileo's tele-
scopes and instruments, and frescoes of the story of his life;
there are these and a hundred other things, that ages have piled
up here, and that we can no more really take in all of, than we
can live the ages.

But because what we do take in we want to make a life of,
and not a delirium, we will settle our own little place here, and
make it warm to us. We will get used to belonging, and to the
fancy of what we may do. We will rest till we are fresh for
it; we will have some pleasant little finger-business to rest in.
In some small feminine content we will forget, between times,
that we are travelers; then we will put up our work, and put
on our boots, and go out for our walk or a drive, and to see
something, as we might at home; and it will be along the sunny
Arno and into the Uffizi Gallery, may be, to look at a picture,
that we know already or that we know we want to know; or it
will be to cross over the Old Bridge and wander into the very
street that Romola lived in, whose ancient buildings lift their
black gloom along the river side; or perhaps, to follow the
narrow, crooked mazes into the heart of the city, and find the
house of the Buonarottis, and see their frescoed history, and
the sketches and studies and autographs of Michael Angelo.

I think we felt richer, all along, in the things we might do,
than in the things we checked off as done.

" I like to have cake in the cupboard," said Emery Ann.
" Who ever heard of turning to, and eating up a whole batch,
hot ? "

Down at the dinner table, or in the general salon, we came
into the world of the knowing ones; people who were always
ready to overwhelm you with some old Perugino, or Masaccio,
or Ghirlandajo, that you had not heard of yet; among whom
the talk ran like a kind of fugue, in which you could detect
pretty well the week old and the yesterday people, by the parts
they took. Or like a general recitative of the House that Jack
built, adapted; so that some would have only learned as far as,
— This is the town where the Medicis reigned, and Michael
Angelo lived and sculptured; and others, away on, — these are

the statues that Michael Angelo wrought, and the pictures that
Del Sarto painted, and the bas-reliefs Della Robbia carved,
and the frescoes Fra Angelico made, and the churches Brunelleschi built; and these are the marbles of John of Bologna
and the bronzes of Benvenuto Cellini in the Loggia that Or-
cagna erected, — and these are the wonderful points and touches
in the statues and pictures and frescoes and carvings, and the
things you have all of you got to discover in the churches and
squares, and loggie and palaces, in the town where Michael Angelo lived, and the Medicis reigned, and the Guelphs and Ghib-
ellines took their turns; that the Emperor Charlemagne restored,
and Attila conquered long ago, and nobody knows who founded.

"I don't feel half qualified to flock and feed with ostriches,"
Stephen Holabird remarked one of those first nights, coming up
into our quiet salon, where Vincenzio had just brought the bright
moderator lamp, and "the Smile" had replenished the gay little
fire, and the worsted work was lying about on the table among
the guide-books. "The Smile" was a squat "little facchino" or
man of burdens, who stoked for our side of the house, and was
all smut, except where he beamed with a row of dazzling teeth
at us every time he came in, like the sun out of a thunder-cloud.

"Ostriches?" repeated Edith, looking up at him; thinking,
I suppose, he meant something about the creams of the last
course, and the walnuts of the dessert, which did n't quite hold
out to our end of the table; and rather wondering, for Stephen
never seemed to care so very much about his eating.

"Yes. Literally, as to their legs; and figuratively as to their
stomachs. People who can take in and digest seven churches
in a day, and stand round to do it. I got awfully plucked to-
night. Those three wise women came down upon me about the
tombs of the Medicis, and Michael Angelo's Night and Morning;
and I did n't know the whole arrangement was in the Church of
San Lorenzo, or that it was altogether anywhere. They just
looked at me — as if I had never heard of the Ten Command-
ments!"

"Like the woman that talked to me about "jade," this morning," said Emery Ann. "She said there was such fine "yard"
in some 'palazzo' or other; and I said that was comfortable,

when the streets were so narrer-contracted ; and then she looked
so disgusted at me, as if I 'd spoke toads to her di'monds, and it
turned out that she was talkin' about crockery ; some old-fashioned
kind that I 'd never heard of. She did n't explain it to me though ;
she turned round and went on about it to another knowing one,
and they aired their information at each other till I guess I made
out pretty much all they 'd picked up, and I war n't mortified a
mite, either. My turn was only just come, you see ; and it came
that way. I know ' jade ' now ; and *they* did n't *alwers*. You
can't begin on a world, till you 're born into it, anyway ; but
there 's some folks that would n't let on they ever *were* born, if
they died for it."

"I get my fun out of it at the other end," said Stephen. " It 's
no use everybody setting up for the same style. There would
not be any particular style about it. So when Lady Clara Very-
very de Very asks me if I 've seen Andrea del Sarto's Madonna
of the Sack, at the Annunziata, and if it is n't wonderful, I reply that the Sack is certainly most extr-o-rd'n'ry ; that there is
evidently a monstrous deal in it ; and then I inquire quite innocently, if she does n't think old Andrew would have made out a
smarter thing if he 'd just had the Sack, and let alone the Lady?
And I 'm sure she does n't know a word about the story, or she
would have come down in a pattering shower of ' so very-very
sad, to be sure, and yet so int'resting, his putting her into all his
pictures ; really, so very-very touching.' But instead of that,
she hushes up and lifts her chin in the air, just enough to go for
dignity in case I did mean to be impertinent, which she is n't
sure of ; and I eat my soup until she or somebody else begins
again with the Fanali, or the Tabernacles, or something."

"Apropos, auntie," said Edith, "did you know that those
pretty, graceful lanterns on the wide balcony over opposite, were
after the real old Florentine Fanali, — the special signs of the
distinguished houses, that only the very high families could
have ? And that the beautiful house itself is a palace, and was
given by Louis Napoleon to Countess ——, a great friend of his
who lent him money when he was poor, and at whose hotel in
Paris the arrangements were all made for the famous Coup
d'État ? "

No; I had not known, but I had recognized something-stately-exquisite in the unknown sign. The Fanali are really lovely things wrought in light iron-work, projected from corners of palaces, or set, as these, upon high, slender shafts above the rails of balconies; with their delicate crowns and pendants, and their finishin gspires, expressing in each artistic line the raying and upspringing of a light or flame, they almost illuminate without the touch of fire. They suggest their purpose; they are a charming last elegance of completion; they sparkle from the solid ponderousness, as if something gave you a live glance from out the old dead solemnity.

Over here, upon this sunshiny, modern mansion that stands in its spacious grounds fenced about with tall rails of gilded iron, they surmount the balustrades with an air of delicate superbness. No one could help but notice them, significant as human port or gesture of a subtile pride.

People never know whom they are building for, or giving to; we were all so daily obliged to Louis Napoleon for putting the lovely Palace just opposite our windows of the Alleanza. It was the only thing between us and the Arno; for the Via Montebello runs parallel with the Lung Arno Nuova, and this house and grounds takes up the intervening square; so that we got the space and the sunshine, as much as the full-dressed major-domo who seemed to be left in sole charge and enjoyment, and who opened the great saloon windows early of a morning and stepped forth upon the stately balcony, while the rooms were airing, like Alexander Selkirk or a tame peacock.

We took the Church of Santa Croce for our first intent of sight-seeing.

We had been five days in Florence, quietly composing ourselves. We had been down to Viessieux', and subscribed to the Library, and brought home Vasari's " Lives of the Painters," and " Romola," and the " Life of Savonarola." We had been reading ourselves back a little, over our worsted work, into the atmosphere and mood of the old City in its old Days. One wants a baptism, as well as a birth. We were just born, as Emery Ann had said, into this world of Italy. We wanted some new pour-

.ing of its water, some fresh anointing of its oil, some gradual opening of our eyes into its different medium, before we could go forth and behold and understand and assimilate. Meanwhile, daily, we astonished our fellow-pensioners, who chattered of so much that they had done, and demanded of us an account of our doing, by our persistent answers of "Nothing yet. We do not feel ready."

I said that about our first *intent* of seeing, because the moment you move toward *one* seeing, among these old, full places, you find upon your path such a crowd of other things among which you cannot walk blindfold. There is a tumult of marvel and interest that surges about you in great waves, among which you can hardly catch your breath. The tide breaks up around you from all the ocean of the past. You are smitten with a surf from far deeps that shines living in the light of the present.

The meanings that cluster thick in the signs that every stone is full of, every wall and niche is made eloquent with, are too many to be taken any real note of, except here and there, when something interprets itself startlingly to you, and you know how all the rest must have been quick once with significance, as born from the thought and new from the hands of the builder. They only appear quaint, worn, confused, ugly enough, perhaps, to the hasty looking that is not seeing, — the sight seeker's glance that expects instant surprise and joy of a pleased and full admiring. I have seen a great many things, and much has spoken to me, since I came quite away, the forms of which stood mute and meaningless before me in the few minutes I had in their presence. I have learned about them since, because I went about among them then. This, I think, is to us unlearned ones, the great use of travel.

See now, this queer blotched, flat old façade of Santa Maria Novella; Michael Angelo's "Bride;" that we passed, driving through the city that morning, and traversing in our way the great piazza that is named from it.

Ancient, battered, dull, — time and weatherworn, — it lifts itself across the head of the pentagonal space which slopes away before it.

These grand old edifices bury their grandeur deep back often among crowding walls, showing a mere front only, along the public way, left unfinished and unadorned perhaps, for centuries after the interior has been elaborated with all the glory of sculpture, and made rich with pictures, and grown dusky and solemn in every tint and curve with the shut air and the long shadow.

Old as it looks, this façade has never been quite completed. But every bit of it has a meaning. Those curious curves that fill the angles, one on either side, between the deep frieze and the lower cornice, and look, — Edith said, — "like the walrus-shapes in geography books," — are the emblematic sails of the Rucellai, whose chapel occupies the right transept within. There are carven circles upon them, — that on the left only is finished, — below which are ancient astronomical instruments fixed upon the wall; a marble gnomon and two bronze armils. These last were for noting the lines of light, — the one at the exact noon point at the moment of the sun's reaching the meridian, — and the other, the equinoxes. There is a hole also, through the wall, made for the passage of a ray from the sun into the nave, where a meridian line was to have been graven upon the pavement, but was never done.

This gathering and manifesting of the truths of the outward heaven, and treasuring their knowledges and observations in the same buildings where they enshrined their memorials of the inward faith, and sought the shining from the inward heaven ; where they made their altars toward the east, and lifted the cross toward the sun rising, seemed full of beautiful correspondence to me; as if it came with a direct instinct, from the harmonies of the heavens and the earth that shall be, — that wait, unapprehended and unevolved, in the foreshadowing mysteries of the heavens and the earth that now are.

I think it was of a lovely ordering and relation, that Galileo divined the central law of the planets from the lamp that swung beneath the solemn dome of a great cathedral.

There are faded frescoes in lunettes over the door-ways ; dim, and not beautiful, until you stop to think what was put into them, and why. And I think that all any artist can do, — of the old days or the new, — is to make lines by which you can

run back into his thought, and follow that out again to the asking
of the time which it ministered to ; and that, in this way only,
the early paintings, stiff and queer, and half-finished, have their
charm and value.

Here, over the great entrance, is the processional Bearing of
the Holy Sacrament into the church on a high holy day, — the
Corpus Christi ; and before it kneels St. Dominick of the lily
and the star, with the angels who ministered to him of the bread
and wine of heaven. When you know the story of it, and see
it put there with the typical pictured ceremony of the carrying
the sign of the Presence into the Cathedral walls, — and when
you find that the vanishing colors over the other door-ways,
represented Aaron with the manna, and Melchisedek with the
bread of the old mystic sacrament offered to Abraham, — you
catch a sentence of the language the primal church was always
speaking to her children, *showing* them the things of the kingdom of heaven.

And these are the things I look for continually, trying rather
to understand the spirit that was in the world and made the liv-
ingness of works, than to search out the technicalities and chro-
nologies of art-history and craft.

We came, without looking for it, down the Via Cerretani, into
the Place of the Dome. Giotto's Tower stood up into the blue
height like a miracle. Its perfect lines rear their lovely parallels, carrying the thought up with them in a half-comprehended
wonder and delight, till they pause short in full power and bold-
ness, and show you suddenly why you wondered and delighted.

" There is n't any great marvel in a *steeple*," said Emery Ann ;
" it runs up to a point, natural enough, and the end of it *is* the
end. But *that* might have clumb forever ! "

" There was to have been a pyramid," said Edith, who had
turned to her little " Florence Hand Book," while we stopped
the carriage to gaze and enjoy. " That would have carried
it twenty-eight metres more."

" It was a Providence they did n't put it on ! " said Emery
Ann.

The clear, beautiful colors of the many marbles ; — the columned corners, deep-grooved with slender panelings in contrast-

ing stones ; — the cornices and mouldings between the stories rich with foilings ; — the tall, delicate gothic windows with their light mullion bars, and arches, and balustrades ; the one upper window in each side especially — wide and high and with exquisite dividing pillar-threads — thrown open freest to where the topmost light comes in ; down below, the niches with the statues of the evangelists, the saints, the prophets and the sibyls, four on each of the four sides, — under these, the bas-reliefs of the Virtues, the Sacraments, the Works of Mercy, and the Beatitudes, in the diamonded panels, and still beneath, the hexagons with the story of human progress in the carvings, from the first age to the art and science of Grecian cultivation, — here was a glory of speech again like the utterances of the marbles at Milan ; rhymed to an inward harmony through the outward law of a measure that the rhymers hardly knew as they handled. Philosophy, Astronomy, Geometry, Music ; the natural ear and understanding ; then the word of the Spirit to the life of man ; the obediences, the virtues, the love and the Benedictions ; after these, the seers of vision, the layers-hold of revelations, — the thrones and the powers of prophecy and sainthood. And the Building — that springs up out of these foundations in humanity, and stands fair and grand, eternal in the heaven !

I talked about this afterward with Miss Euphrasia. She saw what I did in it, she rejoiced especially in the degrees ; the separate marked heights, — of the structure ; lines and divisions, — all of beauty and fitness, — that showed the steps and ranks of attainment upward.

The Miss Horners tell us in their book of Florence, that Mr. Ferguson objects, artistically, to this. " How can he," I asked of Miss Euphrasia, " with the right instinct of art, — when the *truth* is in it ? "

" Many people would say," she answered me, " that the truth of the thing, as we think we find it, is a very pretty fancy ; but as to its being the real fact through whose vitality and actualness the stones were put one upon another, — had to be put, by a law of expression, — all that would be to them less than fancy — mere fantasy."

" But it is there ! " I cried. " It holds together. It is all that *does* hold together. Without it, the masonry is nothing, — would fall apart, — would have refused to be builded. They. *had* to follow the meaning, as the lapidary has to follow the line of cleavage when he shapes a jewel ! "

" They do not know the word that goes forth into the ends of the earth," said Miss Euphrasia, quietly. " And that there can be neither speech nor language, nor any sign, where the voice is not heard."

" Except the Lord build the house they. labor in vain that build it." The words came instantly in my mind and touched themselves in that internal sense, which is the deepest literal, to what Miss·Euphrasia had quoted.

Another time, when I was alone, I turned to them in the beginning of one of those Psalms of David, that were made for " songs of degrees." I paused over that old·heading, wondering what the whole meaning of it was, that they should have been so appointed and used. And then something more flashed upon me and made me see, with such a great fullness, — what David, father of Solomon the Builder — must have seen ; what runs gloriously, wondrously, through all these fifteen Psalms, that the Priests and the Levites used to sing as they went up the steps into the temple. That ·in the first and last, in the upper and lower life, in all the degrees of the building, — one thought flows through, one intent and blessing ; from Him who is the First and Last.

It is in the promise to them that " fear the Lord," that recognize Him. Even the form of the outer living shall be built in a serene and gracious order " as a city that is compact together." It is in the prophecies of redeeming for the nation : — They shall eat of the labor of their hands : the wife shall be as a fruitful vine ; the children shall be like olive plants. " The Lord shall bless them out of Zion, and they shall see the good of Jerusalem all the days of their life." ˙ " There shall be·peace in Jerusalem ; prosperity within her walls and palaces." When a " place " is found out " *for the Lord,* a habitation for the mighty God of Jacob ! "

This is the·New Jerusalem ; the order of the inward and the

outward; the flowing down from the highest into the least, — from the Head even to the feet.

The precious ointment upon the head, that ran down upon the beard, even Aaron's beard, that went down to the skirts of his garments: "As the dew of Hermon that descended from the mountains of Zion, for there the Lord commanded blessing, even life for evermore."

It is *so* full, Rose, that it can neither be said nor written out. It can only be touched in points of light, that leap and answer to each other. It shone here, and it shone there, as I read, and thought, and the answer came to me that this truly, — in all the world and in the life God means to make in it, — is the divine Song of his Degrees.

We did not stay that morning to study the Great Bronze Doors in the Baptistery, over against the beautiful Tower, neither did we enter either of the three buildings then; but in the order of place and of my telling over to you, and in the order of thought as they all seem to me and join together now, they come in here so obviously, that I must just go on with the bits I can say about them.

That again is a good of not telling things just as fast as I do them, which is often quite out of the right succession into which they come in their realities, after I have gathered them together, and they have somewhat interpreted themselves and each other. Which reminds me of how much all that we live works in the same way, ranging itself in its essential relation and economy, not at all always according to the synchronism in days and years. As the Bible words do, also, and the stories and signs written out in the Bible; answering each other and finishing their significances across the generations: which is the wonder and the wholeness of the Word of God.

These great works of men prove themselves after the self-same law; scarcely any were conceived and executed in a human unity of time and purpose; the single thought of a single man hardly ever runs through one of them from beginning to end. They were interrupted, shifted from hand to hand, — the technical designs were changed; but through all lived and persisted that

which had to be said by them; the thought which was above
and beyond any one man's entire ordering.

Giotto meant to have had a spire upon the summit of the
Campanile, but it *finished itself* without the spire, in the hands
of Gaddi. He saw that it was done, as sometimes, with an instant touch or word, and an inspiration to perceive that it has
ended, a great man finishes that which he has to write, or paint,
or say, with a flinging down of brush or pen, or a sublime surprise of silence.

Life itself, I think, with all the press and pain of its durance
and relinquishing, must end so, sometimes.

Perhaps the last mere human experience of the Lord was
that blessed marveling that overswept him at the culmination of
his agony, and broke forth in the high, sudden ecstasy of " It is
finished ! "

The Three Bronze Doors were not made and numbered in
the order of their real argument. A hundred years after Andrea
Pisano had wrought out the history of John the Baptist, comes
Ghiberti with his marvelous thought for the " Gate of Paradise," which was set towards the east. He begins with the
creation of men upon the earth, and carries on through his ten
reliefs, the time-types of event, — the Sin, the Flood, the Faith-
dawning in Abraham, the Divine Leading and Overruling in the
Story of Joseph, the Lawgiving, the Conquering of Joshua, the
uprising of David, — to the glory of the wisdom of Solomon,
and the coming before him of the Sabean Queen.

There it stops. Over it stands the Wisdom that is to be
made manifest, between the figure of the Baptist who pours the
water-chrism upon his head, and a winged celestial presence
waiting on his right hand.

And they call this, which is the Gate of the Beginning, the
" Second Door," because it was carven in the fifteenth century,
and the other had been finished in thirteen hundred and thirty.

The other is the Life of John. The Priest struck dumb in
his office, because of the Voice that was to come.

The women whom the divine Hope drew one toward the
other. The Birth ; the Naming, as the " gracious gift of God ;"
the Crying and Preaching ; the Baptizing. The Recognition of

the Holiest who already stood among them. The rebuke of sin in the high place to the very face of the Herod of the time. The Prison ; the steadfast Prophesying ; the Beheadal. The obtaining of the head, and the Burial of the body by them who had believed.

This is the story of the world's arousal to the truth that accuses, that overthrows, that commands repentance, that smites with fear and shame, and washes with tears, because the coming of the Highest is at hand ; it is the legend of the Second Door that opens for the world.

Around this gate is lovely frame-work of all sweet growth of life and fruit, and forms of birds that come and lodge in the branches. Above it is the solemn sculpture of what always has to be that such a gate may be flung wide, — the martyrdom of the Prophet.

And the last Door is that by which all men may enter, and go in and out and find pasture. It is the Divine Life on earth, from the Annunciation to Mary, to the Descent of the Holy Ghost. Above its twenty panels of most deep and delicate and intricate relief, framed in with foliage and forms of living creatures, among which look forth the images and faces of Prophets, Sibyls, Evangelists, Fathers, is set again the figure of the " greatest Prophet born of woman " — the Forerunner — between a Pharisee and a Sadducee ; preaching to them the Word of Preparation.

And all this stands in the noisy city square, where the common crowd hustles to and fro, and the wind blows dust into the precious bronzes ; and opposite is the unfinished and many times abandoned façade of the Duomo, roughly boarded up ; but above, in the clear air, run the fair, triumphant lines and swing the full voiced bells of Giotto's Campanile ; and the great round of the Cathedral roof swells up over the housetops, — the greater that it is but *just* above, and seems so to rest and brood among them ; and into this church of the Baptist come all the mothers of Florence with every little child that is born there, that they may be named in the name of the Father and of the Son and of the Holy Ghost.

It is the visible Heart of the great, old City.

Crossing the Piazza della Signoria we stopped at Fenzi's and got our letters. Margaret's from Venice was among them, telling me something — directly and indirectly — of what I have written a little way back; the going on of the story that seems to have stood still in the middle, as nevertheless no human story ever does.

Margaret told me of their goings and comings; of their falling in with the people they knew; of the words of her talk with her mother that grew out of that; the rest of it I know, because I was there. There, in the human heart and experience of it, in which I knew Mrs. Regis as well as if she were myself; as she is indeed a certain piece of my possible self, carried out in other circumstances, else I never should have known her at all. In which by the same rule I know Margaret; who is a higher, and fresher, and sweeter possible of me.

I read the letter in the carriage, all the way to the Place and the Cathedral of the Holy Cross.

"What I shall wait for if I have to wait for it all through the world."

Directly over the leaf, her next lines told me, unawares, the strength and beauty of her waiting, that was no mere weak tarrying. A waiting that was a watch and ward, rather, in the true power and holding of the word; — a calm biding that was already a "continuing in."

For she had that to which she belonged; she was like them who "watch for their Lord," to whom He cometh continually, in all things. She had entered into the world, of which her being and so her love, was. She had found out this secret of the soul; this certain shining that illuminates all through the husk of circumstance, — the inevitable might of the growth that shall be, — the power of the substantial and endless life.

She was reading there in Venice just such things as I was reading here; as my mind was full of when her letter came into my hands. Just such things, also, as — whatever text or script of the world might lie before him — Paul Rushleigh would be spelling from Sphinx or Pyramid, or listening out in the sweet and solemn hush laid like a loving memory of God upon the unchanged Mount of Olives or the Galilean Sea.

" The world is full of it," she said, " and I am so glad to think
myself into some company with those who find it. So glad to
have some little sign in me that I am 'minding the same things,'
the things that certainly do keep us together."

It was the wonder of the "stonës of Venice," that she had
been telling me of, right after that proud owning of herself in
what she had said to her mother. Not the faintest gasp of a
spirit-weariness, the merest sigh of a complaint; not even any
deploring of mistake, or any dwelling upon the troublous pause,
as if things had or could pause in a trouble. Just a living
straight on, in noblest confidence that there *was* no mistake, no
stopping. A discerning of life with an insight that, close upon
fifty years, I had just begun to hold with certainty.

Had I been trying to *help* this child, — to *teach* her anything? In the glory of her youth, that was like angelhood, she
stood straight up in the light, and saw, and laid hold for herself,
as only the first sight, cleared from the blessed beginning, can
see ; as only the child-hand, in its purity, can grasp. I thought
of " They who seek Me early." There is a vista through the
wilderness that is all open and beautiful, seen from the first
right turn : afterward, we may search for it with pain, and
tears, and bewilderment.

" These sculptures," she said, " are like Creation. They are
so full of crowding, exquisite, patient detail. It is as if these
carvers had the whole truth to tell, no matter whether men
ever came to read it or not. And the great gateway — the
magnificent portals, — all rich with emblems and ornament —
that are only opened for some very seldom and wonderful entering in, — under which we go through little included leaves, —
they put me in mind of what waits to open, by and by, or once
in a while, in the living that is made to last so long and for so
many, and that though we go in and out by little doors meanwhile, we may see them all " lifted up " some time, and the
' King of Glory ' coming in.

" You see, I send you the big pieces, dear Miss Patience.
You have given me so many ! "

CHAPTER XV.

INVENTIO CRUCIS.

. . . . Santa Croce is the building up of a single thought, as is the church in Milan " to the Virgin that ariseth."

It is the finding and the lifting up in the world's wilderness of the Tree of Life that was for the healing of the nations.

For the True Cross, you know, that the Empress Helena· found (led by a *Judas*, too, to the hill of finding), was, in the legend, the tree that had been growing from the very beginning of the need on earth; planted by seeds from heaven, on the death of Adam, — laid under the tongue that had tasted the forbidden thing, and springing thence, a sign here and there of work and of healing, through the days of prophecy and waiting and unconsciousness, in which it was kept for the day of its sacred rising; the Day of the Suffering of the Son of Man, and the Finishing of the Redemption.

Fitly enough, in the great square before the cathedral, stands the statue of Dante, the poet of Hell and Purgatory and Paradise. White and grand, with the lions at the pedestal-corners, and the eagle at his feet, — signs of the evangels, made since into signs for the banners and the arms of states.

At every step in these realms of sign, where art has made tangible all the thoughts of the ages, one is stopped by the links that reach back and lock together.

The Man, the Lion, the Bull, the Eagle; the four creatures in the vision of Ezekiel, that were given for types by the church to Matthew, Mark, Luke, and John, and taken afterward for emblems by cities and empires that built themselves up under their names for patrons.

The Man or Angel, sign of the Incarnation, for him who

tells the simplest human history of Christ,—who gives also
the full, simple, beautiful word for human living,—the Sermon
on the Mount; the Evangelist of fact and precept.

The Lion, symbol of the Resurrection, from the old fable that
his young are born dead, and that after three days he resuscitates
them by his breath or his roar; this for the writer who begins
with the Voice crying in the Wilderness: Repent and live again,
ye children, for the kingdom of the living is at hand. Who goes
straightway, then, into the stories of restoring; the healing, the
cleansings, the castings out, the liftings up from palsy and fever,
the power on earth that forgave sins by saying to them who
were dying of their trespasses, Rise up and walk! Go into your
house,—the body of your living that is given back to you again!

The Ox or Bullock for Priesthood and Sacrifice, put for Luke,
the setter-forth of the High Priesthood of the Lord.

The Eagle for John, the Apostle of Inspiration, looking steadfast into the light, and flying straight toward the face of the sun.
And with yet another symbolism, I think, of the Lord's own
giving, that people have forgotten to interpret or to make much
account of. The symbol of the divine instinct for every coming
of the Son of Man, and toward all the life of His kingdom, by
which always, " wheresoever the body is, thither shall the eagles
be gathered together."

And so through the adopting and wearing of the nations, and
the crowning by the ages of the seer at whose feet the scutcheons
are laid down, they come back with their primal tokens; emblems of the heavenly seeing, and the crying out of the vision,
from the desolate places, into the hearing of the world.

We stood on the broad pavement between the statue and the
temple, and we read the marble fronting of the church.

Full of signs; the spheres, the triangles, the trefoils; the
arches pointed up over the door-ways, so that still in each a
sculptured arc lies within the two lines of three that would
enfold a perfect circle; the crosses graven in the side gable; the
great one borne by bronze angels that surmounts the apex of
the roof; the Madonna Addolorata,—Lady of Grief,—Mother-
Tenderness which suffers over all suffering,—and waits above
all waiting need,—standing above the adornment of the central

entrance, the Elevation of the Cross in bas-relief. A glory of angels around the cross in the heavens; below, humanity in its miseries, reaching and gazing to the Help. On either hand, above the lesser doors, the Vision of Constantine, and the Finding. All parts of the one Story, repeated also in everything shaped and shrined within the house, from the frescoes in Choir and Sacristy, and the colossal crucifix of Cimabue, to the little crucifix of Donatello in the last chapel of the left transept, concerning which he said, humbly, when he had seen that of his friend and critic, "It is given to Brunelleschi to represent a Christ, to me a boor, only." Not thinking, as we think now, looking at his work kept for a better memorial than he knew, — "Truly, thy self-abandonment was the representing; thy little crucifix presents the Christ indeed."

Out on the pavement, I looked long at that sculpture of the miraculous "Invention;" that testing of the true cross out of the three, by the women healed with its touch, — the dead man raised, who was being carried by to burial. Found by its power.

"It is all they can ever know it by, though they may dig up from their sepulchres a thousand other histories and knowledges," I said.

I thought I spoke to Edith, who had been beside me. Some one answered me as if answering a stranger: "I thank you, that is precisely what it has been saying to me."

I looked up, and found that the lady by my side was Miss Euphrasia.

Yes, that was how the thing that keeps happening had happened again. "Minding the same things." We do not lose each other on this wide, wonderful "Other Side." There is nowhere that we ever shall lose. We shall be always finding by the same sure way.

We waited till we got home, — for Miss Euphrasia was at the Hotel Corona d'Italia, next door to us, — before we asked and told of the between, and the what next; we entered gladly into the now in which we met.

We returned to the old legend together. The Tree of Life that was planted, with Adam's burial, to be the Tree of Sacrifice, and so, forever, the Tree of Life again.

"As He told us all life must be," said Miss Euphrasia. "Every son of man must suffer many things; must even be slain, to be raised again the third day. But whoso loseth his life for that sake shall find it. The life is in the cross; and the cross has always been in the world; the holy, saving thing of it."

"This tree of the true cross was the tree flung into the water of Marah, to sweeten it, the story says," said Edith, who was with us now, inside the church, studying out the old frescoes in the apse.

"Yes, you see it was a *tree* that had to be thrown in; a thing with life in it; a growing thing; not a stone, or a clod," said Miss Euphrasia. "It was the heathen fable, that chained Prometheus to a rock. Not that the rock or the earth is dead; it holds the living strength in it; but that which the earth ' *brings forth* ' is the ' tree bearing fruit after its kind.' That which life in us brings forth, — our doing and bearing, — becomes *our* life, the fibre of us; it was. to the wood of a tree that the Son of Man was bound; the tree of a human life and suffering; with nailing through hands and feet that went the way and did the work of his obedience in it; and the wood of a tree became the sign of sacrifice and saving."

"The story says again that it was a rod of that tree with which Moses smote the rock without calling upon God, and so was forbidden himself to enter the Promised Land." I said to her, "That frightens one, to think how terrible it may be to use the power of life that is given in us, to touch *things* with; even to strike out the truth that is in them, as of our own selves."

"It makes one half afraid to strike at all," said Edith.

"Except as we take the rod from before the Lord," said Miss Euphrasia. "And remember that every rod of power is a stem of the cross, and bear it so."

"It brings us back to the *finding*," I said. "What is given into one's hands is so often a foretelling of what is to be laid upon us."

"Have you heard from Margaret Regis lately?" asked Miss Euphrasia. It seemed like a sudden turn; to herself, perhaps. But I felt the hidden line that drew her that way.

"Yes," I told her. "I have a letter from her in my pocket. She is among the stones of Venice. And she has found her cross; and she is alive with the touch of it; and it is beautiful in her hands."

We had walked across the chancel, before the altar. We had turned into a little chapel in which a picture hung that stopped me short.

A cross, standing up, dark and strong, in a great gloom. A figure of a man, in a friar's robe, borne up in the gloom, floating as if upon it, his arms stretched out toward the arms of the thing he sees in his vision. It was the picture of an ecstasy of Saint Francis of Assisi.

We all stood before the painting, that had but one thing to tell, and told it mightily.

"I wonder how people can talk as if it were a *gay* thing, this going round among the sights!" said Edith to Stephen Holabird, who had been very quiet all the morning.

"I think sight-seeing is the solemnest thing I ever did," said Stephen, with a gravity that covered itself by an odd pretense of irony.

"But all churches are not Santa Croce," said Miss Euphrasia.

"And all seein' is n't signs," said Emery Ann.

There were two more things I must just tell you of. Two pictures of the Virgin, in chapels near the altar on the other side.

One is an Assumption by Allori ; not the assumption of heavenly majesty, it seemed to me; not the rising to be Queen of Heaven; but the *Mother* going, at last, to her joy. She floats upward with a beautiful, rapturous face, and a bounding motion, as if she had-risen from the earth with a spring of ecstacy and release; her crimson robe, color of love and joy, — swelling softly about her, seems to bear her up and enfold her with a living warmth and splendor of beatitude. It is the Glorified Mother ascending to meet her Glorified Child. It is the apotheosis of all motherhood, of all human love that has borne the sword-piercing, and endured unto the end.

The other picture completes the thought, and supplements it with yet a higher. It is Giotto's Coronation. The *young* face in it struck me instantly. It is not here the Sorrowful Mother, on whose head the Saviour sets the crown; not the woman worn with pain and years, who fainted at the foot of the cross; it is not, even, as the Mother alone, He crowns her. She is the Bride, the Lamb's Wife. She stands for the Church by whom the Christ comes into the world, and remains; of whose faithful souls the Lord declares, " Whoso loveth and doeth the will, the same is my brother, and sister, and mother." All relationships join and are fulfilled in the one Love; all the types gather to the one reality and pour themselves back to Him who crowns them with life eternal in his kingdom.

This was a day of rich and happy surprises. When we came back late, to rest and dress for dinner, there were fresh names upon the visitors' board in the little rotunda of the Alleanza, — a navy list — of officers' wives and daughters; fourteen navy ladies had come in a body from Nice, merry and tearful, jolly and grumbling, as navy ladies learn to be. The American ships had been ordered suddenly to the Coast of Cuba, because of the Spanish fuss. They had arrived late last night at the " Corona," and this morning half a dozen of them had spilled over into the Alleanza.

Mrs. Goldthwaite, — Stephen Holabird's sister Barbara, — had left a message for him with the porter, and he rushed off to her room, where he found her, he said, pacing like a panther between her door and window, in a frantic watching for him to come.

" What else had I to do, you know?" she said. " I had unpacked everything, and put on my best long-tailed black silk and my Genoese gold things, and dressed Bud up to the smothering point in a rose colored sash, and there we were, kept on the hob, with the surprise all simmering down. It is the worst thing in the world to keep; it 's like waffles, or omelette soufflée."

Mrs. Barbara Goldthwaite is full of a sweet impetuous-heartedness that brims over in fun and nonsense. And Mrs. Barbara Goldthwaite's little Rosebud is a two year's old joke in golden curls, for whom her pride might feel to the young mother like a foolishness, and her tenderness almost a pain, if she did n't just in self-defense turn them into whimsicality. So too with her wifely joys and anxieties, which she cannot keep down or back.

"Think of fourteen of us, left gasping there like fish out of water; and then packed off all in one box like a lot of sardines," she said, with a quick little tremble in her laugh, and her fun glittering through bright, wet eyes. "I wish they would annex Cuba, — and everything else; and then just anchor the Katahdin and the rest of the navy along shore to keep 'em annexed!"

Miss Euphrasia went to Rome two days after.

In the meanwhile I had just one snatch of talk with her in which we could say anything about Margaret.

"The old engagement has been ended; Harry Mackenzie has married suddenly, I hear."

"Yes, and Paul Rushleigh does not know; and Margaret has refused him for conscience sake, and he has gone off to the East."

There was a room full of people; I spoke fast while there was talking and laughing near.

"But Paul Rushleigh is not in the East! I had a letter from him from Palermo within a week. He has been traveling in Sicily, and is coming back to Naples and Rome. Major —— died at Malta a month ago."

"And you will see him, perhaps? Or you will be writing to him, at any rate?" I spoke excitedly. Possibilities rushed upon me.

But in a minute they did not look quite so possible. Miss Euphrasia answered me quietly.

"He only wrote to tell me about climate and hotels, and those things. He remembered very kindly what I and my little winter cough would be in search of, and what I had wanted to know. And the letter went to the English bankers first. But if I should see him, and if he *should* talk with me, — we must wait for these things, you know; — what is it, after all, dear Miss Patience?" -

"He does not know that she is free; that it was a mistake," I said. "She did not know, herself."

I can put the comma there, in writing it. But there is no proof-reading of speech, and I doubt if it got to Miss Euphrasia's noticing.

I thought of it afterward, remembering that her sweet face looked grave as she heard me, and something between her and myself — I could scarcely tell *in* which of us — made me feel again the hindrance in the nature of things that had checked my impulse when I first spoke to Mrs. Regis, and she had answered me, — "I cannot take it *back* for her, Miss Strong!"

I suppose even Miss Euphrasia would think that Margaret ought to have "known herself." And I was afraid I had not put that comma in.

The great dinner bell was ringing as I had spoken, and everybody began to move. Miss Euphrasia was sitting with us with her bonnet on, having stopped to call on her way home to the Corona. She got up and walked with us among all the crowding, chattering people, up the steep, odd narrow passage that is just like a little street sidewalk inside of a house, and in fact seems to lead up hill between two houses that are joined together for the Pension dell' Alleanza; and when we came to the Rotunda and the door-way, she bade us good-night and went out. There was no chance for any more; even if it had come to me then, or next day when she looked in to say good-bye, — as it did not.

However she knew the chief things; that Margaret was free from the old history; and that in the new she had found and taken up her cross.

And these were the things that I hoped somehow would be borne round to the knowledge of Paul Rushleigh. How could I suppose, then, that that comma, through Miss Euphrasia's missing of it, would make any difference to him?

CHAPTER XVI.

CONVENIENCE.

. . . .

. . . . We had nearly a fortnight after this, again, of a very quiet time, in which the sights, for the most part, waited.

Edith had taken a cold in Santa Croce, and our new friend, Mrs. Goldthwaite, was occupied with her little child, who had been ailing at Nice, and who had several days of really alarming illness after their arrival in Florence.

The weather was very keen. The two climates of Florence, — that of the shady and that of the sunny side, — struggled together in the same streets. The long narrow thoroughfares between the old tall buildings in the heart of the city were just tunnels for the Tramontana to rush through; the poor women sat in their door-ways or at their chestnut stalls, with their little "scaldinos" upon their laps, keeping their fingers warm over them as they knitted; or passed you in the way, holding them by their big round bails under their aprons. The little earthen vessel, with its burning charcoal, is hearth and home to the poorer sort, here in these Italian cities, where they do not recognize the winter that yet pounces down in fierce gusts upon them. From these cold, dark ventiducts you may come out suddenly upon a bright warm corner of an open square, where basketfuls of carnations and tuberoses and violets are selling; and out on the Lung 'Arno it is like a day in early June at home, when you find your clothing suddenly too warm and heavy; and the glow of light on river and pavement smites back with a white dazzle upon your eyes.

We went on with our books and our worsted work, — Edith is doing a great heap of violets with deep green clustering leaves, on a cream-white ground, for a cushion for her mother's drawing room; — and we took our painting lessons from bewitching little Madame Tecchi, who always came in late and flushed and lovely from her morning's work among the "aingeels " in the "galérie ; " and Edith and Stephen did their Italian exercises with Signorina Bianchi ; and as the cold wore off, the old Abbate came back to the singing lessons ; — to the "Mia Madre," and " Vergin' Rosa," — and the fiery interjected admonition, " With all your *soul*, mademoiselle ! Now ! with all your *soul!* " at the culminating passages of power and pathos ; and then when it was over, to make the regular little low bow, with a sweep of his dropped eyelids and his clerical hat at the same time and in the same curve, as he bade " buon giorno " to us all, and drew the line again that separated him from all soul and presence except in the recognitions of courtesy and the fulfilling of his set vocation.

Emery Ann was very sober and absorbed in these days over the " Life of Savonarola." " There was good yeast enough in him," she said one afternoon as she shut the book. " I don't see why the whole three measures was n't leavened that time."

" It has to be three measures of *meal*," I answered. " Three measures of stones, or even of grain in the husks, — would n't leaven, you know."

" No, nor *meal* in a cold night away from the fire," she said, perceiving and assenting. " There 's two parts to it, and more, finally. But that 's what puzzles me. Why ain't the Lord looking out for both sides at the same time, you see ? A woman has to, when she mixes things."

" Don't you forget some of your ' more, finallies,' Miss Emery Ann ? " asked Barbara Goldthwaite, who was sitting with us. " It is an *overnight mixing*, you know. It is n't morning yet. And perhaps the great world measures are n't even all stirred in."

" That 's so," said Emery Ann, and went back, peacefully, into the fifteenth century.

I was trying to copy in water-colors an oil painting of the head of Raphael's Madonna del Gran Duca, in the Pitti. Madame Tecchi had brought it to me, and assured me I could do it " verra naïce." And very nice work I found it. I think I know more about Raphael's pictures, — and about all the won-

derful old simplicities in pictures, — for the studying of that one
calm, sweet face, and the infinitude of tints and touches that had
to make — and define — the quietness of it. Tameness, I might
have called it, — as I have called dozens of Madonna faces tame
— if I had not been set to work at it. It would have been so
much easier to make it something else ! Just as it would a tame
life, you know !

It was a good fortnight; a laying up of readiness. I did not
dare to tell people that I spent those in-door mornings when they
were learning art and paying homage in the galleries, trying to
make a picture; trying to copy Raphael. But then you don't
always tell people what you have been attempting on your small
personal account in the world, instead of fathoming the last
" Science Monthly," or posting yourself in politics, or going to
a Social Reform Convention or even what little Sabbaths of your
own you kept the Sundays that you stayed away from church.

I am very sure, I say, that I got farther *in*, toward where
Raphael had been beyond the world, by doing imperfectly a
little bit with all my might myself, than I should have got by
crying " Master ! Master ! " before his miracles, for a twelve-
month.

It was a good fortnight, getting acquainted with Barbara Goldthwaite and her baby. They are better, after all, than the painted
Madonnas. They are the very, beautiful thing itself, — the
Mother-and-Child-Story, — that the old artists looked about to
find, in the real, in their day, before they ever dared to paint it.
The Lord is always telling it over again ; always putting into a
human miracle-play that coming of Himself into his world,
which is a fresh possibility and hope with every little child that
is born in it.

I had two letters from Miss Euphrasia and one more from
Margaret toward the end of the time. Miss Euphrasia was
stopping at Siena. She found it pleasant there for climate and
for quiet; and she told me of Sodoma's frescoes, of the sweet
musical Tuscan speech, of the Gothic architecture. But not
yet anything more of Paul Rushleigh, except that she had heard
from him as still at Rome, very busy with the Archæological Society and its excursions. These were keeping him there; he

ould very likely stay all winter. How did he know, I thought, hat was keeping him there? I grew quiet about any small terference that I had been uneasy for. I put my fingers ou e little map of Italy in my Baedeker. I touched Venezia, irenze, Siena, Roma. I could clasp them all. Black lines arked the chain of swift rails that joined them. And through e air ran fine telegraph threads, and the post rushed to and o daily, scattering white messages and printed news; and the owds were drifting up and down. No; there was no far sep-ateness, no hopeless missing. People would be kept, and sent. ives and their links are not unorganized, unarranged for, where ery commonest doing falls into sure system, and plays in an evitable convenience.

Convenience. That is Emery Ann's word, in its purest ety-ology, yet innocently of all word-science. The coming to-ether of things; the "never raining without a pour;" the ravitation of events.

We were "in the middle of a convenience" these two weeks, though part of it, indeed, seemed to slip away before the rest egan. There are no perfect conveniences in this world; none, least, so pettily perfect that we can see round them. The orld itself can't be seen round. The biggest map you can ake of it is a hemisphere. Because of its absolute con-ven-nce; its entire central consistence. Because there is but one ctual stand-point, you seem to have antipodes.

Miss Euphrasia had come and gone,—on her way toward aul Rushleigh; holding in her hand a thread of communica-on, that,—spite of my faith that if it had not been that, it ould have been, at the real need and fitting, some other; and itself the line of the Lord's own engineering, no cable stronger r more surely flung,—seemed the slight, critical, hair-fibre pon which all that concerned these two might hang; by whose reaking or non-joining, everything might drift away again into deeper and longer uncertainty.

I was holding my breath, as it were, in my letters to Siena, st I should sway disastrously, the cobweb thread. I did not are say "Rome" in my writing to Venice, off there in the orth; I sat between, listening both ways.

When, all at once, as we were going out through the green little arcade of the Alleanza entrance, one morning, Margaret Regis and her step-mother met us face to face, coming in through the iron gate-way.

" Margaret ! "

" Edith ! "

" Dear Miss Patience ! "

" Back from Venice ! "

" Yes; last night."

" And your rooms ? "

" At Hotel Vittoria."

" We came down at once to find you.   You are going out ? "

" So nice that we had *not* gone ! "

" We *wanted* you ! "   Margaret whispered among the quickly interchanged sentences.

" It was getting very cold at Venice," Mrs. Regis said.

She looked paler, I could see, than when she had left us.

" Mamma did not feel as if Venice suited her, at last," said Margaret, as we passed back into the little salon.

Barbara Goldthwaite had slipped away, and taken Stephen with her, after the first greeting and introduction.

" We will leave the Uffizi till another day," she said. " Stevie and I will just go and look at the mosaics in the Acciajoli, — and perhaps walk out on the Ponte Vecchio.   We 'll all find each other again at lunch."

Barbara Goldthwaite is never in the way, a minute; she never blunders in her tact.   But Stephen laughs about her old blunders, and bluntness, — the same thing, I fancy, — when she was blundering up to what she is now.

" That was because," Barbara says, " I drove my screws with a hammer.   I had n't got my whole tool-box then."

CHAPTER XVII.

MADONNA DEL CARDELLINO.

. . . .

. . . . THEY "wanted me." And yet they did not say why; or anything about it. But I do take that sort of wanting to mean a great deal. It was the way mother used to want me, when she would say, from her room across to mine, — "Are you there, Pashie?" "Yes, mother; would you like anything?" "That's all; just to know that you are handy." And how contented-sweet she made the words sound!

Those little things are what make me sure, to-day, that she is "there." And "that is all." Just to know it. Why that is all there is between God and us, even.

We went, all together, to the Uffizi gallery the next morning.

I had an hour first, after breakfast, at my Madonna. How nice it is getting up to pleasant work that you have put by the night before! How nice the busy Mondays are, even, after the Sunday stops! The last part of the verse about them that "die in the Lord," is the beauty of it, and has the promise to our living natures: "They rest" — not "cease" — from their labors, — and their "*works do follow them.*" That is the Rest of God; the evening and the morning that make his Days, after which He created ours. The pause that is only *poise;* and then the brightness and the betterness of the beginning again. You begin farther on, always. You have gone a little way, somehow, while you seemed to be altogether stopping; and your work has followed you. You and it have ripened in the night.

I must tell you a little bit, now I have happened upon it, about those Florence mornings.

Certainly, it was more like death and the resurrection than the ordinary analogue of sleep and waking, — that going into the little stone bedrooms, dark and chill, — the very walls radiating a smiting cold upon us notwithstanding the fires we always kindled, — out of our cheery salon that had been warm all day with a wood blaze, and a sun blaze, and our new busyness; creeping into what we called our " catafalques," — the narrow, high, straight-draperied single beds, where we were glad to draw the woolen damask across and pin it together as close as its dimensions would allow, and where many a night Emery Ann has slept with a veil on, because " her nose waked her up with the nip in the end of it; " and then the shine and the stir beginning gay and broad about us; the clear blue filling the window panes, and for a trumpet of awakening, the cries of " English bread " and " chestnuts," and the man who invariably began his shout of " Hear *me* sneeze! " at the first dawn, and overbore everybody's else with it until all the breakfast fires were supposed to be lighted. We never *could* make anything else out of it, we heard it so distinct in our own tongue; though we soon found out that he was a match-seller, and that his call was really " Fiamm*i*ceri! Fiamm*i*ceri! "

There was another that burst tremendously and peremptorily upon our ears one morning, and that was as " plain as day," Emery Ann said; which is n't so nonsensical as you might make it out, since plain is plain, whether to sight or hearing; and clear is clear, in different ways, though you might n't say that crab-apple jelly was as clear as a bell. I wish I knew what the vender really did vociferate; no doubt it would make it still funnier; but he went up and down, like an official of some S. F. P. C. T. A. (or ever so much more of it in Italian); ordering, " Give that horse-some-meat! *Give*-that-horse-some-of-that-roast-beef! " And another piped shrilly and plaintively, " Hen lost! hen lost in the hay! "

How could one help it, you see? One's tongue is also one's natural ear; and has been since the days of the hearing of the Parthians and the Cretans and the Mesopotamians; and will be, — yes! in that real morning when we shall wake up to just what we have known before, and nothing different, though it came by the voice of Gabriel!

Emery Ann, being truly of the Saints, is of the first rising.

I hear her go stealthily through the shuttered darkness of the
salon, across to Edith's room, and I know she is busy at the re-
fractory little corner fire-place, setting the sticks carefully on
end in a cone, the only way they will burn, and putting the
kindlings in the middle; and then she steals forth again, leaving a gentle sound of crackling behind her, and gets at the big-
ger chimney triangle of the salon.

. Then I say gently, "Coaxing up the crater, Emery Ann?"

"Yes, I've just touched off Etna, and now I've begun on
Vesuvius!"

And presently they roar cheerfully, with half a basket of
wood apiece at three francs the basket, and she puts back the
shutters, and the day is begun.

We ring for Vincenzio, when we are ready for our breakfast;
and he brings us on a tray, hot coffee, eggs, and petits pains,
with three prints of saltless butter. Emery Ann "brades"
these last with the essential condiment, and we put down the
rolls to brown and crisp upon the hearth. We sit round the
corner, with our feet converging toward the fire, and the table
behind us from which we help ourselves into our plates set in
our laps.

After breakfast, and the sending away, upon certain days,
Emery Ann locks the door upon Vincenzio, and enacts a mystery. She produces a broom from within a wardrobe, and a
dust-pan from under a sideboard; a handful of salt from a bag
in the big willow basket, wherewith she sows the carpet —
dusty with years in which there have been no shakings, — and
enters straightway into her Paradise of cleansing. "Making,"
as she says, " square corners, instead of round."

After which Edith and I, emerging from our bedrooms again,
set out the photographs and arrange the flowers, and the piles
of books, and put the "chirpy" look to everything.

Vincenzio caught us all at it one morning, when he came
back suddenly, — a deliberate suddenness, I believe, — with the
unimpeachable and exasperating " Est-ce que vous avez sonné,
madame?" And he never respected us much after that, but
answered us when we did ring with an air of half insolent, half
perplexed consciousness that there was some mistake in our

30

mutual positions; though we did occupy a salon, and use the dear Italian fire-wood with so truly an American freedom.

Until one day, he came up, actually pale, with the card of " La Principessa M—— née C——," and the announcement, as if it were of a cyclone or a flood, that could not be helped, but that must overwhelm us at its pleasure, " Et, madame, elle *monte,* — à present ! "

I met her quietly at the door, — I had taken a note of introduction· to her from our dear Dr. J——, at home, — she is interested in certain things that he knew I could tell her about, — and I was expecting her to come; — and Vincenzio disappeared with wide eyes and a suppressed gasp, and waited upon us from that time forth with an obsequious acceptation of a mystery which he despaired of comprehending, but which was clearly acquitted of all ignominy. " But these are always so queer, these Americans ! " I suppose he said to himself.

We took up the life of Florence together, letting our own life, in its quiet, unspoken consciousness, run on underneath; and we went down to the Uffizi.

" What is *that ?* " says Emery Ann, toiling up breathless to the great landing between the double staircases with the hundred and twenty-six steps, and stopping before, or beneath, an ancient sculpture all knots and twists of naked muscle.

" That — is 'An Athlete,' " replied Stephen, glancing at his " Guide." " A man of strength. An old time combatant."

" I should think so," panted the excellent woman. " And a good place for him ! Though you don't need the hint, finally, from anything but your *own* muscles, coming up here ! "

A great, black Mars, in basalt, and a Bacchus, lift themselves in opposite corners, grandly; and underneath, the tender little life of flowers, — the breath of to-day, and yet a mightier presence in that vital breath, — fills the air and the sight with pleasantness, where an old man sits selling violets, carnations, and tuberoses, to the comers up and down.

Through the vestibule, full of Medicis, — Lawrence the Magnificent, the Cosmos, Cardinal Leopold, and the rest; Roman emperors and gods, a wild boar, a fierce, strong horse, and other great beasts in marble, — we got into the eastern corridor and stood at the north end of its vast length, among the pictures of Cimabue and Giotto, and the old Sienese painters; stiff, quaint, sweet; with great intents in their rudimental lines, great, reverent care in their patient finish, holy and blessed conceptions far beyond, but inextricable from their rigid attitudes and groupings.

You feel yourself, among them, in company with the first intense, realizing apprehensions of a Divineness that had come into the world close before their time in it, with the touch of which their time was warm. I think it needs nothing better than to pass from the presence of these old Romans and their deities, their men of strength and their wild beasts, to these pure Virgins listening to the first promise of a coming Redemption, — these Madonnas rejoicing and worshiping above the cradled Child, — these scenes on the Mount of Olives, — in the Garden, at the Cross, — these raptured Saints of the new Revelation, — to make one see, as by the line of color where a sweet, fresh stream flows down with power into a troubled one, — that into a wild, base, self-darkened, stormy, material world, had come, at a definite point in history, a sudden, strange Peace and Good Will, that could be nothing less than a gospel from beyond it.

Not quite half-way down the long gallery-stretch, stands, on the left, before you come to the double doors that lead into the lovely Tribune, — the Tabernacle of Fra Angelico, with its great leaves apart, upon whose panels within are painted Saint Mark of the Lion, and John, the Voice of the Wilderness; at the back the central picture of the Holy Mother and the Child, whose word is for the raising of the world; and about them, as a celestial halo, the frame-work of the tender "incomparable sweet" angels, that are copied everywhere, and, — I had almost said, — *never* copied. Because how can common artist, with common pigments, get through line and shadow and ever so carefully mixed tint, what came into the soul of John of Fiesole by prayer?

The tender depth of the eyes, their very outward curves of lid and orbit touched with such strong softness, — the gentle brows and the wonderful blessedness that broadens them; —

the hair like sun-filaments ; — the clear tongue of flame that at once springs from and descends upon each forehead at the parting of the locks, — the golden and purple and crimson wings ; — the uplifted, or softly clasping, or dropping arms, with trumpet, or cymbals, or viol, or tambour, or drum, or harp ; — the robes of heavenly colors, — rose, or blue, or green, or violet ; or chaste, sweet brown, with saffron lights, that I thought loveliest of all, — folding and floating about the figures with some glad motion or ecstatic rest interpreted in every line ; — the feet, shod with a self-same glory as the glory of the raiment, set upon clouds that upbear while they are pressed upon ; — from head to foot each is, in all these, a beautiful apocalypse, perfect in every type of form, and radiant with the meanings of heaven.

·I must tell you here, where it seems most fitly to belong, that there is one painter in Florence, — and that is why I only "almost" said that Fra Giovanni's angels are never copied, — who puts upon paper, in marvelous acquarella, the very visions of Angelico himself; which must be, yet, his own present visions also, — and so, not copied, after all, and I said true. You cannot think of *paint* as you look at them ; you cannot even think of *things ;* the faces are spirit ; the robes are color, — not colored stuff ; light and presence are before you, but they come neither of, nor to, the touch ; any more than do his exquisite flowers, that are *born* seemingly, as real flowers are that apparition themselves out of the unseen, — stopping on the very threshold, but half-materialized, — the nearest things in nature to the super-nature.

Almost the intensest pleasure, — not the deepest or grandest, of course, but the keenest, in its moment and way, — that I had in Florence, I had in Rocchi's studio.

From the Tabernacle we were moved to find our way as straight as might be, to the Hall of the Ancient Masters, to see in direct sequence with this the Blessed Angelico's work of the Virgin's Coronation, before which we stood in an amaze at the breadth of glory which possessed him, when he got and seized and held the glimpse of that sea of angel faces, — that thronging High-Court of Heaven, blossoming tier above tier in raptures and sweetnesses, and still tumults of joy, like the infinite Celestial Rose of Dante's Paradise.

To get there, we went through the Tribune. We pulled apart the silent swinging doors, and entered the little octagon hall, full of pictures, full of people, full of restrained light, that threw soft untraceable shade, full of silence, of an absorbed hush, a slow-breathing awe and delight. For here are things that make the new, rushing world stand still, in presence of what an older, slower, mightier world did.

I was just turning, drawn by the one purest, brightest marvel of the place, — to where at the left as we came in, one easel held the picture, most fair in color, shining upon you that way the moment you approach, yet fairer in its deep, gracious sign, — Raphael's Madonna of the Goldfinch, — when a curious, startling, smothered sound from Emery Ann behind me, and her violent turning round and pushing at the door again, turned me about in anxiety. "What is it, Emery Ann? Is anything the matter? Where are you going?" I said hurriedly, as I followed her.

"Let me out!" was all her answer, as she struggled at the second door, and escaped into the gallery. Here she made straight for a bench upon the opposite side, sat herself down upon it with a jounce, as one has seen a child set down into a safe and penitential place out of some mischief, and covered up her face with her hands. Her old forehead was as red as flame.

I was frightened. I thought of apoplexy, or something. I began at her bonnet strings.

"Let me alone," she said. "It ain't me! It's *them!*" Was the dear old thing gone crazy?

I tried a severe authoritativeness. "Emery Ann Tudor! *What?*"

"It ain't to be spoken of. Not an identical stitch on!" with a hollow horror, was all she could say. She did not know that two or three of the others had come around her, or she would not have said that.

A queer, abashed look stole over Stephen's face, and he walked away from us. Edith, from some sympathetic certainty, had stayed by the door, and as Stephen returned toward her, she moved down a little and began gazing at a "Credi."

"It is the Titians, — the Venuses," said Margaret with a

quiet directness ; but the pure blood mounted to her cheek also.
" Why will they let them be there ? "

I had not seen them. That was my good fortune, happening
to turn as I entered, and catching glimpse of the sweet glory of
Raphael.

" But you have n't found out what *else* is there," I said, comforting Emery Ann, persuasively. " I had just come straight upon
a beautiful — heavenly thing ! "

" Forzino," she gasped, wretchedly. " But I could n't have
the face — my gracious ! It would put a Hottentot out of
countenance ! " she broke forth again, indignantly.

" Don't look ! That is not necessary. Come straight to the
beautiful picture with me."

" Not look ! as if folks could know who *had n't* looked ! I
wouldn't *be* there, again, five minutes, for a farm ! "

" But this fuss, dear Emery Ann, is n't it worse ? " I ventured, gently.

" Don't make it, then. I 'll stay here."

A lady, well, yes, — a Massachusetts lady, — though I don't
for a minute allow her to represent Massachusetts, or its art-
culture, any more than I let those Titians stand to me for the
genius of picture ; a woman of energetic, and it seemed to me
rather recent, enthusiasm in these things ; a Mrs. Megilp, who
had met Barbara Goldthwaite somewhere, once, — had attached
herself to our party. They two, also, stood by.

" Why one never *thinks* of such a thing ! " said at last, with
high, superior dignity, the cool æsthetic dame, who had stared,
thus far, a little aloof, at Emery Ann's absurdity. " It never
occurs to me."

" Never occurs to you, ma'am ? What *does* occur to you ? "

" The art ; the beauty ; the inspiration ; the wonder of the
coloring ; the " —

" I wish there was a man here, for a minute, to say the
devil! " interrupted Emery Ann, furious.

" One does not descend to the devil," retorted the sublime
disciple with an emphasized calmness, and apparently having
quite the better, in word and temper, for the instant. " One
loses," she continued, addressing Barbara and me now, as if

quite done with Emery Ann, — "One loses the literalness, don't you think, — the subject, indeed, — in the mastership of the art? It suggests to me nothing but itself," concluded the woman of self-eliminating imagination.

"Which scarcely says so very much for the art, after all, perhaps," remarked Barbara Goldthwaite.

Emery Ann choked. I turned to look at her, with new surprise. A new mood had come over her; the tears were starting; her face was working curiously in her battle to keep them back, but there was a deep, pitiful sorrow having its way suddenly, in which the queer twitch and down-drawing of her eyebrows and her homely, good mouth failed to look ridiculous. " I can't help it, and it don't signify·! " she said, half laughing at herself.

" Hysterical! " observed the æsthetic lady, with a mansard-roof expression, and tore herself away.

" It was the very thing Savinairalow tried to burn up out of the world three hundred years ago," moaned Emery Ann. "And here it is, kep' over till now, and women comin' from *Boston* to look at it! More, finally. Actually to make a kind of piousness out of it. 'T won't *do* to do anything but fall down and worship the brazen image that Neppercutnuzzer the · King has sot up ! "

I did not know what more to say to her. I was very glad to see Edith and Stephen Holabird walking up the gallery again toward us.

" We are going to the little Room of Gems, Miss Emery Ann," said Stephen. " You will be delighted with the crystals and the lapis lazuli, and the gold things. There is a head cut out of a turquoise with diamond eyes. Won't you come? "

" It sounds like a kind of a safe place," whispered the hard bestead Puritan woman to me, wiping her eyes, and hushing herself up like the same unlucky child she had set down so hard upon the bench, — " And I suppose I 've got to go somewheres."

Margaret and Barbara and I went back to the Madonna del Cardellino.

But I must turn wholly away now, from the episode of our interruption, as we did from what Barbara called the Veni, and put the dear little Goldfinch into a quite separate paragraph.

For the Goldfinch, — the little, fluttering bird, — in the hand of the infant Baptist, — is the centre, as it is the name, of the holy, exquisite myth-picture.

Mary has an open book in her hand; is it for her own pondering, or has she just been teaching the Boy something of that which is already written? The Boy whom it became from the beginning to fulfill all order and righteousness; to *grow* in stature and in knowledge, though He came forth from the eternity of the Father's own greatness and wisdom?

The little John brings a bird in his hand. He holds it forth to the Christ-cousin, a living word, as if he were feeling even then that the interpretation of all life, the baptism of inner fire, were waiting in that baby Presence to meet and touch the least forms into an electric power and recognition. One thinks that he might often come so, with a flower, an insect, a grass-blade, a shining stone; each new wonder that his child search encountered in the new, wonderful world.

But the large, tender look in the Christ-eyes! The brooding, cherishing, protecting gesture of the little hand, as He turns from Mary's knee and holds it bent above the tiny creature!

"Not one of these shall fall to the ground without your Father!"

The Father in Him says the word; as plainly as that Son of Man spoke it afterward to the Twelve.

I cannot tell you the full Divineness, that seems to lighten and flow forth from the face into the act. "I *would* gather you!" "Ye are of more value than many of these." "Your Father feedeth them, shall He not much more feed you?" It is the Lord, touched with His own sign, moved with the showing of His own dear meanings in the thing He has created. "Could ye not read it when I have put it there so plain? If I have given you earthly things and ye comprehend them not, how shall ye understand when I come to tell you of heavenly things?

Mary's robe — blue, beautiful, glowing-soft — is like the depth of heaven, — the lovely fullness of the mystery that waits.

CHAPTER XVIII.

A NEW MONNA BRIGIDA.

. . . .

. . . . I DID not tell Emery Ann what the Convent of San Marco was, the afternoon we went there. I carefully guarded against her finding out beforehand. We all spoke of it as the Museum of St. Mark, which she, not being given at all to the study of the guide-books, but just going where she was taken, and seeing, as it were, " the passing," as it came along, did not associate with the monastery of the Dominican she had been reading so earnestly about, who thundered at the vices of priests and princes, scourged at the beasts in the Temple, preached like another John, to his Piagnoni, and persuaded the people to burn their trinkets, their falsities and fripperies of dress and their elegant immoralities of art in the public squares. I had a feeling that I should like to have her really come upon the central interest of the place with an unprepared, and so unspoiled feeling. The expecting of an impression, even in the things most vital to ourselves, is so often the quenching of the possibility ; Emery Ann should not be disappointed of this, that would be so great to her.

We had come at a wrong hour, — or upon a wrong day ; it was a festa, or something ; after a cold drive, and the dismissal of our voiture, we knocked at the great cloister gate, to be told by a charmingly pretty little dark-eyed portière, that " non si lascia entrare." But Margaret's graceful persuasion in some bits of Italian, and a five-franc piece from Stephen, let in our party, and one or two more, though the heavy barrier was swung to in the faces of another advancing group, who would willingly have taken advantage of the opening.

Shall we ever forget the *cold* of the place that day ? It was like the chill of all the dead centuries. I assure you, Rose, the shrine pilgrims, with peas in their shoes, are not to be name above us, who have taken the winter months for our art an hero pilgrimage through the churches, and palaces, and gallerie of this bright, old, dusty, blossoming, wonderful, pinching, per ishing Florence!

The Last Supper of Ghirlandajo covers the end wall in th empty little refectory at the foot of the great stairs. We wer put in there to wonder. We stood and did it after our differen ways.

A peacock with folded, trailing feathers, sits upon the ledg of an open window in the Supper Room, in the picture. Tw cats, — I think it was, — occupied the foreground. I was look ing at these and trying to think why it was such an almost in variable thing with the old painters, to put some such animal into the most sacred scenes, when Stephen Holabird asked th question.

"It does n't sound reverential, — but — in the name of al that is, *why cats?* Does anybody know?"

Suddenly it seemed to me that I did know. Something mad me think of the little goldfinch in the Madonna picture. Of the living things that are put into the world, made part and par cel of its reality, signs and outcomes of its higher and deepe ranges. Moving in the line of our own living, having to do mutely and disregarded, but not insignificantly, with its in tensest scenes. Is n't it because —

Margaret Regis interrupted my thinking, and finished it.

"The dogs eat of the crumbs that fall from the table," she said.

That was it. The Divine coming into the world to save the world, to sup with it, to suffer with it, reaches even to the low est. The Supper is for them also. Every spirit is to receive, — "in its own order."

And the Peacock with its folded glories following *after*, is fo the immortality that the mortal shall put on.

Also, dear friend, the *eyes*, — the insights! The living creat ures "full of eyes," before and behind! The mysteries of time made clear and beautiful in the vision of the hereafter! The life eternal, — that is to know the things the Father doeth, and the Christ He doeth them by!

Up the stairs, and along the great corridors, whose walls were once all aflame with heavenly phantasms from Fra Angelico's soul and pencil, and where the softened colors now seem to tell how the beatific visions are fading out of a world gone back into its poor, positive living, — we came to the Gallery of the Banners ; where in the rainbow light of all the colors of Italy, — the silken splendor of its many flags, that, draped about their gilded and burnished staves, lean forward from the walls to make the stately avenue of approach, — looks forth from its throned repose in the far, deep end, the face of Dante in white marble.

Set here at last, with the tardy homage of the centuries bending about it in these ensigns of every city and guild that bring their honor to him in this Florence that sent him out a wanderer upon the land, almost six hundred years ago.

The stillness, the radiance, the long remoteness of the room are strangely impressive. He holds mute, splendid court here ; and strangers from the new side of the planet, that he never dreamed of, — for fleshly habitation, — come softly into the presence of the seer who dreamed out Hell and Paradise ; and planted his Purgatorio — who knows with what blind prophecy of the long, hard working out of human weird ? — upon their hemisphere.

In and out of little cells ; looking in at the double chambers, where Cosmo of the Medici had his oftentime habitation, — lingering in Angelico's own, where stands his Madonna of the Star with the light raying all about her, and the holy Child just sweetly *cuddled* in her neck as her cheek leans down upon the little head laid there so baby-like and tender, — we kept on, Emery Ann not yet knowing, or putting the clews together, — we had seen so many Angelicos and Bartolommeos everywhere before ; — and at last, in the two small stone-walled closets, with their narrow clefts of window looking down upon the city, — with the desk and the manuscripts, — the glass case with the hair shirt in it, — the crucifix, — the old picture of his own martyrdom, and his portrait, we stood where the soul of Savonarola had, in the body, stood, and knelt, and mightily mused and struggled, and had left a presence in the very air to meet us at this hour.

Whether it were this presence, which had verily put a soul in things, or a certain unspoken awe that touched her feeling, from the feeling of us who knew, — Emery Ann, as she came in, stopped short in the middle of the first tiny apartment, gave a glance about her, and without a single object having clearly interpreted itself or been yet alluded to, caught me by the arm and whispered, — " What is there — or whatever *was* there — *here* ? "

" Why, what makes you think to ask ? " I returned, following with a keen interest my own experiment. " These are all cells of monks who lived here once. This museum was an old convent."

" But somebody, I 'm sure, did something here. It kind of creeps through me. Who was it ? "

" Jerome Savonarola. Those are his writings. That is his crucifix. That " —

But Emery Ann had started away. Rushed for a step or two ; as far as she could rush, in the narrow place. As far as she could get, away from any other person in our little group. She stood still, with her back to us, just within the door-way we had entered by, her face toward the side wall. As if there had been a picture there to look at, where there was nothing.

"It ain't fit!" I heard her say, under her breath, presently, as I waited. And she marched forth into the corridor.

Stephen and the girls and Barbara Goldthwaite were talking together in the inner cell. Not chattering ; but yet, it seemed to me, somehow, as if there ought to be silence. And Emery Ann, I think, could not bear it. That, and something else, also, which was most pathetically queer.

She had been following up the Life of Savinairolow, as she persists in calling him, with Mrs. Lewes's " Romola," which I put into her hands afterward. Her unspoiled imagination had carried her into that great romance, as if she had lived that life among the Florentine dames and their quickenings of conscience under the new, strong preaching in the old republic. I had asked her one day, slily, what she thought of Monna Brigida and her friend Monna Berta.

" They was fools ! " she answered, with that energy in which her syntax so sublimely swamped. " Folks in story-books always is. You want so to get behind 'em and give 'em a shove, when they won't do such a little easy thing that their very souls depends on! And you can't; any more than you could behind a woman in a looking-glass!" And there, all at once, she had hushed herself, and turned away, with her elbow on her knee, and the color coming suddenly under the edges of the brown front where her supporting fingers pressed wrinkles up into her temples.

" Folks ought to hold their tongues, and go in one at a time, she said to me, when we had come out of the cells, and I found her waiting in the corridor. " It's like the tomb and the angels, — it don't want explanations. Don't you say anything." And she slipped by me and disappeared, alone, into the chamber.

Emery Ann can't have the tears come for a minute, without looking as if she had cried for an hour. They come so in earnest. When she overtook us, or rather when she came slowly at a distance behind us, again, and I stopped for her, — the end of her nose was red, and her barège veil was pulled down across her forehead and eyes.

"I'm scairt to death for what they'll think of it. But I don't care! I've give the woman in the looking-glass the shove!"

" Emery"— I was going to utter her name inquiringly.

"'Sh! I won't say another blessed word till we get home!" And she sniffed resolutely, and walked on.

We had half an hour to dress for dinner, after we got back to the Alleanza.

I was in Edith's room, when Emery Ann called to me from our opposite door across the salon. I went to her. She had got her black silk skirt on; the corsage with collar and cuffs pinned in, lay upon the bed. She, in flannel sack, with soft white hair about her face, and, I must say, her emotions still crimson in the end of her nose, was standing beside it.

" Will you send some dinner up to me, Patience, or *what* will you do with me? I guess it's your job, now, after all. I don't darst to look in the glass, — for I've clear shoved myself out of it!"

"What have you done? Where is —?" It flashed across me, just as she cut me short with her answer.

"I shan't ever tell you what I've done with that half-piece, so you need n't ask me! But I rolled it up tidy like a bundle from a shop. They 'll think I lost it, I presume."

She had left it behind her in Savonarola's cell!

O little seed of everlasting truth! O fruit sprung forth, — small, beautiful, — after four hundred years!

I combed the soft shining, hair in smooth curves about her temples. I pinned up a delicate little thread lace face-veil into a head-dress with wide barbe ends to fall behind, and with a hair-pin or two fastened it at the sides and caught it to a point in front. And the tears came into my own eyes as I did so, and then stood back and looked at her, — my dear good Emery Ann, glorified. Every trace of commonness had vanished with the stiff brown satin braid and the wig front. She had got her halo on. All the quiet, homely saintliness of her life was shining about her placid forehead and softening in her rugged features, in that whiteness. The red had gone down out of her nose now, as she had grown calm with her confidence in me, and through my calm taking of it. I could have been proud of my elderly *lady*, if I had not seen something so much more than any mere ladyhood in her changed look.

But all I said to her was, "It is a thousand times nicer. And you need n't mind it a bit. It 's the fashion to come out in gray hair. People do it every day. Come to the glass, and look."

"I guess I 'd as well not," she answered. "I really mean it; and I might get frightened out of it."

So she left me, and went to sit down in the salon.

I was putting on my own cap, when I heard, in a flustered tone and with a sudden movement, —

"I ask your pardon, ma'am, — why, where under the —? 'T aiu't anybody! Patience, there 's a ghost in the room!"

She had crossed in front of the long mirror, and got a glimpse of herself; then, as she had moved on and spoken, the apparition had vanished. Of course, it came to her directly, what it was; and I think she went back.

"Monna' Brigida *was* a fool! But there! if you don 't look

out, it's the frying-pan and the fire, I guess! It's a snare, any-way." And she sat down again.

That night, after they had all complimented her and con-gratulated her, — "As if," she said, "she had done it for the *im-provement!*" she took off her lace, and brushed out the gray locks, very meekly.

"It gets taken out of you, finally," she said to me. "There ain't much credit in it when the givin' up is all given back in spite of you. It's the power and the glory; and it ain't yourn. The very hairs of your head *air* all numbered, certain; and you'll have what belongs to you, and be made the best of, if you'll let it all go, and leave the Lord alone. Only — folks mostly *air* fools. And there's more than one kind of half-pieces!"

"Did you know Carlyle said that?" asked I, provoking a diversion.

"What? about half-pieces?"

"No; about fools."

"I did n't know he said anything. Who was he?"

"He is a great English philosopher, who defines his own nation as so many 'millions of people, mostly fools.'"

"He is n't so particular as he might be. I was n't talkin' of millions. I was talkin' of *ones*. Accordin' to my experience, an *individual* is two thirds a fool, — if the other third could only find it out. Or three quarters, finally. And *that's* the comfort of the tares and the wheat."

"But, Emery Ann!" said I, "what *was* the giving up? I never supposed you thought much" —

'There's where you don't know anything at all about it," she took me up quickly. "The old adversary may go about like a roaring lion, but he don't always roar. That's the mean-ness of him. I tell you it's folks that has n't got a thing that's the most tempted by it. It's the covetousness that's the idola-try. I'll just mortify myself by saying it: I've been all my life long trying to be good-looking, and never made out, — there!"

Just think of that! Emery Ann's stubby old "front," and her clumsy satin braid, snares of the adversary! "All her life long trying to be good-looking," and missing it all the time! Truly the signs matter little; the story of souls is much the same. Forms, — fames, — merchandises; it is in none of these things, but in the coveting, — the longing that takes up the heart.

And now she had bravely laid down her life, — and found it. And now she was meek and ashamed in the finding. I was ashamed before her, when I took off my small brown "band," sprinkled with my own "saved" gray hair.

"It is but one little tail," I said, humbly. "I can't do very well without that to pin to."

"A pig has only one little tail," Emery Ann answered me, with uncompromising solemnity. "But that makes all the difference."

And we got into our catafalques.

CHAPTER XIX.

HEART'S-EASE; AND WHEAT GRAINS.

. . . .

. . . . ˉBARBARA GOLDTHWAITE brought into our room a quantity of pretty things she had bought in Genoa. "You are fascinated out of your last centime, there," she said, as she spread them out before us.

Mrs. Regis and Margaret were with me. They had come round from the Victoria to the Corona d'Italia, next door; and they were in every day when we were not all out somewhere together. Mrs. Regis still looked pale. Venice had not agreed with her. The subtle poison that lurks about, more or less, in all the air of Italy, was depressing her physically. Beside that, there was something, I could see, taxing her inwardly; wearing her, as with some questioning discomfort. Now and then, I caught her eyes resting upon Margaret, or following her, as she occupied herself genuinely with any pleasant interest of the hour, — tracing pictures of the same hand, and the inspiration of them, through chamber after chamber of one of the great galleries, — sketching, with me, of a morning, some lovely outline of a Fra Angelico, — reading aloud with us from the old volumes of Vasari, or from Mrs. Jameson's and Lady Eastlake's writings about Art, — or, as now, busy and pleased with something of ornament simply exquisite to look at; and it seemed as if the girl were a kind of riddle to her, the woman who had known the world for five-and-twenty years of clever, society-seasoned womanhood.

We had been following out certain mentions and meanings in our different books that morning; and we were just criticising a criticism, when Barbara Goldthwaite entered, her hands full with a dozen little crimson-satin paper boxes.

31

"I know it's dreadfully degenerate and rococo of me," she said; "but just put away your real sublimities a minute and see if you can't get captivated too with this lovely trash!" And five women of us, — of tolerably good sense, and in a way of some serious culture, — were round her and her jeweler's packages in a moment.

"This is for Bud, when she's really grown up into Rose Goldthwaite, — my little Golden Rose." It was a bracelet of gold filagree, — rose leaves wreathed together, and clasped with a tiny cluster of flowers and buds. "I think it's the loveliest name in all the world. It always means the daintiest possible things to me; — the "Rose Enthroned;" the apex of evolution. Rosa Mundi, my sister, lives in a Horseshoe, I must tell you, and she has so many neighbors she does n't know what to do. This is for her; and it has got a whole Apocalypse Explained in it."

It was a silver horseshoe, with shining specks of diamonds for nails. In the middle, throwing tiny sprays and leaf-tips across it, was a golden rose; dependent from the two ends of the shoe by a silver chain hung a tiny globe of silver, with raised figures on it of dead gold, — shaped like the great continents; the ocean spaces, burnished silver.

"Is n't that a pretty illustration?" Barbara asked. "I *made* the man undertake these things, though he said he had no patterns; they were quite out of his way of manufacture. They turn out such stereotyped things! Pansies and daisies, — I beg your pardon, Marguerite; I've some delighteous things in daisies, too, — for everybody! I just told him I'd come four thousand miles, more or less, to get them. You see, there's the horseshoe; that's the principle of good neighborhood as set forth by Rosa Mundi; and that, once established, holds the world to its blessed ends. And the world then, — I could n't make it literally blossom like the rose, but I had it put into the same preciousness, — comes out after a rose-fashion, and gets drawn up into the millenium! Now here's mamma's; this dear little silver dove, with outstretched wings. That's the Holy Bird, is n't it?

"And the forget-me-nots are for Ruthie; and this is for Bud

again, when she is grown up;" (that came in at every other
article;) "and see these daisy ear-rings and this feronière! I
shall have to keep them myself, I guess, though Harry did have
this bunch of barberries made for me, too! Well, they 'll all
be Rosebud's, by and by! No; I 'll keep the daisies for you,
Margaret, for a wedding gift! I know you 'll never buy silver
daisies for yourself."

A flush came — gently, not stormily — up into Margaret's
face. She made no answer, but turned to her step-mother with
a wreath of golden pansies she had taken in her hand. She
laid them over Mrs. Regis's forehead, against the rich coil of her
dark hair.

"I should like to see you wear a thing like this, mamma,"
she said.

"When you wear your daisies?" said Mrs. Regis, meeting
the young girl's eyes, slowly, as she searched them.

"Yes, perhaps, if I ever do," Margaret answered, simply, not
taking her own eyes away.

Mrs. Regis's very lips were pale for a moment, but she smiled,
and the talk was ended.

Heart's-ease. I thought that was what Margaret meant.
Would Mrs. Regis wear it then?

But I knew from something quick and subtile in the lines of
the sweet, strong, young face, that there was in the heart of the
child a clear, calm confession of the sole giving that might ever
crown her with her own name flower, — the pure, steadfast marguerites.

We went back for a few minutes to our books again.

We had come across two little bits that morning that went
into the treasure bag of thoughts to keep; one of suggestion,
the other of contradiction. And we had stopped to talk about
them, when Barbara came with her silver globes and golden
roses.

We were following up Perugino. But looking along through
Mrs. Jameson, there fell under my eye a sentence about an
illumination in the MS. of Queen Mary's Prayer Book in the
British Museum. It is of "Joseph dropping wheat into the
river, that it might float to his father's country, and tell him
that there was wheat in Egypt."

I find in my own little memorandum, made that day, this line written; I don't know, — for the book is not by me now, — whether quoted by Mrs. Jameson, or just *reminded* to myself. I only know that it reminded me again of a whole blessed interpretation of Joseph's story that comforted me once against, perhaps, some needless things of my greatest sorrow: " And when Jacob *saw* that there was wheat in Egypt." Love lifted up, — even love gone away from us through negligences or ignorances, — goes yet to prepare a place for us. And it sends us word; it drops sweet grains into the river that we may *see* the wheat that is in Egypt.

I said something of it, with a more every-day application, as I laid down the volume.

" That is how things taken away, — forfeited, even, — things that our own mistaken living banishes and misses, — drop back a promise toward us. It is never to taunt us, but to tell us what still may bé, that the drifting corn comes by upon the river."

" You good people always seem so sure of these things," said Mrs. Regis. ,But she did not say it cynically. I thought she would not have said it at all, if she had been impatient of my word.

" I thought it was we *bad* people I was taking comfort for," I answered, smiling.

" Bad or good, I think people are very happy who have such things come to them. I have no doubt there *is* corn in Egypt, — as a theory; but I might stand a long while by the river, I'm afraid, before the grains would begin to drift down to me. I should not know when or how to look for them."

" Miss Euphrasia would say, ' Shun evil as sin, and look to the Lord.' That is both how and where."

" That is a remarkable saying," observed Mrs. Regis, thoughtfully. And then again, when nothing more had been spoken immediately, — " Remarkable in this; its two words of qualification. ' As Sin.' We are all ready enough to shun evil as evil, — even evil as ugliness or inconvenience, I suppose. Who said that, Miss Patience ? For you spoke as if you quoted it from farther back than Miss Euphrasia."

" Emanuel Swedenborg."

"Ah! Yes." It was here that Barbara had come in, and we had laid by our reading, and gathered about her, with that willingness, perhaps, which people feel to turn down a leaf sometimes at a thought they have been making special pause upon.

" This other page that we had just stopped at," I said, taking up the volume of our regular reading as we settled down again, " puts in mind by its very contradiction of the thing that we were talking of. Perugino knew better than Lady Eastlake what he was about."

It was a reference to her criticism of his Ascension in the Museum at Lyons. She objects to his representing the Lord as *lingering* above those He leaves ; poised, as it were, reluctant, with his outstretched hands of blessing over them ; delaying to pass out of their sight into his glory ; "sacrificing sublimity," she says, " in the upper part of the picture."

" I disagree with that utterly," I exclaimed warmly. " I wish I could see the painting. But from the etching it seems to me the very most beautiful conception possible of the Ascension. It is as if He did *not* go away ; were not *going*, but were with them always — only a little raised above — unto the end of the world. He, and the angels with Him, *rest* in calm attitudes, over the uplifted heads and reaching hands below. It is not only He that lingers ; but all heaven comes down and waits ! It is the nearness of the Shining Shore ! He is exalted, that He may shed forth this that ye do see and hear ! He dropped back his promise to the world, from the very death into which they thought they had sent Him ! Was not this like the wheat out of Egypt ? "

" After that," said Mrs. Regis, who had taken the book, and examined the etching, — " such a comment as comes next sounds like a glib blasphemy. It says here, — speaking of Raphael's design for the Ascension executed as one of the series of tapestries, as also not impressive, — ' The Saviour soars' with a leisurely confidence of being *en évidence* to those below ! "

" They forget what they are putting into such words," I answered quickly. " And yet the truth would say itself, even

through misapprehension ! ' Lifted up' for the very purpose
that we might look upon Him ! Not that He should be taken
out of our sight ! ".

Mrs. Regis shut the book as she laid it back upon the table by
me. I did not open it. We let the reading end there.

We had what Barbara called a " delectable freeze " in the
Accademia, one morning.

It is away down in the Via Ricasoli. Block behind block of
tall grim old houses, with mere crevices of street-way between
them, and these crevices running east and west, — so that never
the sun, but always the fierce Tramontana, sweeping from the
Apennines to the sea, pours down along their gloomy depth, —
lie between the broad, warm aisle of the Arno and the Square
of St. Mark, on which the academy building corners. We were
half frozen when we got there, for the Tramontana was at its
fiercest; and as we entered the great vestibule, and the still,
tomb-like frigor of the stone walls, that are built on purpose
never to be warmed, received us from the buffet of the rushing
cold without, a porter, moved with compassion — or the hope of
francs — by the blue points of our noses, offered us a couple of
scaldinos.

I never saw ladies carry scaldinos about in any picture gallery we ever entered ; we had no precedent for it ; indeed,
when we told what we had done at the dinner table that evening in reply to " Lady Clara's " remark that she was " very-
very sure we must have been petrified," there was a little
shout of amusement all around, and " Lady Clara," who did
not shout, nor even smile, said " How very-very amusing !
Really, quite extr-o-rd'nr'y ! " automatically, between her spoon-
fuls of soup. — But we took them with an unhesitating grati-
tude, as we would have taken any sort of salvation in a last
emergency, and by thawing our hands and faces over the glowing coals as we walked about, or one foot at a time when we
set them on the floor to pause before a picture, and taking
turns with each other in possession of them, we remained an
hour or two in the galleries and departed at length by our
own volition, and were not carried out in stiffened lengths like
marble monoliths.

I was struck with the grandeur and the antithesis of the two statues, Jeremiah and Archimedes, placed on either side the entrance into the long hall of sculpture.

The splendid majesty of the Prophet; his uplifted look, searching the heavens, receiving thence the direct inspiration of things divine; — the Philosopher, grand, too, but with the obscured, laboring look of him, who has all *matter* to toil through before he may reach the answer to his questions; his eyes bent downward, reasoning into the earth, — weighing the body of the world. "They are the opposite ends of the Problem," I said to myself; "they stand well, the one over against the other."

Up in the great Hall of Large Pictures, we saw things of which I must tell you briefly, because I have other matters waiting for another letter, that perhaps, if my letters were chapters in a book, you might "skip to;" but which, as it is, will peaceably bide their time, since they must sail across the ocean to you in a separate ship; and I have you now safely, to show you in my own way six works, — yes seven, — of the one hundred and twenty-four that are here. And I will not tell you a word about them, but that which they in the merest noting, tell themselves.

A picture of the fifteenth century, by Fabriano, — a great gorgeous canvas, all gleaming with color and with real gold. A magnificent caravan; camels, elephants, slaves, and a gathering of people; the beasts caparisoned and laden richly. Three kings, splendid in crimson and purple and gold, — this, as I said, wherever it occurs in the picture, being real, precious blazonry, shining pure and untarnished after the four hundred years. Gifts upon the ground, laid down in offering, but also as if cast aside, almost, and forgotten, in the gracious, wonderful Infant Presence. A grand, gray old man, with massive head, kneeling before the tiny Child; his robes sweeping the stable floor; his head bowed, his lips pressed to the little baby feet that were to walk Palestine up and down on merciful errands, and be nailed through to the beam of the Cross. The baby's hand, so small and tender, laid upon the grand, bald head; God's touch in the little palm; an Infinite blessing in the outspread fingers; the same grace one recognizes, wide and mighty to overshelter a universe,

— that is in the sign of the same baby hand held over Raphael's little bird. The placid face of a red cow, with large eyes almost human in their gazing, reaches forward, through the manger, looking on; as with the dim, far-off wistfulness of the beasts, toward something which had come upon the earth, and was to reach down, in the new, blessed order, to them also, beneath the table of the Supper of the Lord.

Another Nativity, by Ghirlandajo:— it hangs near by the first. Here are the shepherds worshiping. A little bird has hopped close to the Virgin's foot, and looks up, with that spirit look, that the winged things have, at the Child; an ass, with meek face, waits patiently; the Friend and Helper of all the burdened and lowly, has come at last into his world in that cradle of a human birth.

A Holy Trinity, by Albertinelli:— the Son, crucified; the Father, with widespread arms and bending head leaning close above him out of the heavens; the Dove, hovering over the head of the Christ, flutters forth from the Father's bosom.

An Annunciation, by Allori:— the Virgin just risen from a rush-bottomed chair, has at her feet a great round basket full of woman's work; two large pins or needles thrust in among the loosely piled materials. The Angel Gabriel, beautiful, noble in face, strong-winged, majestic, — alights before her in the midst of her simple, ordinary avocation; an olive branch droops before him, as in salute, from one hand, while he lifts the other toward the great glory that is breaking above her in the open heaven, and whose flood of excelling brightness overshadows her already. Cherub faces gleaming through the clouds; the unseen quickening, throbbing into vision; flowers fallen, like a rain, upon the floor.

Two Saint Francises, by Cigoli : — separated by a picture one does not care for, — a Susannah, by somebody; — the second as you come to it, revealing itself instantly as the sequel, in the same thought and touch as the first. In one, the saint upon his tnees, imploring, *reaching*, with his whole spirit toward heaven ; heaven closed and hidden. A face of utter, agonized beseeching ; a longing, straining, out of the flesh into the infinite and holy ; — strong, wasted features ; — great, — strangely great, — deep, dark eyes ; their lids crimson-heavy with tears and watching ; the gaze fixed, and far ; absolutely alone from the world, his solitary, kneeling man, and present before God and the Lord, desiring from Him the great showing of his presence. — In the other picture : — kneeling again ; but with hands crossed quietly upon his breast, — the straining subsided, — an awed, hushed sense upon him of the Divine *come* unto him ; shafts of light descending in quick lines toward hands, feet, breast ; the Stigmata, — the holy signs, set upon him: But he had received the Lord's wounds before, into his soul.

The seventh is Carlo Dolce's Creator. I do not think it so strange as many do, that these old artists, in the old church, gave typical form to the thought of the Almighty Father. When you consider, you see that we cannot possibly *have* thought *without* form. It was the *graven* image that was forbidden, as dear Emery Ann is continually saying ; the hard, fixed, *finished* representation, that may as really be so in idea as in marble. Graven creeds and conditions — emptied of the spirit that gave them fluency and expansion — are worse images, because they get into men's minds, than any that can be made for the mere senses. It is forever by the things that are seen in the creation of the world, that we understand the invisible things of Him ; even his eternal power and Godhead. You cannot think of any abstract thing without an image ; of faith without a leaning and a holding, — a grasping of the hem of a divine Garment, — an attitude and act of the spirit ; of hope without a " reaching forward to the things that are before."— And if we analyze our thought of God, we find it in some clear and awful shadow of the divinest that we know, — the human. I think, ever since I left off saying my prayers at my mother's knee I have had to say them at God's knee ! And is that wicked ?

Here, in the picture, are vast, rolling clouds ; an Arm resting in embrace about some shadowy globe-form ; a Face looking forth from above, like the Face of Jesus. The Word, by *whom* also, He did make the worlds. The Human of God, tender with the thought of the humanity to be created, — of the relation to be between Himself and it, born from Himself. Alone; darkness and light seething together about Him; but all the manifoldness of love and life that shall be, breathing and moving in Him : an infinite, yearning solicitude, almost awe at his own Act, feeling the history " from the foundation," of souls that should go forth from Him ; and through their depths of discipline, — of sin, and pain, and love, and joy, come struggling and trembling back to Him again. The Lamb slain from the beginning with the dying of his own creation, that must be, for it to be born forever into His Life.

There was all this in the picture to me ; just because it was such a face of human grace and tenderness: so soft and deep with color and shadow ; so feminine of outline, as Carlo Dolce's faces are ; so strange, at first glance, and lacking, as an impersonation of Almightiness. It grew upon me. I did not see anything there at first but a face that looked like the face of the Saviour, sweet and earnest. The Catalogue told me the Name ; and then it came and came to me, as I stood and searched ; how the Face of the Son of Man is the Face of the Father of Spirits ; how the utmost tenderness and humanness were in the giving of a life out of Himself to grow and endure until it came to know His own ; how that not Might, but Love, — even to Pain, — was that which brought forth the worlds ; and that to create, was to be the Mother, also, of His creation.

Up-stairs, in the little gallery of the moderns, hangs the New Testament to this beautiful old Genesis, — Vogel's Jesus blessing the Children. Not babies brought in arms; children clustered, of their own accord, all about Him; one sweet, girl-face looking up into his eyes, — a pure, fearless, lovely-modest gaze. One little thing climbed and nestled close, with cheek against his bosom ; others upon his knees ; one, — an *older* one, — kneeling, with face hidden against his garment ; as if khowing already something of Peter's " Depart from me ; " and yet — clinging. One looks until one feels one's self *in* the picture, among the children, become before Him, as a little, sorry, comforted, glad child.

CHAPTER XX.

WAITINGS; AND STRENGTHS.

. . . .

, ... " I DON'T believe in it ! More and more, I don't believe in it ! You 'll be sick of hearing me say so ; but it 's
' graven images ' all through the world. Folks making things
to look like something. They might have the real things at the
same pains. That table cost more than the pearls and the
shells and the ribbons would."

We were standing before a wonderful porphyry table in the
Pitti Palace ; its polished surface, of itself so precious, is inlaid
with what seem like strings of fair, round, enormous pearls,
loops of shining ribbons, branches of coral, and exquisite sea-
shells, — flung down upon it in a rich grace of confusion. All
made of gems and rare minerals, worked into a mosaic of mimic
form that mocks at fact.

" Though I don't know as the real things are the most to be
wanted, — that kind ; " she went on. " Or else the Lord
would n't have hid 'em away in the caves of the earth, and at
the bottom of the sea. Except, forzino, because the real realness is hid away, that way, too." Emery Ann, also, in a kind
of head foremost fashion, was beginning to blunder through the
signs, and to touch bottom only at the things they stand for.

" But just see ! For all these painted mothers and children,
there might be real, live, happy ones, picked out of dirt and
misery. For that painted Mary Magdaleen " (it was Titian's
miracle, with the river of golden hair), " there might be a thousand saved women. And for pictures of trees, and mountains,
and pastures, — and *cattle*-pieces, and ' *still* life ! ' mugs and loaves
and fruit and things " — (I wish I could note down her emphasis of contempt on these words) — " that they paint nowa-

days,—lots of poor folks might have a little garden spot, truly, before their doors; not freskered; and bread and tea, and a cow to keep! I believe the Lord meant us to work in the real things, when *He* made the first things beautiful, and told folks to take hold and multiply!" Emery Ann gave herself rein almost to eloquence.

"But," said Barbara Goldthwaite, "the Lord made this power also,—to paint, and sculpture, and reproduce beautiful images of things."

"And warned and commanded against putting them in the place of *His* things, and falling down and worshiping 'em."

"But He does give the genius, and it is meant for something."

"Like enough. He gave Peter once a miraculous draught of fishes; and frightened him half out of his sinful wits. And then what? Keep on there, in his little boat, dragging 'em up like that, for a trade, out of Galilee? No; go to work and fish men!"

Emery Ann is a terrible Radical; but it is n't, with her, all tearing up. She has got hold of a root of something, that is fast; a root like the mustard-tree, that should grow till all the fowls of the air come and build in its branches.

Do you think it strange, or forced, that we run so continually into thoughts and talks like these? If people heartily *want* to know the secrets of life, it quickens so all around them! And if two or three together, are in any earnest, — why, that is the promise again. The Giving is right in the midst of them. It comes, again and again, as the loaves were fed out. It is no praise; no betterness; no setting up to anything. It is just sitting *down*, low, upon the grass. It is as simple — and as daily — as daily bread.

"But, Miss Emery Ann," said Stephen, "what do you do about occupation, and the need of work and the pay for it which is men's living, — each one earning in the way he can? Ever so many men, they say, worked at that table for twenty years; it was their 'bread and tea,' or whatever they had."

I could have put in a word there, but I would not. It had begun with Emery Ann. I thought it would be given her what she should say.

"I can't argue it clear out," she answered. "I can't provide for everything, all through. And we ain't expected to stop and do that. But I guess it would turn out to be provided. 'T ain't bread alone."

That was about as near as she ever comes, in common talk, to Scripture quoting.

"Things are added! And I don't suppose we know, — because we've never thoroughly tried — *what* things. They're prepared; only the people won't come to the supper. If the whole world, — I ain't saying but what there 'd be hardships for somebody, like enough, beginning now, in the sort of world it's come to ; — but if the whole world, ever since Adam, had done the real things, — the 'will-as-'t is-in-heaven,' — it would have been more of an *inside* world, I think 's likely ; and who knows but what, instead of hammering 'em out of marble, and putting 'em onto cloth with paints, to fade out as fast as they went on, — there might n't have been a coming of things into the world by the inside doors, that never *have* come, and that it has n't ever come into folks' heads to invent or contrive? And that 's Bible, too! You can't keep from stubbing up against the Bible. Instead of that, it 's been mostly thieves and robbers, climbing up the outside walls! I don't believe in 'em as a general thing, and I can't; I won't, finally, — not in the *trade* of it! I 'd believe in a real message, now and then, like that little John and Jesus, with the bird."

I had bought a beautiful large photograph of the Madonna del Cardellino, and hung it up in our salon; and a dozen times a day, I would find Emery Ann standing before it, with a look upon her dear, old face that she knew nothing of, and her hand just lifted and curved a little against her bosom, in unconscious repetition of what touched her ; as she used, I was reminded, to move her lips silently, after every syllable, when Eliphalet was a little boy, saying his Sunday hymns. But I could never persuade her into the Tribune, to see the real Raphael, in its glory of color.

"I don't care for the color," she said. "I 've got the Gospel of it, and that 's enough. And I won't go near those *Titans!*"

" Shall we have time for the Galileo Tribune?" asked Margaret, as we came down the stairs, and forth into the great paved court-yard of the Pitti.

" Oh, yes, — if you please," said Stephen Holabird. "I want so very much to see the anatomical wax-works."

It was all near by, in the Museum of Physic and Natural History.

" You are not too cold, mamma? It is such a beautiful morning!" Margaret said, with a ring both sweet and glad, in her voice, as we crossed, in the broad sunshine, to the Via Romana.

We got into the Tribuna, upon the first floor, after a pause before the huge, rude, wonderful planetarium that stands in an alcove without; its iron arms still and rusted, its ponderous globes motionless forever, a monument, only, of the grand, early inspiration that worked toward an illustration of the poise and mechanism of the worlds.

In the beautiful double room, with its mosaic pavements, its walls alive with the pictured life of the hero-philosopher, — the cabinets of instruments constructed and used by himself, surrounding us, — his great figure, in marble, fronting us from the farther end, and overshadowing us when we stood before it, our heads just level, "as was fitting," Margaret said, with his calmly-planted feet, — we spent a long time; returning to wait there, after we had walked through the mineralogical rooms above, rich with richest gatherings of ores and crystals and metal masses, priceless in pure deposit, and curious fossils, and stones that we only knew by strange and mystical name, — while Stephen went back and lingered in the anatomical chambers.

Margaret Regis was so genuinely and tirelessly occupied with it! She stood before the frescoes of the great Experiments, — of the Presenting of the Telescope to the Doge and the Council of Ten, — of the watching of the swinging lamps in the Cathedral of Pisa, — and again beneath the statue of the man, whose thought was in and beyond it all, and of which it was only a scanty record, — as if Time and Man were there, an actual presence, into which she entered, with delight of reverence.

" I do not understand the child!" Mrs. Regis said to me, half weariedly. " Her whole mind, for the moment, is in this. She is so changed! She used to be restless, captious, impatient of unsettled things. And now — when *everything* is unsettled — she *strengthens* under it!"

We were just opposite a picture of Galileo, with his instruments, among the Savans, — or the Ten of Venice, it might be, who were not so learned, — I won't be sure. His great telescope, out of use, rests upon its pivot, its end swung away from the window against the blank of wall. Some old dignitary, with a face of magnificent cavil, has stealthily stooped to it, to try what he may see through the new, magical tube. The blankness of his expression, repeating that of the dead barrier, which blocks out earth and stars, mingling with the perverse satisfaction that seems to say, — " After all, there is nothing there!" is a glorious satire.

" It is a question of the poise, — like *that*," I said. " We can look through our present just as it happens — or as it seems — to point, — against a wall; or we can lift it up toward the heavens. Margaret makes me think of nothing so much as Isaiah's song, — 'The Creator of *the ends of the earth*,' — the Planner of what is to come of it all, — 'faileth not;' and 'they that *wait on the Lord* shall renew their strength!' It is the grand reversal of Solomon's half proverb, — 'Hope deferred maketh the heart sick.'"

" I *must* talk with you!" Mrs. Regis exclaimed, impulsively, under her breath. "I have been waiting, waiting, till I *am* heart-sick! Though," and she smiled strangely, "whether it is a *hope* deferred, — if a hope must be a wish, — I cannot tell. I wrote to Paul Rushleigh, Miss Patience, from Venice. I sent two letters, — one to Cairo, one to Beyrout. And I have heard nothing."

" My dear Mrs. Regis! Paul Rushleigh is in Rome. Why have you never named his name before?"

CHAPTER XXI.

SET STEADFASTLY.

. . . .

. . . . THE children came up, —'I call Edith and Stephen the children, — and said they were going into the Boboli Gardens.

We had looked down from the windows of the Pitti that morning into the lovely shades and recesses, upon the climbing heights, the long walks, the gleaming beauty of numberless statues white against the evergreens that make the enchantment of this vast old pleasure-ground which as yet we had not entered; notwithstanding Edith's memory-dream of it from her childhood, for whose sake it was "one of the things that made her want to come to Europe." It was Thursday to-day, and the place was open. We had always happened upon a wrong day, when we had been close by, before, and had not cared to delay for a permission.

How can one keep on chaperoning, when one is tired off one's feet, and the chances, that are not to be unkindly refused or neglected, turn up rightly for feet and eyes that are younger?

It began this morning that Edith and Stephen got a fashion, with a precedent, for strolling off together, in the fine middays, when the other sight-seeing was over, into the "dear old Boboli;" "among the gods and the fairies," they said. Stephen got a month's permission from the prefect at the palace, and thenceforth, — as "All Print" to Mr. Silas Wegg, — all Dream Land in actual territory, was open to them.

One day, in these times, — and not long after, — our little party being variously scattered, Mrs. Regis and I found ourselves in the old splendid church of the Annunziata.

Christmas was over; we had made a stocking-holiday of it, in memory of home, and turned it into a "mosaic dispensation," Barbara Goldthwaite said; for Stephen had put in her stocking

a Florentine mosaic paper-weight inlaid with jessamine flowers;
and she had dropped into his a pair of sleeve-buttons; and
the boy had taken Christmas privilege and given Edith a tiny
brooch with little blue forget-me-nots; and Mrs. Regis had surprised me utterly with an exquisite portfolio, upon whose cover
was a white branch of Annunciation lilies. Christmas was over,
and the New Year; and the Epiphany; but the crimson silken
curtains still festooned the chapels of the Annunziata, and swung
along the height of the nave, and reddened richly the light that
fell upon the silver lilies on the Virgin's Altar.

We were fond of this old church; not because it is the
aristocratic worshiping place of all the chief Florentines; not
for the dazzle of its jewels and precious metals; nor even for
Del Sarto's Madonna del Sacco — which I have seen far more
satisfactorily in engraving, — over the cloister door; but for
that vast old cloister itself, stretching down with its wide pavement and its many pillars and its groined roof, such a grand,
quiet vista, with dim pictures all along its wall, from the north
transept to the front : — for the court-yard, with its beautiful
frescoes, sheltered behind glass screens; where we wondered at
the Nativity of the Virgin, in which, by the chimney-side, where
a woman sits and washes the child, a lovely little maiden form
stands like a vision, — we questioned whether of what the baby
should be in her coming sweet separate girlhood; where another
of Del Sarto's pictures shows St. Philip raising a dead boy to
life, and, — as in many of these painted miracle-scenes, — the
living figure stands beside the dead one; the real shape, not the
corpse reanimated : — for the many, small, secluded chapels, on
either side the un-aisled nave, with their little inner archways
that pass from one to another; these suggested even better and
more than they really satisfied us with.

It was here that I had the fancy of what such a church, made
truly holy with the holiness of art, — with "messages," as Emery
Ann had called them, — might be to believers of any faith, and
all; how from one to another of these separate niches, one
might pass and find a reminding, a re-presenting, of the Acts
and Moments of the Gospels; sweet, solemn scenes, shutting
one into each most beautiful comforting instant of the Lord's

32

Life on earth; in the presence of which one could forget the human counting of centuries in the ever during Now; where the word and the gift might seem fresh again, given to the soul's fresh need. Where, penitent, it could hide and kneel in company with the Magdalen; or weep with Peter under the look of Jesus; or, storm beaten, could grow calm before the Form upon the waters, and almost hear the accent — " It is I; be not afraid; " or sick of the palsy, find the Healer bending above the bed " let down before Him where He was; " or sorrowing and imploring, receive its dead again at the gate of Nain, or the tomb of Lazarus. I knew it must have been the first intent of them; before they were made into mere gorgeous burial places and monuments for common-lordly men.

We sat down in a shaded archway, upon a low step that led upward to a shrine.

Near by was a confessional; a dark-robed priest had just gone in, upon his side; the sign was put up that he was there, and waiting; but the penitent side was for a while vacant.

Mrs. Regis said to me what is so apt to be said, at sight of these tangible helps, by those who have not found the living reality in their own faith that is *more* than tangible.

" I half envy these Romanists; who have something to come to! Some one whom they can really *tell*, — what is not known beforehand. I think that is all that makes it telling, — or confessing."

" Yes. God knows it all beforehand. Perhaps that was one of the things that He came into the human for. That He might show us how he *could* be human to us. Perhaps the Christ-Nature in Him puts the Omniscience behind Him, and listens to us just as Christ listened in the body. It may be part of that Life of which he said, ' I have power to lay it down, and I have power to take it again.' At any rate, it is always *confession;* and that means more than telling."

" I don't understand."

" Committal; trust; " I said. " Giving freely up, in order to be set free. You know they call the crypts and shrines where saints and martyrs are buried in these old cathedrals, ' confessions.' The confession of St. Paul and of St. Peter are in their churches at Rome. Something laid down before the Lord ; 'committed to Him until that day.' It has struck me very much that it should be the same word that we use for bringing the wants and wrongs of life, and giving them up, to the dealing of the Lord. They are laid down, — buried, then, the body and burden of them, which is always some slain right ; and the remission, — the making up and giving back again, — is trusted to Him. The pure life — the martyr-confession — is the same ; a rendering up to the sure faith of Him ; "into thy hands I commit my spirit," is always the martyr-witness. We can let our thoughts and memories lie before Him so, without a word."

" You give me a new idea of prayer," Mrs. Regis answered me.

" Perhaps the very best idea of it is just a thinking toward God ; and a waiting for what He will think back to us, and do ; not a trying to tell Him anything."

" I do not suppose," said Mrs. Regis, " that I shall ever be what is called a religious woman. I have no religious sentiment. I am only not satisfied unless things are fair, and straight, and — comfortable. I think it grows upon me ; and gets deeper, — and larger round ; and so, perplexing. The longer I live, the larger circumference I want, of what Emery Ann would call ' tidiness ; ' things cleared up. I have a great sympathy with Pleasant Riderhood," she ended, slightly laughing ; " who could n't get into a row with an easy mind, until she had twisted up her back hair."

As we walked down the church again, — that last little incongruity of her speech having, as it were, admonished us that we were getting back into our every day — and should leave the shrine, perhaps, for the street, with it, —

" I shall not be comfortable," she said, seriously and quietly, " until I have taken Margaret to Rome. And the child argues so for staying here! I know she thinks it might not be well for me ; for certainly, Italy has not agreed with me !"

Her high look, — her pale, handsome face, — the struggle and the secret that made her lip tremulous and tender underneath its calm restraint, — the very things in her bearing that seemed to shut off notice and sympathy, overcame their own barriers with me.

"Dear Mrs. Regis!" I cried softly, the understanding and the honor of her that were alive in me in spite of her ignoring, rushing through voice and words, — "God has made you of too noble substance to be comfortable at last, with less than perfect self-forgetting!"

She lifted the great leathern curtain before which we stood, and we passed into the square.

It was almost three weeks longer, before they went away. She grew paler, as she insisted, day by day, against Margaret's increasing unwillingness for her sake; but she never yielded, or faltered; her face was as that of one set steadfastly to go to up Jerusalem.

CHAPTER XXII.

A COMMA.

. . . .

. . . . Miss Euphrasia Kirkbright followed Mr. Shea's interpreting clerk up the fifth dark, dingy, Roman staircase of uncleansed stone that she had climbed that morning.

She had been at Hotel de Londres, in the Piazza di Spagna, since her arrival. There she had got tired of paying twenty francs a day ; tired also of the long six-o'clock dinners ; tired of the dress and the bustle, and the loneliness. This last she had begun to escape from in a growing intimacy with a lovely English lady and her invalid daughter, whom she had first met in Siena, and who had come down to Rome just after herself; and the three were planning an escape now, together, into apartments.

Miss Euphrasia had gone to the house agent, been courteously fitted out with a list of lodgings and the attendant above mentioned, and had been taken the inevitable preparatory round which they so well understand how to lead one, through useless investigations of damp, dirty, cheerless, impossible rooms, until, at the end of hope and patience, her mind brought to that point whence the rebound of a comparative satisfaction would become certain decision, she was ushered up this last dark old passage and ascent, that she was already firmly resolved should be the last.

The words were on her lips, — "It is hardly worth while ; it seems like all the rest ; I do not think we can suit ourselves ; " when a door was thrown open before her into a large, light, square room, with three casement windows to the floor, and a blaze of Roman sunshine, — the one antidote to all Roman horrors and distastes, — rushed gorgeously upon her, and took her into its welcoming embrace. The sunshine poured into and around, — filling it up like a great reservoir, — the Forum of Trajan ; and the long, deep, railed excavation around which runs the street of the square, — with its clustering fragments of mighty columns, like the stumps of a magnificent old hewn-down forest, — its mysterious half arches, through which plunge pathways into subterranean aisles, and chambers yet unexplored, — and its one perfect pillar standing up straight into the light, — was directly before her as she walked to the middle of the three windows and gazed forth.

It was just past high noon, and the sun, southing and wester-ing, had fairly taken possession for all the long remaining hours of this whole front of building on the northeasterly side of the piazza. That is another of the " tricks and the manners " of house-showing ! They take you — where they mean *you* to take — just in the right moment to meet the sun. Close by upon the right rose a church tower ; beyond the column showed the great dome and lantern of Santa Maria di Loreto.

Miss Euphrasia stood, delighting in this grand opening, think-ing how far pleasanter its outlook was into the real old Rome, than the hotel frontage upon the gay Piazza di Spagna, and won-dering how she should find out as to its salubrity, so near the excavations, when as she turned to put some cautious questions to her attendant, and found that he had left her by herself in the salon, she encountered at the same moment, just entering from a farther room of the suite, General Paul Rushleigh.

They met eagerly, with outstretched hands and a quick greet-ing.

" You are before me here," said Miss Euphrasia, then.

" No," he answered, " I was looking at the apartment for an acquaintance at the ' Amérique,' a St. Louis gentleman and his wife. But there are more rooms than they need. Three or four persons would be nicely accommodated. There are three sleeping rooms, a dining-room, and a servant's room outside the kitchen. Are *you* house hunting ? "

" Yes. Do you think the situation safe ? "

" Especially so ; Murray indorses the Piazza Trajano as one of the most healthy situations in Rome. These rooms are just vacated by an English officer and his family. My St. Louis friend had an engagement this morning that could not be put off, and I came to examine for him, but it is too large a suite. You have a party?"

"Two ladies beside myself, and their maid."

Miss Euphrasia spoke a little absently, and with an instant's delay; she was considering.

Some sudden interest, checked by a slight hesitation, appeared in General Rushleigh's manner.

"Two ladies? — Might I ask — ?"

"Oh, they are not any of our old friends. Two English ladies, mother and daughter. I think the rooms will do," she said, returning to her consideration of the business question. Some instant reminder, and as instant an impulse to avoidance of the subject, seemed to have moved her in her direct reply, and then in the dropping of further allusion.

"Have you met our old friends lately?" asked General Rushleigh, quietly.

"I saw Miss Strong and her party in Florence."

"Mrs. Regis?"

"Mrs. Regis and her daughter were in Venice."

Paul Rushleigh cut straight through her reserve, and her short answers.

"Dear Miss Euphrasia, I think you have a consciousness of something that holds you back a little from me. And why have you not left some word for me, before now, at the bankers?"

"Last week you were in the country."

"Oh, you heard? Yes, we went out to Amelia, to see the Cyclopean walls."

"Are they not very wonderful?"

"Amazing. It is difficult to imagine what enginery they could have employed. The farther back you go in research among the works of remote ages, the more ponderous the traces of them become. And to-day, from among those old Umbrian mountains down here to Rome, run the light tracks of the rail, and the threads of the telegraph. It is such a contrast of powers."

"Yes. As human life gets hold of the essential, the work in

the material must take a more transitory character. The greatest things are shown by the slightest mechanism, — the most
fleeting signs. Clouds, flowers, waves, — the might of sunlight
and storms; they are all of the things that drift and pass away
most easily; but the word in them never passes away! I think
the world is very near, — physically, — coming to a living in
the very powers and secrets of life; and very near, — spiritually,
— to a possible forfeiting of it for cycles more to come!"

"Now you are Miss Euphrasia again. But it is n't Cyclopean walls that I am thinking mostly of with you at this moment. Have you anything to tell me of my friends? There
need be no wall between you and me. It is a mistake — between real friends — to shun a thing because you know it is
most real. I must always wish to know of Mrs. Regis and her
daughter."

"And yet — you are staying on here, at Rome, and they in
Venice? I do not think I can tell you of them, Paul. It is
rather you who might tell me. There is a puzzle in it."

"I asked Miss Regis to be my wife; and she told me it was
impossible. It is not possible, therefore, that I can follow them
about, — just now; but it is impossible, also, that she can be
less than a very dear interest in life to me, though she will be
only a friend."

General Rushleigh spoke with manly composure; his love
had been too great and manly a thing to be shy or silly about.

"I believe you asked her just before it might have been possible. Miss Patience thinks" — she stopped short.

"I beg you to go on. What does Miss Patience think?"

"That she did not understand herself. That circumstances
were in the way. I will tell you the exact words. . For it was
a kind of a message, if I should have opportunity. And that
was what held me back. She said, 'She did not know herself.'"

General Rushleigh's face took a surprised, incredulous, almost annoyed expression. Miss Euphrasia felt hers color up.

"Miss Patience told me that before," he said. "I do not understand. I had a most clear, true, final answer, as I then assured her."

" But, — I really do not know what to say, Paul ; it is such
a strange thing for me to meddle with, — it was too *soon !* It
was just because she *is* so true ! Why did you not wait? That
old — obligation " —

"You do not think I spoke before I knew *that* was canceled!
When I had waited months ? "

" You knew ? "

" Yes ; from Margaret. When the Mackenzie engagement
was first made known. And then, as you see, I waited. I did
not even come to them at once. No ; it was quite certain. It
was quite ended."

" I can only beg your pardon. I do not think I comprehend
at all," said poor Miss Euphrasia. " I did not know — I do not
see — I think there must be something which Miss Patience
knows that we do not, or else that she knows something less
than she supposes."

And then, naturally, it was Paul Rushleigh's turn to look ex-
tremely uncomprehending.

" Is it that madame will be pleased to take the apartment ? "
inquired the interpreting agent, returning from his talk below
with the padrona.

CHAPTER XXIII.

FROM ARNO TO TIBER.

. . . .

. . . . THE threads had all come back to me. But what was I to do with them?

It was all plain enough to me, now; and I could see how it was exactly plain to no one else. I understood now Paul Rushleigh's staying away, after Mrs. Regis's letter, and I understood his coming. I understood his changed manner at Lugano; relieved of a curb that he had put upon himself, and full of a new, glad, hopeful purpose. I understood his earnestness in asking Margaret about her letters, that morning at Villa Ciani, and his cleared look, returning to its satisfied assurance, when she had told him of the large packet that had come by the way of England. I could see his whole course in its patient strength, its generous delay, its one plain, straightforward confession, its silence since, receiving Margaret's "impossible," as the word of a woman whose words were not spoken lightly, but out of her very life.

I could see, — I saw instantly, — what had been Miss Euphrasia's singular misapprehension. Only once, in all my knowledge of General Rushleigh, had he uttered in my hearing that name of his sister, — Margaret. But it came back to me instantly. Because it had been spoken in the presence of this other Margaret, as a Catholic believer might speak the name of Mary. As the name of all womanhood to him. Maybe Miss Euphrasia had never heard him speak it quite like that. Maybe she had known him with an intimacy apart from much intimacy with his family. And Margaret Regis was the only Margaret in her thought.

Margaret Rushleigh had written to her brother; and his letters had come straight and safe, while ours had miscarried.

It was a very simple little thing. Paul Rushleigh thought he had made sure, and he had waited. How could he guess that Margaret's release had come within that very hour in which she had sent him from her?

And how, now, was he to be made to guess it?

Do you see, it came back upon me like a judgment, all my fault-finding with people in stories, and with people in real life, that they do not take a plain thing right up and handle it as it should be handled? There is so much more in all the delicate, mixed motives of living, than the blunt impulse that would drive at a fact, because it is a fact, like driving at a nail with a hammer. Such a fine, intangible thing may hinder, — may neutralize, — the possibility of using a knowledge; of clearing, point-blank, a mistake.

How could we outside women keep *at* Paul Rushleigh with our little patches of amendment, our tardy bits of gratuitous information? What becoming opportunity or excuse might there be, again, for any of us?

To think that he should have supposed I sent that message after him again, — just what, and no more than, I had said to him when we stood by the sun-dial.

Two old maids of us! My cheeks and ears burned with mortification.

I began to be half provoked with Paul Rushleigh, too. Why would he persist in believing it to be all so utterly ended? Why would he not, like other drowning men, catch at a straw, — a floating thread? He might find it a good stout line to save his life by.

But what if he were not drowning, so very much? He was only a man after all. And it was three months since that morning at Beau Séjour. I began to think of that, at last, in my chagrin and irritation.

I put Miss Euphrasia's letter away to cool. For I felt as if it were that which was like a burning thing and a shame and a trouble; before which my ears and face tingled, and my very heart grew hot. I could not discuss it with myself any more.

Things do cool down. And snarls unsnarl just by putting quietly away.

A few days later I saw something, which had not in any way occurred to me before.

Mrs. Regis was the one to know. Because she was just the only one, now, supposed not to know. Because of her infinite tact : because of the divine uncomfortableness that was besetting her, and that would not let her go till she had paid the uttermost farthing. Because her face was set towards Rome, and she had had no word with Paul Rushleigh since that October morning, when he had " had nothing to ask of her friendship except itself." She, alone, stood on the old basis with him. To her, alone, would come natural and fitting opportunity to speak of Margaret and of what had happened with Margaret, and of the when and the how.

She was elected to the full sacrifice. I could put into her hands the wood for the altar, and the cords for the binding. It was all there was for me to do.

I told her of Miss Euphrasia's letter. Of her having met General Rushleigh in Rome, and of his having spoken of her and of Margaret. I told her that it appeared in this conversation, that his own letters from home coming straighter than ours, had given him information weeks before which had arrived to them only just as he had left Lugano. That he had known of the Mackenzie affair, — and had supposed Margaret to know of it, — all the time he had been with us at the Lake. That this appeared to me, but that he was still, evidently, unconscious of what had been her real position. · I put this all together before her, with the simplest directness. And I made no comment whatever after I had done so.

She took it as I had given it ; only saying that she thanked me for letting her know ; that her mind was quite made up to be in Rome by the next Friday night.

We talked then of other things for a while; and then I got up to go ; for it was in her own room that I had been sitting with her.

She got up and came to me, and laid her hand upon the curtain with mine, as I was about to draw aside the portière.

"I thank you," she said, "because you have believed in me as I ought to be ; not as I might be, if I failed of myself."

There was not the least effusion in her manner; she put me off, slightly, as it were, with her old dignity, even while she spoke straight out of her heart into mine.

And then, holding the curtain to detain me, she said:—

"There is a possible jealousy, Miss Patience, of something coming very close to one in a younger and more fortunate life, which has never come perfectly to one's self."

She had made a beautiful friendship in her later years, which had been like to satisfy her; and this friendship was turning into love, close beside her, for a girl,—her husband's child. It was hard; hard enough to tempt her to an ungenerousness. Was this how she looked at it. now, in very truth? Or how, with a woman's lawful reserve, she covered a keener struggle from me, that. she would not, now, in her pride, ever look at, any more searchingly, herself?

After the Regises had gone we all began to get restless of Florence.

Barbara Goldthwaite would not go to Rome. She had her child to think of. She said she was "getting tired of the dust and ashes of Italy." But perhaps that was because it was just now such desperately cold dust and ashes. She would go back to Nice. The other navy ladies were leaving, some for Rome, some for Venice, some for the warm shores of Castellamare and Sorrento. In Italy, in winter, everybody is rushing about after the Italian climate. "Which, as you dream of it," somebody told us, "you don't really get, unless you keep on to Egypt."

We had come for climate; and yet we had stayed on, in this bleak Florence: and now here were the bitterest chills of all; the mountain winds of the late January; and February to come. It was a cold year; we heard of snow on Vesuvius; still the spring came earlier in Rome. We began to long to go and meet it. And to be so near, once in one's life, and not to see the Coliseum and St. Peter's and the Pantheon!

We began to be tired of things; of losing our lunches by the sight-seeing that had to be done miles away, or hurrying back to the sameness that made the luncheon table irksome. We were tired of the alternative that had seemed nice to us; of

making our own lunches of orangeade and biscuits and " patisserie "— the funniest patisserie sometimes, with sardines tucked
away in tartines of puffed paste! We were impatient of a
dozen discomforts that are inevitable, in one way or another,
in pension living, and that in the tenth week of our stay oppressed us as they had not at all done in the first.

We were tired of Lady Clara Very-very de Very, and we
missed the pleasant English clergyman and his gentle wife and
bright young daughter who had made our dinner party at the
cosy inner table so friendlike and homely, and who had also
gone off to Rome. We were tired of the man in the Greek cap
at the large table d'hote to which we had been transferred;
even of the mirthsome young Russian countess, who sat by him
opposite us, and glanced at him cautiously from the corners of
her eyes, and smiled "under her complexion," as Barbara said
when the clear skin just trembled with an expression that the
muscles were not allowed to play with. The Effendi in the
Greek cap had a spasmodic smile which was enough. It was
that which taxed all our muscles and our politeness. We could
not tell whether it was a chronic infirmity, or an amused scorn.

"Who is he?" we said to each other, daily, for a while.

"He does n't see anybody; he just sits and contorts!" said
Edith.

"He is n't in this world at all," said Emery Ann.

"Then I wish he would n't eat his dinner in this world," said
Stephen.

"He's got a familiar." "He's the wandering Jew."

"Pshaw!" said Barbara. "He's a Greek; and talks in triangles. That's all."

"And smiles in polyhedrons," said Edith.

Emery Ann was tired of "making square corners of round;"
of locking the door upon Vincenzio, and surreptitiously washing
up the hearth with a towel.

"We may rush to evils that we know not of," I told her.

"Yes," she said; "but it's a relief to begin in a new spot,
now and then. You get kind of tired of the same put-upances.
And I always was partial to new beginnings, even amongst the
same old things, at home."

"Oh, Emery Ann," cried Edith, "that you should own up to liking changes, just for changing! I thought it was only we young ones who wanted novelties, and who had to be at the trouble of inventing reasons for them!"

"Why should n't folks like novelty? The Lord does, and makes it. Or else, why do we have mornings?"

So we began to do up, in a hurry, the things that remained. "The catch-all packing," Barbara Goldthwaite called it; the last big basket into which we tumbled things heterogeneously that are to be brought to light and sorted after you get there.

After we get *where*, Rose? Shall I ever catch quite up, again? For we are here, — well, you know where, by the post-marks and the bankers; — and have n't I kept faithfully to my straightforwardness?

Pretty soon, I think, I shall have to take to rapid groupings and etchings; to touching here and there that I shall fill up in the talks, that are now not so very very many weeks off. That will do to end with, which would have been a wretched shirk in the beginning. You can scramble your cake together at the last, and perhaps it will be all the better for it; but you must beat your eggs and mix your spices patiently in the preliminary.

And when we come to the great things of Rome! Where the dust and crumbles of ages are the innumerable texts for life-long research, the parables of time and history!

Dante gave it up at the fourth canto; in the edge of the very first circle; as soon as the mighty "*ones*" began to crowd about him, out of the confusion of the millions, in the light of the "fire that overcame a hemisphere of darkness." It is easy enough to sum up the "thick crowded forest;" but the multitude that separates with separate "great authority" of presence, — there even he has to simply name them, and confess,

> "I cannot all of them portray in full,
> Because so drives me onward the long theme
> That many times the word comes short of fact."

Our own little story — which you care for because it is ours — alights presently in Rome; where it touches, I shall touch, in the simple, inevitable way, that I did there; but to *tell* Rome!

Or to find out ever so little about it among its buried and re-
buried hills! A thousand and one nights for a thousand and
three hundred years of story, and a thousand and five hundred
more of fading away and covering up in dust!

We made haste to see the marble mausoleum of the Medicis,
where from the deep brilliancy of the polished precious stone,
in whose niches rest the sarcophagi of the princes, comes back
reflected pictures of your own face and the moving group of
visitors about you, in the gorgeous octagon, as you gaze; the
old greatness, deeper buried than it knew, in the very splendor
of its own entombing, lost sight of in the mere flitting wonder
and self-pleasing of to-day. We went into the other chapel,
where the dead Julian and Lorenzo lie, with the living sculptures of Michael Angelo above them. Day and Night; Evening and Dawn; marble truths and prophecies of the restless
Darkness, the sure coming and avenging Light. The Day
wakes up as if to a pain; there is a dread and a delay of waking; the master told with his chisel what he dared not tell in
word; the after years can read it plainly; and the Medici sleep
on in their dust of pride, unconscious of the immortal satire.

We took a pleasant morning for a last drive to San Miniato
upon the hill of the cypresses and the crosses; to stand upon the
Terrace of Michael Angelo that overlooks the city and the valley from the Apennines to the Maritime Alps, — to see again
the old, quaint church and the sunny burial ground with lovely
sculptures, and queer fantastic ornaments of false trees; large
weeping willows, actually planted before the tombs, but made
leaf by leaf of tiny green glass beads, strung together by the
hands of nuns! There was something in it of the sort of memory that shuts itself up to a slow useless weaving; a mock life
making mock tribute to dead things.

We had never been inside the Palazzo Vecchio; this, at the very
end, which was the best, we did. We had known it gradually,
with a gradual liking that was at first almost unliking, of its odd,
uncouth tower, set with such seeming want of symmetry neither
centre-wise nor corner-wise, but *any*-wise, just *not* in the middle
of the heavy, overhanging battlemented front, arched and loop-

holed and machicolated, — the old clock telling the hours of to-day from the base of its square shaft about which, a little nearer the midway, was a projecting, arched and battlemented gallery like that which surmounts the edifice itself; and over that the belfry, the blunt spire, and the staff, up which, not content with its repeated effigies below, — climbs, queer and ratlike in the distance, the lion of the Florentine banner.

Clear above the tops of the houses, rising from the crown of fortress wall, you see the singular column from every quarter, as you come and go, — the watch-tower through the centuries, of the city. Taller than the Campanile, outreaching the peaked lantern of the Duomo, separate, unique, — it asserts itself continually to you, and grows in its strange beauty and even to a homelike dearness. And when it had grown to this with us, and when living into its history, in the books we had been reading, we had filled the Old Palace and its square with memories, — of times when at the sound of one of its great bells the people used to say to one another: "The cow lows!" and when the other, the Bell of the Lion, pealed out the victories, — when from the vanished platform of the ringhiere the Signory used to address the people in the Piazza standing among the splendid marbles of Michael Angelo and John of Bologna; — when Savonarola lay in an inner dungeon there for forty days between his tortures, — days that perhaps he counted as we are reminded to count them now, after the Forty Days of fasting and infernal besetting in the Wilderness, — when a score and a half years later the thing he preached was made a proclamation from this very palace front, and " Christ the Redeemer " was chosen King of Florence; — after all this had grown real to us, we came last to enter reverently the old interior; to stand in the beautiful, dim court-yard, with its colonnaded walls all painted with pictures of German cities, fading out now, but bright when one of the Medici married his German wife, the niece of Charles the Fifth, and brought her here, — its lovely porphyry fountain in the middle with its bronze figure of the boy and dolphin, where the cool water continually plashes in the shadow and stillness from the nostrils of the captured fish, — with its great staircase ascending from the gloom of the arch beyond to the chambers of the Sig-

33

nory. To walk up and down the vast, empty, echoing Hall of the Five Hundred, with its great raised dais at one end, — the utterly bare, dead space relieved by nothing but the frescoes of the lofty walls, tumultuous with battle pieces; to pass from this to the Hall of the Two Hundred, or the Lesser Council; to climb, then, more great stairs to the Audience Chamber, and the remote little Chapel with its fresco of the Annunciation, by Ghirlandajo, at one end, and John of Bologna's Crucifix at the other; its low door-way surmounted by the initials of the Saviour, and the motto "Christ our Lord reigns forever."

Emery Ann was greatly impressed by this inscription, and the story of the proclamation. She stood in the outer room before it, looking up at the Latin words, and saying to herself, — slowly, and repeatedly, — "They almost done it, then. They almost done it!"

We came out somewhere, suddenly, in a gallery or ante-room, whence a window-aperture stood open to some interior space; approaching and looking through, we found ourselves high up in the great side wall of the Sala del Cinque Cento; then we got out upon a little corridor or balcony, into the open air; and the city and the streets were beneath us. Our guide led us into a small chamber on this wall, where he showed us an exquisite little carved model for the façade of the Duomo, waiting so long; pillared and sculptured and frescoed; the Father, Moses, Christ, above the central door-way; the Madonna of the Flowers, in fresco, in the apex; the Lions of Florence couched upon the pilasters. Everywhere the Lion; everywhere the Lily; in this Florence, that, as Emery Ann says, "almost done it," once!

When, — and where, — shall the real City of the Lion and the Lily be?

The children went once more to Fiesole, where I did not go at all; they took Emery Ann with them this last time, and came back in highest fun and spirits. They had been in the old ruin of the Roman amphitheatre, had groped their way down the subterranean passages to where the wild beasts were kept of old; had crept out to the daylight again; meeting

in the narrow tunnel another party of sight-seers coming in.
"More wild beasts," said Emery Ann, quite simply and spon-
taneously, as they scrambled past each other; and everybody
shouted except herself. They had lunched at a wretched little
café, where they had some wine and lignum vitæ cheese.
"Pity the old Romans had n't built their walls with this,"
quoth Stephen, in deliberate English, with an admiring gesture
to the garçon; "they would n't have crumbled to this day! The
mightiest mite could not have forced his way through them."
And the flattered garçon smiled, and answered "si, signore."
Emery Ann disputed the bill. It was exorbitant, — four francs
apiece. "But," she expostulated in her separate and particular Tuscan, "it is *absurdo, ridiculoso*. It is an imposi-
tienzo! It was n't worth four centesimos!" And the same
garçon shook his head, shrugged his shoulders, spread his hands,
did n't comprehend, and smiled inexorably.

Edith and Stephen found violets in the Boboli gardens, to
press in their leaf-books; we bought our last Florentine keep-
sakes in the old booth-like shops on the Ponte Vecchio; we
hurried one fearfully cold day to the Church of Santo Spirito,
wherein I remember of the frescoes only some queer predellas
in one of which St. John's eagle stands upon the ground,
flapping his wings and stretching his neck, with an air of great
bustle and importance, so that Stephen cried out, very irrever-
ently, "Why, that 's the Raven! I 'm a Polly! I 'm a Kettle!
I 'm a Polly-put-the-devil-on-we'll all have tea!" And in
another a very funny angel in red boots, making wonderful
haste with a very skittish step, leading off before a Tobias or
somebody.

But near the door, a beautiful copy, in purest marble, of a
statue of Christ by Michael Angelo, made amends and satisfied
me. Young; simply noble; sweetly grand; of a tender, patient majesty; without conventional accessory or circumstance;
it is only, and divinely, the Son of Man

We spent our last evening all together, in our bright salon;
we ordered up champagne and crema montata; we made Cram-
bos; we sat upon our corded trunks at the door-way, and repeated our good-byes.

"I hope Mrs. Barbary," said Emery Ann to Mrs. Goldthwaite, whom she greatly admires, — "we shall come across
you and little Bud again, somewheres!"

" I hope só," returned Barbara. " If not in this old world,
in another and a better — hemisphere!"

" Where Barberries are indigenous," concluded Stephen.

We fee'd the expectant crowd of servants, who had had five
francs apiece at Christmas, and porterage and special douceurs
at other times ; we breakfasted in the dim, early morning; we
were put into our voiture by the polite and kindly host himself,
and our different bags and wraps brought after us by as
many different hands ; last of all the perfidious and mercenary
"Smile," who had pocketed his four francs ten hours before,
hung upon the step with a thunderous frown eclipsing his dis-
tinctive beam, demanding "pour boire" for having helped
down with a trunk! That really grieved us; we had believed
in him ; and however occupied with talk, work, or books, had
never failed of our returning smile and our "grazie," when
he brought us up a basket full of wood, and spoiled our fire,
which we had immediately on his departure regularly to re-
build. We had believed in him ; we gave up our extorted
franc and our faith at the same moment. Stephen came out,
too late to save us, and jumped upon the box; we were driven
off in a hurry ; at the station Stephen bought our tickets, had
our baggage weighed and registered, put into our hands at parting a white basket, in which we found afterward delicious
oranges and figs and a "pane santo" from Barbara; in half an
hour we were gliding slowly forth alongside the walls of Florence, looking back as we skirted them, with a tender regretful
delight, upon the swelling Duomo that always seems to float like
a great balloon just above the crowded city roofs, — upon the
quaint, gray majesty of the Palazzo Vecchio tower, — and to
the glorious Campanile cutting with its pure shaft the clear
winter sky.

For the first time we three feminine voyagers were *en route*
alone. Stephen was to go the next day as far as Genoa with his
sister ; then he was to come down to Rome by steamer to Civita
Vecchia.

But we were, per pleasant force, in a first class carriage. It is a long day's travel from Florence to Rome, and only the first class trains go through express. We resigned ourselves to the cheerful necessity, intending to do our economy on the short trips back through Northern Italy. But that did not end exactly so, either.

The whole journey is a fit, gradual approach. I felt Rome away off even among the Tuscan hills, and more and more as we penetrated into the Umbrian Mountains.

A country growing strange, dreary, like a weird dream; few persons even about the stations, that were mere stopping places; little life; no bustle. Like a progress into a fairy tale; over the hills and far away; really *into* the great, distant, visionful Past.

Every little way the locomotive whistled through the heart of a mountain tunnel; it was like a rat, squeaking in a burrow. Man is but a small creature, building and tunneling in almighty masonries.

Beautiful, far heights and green valley reaches for a while; hills fair with vineyards or silver dusky with the olive; monasteries and citadels, stretching their walls along the shoulders of remote eminences, — separate and far apart. Churches, cathedrals, lifting their towers into the silent air, above quaint, silent, slumberous, antiquated cities.

Shining up to us suddenly, in its broad, exquisite beauty, — glittering among the hills in a hot glow of meridian sunshine, — a liquid splendor, — a still, magical delight, — we came all at once upon the Lake of Thrasymene! Taking us, as with a great stride, deeper into the olden dream; hushed into its quietude from its own, far back, bloody tumult; sleeping at the foot of the woody defiles down which the misled Roman legions poured, while the army of the Carthaginian watched for them from the middle heights; the green, gentle brook-threaded defiles, that ran then red with blood to the blue water! Mute, now, over its old, deadly secret; sweetened again, as if the secret were not there; pure as sapphire under a sapphire heaven; with its mossy islands and its distant-rimming hills, looking like a fair untrodden creation, waiting for its first humanity. And who can tell what it *is* waiting for? Who can tell what of humanity, indeed, it images, sweetened from the old horror, kept for a more blessed time?

Rocky shapes, wild, stupendous, desolate; snow-blasts fluttering among their peaks like phantoms; murky, gusty, brown vapors sweeping round them. Slopes and steeps calcined with old fire; powdered with gray, red drifts. Huge volcanic wastes, like wastes of Time far back of History. The very face of nature saying continually, " This was; but it is over now."

A deep ravine we crossed, broad and dry; dead with white, bare stones; some wide stream had rushed there once; now there was not even a trickle, nor did a blade of anything grow up to take the place of the water. " The bed of a great river, auntie!" Edith cried, discovering with curious awe. " The river's been up and dressed, then, I guess, sometime," commented Emery Ann.

Green-forested hillsides again, ruggedly overhung and battlemented; towns or villages, ruined and hushed, nestled or perched among them, high above the valleys; held, perhaps, in a loop of defensive wall dropped around them from the bastions of a crumbling, ancient castle mass; others, again, built all up a cliff-side, like nests against the rock.

Emery Ann and Edith watched all along for Udolpho, which they were resolved to locate. They placed it and plucked it off again, point after point; at last, dreariest, wildest, most unapproachable of all, — they declared *that* was it, " finally; " a huge towering thing in the clouds, at the top of a tremendous pinnacle, frowning and frightful and tempest-scarred.

Deeper, yet, among volcanic hills; leaden, black, yellow, with colors of smelting and burning. Enormous cinder-heaps, — sometimes all silver-filagreed, — ash-frosted, like white lichen. Splintered, filamented, like asbestos; needled, like crystals.

After a while, darkness, like a sleep without a dream; then, walls, and thickening shadows, and glimmering lights; the feeling of a huge presence, such as you have only in approaching a great city by night; a slackening speed, a final stop.

And this was Rome.

In the starlight, and by the irregular lamps, as we were driven from the distant railway station to the hotel in Via Babuino to which we had telegraphed for rooms, we caught mingled glimpses of poor, confused, common buildings, and tall, ghostly fragments of black ruins.

Was this the way it was to look by daylight, and always?

We did not know that the whole wide quarter that we were traversing, was a tract in process of gradual excavation; that the old, old, dingy, *modern* Italian walls and buildings were giving way to the unearthing of older, more curiously precious remains; that here, between the Viminal and Quirinal Hills, we had steamed straight in to the Baths of Diocletian!

CHAPTER XXIV.

DUE, PIAZZA BARBERINI.

. . . .

EDITH TO MISTRESS BARBARA.

> Rome: January,—last day but one;
> Happy New Year a twelfth part done;
> Carnival season just begun.

Dear friend,
  Perpend:

Our Roman advent to rehearse,
Wegg-wise, I drop to easy verse;
Firing a small poetic flambeau
In honor of our blessed Crambo;
(Some name, I trow, of cheerful saint,
Or ought to be so, if it ain't;)
To set you forth, with smile and tear,
Our trials and our triumphs here, —
And thank you in particular metre,
For that sweet cake, — was never sweeter!
Which, ere we left the Arno's banks,
Came — grace of grace — *too late* for thanks.

'T is the first moment we have found
To sit us down and look around,
And but that we paid fares for Rome,
And *have* seen Trajan's column rearing
Its proud old shaft, — for all appearing,
We might well dream we were at home.

On Wednesday night was all but weeping:
Last eve beheld us at housekeeping!
Poor Emery Ann just stared and laughed
The livelong day, and thought us daft;
So "rapid" we rushed and rallied round,
House, and dinner, and fire-wood found, —
Candles, and coffee, — salt and spice, —
All things essential, and some things nice, —
Butter and matches, rolls and cream,
Tumbling in, in a steady stream,
Ordered quick to our mansion tiny,
Due, Piazza Barberini.
Sure, Cinderella's old godmother
Lent us her wand, or charmed another!

'Twas half despair, and half 't was pique;
They treated us mean at the D'Amérique!
They showed us up one-and-eighty stairs;
They left us no breath to say our prayers;
They stowed us away in a northeast corner,
In the very teeth of the Tramontana;
Small space they gave us to turn about,
Then they lit a fire, and they smoked us out.
These were the lodgings, sweet and sunny,
They *promised* us for our paper money!

We strode forth silent, that bright next day,
Hired a fiacre and rattled away.
Two hours after we called for the bill:
Perhaps that clerk may be gaping still!
' We have an apartment. Please send our boxes.'
His face was as long, when he heard that ' please '
Blandly breathed, as La Fontaine's fox's
When in the — Tiber? he dropped the cheese.

I believe, after all, I have mixed the fables.
No matter: we quietly turned the tables;
Spread our own; and when five hours struck,
Sat down to soup, and cutlets, and duck.

Believe we are jolly! Four carcel lamps,
Four bright fires to keep out the damps, —
Bran new carpet, and curtains, and sich,
Just left by a countess. We *do* feel rich!
Wardrobes, bureaus, mirrors, and china, —
Linen, silver, —no need to be finer, —
Sun streaming in at the window all day,
And ten francs only, apiece, to pay.
This reckons sunshine, and service, and rent,
And woodpile, and dinners, and things that are sent.

I know you 'll be glad. We 've taken, moreover,
A two month's lease of this patch of clover,
To browse till April. And now, my dear,
If you and Bud could be only here!
But — a rivedervi! And each to each,
Without mere fashion or trick of speech,
Our hearty love! We shall not forget you,
Nor the happy chance by which we met you.
Friends once, friends always, if you 'll agree,
By Arno, or Tiber, or over the sea;
And as well for its own delicious sake,
As friendship's, — we 'll *never* forget that *Cake!*
          Yours, for the song,
          And the days that are long, —
                    Emery Ann —
                    Aunt Patience — and
                              EDITH STRONG.

I don't know that I can do a bit better than that, Rose! It was just how it was; and the child's nonsense-rhyme has in it all the sense of our glee and fun and splendid recklessness as we committed ourselves to cheerful fate, took the sunny lodgings, and rushed round *Rome* — think of *that!* bespeaking our groceries, and dinners, our cream and butter from the English dairy, and our *petits pains* from the French bakery. In the dairy, drinking cream, we met fair-haired, sweet-voiced Mrs. Blaiseley, the English rector's wife. We fell upon the Fountain of Trevi. "Fancy," as the English say, coming upon that gorgeous pile of rocks and water, stone gods and horses, and monsters and men, and palace front, by accident and unawares!

"What *is* it?" I cried, as the carriage rounded swiftly the shady turn, and the splendid confusion filled up suddenly all the space at our left as we swept between the tall, overglooming buildings.

"Dhat," said our English speaking clerk, "ees dhe founteen of Trevi. Dhe Aqua Virgo, dhe baste watter een Rŏm."

The best water in Rome came plunging down with a shout of plenty among the heaped up artificial · crags, tumbling hither and thither, over Triton's shoulders and around Neptune's feet, washing his car-wheels and the feet of his horses, losing and finding itself in turns and falls, raining down rock faces, and trickling through crevices, till it gathered itself deep down in its low, unnoticed basin.

"That is what Mistress Barbara would call mag-nif-icendous!" said Edith, catching her breath again in the Via della Stamperia, as we were whisked away, across to the Via del Tritone and round — *home*.

Edith greatly admires her "Mistress Barbara;" looking up to her from that near but reverential level of just-grown girlhood that regards young matronhood with an awe of mystery and a half-conscious thrill of prophecy. She has been very constantly with her; Barbara, on her side, petting and appropriating her with an indescribable air of representative, official, *de corps* reception and fellowship, as if the whole body of dames in her recognized in Edith the whole advancing sisterhood of demoiselles, or as if — pshaw! Edith is so emphatic-

ally and simply, a *girl!* But hence, the Crambo letter, in
which the child ambitiously did her brightest; and more, in that
line, than I knew was in her.

Emery Ann was perfectly happy. She had got breakfast
dishes to wash again; much to the unwilling amaze of Eligia,
the little serving-maiden, who came with the other furnishings,
a part of the lease; who wore an enormous cushion of false,
black hair on the back of her head, and made nothing of rushing down to the Corso without additional covering, for the least
little errand that she could persuade me into believing I needed
done; who spoke not a word of English, but who received
orders delightedly through Edith's broken interpretation; who
made up her charcoal fire at a minute's notice in one of the
round holes of the great brick structure like a rostrum, that
was built across one half the kitchen, and fanned it with a
huge "ventolo," at another hole beneath; who found all sorts of
people among her own relations to meet our exigencies, — from
washing our clothes to carrying off the scraps when the dinner
of one day had duly served the lunch of the next; coming
sweetly and unblushingly for "soldi" at the end of the week,
for the remuneration of the last named individual; who told us
of "Carlo Dolce," — a Carlo who brought sweetmeats from
door to door after the dinner hours, and whom Edith summoned;
from whom we bought lovely candied fruits, — nuts, dates,
grapes, oranges, luscious and sparkling, strung daintily upon
straws at a sou the straw; so that at dessert, when he came in
and stood with his pyramidal tray, we plundered it at our choice
of a great plateful of confections for about a franc; — who —
meaning Eligia again — drew up water for us from the mysterious depths of the great central well of the high building into
which the windows of three stories looked, and into which we
doubted many scraps from many apartments drifted, or at our
misgiving of this, brought it cheerfully in a bucket from the
fountain of the Triton in the sunny piazza; — who disappeared
continually during the great Carnival week, and reappeared
demurely at her duties with the black mass of her back hair
innocently full of confetti; who welcomed our advent as if we
were the angels she had been looking for through a life-time,

and shed real tears at our departure, following us to the Hotel
della Pace with a great dish of "nocche"—a detestable preparation of potatoes—which her "zia" had made for us upon
an unlucky inquiry about what the thing was which we had
heard somebody praise by name; and who went on doubtless
serving a long succession after us, with the same especial, smiling, spontaneous, uncalculating zeal at a franc a day, perquis-
ites for her entire, remotest family connections, and a generous
douceur with the good-bye.

Emery Ann bought a feather duster. She insisted upon buying that, and nothing else, from a man who came to the carriage as we waited before the house agent's one morning, to try
to sell us a whole tray full of pretty wares,—pictures, vases,
statuettes, I know not what, for Roman souvenirs. He had it in
his hand to flick the imaginary dust from every object that he
held up to a buyer's notice. It was his baton,—his wand,—
his caduceus,—his talisman of trade,—without which his trade
was gone; but nothing else would Emery Ann have. She had
not seen a feather duster for a half year; and she had just got
back into the sweetness of a domestic empire. She paid twice
as much for it as she would have had to pay in a shop, and she
rode home, holding it straight up in her right hand, like a
sceptre.

Emery Ann trimmed the great lamps; looked after the cupboard; kept the fire bright at evening so that it flashed up re-
splendently into the broad mirror that reached from mantel to
ceiling; made tea when Eligia brought in the tray at eight
o'clock; reigned again over her queendom, in short, which was
home and comfort wherever she could make it. She was delighted with Rome; she would have been delighted with those
six rooms anywhere. Anywhere across the water from New
England, I mean; at home she would have scouted their "put-
upances."

We were at the top of the great slope of the Piazza Barberini; the Palace on our left, up the hill; the Church of the
Capuchins with its cemetery walled with friars' bones, and its
glorious Guido picture,—the Archangel Michael,—on the
right. Between, on either side the block of which we occupied

the apex, ran the streets of San Nicolà, full of artists' studios, — and San Basilio, where our American minister lives just round the corner; both leading off toward gardens and villas and the Pincian Hill. Half the carriages in Rome seemed to roll under our little balcony of a bright afternoon, and from the long salon window we could not help looking right down into the faces and laps of the occupants. "A great place for passing," Emery Ann said. "Only it was all strange passing, after all." "And passing strange," transposed Edith.

The old fountain of the Triton showed its glory to me as I sat there watching it into the late afternoon, and through the lingering light of our first sunset in Rome. As the last rays shot across the tops of the farther buildings, the spray, that had been like star-dust with its full illumination, caught now and again at its highest leaps only, the retreating splendor, and sparkled out into gladness. Then it played on, at intervals, too low to be shone upon. It was heart and life at sunset time. It was the joy of oldening years, that only springs now and then into a shimmer of its all-day gladness, — playing on, for the most part, in a shadow. But how lovely that momentary flash and crown are! How they tell of the morning; when from the east the glory shall come again, — rising, not setting, — and the quick pulses that have *lived all night* shall catch it for longer and longer, brighter and brighter, till every drop of being sparkles through and through again!

The second evening that we were there, Edith sat at the window at five o'clock, watching for the dinner-box.

The dinner-box is a huge tin receptacle, borne from the trattoria upon the head of a man, — *our* man was the shiniest, jolliest, broad-as-longest fellow that rolled up the square of a whole afternoon, when the peripatetic kitchens with their movable feasts sailed about and in and out the dingy staircase entrances like a fleet of tin arks in a trade wind, — and containing three — five — seven courses as you please and pay, piled in about a pot of burning charcoal.

Emery Ann was setting the table in the adjoining room.

The piazza was gay; for a stream of carriages was pouring down from the Villa Ludovisi road and from the way of the

Pincian; and the English hunt, that we had seen a party mount for under our windows in the morning, was returning, and their grooms and carriages were waiting for them again before the fountain.

In the midst of all an open fiacre cut straight through the throng in the reverse direction and came up from the Via Felice toward our own door.

Edith started to her feet, waved her two hands eagerly, and struggled with the heavy casement latch.

"It is Margaret," she cried. " Run down, Emery Ann, please, and stop her! I shall never get this window open, and she may n't see. Oh, yes; she is turning; she is come on purpose; how *did* she know?" And before she could run through to the big, black door that opened from our dining room to our landing, and shove the bar, the cord that hung there was pulled and the bell sounded above her head.

"How perfectly lovely! When did you find out? We were coming to-morrow, ourselves. We looked you up at Spada Flamini's."

"And so did we. And — how perfectly lovely, too! Why Miss Emery Ann! This is really being settled!"

"About as much settled as a fly on the ceiling," said Emery Ann, following us into the salon, with a handful of silver spoons. " But the *things* are fixed, — for as long as we stay."

"And it looks so homelike! Why, it does n't seem like a Roman apartment! This is such a cosy little salon. Ours is a league, or so, across."

"Just enough like home to make folks homesick," persisted Emery Ann, "when they stop to think of it. Only you don't stop. You can't even sit down and make believe. There are so many *must-y* places. You can't mend a petticoat in peace, because of the ruins, or the tombs, or the churches, that you 've got to go to, because you came a purpose, and that 't would be ridickleous not to see. I'm see-sick!"

"It's a see o' troubles, is n't it, Emery Ann?" said Edith. " But the only way is to take arms bravely against it, and by opposing, end them."

"Tackle 'em all, you mean. Well, we 're doing it. But I guess all these freezing churches 'll be" —

" A die o' sees," suggested Margaret, laughing. " What have you done to her, Miss Patience ? "

" Taken her out this morning on the Appian Way, as far as Cecilia Metella's tomb, and then back and around the walls, from the Gate of Sebastian to the Gate of St. Paul, and out from there to the Church of San Paolo."

" When she wanted to put a new braid on her alpaca walking skirt," said Edith.

" It 'll seem real good to sit down and darn a lot of stockings again, if I ever do," said Emery Ann.

" And in the mean time, while you can't do any better, San Paolo is a beautiful sight to see, and the old walls of Rome are pretty well worth while," said Edith.

" Yes, an awful while," said Emery Ann. " I 'm inclined to think they 're as interesting as any of it. For you can kind of imagine it 's all in there, just as it was then, when the old savages were battering to get in."

" And the modern savages had n't got in, and made a show and promenade of it," said I.

" It don't appear to me," said Emery Ann, " that after it was dead and buried it was ever meant to be dug up again. They 're diggin' up death with it, you see; folks come here to get poisoned, breathin' heathen dust and ashes. 'T was done with; they 'd better let it stay done."

" And stay at home themselves, — and darn their stockings ? "

" Well, yes, Miss Margaret," said Emery Ann, smiling upon the girl with a pleased understanding, out of her affected grimness. " If they 've got holes in 'em, and they mostly have. Especially our folks that are traipsin' everywheres. Tearing over Europe, the biggest part of them, like cats over the roofs of strange houses. I 'm inclined to think America 's about the best place to live in, particularly for Americans. It 's well enough, I suppose, if you want to get an education, or to make a splurge with a little money, or get rid of your obligations and be accountable to nobody ; it 's cheap to come abroad and do it. But if you want to be tired, — or sick, — or die, — or have dipped toast for breakfast, — you got to get home again to do it decently. And there 's the trotter-here man ! " she broke off, as a great clatter and chatter arose in the farther room. "And Elijah"—(she would always speak of our scatter-witted little Italian serving-maid as if she had been a Hebrew prophet), "will be *sure* to spill the soup into the pudding!"

"And you are in an apartment, too? You have n't been able to tell us a word. And where is it? And where is Mrs. Regis?"

"Mamma has a cold," she said, and her face shaded a little anxiously. "But she insists upon sending me out, when she cannot go herself. We have a nice English maid, beside our Italian Gigia;—quite a *bonne* for me,—and she sits in the carriage. Mamma declares she is quite happy with her book,—we keep supplied from Piale's,—I have just come from exchanging some;—and that she won't be happy unless I go off and leave her, for a little while, at least. We are in Via de' Crociferi; just back of the Fountain of Trevi; they pull the delicious water all the way up in buckets on a slanting rope. You go through a great wilderness of an old house before you get to our rooms, but they are *so* wide and sunny! Three windows in each, looking over the great, red-tiled roofs right into the south sky full of sunshine. You can't tell which it is most of,—that, or the south sunshine pouring in. And yet,—mamma is n't well;" she said again, the shadow reverting with the word. "I almost wish we had not come to Rome. But I am glad you are here! She hopes you will come and see her; and she means to ask you to let me go about with you. If she would only just believe that I am not in any hurry to go about!"

"Have you seen Miss Euphrasia?"

"Once,—yes; we met her in the Palace of the Cæsars. Does n't that sound sublimely odd? And she came for a call afterward, and we were out. We have hardly been out,—that is, mamma has hardly been,—since that first week; and we have not returned it. People are so busy in Rome. I suppose she thinks we are doing everything else. Now, I shall not interrupt your dinner. Ours is at half-past six; mamma likes it late. I just came to let you know. It is *good* to have you, dear Miss Patience!"

And with a kiss she went off with Edith, who bade her good-bye upon the stairs.

Emery Ann, fidgeting over the four courses, cooling in their little dishes, called us to dinner. As I helped the soup, I thought to myself, — " The Forum of Trajan ; the Square of the Barberini ; and the Fountain of Trevi. A wide neighborhood ; but we are neighbors. And what are we all here for, I wonder ? "

Evidently, they had not seen Paul Rushleigh.

Afterwards I learned that he had been away from the city again ; gone with a party to Palestrina.

34

CHAPTER XXV.

THE BEAUTIFUL ROUND.

. . . .

. . . . Patience Strong was by herself in the background. Only there is not any background to it.

I was quite away, however, in the circumference; looking at the tomb of Raphael. But I ought to go back and bring you in from the street, as we came.

We had been round to the Via Condotti, for our letters; and then were driven back, through the streets and squares beyond the Corso, toward Ruined Rome, — the Forum, the Coliseum, the Temples, the great Baths, the Hill of the Cæsars.

It was our first going there. We had dim notion of the topography. . We had told the man to drive to the Roman Forum. It scarcely occurred to us, that being *our* definite object, that anything else of wonder would lie, in a kind of awful disregard upon our way; would stop us with splendid shock of surprise as it did. In the very thick of the city, where palaces, churches, colleges-buildings, convents, shut in against each other with a dim, confused crowding, the way opened out to a small square, in the midst of which an old, curious, massive fountain played in the gloom.

But what was this looming upon us, above and beyond the fountain? What was this pile that looked over at our puny coming like the Face of the Ages? This front, worn with Time, crumbling to a surface roughness, but solid, like the surface-crumbled hills; dark, solemn, waiting; a vast porchway, pillared with majesty; a rough swell of architecture beyond, losing itself among the throng of buildings, showing itself here and there, uncovered of finish or ornament, its glorious bronze-sheathing stripped off long ago to make altar ornaments for a newer temple, — cannon for the Castle of the Holy Angel, built above an Emperor's tomb? I have told you. It was the Pantheon.

We forgot everything else. We got out of our little, miserable carriage : we walked with insignificant feet up the five great steps ; we passed between the august columns ; we crossed the deep platform behind them ; we entered through the wide, lofty, silent door-way ; we came into a sphere, like the sphere of the heavens !

A shining pavement, of porphyry and marbles, so solid that no tread sounds upon it, more than upon velvet. Walls, — a far away horizon, — reaching up their wide-swept circle, with no break of any support between, to the Dome that simply rounds them in. It is *all* a Dome. You know it; and I knew it; but neither of us knew anything in that time we thought we did. One must stand here, within, beneath it, to know it at all.

Overhead, — far overhead, — the one Opening, from the mid-heaven down. The Light all pouring in at its single, sacred aperture ; softening, spreading as it flows, filling the still interior ; the Blue, like the curtain of the Tabernacle firmamenting it across !

I do not care what they built it for. I do not care for the disputes, the comparisons. I see what *is* built. Whether a bath for mere bodily luxury, or a temple to all the gods, was planned and meant, something infinitely more turned out, and has lasted for the generations. Something that receives the soul into itself and floods it with a presence ; that interprets worship and oneness and answer ; that tells, beyond all heathen pantheism, of a divine singleness and plenitude ; in this, — that a temple for *all* the gods finds but its one opening, after all, into the central heaven ; one single source and down-coming of a universal filling and abiding. The Cathedral of Milan is a History of the Race : the Pantheon of Rome is a Revelation of God.

And under the typical light, lie fitly the tombs of them in whose souls it shined.

I walked quietly around the margin under the walls, niched and recessed and altared. I found the Virgin and the Child, sculptured above the burial place of the man who delighted to paint his visions of Mary and the Christ. It was while I paused there, trying to read the Latin words of the inscription, that some inner touch made me turn to what no movement or sound could have called me. I saw, standing right under the circle of blue, in the heart and midst of the inexpressibly soft and tender light, — hand laid in hand, face lifted to face, with no surprise, no hesitation, no recalling, it almost seemed, — as if they had stood there ages before, and in the perfect round of things had never been lost, and could never have strayed away, — two quiet figures: Margaret and Paul.

I did not hear a word they said. I do not know whether they said anything. The greeting, of course, was the thing of the moment: but after their hands parted, they stood there, side by side.

The Pantheon read me its second, beautiful meaning; like the second part of the Law of God.

The human part of it, under the divine supremeness. The perfect round of our safety, out of which we cannot stray or lose anything that is to come to us. In which the partings, the distances, the silences, the turnings away, are mere seemings in a little seeming space, — a real space holding all and keeping all one in a single Thought; returning and controling all into a sure harmony and perfect finding; in whose great

> "Circle, year by year,
> We're nearer on the other side,
> The farther we are sundered here."

It was in Margaret's face, as they turned presently, and walked toward me.

Calm and sure and satisfied; no heightened color, no excitement; no beginning again of a feverish, uncertain story. A simple recovering, in its place and time, in the very spirit of all her waiting, of the thing she had been waiting for.

Would it have been so elsewhere, I wondered? Or was it, in this wonderful place, more like a meeting in a dream, — a finding in eternity?

All helped, doubtless; was meant to help. But, as it began then there, it went on day by day.

General Rushleigh went on to the Coliseum with us. That was a day of days!

Who says we are shut out, — we to whom the principal action of the beautiful story does not seem to come? It was as much mine as theirs.

I felt as serene as Margaret. Nothing troubled me for them. I hurried into no fancies, no anxieties. I asked no restless, inward questions.

I think Paul Rushleigh's quietness, being a man's, was different. He was strong: he could meet this girl, whom perhaps he would not have gone to meet, without trembling, without retreating. The noblest of him could put down the least, the selfish; could be glad in the nobleness of her presence, since it had come. He could take this day, though there might be days beyond into which its glory was not to reach. Because his love also had been high enough to say, — "You may leave me, but I can never let you go."

But Margaret's sweet certainty, — her resting in the right that was sure to come, — I hardly think that was all his. He could bear, — for he was strong; and he could take a part, without churlish rejection, although the whole were hopelessly put off; for he was of fine nature: but that wordless patience, so glad even in its waiting, — I do not quite think he had entered into that; if a man ever does in his attitude and relation toward woman. He may, in his relation toward God; in his faith, for his life, in the heavenly wisdom; even in his losing and utter giving up of this very human love; because, in his attitude toward God, he is of the feminine.

I thought this the more, and was the more sure of it, when the days went on, and I continued to see them together.

What a sunshine it was that fell down in a glory over the gardens that grow among the palaces of the Cæsars, — upon the old arches, mighty in decay, — upon the temple fragments; the long excavation of the basilica; into the huge hollow of the Roman Forum with its pillars and fractions of wall, and massive steps, and open blanks, and its lonely, lofty column standing apart; — upon the vast ellipse and beautiful, broken outline of

Streaming into the great arena; glowing upon tier above tier
of the amphitheatre slopes; shut out of the rough huge-piled
staircases that mount up through the archways and from the
long galleries; meeting and flowing about you again as you come
out from these upon the dizzy parapets and platforms; lighting
up the endless Campagna as if just there a whole summer had
dropped down in one horizon upon the earth; holding the towers and spires and gate-ways and old walls of Rome, spread out
beneath you, in that wide shining that takes in the evil and the
good!

Something independent of time and circumstance seemed to
set free to the perfect enjoyment of that which was so apart from
time and present circumstance. The long, long stillness and
desertness, since human fears and agonies had been borne here,
— the beauty and the calm that rested upon it all, after the slow
centuries, like that we had seen in like wise, upon the blue lake
of Thrasymene, — these seemed to put off, to counteract, the little crises and perplexities of to-day; to make it seem little matter in the midst of verities — ourselves verities also, after all —
what doubt might be, of mere particular, in the moment, or
might wait decision in moments still to come.

We had done and seen enough doubtless, when we came forth
from the dusk archway to the warm street space again, and found
our carriage waiting by the Meta Sudans, — the great, dry, rock-
rimmed basin, with its ruined cone, through which the water
played to fill it for the use of the combatants when they rushed
forth panting and sweating from their hot encounters in the
arena. We were tired enough, doubtless, had we known it; but
there was the lovely day; there was the pleasant, green-walled
road, running along under the Palatine Hill from the Arch of
Constantine: there, beyond, we knew, — just a short drive
farther, — were the Baths of Caracalla, with the marvelous sunshine and the sweet, sweet air filling the old, deep reservoirs
and magnificent, roofless halls, and playing among the broken,
ivied masonry. The spell was upon us; we could not yet return
to common things.

Only Margaret hesitated, thinking of her mother. But we
were sure that Mrs. Regis would wish her to have the hour

longer ; I told her so, quite confidently.   She had the rest of us
to consider, too ; our great pleasure against an hour's delay ;
and we took the way of San Gregorio, past the church of his
name, where they keep the table at which, they tell you, the
Saint fed every morning the twelve poor pilgrims, and once an
angel came to make the thirteenth.

"After that," said Margaret, "I wonder people should dislike
to sit down thirteen at table.   There might always, you know,
with thirteen souls, be *one* angel among them ! "

"Perhaps that is the very thing the superstition came from,"
said General Rushleigh.   "People are so strangely afraid after
all, even when they seem quite ready,—of turning into angels ! "

"Well," remarked Emery Ann, "I think if I was a *caterpil-
lar*, and *knew* about it, I should most dread to leave off crawling
and gnawing, and roll myself up into my coffin, even to turn
into a butterfly.   I don't believe I should ever make up my
mind to do it, finally."

"That's why, I suppose," said Edith, "they have n't any minds
given them to make up.   And we, who have the minds, have n't
the responsibility."

The green roadside was sprinkled with tiny daisies, and pretty
ferns grew in the old walls, hung richly often with vines, and
shaded with evergreen shrubs.   We turned off at the angle where
the roads divide that lead to the neighboring, yet far apart,
gates of San Paolo on the right, and San Sebastiano on the left.
A few minutes more brought us to a great gate in a high wall,
guarded ; through which we were admitted into the area of ruin
nearly a quarter of a mile square according to the plan, and
stretching its stately wreck of walls, mingled with wild green
growths and crowned with loveliest hanging gardens of thick
leafage and streaming vines in apparently indefinite vistas back
against wooded hills and vineyard slopes, themselves marked
here and there with some old church or historic fragment seen
through the irregular, beautiful framework that time and destruction and gradual softening of vegetation have broken and
moulded the massive architecture into.

I have made a lumbering description of it; but how can I
touch it to its delicate detail, that fills and finishes the unspeak-

able grandeur to a bewilderment of fairylike loveliness and enchantment ?

Open to the bare, blue sky, from floors whose rich mosaics still lie in patches, like sheltered snows unmelted by decay ; vast masses of masonry lifting themselves up to dizzy height; these draperied in every crevice and from their distant, softly outlined ramparts and in their superbly impending arches, with every exuberant and delicate and glorious thing, that springs from seed and takes life in this quickening and kindling air ; — precious sculptures rescued from burial and forgetfulness, set here and there, to show, fragmentarily, what the old patient world was full of, whose men were content to spend life-time after life-time in their slow chiseling ; enormous inclosures marked out to make you feel what space is ; — long shallow steps dividing one from another, down which you pass thinking how the swimmers plunged here into the splendid natatorium, or perhaps the gladiators had their games, or may be, as Murray concludes, the warm vapors filled the voluptuous calidarium ; — windings and turnings from apartment to apartment, where weed-grown orifices show how the plentiful streams came into the luxurious private baths ; stair-ways ascending where one hardly dares to climb, and where in some places it is forbidden with a warning ; and all this so utterly still except for the voices and footsteps of curious visitors like yourselves, or the song of some bird or the cry of a crow through the reposeful air ; — it is a dream, which can be only dreamed out by sleep-walking there.

We strayed away from each other, singly, or by twos ; we met again at points where we exclaimed to each other at the new beauty of grouping and outlook that we found, — the pictures into which the mighty scene-work shifted itself as we moved.

Margaret and Paul Rushleigh kept together. She avoided him with no conscious shyness; he delivered himself up to the delight of the moment. They seemed not to think of any need of purposely breaking or measuring the pleasant intercourse. Nobody would suppose that the last time they were together, he had asked and she had answered a question which separates or joins two lives. Simply, their lives were *not* separate, whatever had been said or unsaid, and never could be.

Yet how, with the need of word and act and form, and the hindering that had come so subtly and strangely between them, — was this interior truth to reach its clear acknowledgment? They could not *drift*, — through this mortal world, at least, — in a bliss of chance meetings, and unspoken relation. Paul, — the man, — *would* not drift so. He must either speak once more, or leave her again and altogether, when the first delusive gladness changed to sober recollection and a realizing of the " impossible."

And how many little things occurring, or failing to occur, might prevent his word ; his divining that it might be differently heard ?

For Margaret was almost too frankly-friendly; as if — he might think — with one short pain, one hard and final certainty — any different attitude had been forever set aside between them ; as if, *would* he come back so, he might be still what she had told him with such pathos of regret, she had at first so " counted him " to be — her friend !

How much of this would he bear? How much could he understand ?

And what could anybody do, but their two selves ?

We came back all the way around the Cœlian. Out to the farthest point we went, passing the site of the Fountain of Egeria — turning homeward at last through the Square of St. John Lateran, before the long, beautiful front of the church, pillared, balconied, deeply-arched, with the Christian monogram upon its entablature, and white marble figures of Christ and His Twelve, standing colossal in high air, above its balustrade. Then along the Via di San Giovanni straight from the Church to the Coliseum again ; past the old St. Clement, — church of three ages, buried over and over again and open still to the deepest foundation ; through the Forum once more, upon which one comes again and again, with the self-same thrill of strange realization and incredible familiarity ; and so, at last, into the modern, crowded streets.

We left General Rushleigh in the Piazza Trajano. As he alighted from the driver's box, he came round quickly to the side of the carriage, — the side where Margaret sat, — to say good-morning.

With his hat still raised, and his hand still lingering upon the carriage-edge, he asked of her at the very last, a little hurriedly, —

" Will Mrs. Regis see me, do you think, if I call ? "

" I am sure she will, — after a little while," Margaret answered, readily and simply.

I could have almost quarreled with her for that added "little while," which seemed a put-off. I knew it was a quick consideration for her mother, whose nicety about all her personalities Margaret so well understood. Mrs. Regis had been looking unlike herself for a day or two ; her cold, or whatever it was, had affected her face and eyes ; she was not really in visitable condition.

Paul Rushleigh only bowed. He looked a shade disappointed. He repeated his good-morning, and went away.

After that Margaret did not leave Mrs. Regis for nearly a week, except to go down to the library at Piale's. I wondered what Paul Rushleigh did those days. His card came up to Mrs. Regis the second morning, with a basket of cool, white grapes, — overlaid with fresh violets ; but we neither met him nor heard from him otherwise. I myself was not well ; my day among the ruins, I thought, had over-tired me. I went once or twice to Via Crociferi ; Mrs. Regis grew worse. Her face swelled fearfully ; there were great red circles around her eyes that spread themselves into forehead and cheeks. She was weak ; prostrated with the insidious Roman debility. Margaret sat by her, tended her, read to her ; she urged her to see a physician. But this Mrs. Regis persistently refused. " He would order me to leave Rome," she said to me, when Margaret was out of the room.

It was partly impatience, I thought, and anxiety to be well, that aggravated her ailment. The days went on, and I felt as if Margaret's peace were almost unnatural. She gave me the key to it, when I ventured once to say, — "This is one of the inexplicable things ; just as we were all met together, and had

had such a beautiful beginning." "It is so plainly a thing that nobody could help," the girl answered. "And those things must happen right! It was *you* taught me that, Miss Patience."

She had received through my word a virtual principle into her simple, true child-heart, — and it had almost straightway sprung up thence in a body of grace that startled me. Yet it was only what *must* grow from it, if the seed-principle be alive, and not just a dry, perished grain. Ah, though they be the seed of life, we keep our principles in glass jars, so, the most of us, that we wonder when some true young soul puts them fearlessly into the soil of every-day living, and the white, perfect bloom comes up and shows back our faith to our faces!

CHAPTER XXVI.

CATHEDRAL AND CARNIVAL.

. . . .
. . . . "But it is not altogether that," said Miss Euphrasia.

I had come down alone to the Piazza Trajano that morning. Stephen Holabird was now in Rome, and he and Emery Ann and Edith had gone together, with a permission, out to the Villa Ludovisi, to see Guido's Aurora and the gardens. Edith and Stephen are so fond of gardens. Well, they are at the paradisiacal age; the young Adam and Eve are strong in them. You mind, I mean as of the race simply; representatively man and woman; it would be too absurd to talk of anything else! I insist on this representative age in which we ought to *protect* these young folks; not cast them out of the garden by giving them beforetime of the Tree of Knowledge. It is a beautiful and a holy time; it comes again, too, — a Paradise Regained, after the heat, and fever, and disappointment, and mere prose of life are over!

I had came down to sit in the sunshine with Miss Euphrasia, and look at the Column of Trajan. We felt, as we sat quiet and homelike in the wide, balconied windows, before which, a little distance up the square, it rose, as if that, of all the glories and antiquities of Rome, belonged to us. It was built into ourselves, by our unhurried possession of it in restful hours. From base to tip, we followed the mighty grace of its scroll of sculpture, that unrolls the story of a conquering reign; we were never tired of the beauty of it, touched anew by each new morning sun; the beauty and power that had stood there seventeen hundred years, monument of the memory of the "Senate and the Roman People," for the Emperor who has been dust with them and the deeds that the shaft stands for, all that hoary while.

And yet, Miss Euphrasia Kirkbright and I, sitting in the sunshine, gazing at Trajan's pillar, were moved just as deeply, just as anxiously, to-day, for two little human histories that we thought were meant to become one, and that some sand grain of time or chance might seem to separate, as if to-day were all, and finished it.

"It is not altogether that; it is also that she does not know. She has no idea that he had heard it all long first; and that at this moment he supposes her to have known it then. They have met in a quite new order of things, she imagines; the coming right that she trusts in, she believes to see already begun."

"And Mrs. Regis's illness is keeping her so shut up ; shutting him out, too; and *we* know, — we and she."

"One cannot rush at a man with all one knows," said Miss Euphrasia.

She blushed a little as she said it, — and I felt the color, too. We stopped talking about it ; we had not said much ; I had just managed to touch the subject so as to tell her of the mistake she herself had fallen into. We maiden women have a reverence for the things hidden and sacred ; they have been hidden and sacred to us so long.

Miss Euphrasia laid down her work ; she had a little cough that often interrupted her, — the cough she had come to Rome for, — and it interrupted her now. There are different kinds of coughs, as there are different other expressions. Hers was really a cheerful little affair ; not lackadaisical, or complaining, or rebellious with a kind of angry struggle. It was even brisk and business-like, though gentle ; as if it said, — Yes, I know this little bother is to be expected; it all comes in the day's work ; it's done now, and attended to; I'm all right and bright to go on, and we shall go on all the better. It made a natural period, too, to many things.

She took up her knitting pins again, as the tickling strangle subsided, and looked forth cheerily, with the water in her eyes, at the great column.

"I would rather see that," she said, lifting her handkerchief to brush away the dimming drops — "every day and all day, as I do see it, than have what Emery Ann calls a 'wink' at every one of the hundred and eighteen churches of Rome. It is a terrible strain and surfeit, this sight-seeing. I began with 'the level best' insanity. I have had to give it up. The things oppressed me. Murray was a weight on my mind."

"That dreadful little Pineider is worse," I said, "with his eight days! It's like the first chapter of Genesis; the days should be æons. Will you believe that I really have n't seen St. Peter's yet?"

"I keep St. Peter's for the cold days. I like to go there and sit, in the shelter, and look — you would wonder if I told you what I look at most."

"I should not know enough to wonder. St. Peter's is a mighty phantom to me. I believe I have been keeping it, in the fear of a disappointment."

"We might go there to-day," said Miss Euphrasia. At that moment the bell sounded on the landing. The English ladies were out. We were in Miss Euphrasia's own inner room; between it and the large salon she had a small lobby-like space which she had made pretty with flowers, and used for her separate little reception parlor. In this we heard footsteps presently; the maid servant appeared between the curtains of the portière and announced, with sweet Italianizing, —

"Signor Rossili."

We had run away from him as a topic of conversation, to the Church of St. Peter; we were just on the point of running actually away to St. Peter's itself, to escape, I think, sitting there looking at each other with the same subject half dismissed in both our minds; and with the frequent inexplicable magnetism of things thought of and coming, here he was bodily.

"We were speaking of you just now," said Miss Euphrasia, as people always say. She did not blush at all at that; she hid quite safely behind the every-day human experience.

"And I have been speaking of you," returned General Rushleigh. "I have just come from Via 'de' Crociferi."

"Have you seen them?" I asked, somewhat eagerly.

"Miss Margaret only, at the door. Her mother was not able to receive me."

"It is such a trouble," I answered him quickly, — "'so tiresome,' — as the English say, — that their salon is the first room from the corridor. Mrs. Regis lies there on the sofa all day, and of course nobody can be admitted, unless to her."

" Miss Margaret told me that her mother would like to see you, Miss Euphrasia. And as I could do no other service, I came round to tell you. Some time to-day, perhaps " —

" I will go indeed," replied Miss Kirkbright. " We were just thinking of setting out — but that of course is of no consequence, — for an hour at St. Peter's. I mean — my day was quite unappropriated," she adding, smiling at her own unwonted awkwardness.

" And why not ? " asked General Rushleigh. " An hour at St. Peter's is *not* exactly of no consequence. And — as my day, too, is unappropriated, — might I go with you ? "

As we went along in the carriage, I found myself, all the way, *understanding* my friends, as my trick is ; getting beneath, — for what else is understanding ? — and feeling upon myself their circumstance, — recognizing in myself their motive and movement.

I knew what Mrs. Regis's mood was, by her sending for Miss Euphrasia. Something in her turned newly, and finely, and truly, to the best ; some fresh resolve, some quiet submission, — some reward of fellowship, consequently, which is the real communion of the saints — of them who are *being made* holy, — gave her the restful longing that claims companionhood with them who are above and farther within ; the desire, felt only from some small quickening of the spirit, toward souls in whom it largely moves. We do not know how to pray "Make us to be numbered with thy saints," until we first feel shining into ourselves some beam of the glory everlasting.

Paul Rushleigh had been doing little, I fancy, in these days in which we had known little of him. They were calendared by those calls of inquiry at the door, those sendings up of violets and roses and sweet fruits ; between, he lived them as he could. I think the Archæological people saw little of him in those days. He came to us to-day simply because he could not stay with Margaret and her mother. We were next. He could not keep utterly away.

" I did not tell you all the message, Miss Euphrasia," he said, after the silence in which these thoughts had possessed me. " She said her mother wanted you to come and bring her some of your heavenly-mindedness."

He smiled as he repeated Margaret's words.

How well I knew it! To be in a humor for heavenly-mindedness is surely to have some of it already. It is to him that hath that more can be given.

"Margaret is anxious about her mother," I said. Miss Euphrasia had answered nothing but a smile again to that message about heavenly-mindedness. She never speaks anything but words. She never disclaims; she never utters mechanically; she is never embarrassed into nonsense. "Mere words?" she repeated that expression to me once with questioning emphasis. "Words are everything. They are *worth;* they are what *is;* they are the original values. Verbum, — verum; it is the one root."

I think I spoke from the absurd feeling which I cannot keep so clear from, that something had got to be said; that it is like shutting a door in a friend's face to sit silent when he has spoken. So I blundered.

"I think she feels that they ought to go away from Rome." Then I could have bitten my tongue; for there was nothing more to be explained about it, and I discerned instantly what color, aside from the daughterly anxiety, such a feeling of Margaret's might wear to him. But he said nothing. He did not even pursue the subject of Mrs. Regis's health. I could see that he was trying some question in his own mind. I struggled against "understanding" him, lest the magnetism between us should move in him to the idea that I was afraid of.

I was glad that, driving rapidly, we came presently to the beautiful bridge of St. Angelo, which no one can approach without a summons of thought, from whatever abstraction, to itself and what it leads to.

Broad, low sprung over its five arches, its stone parapets stretching fair from side to side of the river, its piers the pedestals of colossal statues, — St. Peter and St. Paul guarding the entrance, and five angels beyond them on either hand bearing separate emblems of Christ's Passion,—the Crown, the Cross, the spear, the nails, the sponge, the reed, the scourge, the scroll, and other two, I know not what, unless the robe of mockery and the cord that bound him in the garden;—crossing to the foot of the Castle fortifications above which against the clear, bright heavens stands the round mass of the tower with its chapel at top, summit-crowned with the figure of the alighted Angel sheathing the red sword of plague; beyond it, at the left, St. Peter's Dome and the Hill of the Vatican;—there is something in the grouping and in the approach, that gives this farthest tongue of the city beyond the Tiber a wonderful, arresting power and charm; a claiming instantly to itself, away from the heathen Rome down opposite among the ancient hills, a focal interest and veneration; outskirt as it is of the City of the Emperors, but centre, for ages, of the Christian World.

It had been difficult for me to get rid of the childish notion that St. Peter's must be in the actual middle of Rome; I had always, when I thought about it, had to stop and pick it up, out of my imagination, and set it there beyond, with the force with which one rectifies, difficultly, a consciously wrong mental picture. But now it placed itself, forever; beyond that fair, angel-sentineled bridge, beyond the tower upon the tomb, and the chapel upon the tower,— away under the right hand and the sheathing sword and the stretching wings of Michael the arch-seraph; now, for always, I saw it, fronting upon its glorious open Court, whose wide area seems for the welcoming of the nations, — its colonnades reaching themselves afar on either side, with invitation, —above them a multitude of statues, figures of saints that walk as it were serene heights of heavenly battlements, — its fountains of pure water rushing up into the light, like the waters of Life springing everywhere in the courtways of Jerusalem the Golden!

"It *might* be," said Miss Euphrasia, "the typical Temple of all the earth!"

"Oh, the fountains! And the great space! And the sweep of those galleries and their pillars! 'Whosoever will — let him come!'" I said, half breathless.

"'And drink freely,'" General Rushleigh finished it for me.

" It just speaks that. I could think of nothing the first time I saw it, but of the Jews' temple in the 'last great day of the feast,' when they were bringing the waters from Siloam, and He stood and cried : ' If any man thirst, let him come unto me ! '

A city within a city. That is St. Peter's.

A gorgeous city, whose solemn avenues are for altars ; where men walk or pause for worship ; where there is not labor nor traffic, nor dwelling built for the body. Sculptured masses, — piers of the great architecture, — stand along the aisles, making them like streets of temples ; dividing the immense space so that it is in *spaces* only that you measure and conceive of it. So that people entering in with the common fancy, agape for some untold, immediate enormousness, think they are disappointed, cheated somehow. My own first impulse was to wish them all away, for an instant at least, that I might see the whole ; as one wishes away the piece of the marble — however disguised into an accessory of the subject — that holds the chiseled thought in its bodily poise and will not let it absolutely free.

General Rushleigh looked at me. I looked on, and on ; I moved, and gazed, and moved again. He followed, interested to discover my genuine, fresh impression. I would not let it escape me, for I knew I had got no true impression yet.

After a while, seeing I said nothing, he asked me : —

" Is it different from what you had expected ! Does it disappoint you ? "

Then I knew what it did do. As soon as he spoke the word, I knew that the grand perplexity was not disappointment.

" It *baffles* me," I said. " As the Alps do, crowding each other out of sight. Where one mightiness hinders from another, and the *whole* is never seen by any mortal eye ! "

" I waited for your definition of it," he said.

We wandered slowly up the nave, through that world of statues, reliefs, mosaics ; histories, and monuments, covering the walls, crowding chapels and niches, clustering around huge pedestals ; we came forth, almost blunted to sublimity, by the vast scale to which we had set perception and comparison, — and this shows how the spirit plays in any key, proportions itself to universe or atom, and asserts divinity in itself, — under the Dome and the Altar-Canopy ; where balconied buttresses like towers, support the enormous vault, and underneath are themselves hollowed into temple niches that hold statues seventeen feet in height. Here again, grandeur intercepts grandeur; there is a firmament below a firmament, and up into the concave of the one from the zenith summit of the other, from out of the golden leafage and gorgeous ornament of the baldacchino into the high mid-space of the cupola, — reaches the golden Cross, one hundred feet above the pavement. And beyond all, they tell you, between this blazoned, interior dome, — pictured in mosaic from base to lantern, with figures of Evangelists, Apostles, the Virgin, the Saviour, and the Almighty Form looking down over all, — and the giddy, topmost ball, to which as through interstellar spaces, a staircase winds between the spheres, — stretches a third encompassing round between the altar and the blessed depth of heaven.

"How much they put in the way!" I said to Paul Rushleigh.

"Cumbered with much serving," answered Paul, "The Romish Church has always been a Martha. The simple heathen thought was better. The Pantheon is clearer than St. Peter's."

"There is nothing of human building so great as the Pantheon !" I exclaimed.

"And yet, Michael Angelo did what he said he would; he raised the Pantheon into the air ! Do you know this Dome is larger than that whole structure?"

"No," I said stoutly. "Feet are nothing. The Pantheon is the greater thing !" Paul Rushleigh smiled and let it go.

We sat down in the left transept, near the door of the sacristy. We had brought in camp-stools from a stack outside, which an old man kept to let to visitors. All around us stood the confessionals, between the chapels ; ticketed with advertisements of different languages, in which penitents might whisper their sins and receive the priestly absolution. Before us, in the centre, was the high altar, beneath the Dome and its own gorgeous baldacchino. Under that, the "Confession," — the tomb of St. Peter, with the ninety-three lamps always burning about it, and the marble Pope always kneeling at its door between the marble stairs. To the left the great space of the Tribune, — the head of the architectural cross; set round with tombs and shrines and sculptures; at whose far end stands the chair of St. Peter, — the real seat, as the Church holds it, built over with a chair of bronze. Like the stone of Scone in Westminster Abbey, inclosed within the Coronation Chair of English monarchs. Everything built about and about, to keep it safe!

Opposite, the other transept shut off with a temporary screen. This was where they held the famous Ecumenical Council. Upon the screen, freshly frescoed, was the figure of Christ, — the Ascended, yet Ever-Abiding; and over the door-way the Latin words of the Promise: "Lo, I am with you always, even unto the end of the world." A simple form, benignant and meek of air, in the midst of all the oppression of the surrounding splendor. Not painted by any famous hand; not meant to stay there among the things fashioned for the ages; and yet the thing of all that spoke most surely of enduring.

"How that stands like a Defense," I said, "between the Church and Church Authority! How their quoting of His own words neutralizes the tyranny of their dogma!"

"That is the thing I told you I liked the best to look at," said Miss Euphrasia.

"In the midst of all the burden of their ceremony; in the face of their councils, — that simple Presence and the promise of it," said Paul Rushleigh. "One wonders how they dared to put it there. It seems to tell the world just what they hide from it. It is like Jesus of Galilee in his peasant robe, standing in the Temple at Jerusalem, saying, "I am the Light of the World."

"It makes one feel how the world is safe after all," said Miss Euphrasia.

"Yes," he said, with kindling warmth. "They may manufacture what they please, in behind there, and command men outside to believe; but those words, in the face of the shut-out, waiting world, are stronger: 'Lo, *I* am with you always!'"

Coming down the long nave again, General Rushleigh was again by my side. It began to seem to me that he kept near me with a kind of sense of something I might have to give him, — a waiting for something I might possibly say; I felt that one thing was between us; a thing that neither of us found direct reason to bring to speech. As we stopped within the entrance for Miss Euphrasia, who had lingered among the sculptures in the chapels near the door, he said to me, at last.

"Do you feel *anxious* about Mrs. Regis?"

"Everything makes me anxious in Rome," I answered. "And Mrs. Regis has not not been well for a long while before. I think she ought to be out of Italy."

"I think sometimes, Miss Patience, that I ought also to be out of Italy; that I ought not to have met them here again. For we have met, and we have not met. I had better go off up the Nile, after all, perhaps. And yet, I have not liked to leave while she was ill."

"Do *not* leave, General Rushleigh."

It was all I could say.

"Do you tell me that? Being a woman, you may understand best. Do I disturb them, do you think? I know it cannot be quite the old relation. It is too soon, perhaps. But I cannot stand outside of where I was before in their friendship! I do not come asking for anything else. I hope they don't misgive me, Miss Patience!"

I think those were just the words he said. They look strangely meek now that I have written them down; but you would not have felt them meek if you had stood there with Paul Rushleigh. They came in brief, strong sentences, full of a strong man's conscious honor and great pride.

I was even touched in my own pride. Did he mean to tell me that for them? That he did not come asking anything but mere friendship any more?

But I knew better. By an insight deeper than any words we ventured on between us, I knew a great deal better.

That miserable shut door; and Mrs. Regis with her poor, strangely disfigured face! And this man that would not guess anything, and would not let Margaret be a mere woman, who might have acted in a mistake! He set her so high that he set her hopelessly away from him. I did not believe in that "friendship" that he took this posture of being satisfied with. But if a man *tells* you it is all he wants, how are you to convey to him that a great deal more may be ready for him? I have pity on the people in the novels, now, who act as if they were in a nightmare.

I answered to his last words, which I have left whole paragraphs behind: —

"I hope they don't misgive me, Miss Patience."

"Was there anything like that in Margaret," I asked, half indignantly, "the day we met you in the Pantheon? All that perfect, lovely, happy day?" I heaped the adjectives like reproaches.

"No; that was a day of heaven. But Miss Regis is simply just what and where she always was; and perhaps she cannot always — when there is time to consider — forget — what I wish to heaven she might forget!"

I had no doubt he did. I have no doubt men often do. That they might begin all over again, and be wiser.

Miss Euphrasia came up. I had only time for one word more.

"Do not leave Rome," I repeated. "We may all need you. If Mrs. Regis would only see a physician" —

"Do you mean that she has *not* seen one? What are you all thinking of?"

I was anxious as he was. But it was too absurd. Just as if I could have told him *that!*

What I did tell him was, that she was afraid of being ordered off.

"And you know she has been shut up almost ever since she came," I said. "The air is good in those high rooms. And they have the best water, — the Acqua Vergine. The mischief was in her first week; she rushed about among the ruins, and she had not been well in Venice."

"Venice is poisonous this year!"

"It is just like poison, — this that has affected her; she brought home scraps of weeds and vines from the Coliseum; she dug them from little crannies and hidden, damp places, — the few that she could find, since they have scraped it! And she kept them in a basin in her room, waiting to feel able to press them or set them out in earth. Margaret thinks that was bad; she did not know of it for several days. Then her gloves, and her handkerchief, in which she tied them! It was all an imprudence, — everything was a risk."

"Will you take me round there?" Miss Euphrasia asked. "We could stop at Spada-Flamini's and get their letters with ours."

"Yes; let us make haste; we must have had far more than our hour here; and the children will be at home, wanting their lunch."

It appeared that General Rushleigh had forgotten his own mail until now. We ordered the driver to take us round by the Via Condotti.

The Carnival was raging along the Corso. We always took the back streets in our drives, only crossing it when we must. We met everywhere groups of maskers, going and returning; everywhere carriages dashed about, gay with flags and flowers and young faces looking out from pink and blue and white and cherry-colored dominos. But the old prestige of the gala time has faded down. If all the former grace of its festivity had been still about it, we should yet have wanted time and money most for other things; but degenerated into the boisterous, dusty, uncomfortable, dangerous thing it is, we simply kept as clear of it as we could. Stephen would put on an old hat and coat and go down among it, to come back and tell us funny stories; and Eligia rushed in, day after day, just in time for dinner duties, her hair always lime-powdered, and the coriandoli sticking in it behind; and we watched the impromptu dances and gay jokes of the common people in the piazza from our windows; and these things quite satisfied us with the Saturnalia.

We followed the river, and came up by the Via di Ripetta to the Piazza del Popolo, where three great streets — di Ripetta, — del Babuino, and the central Corso, — diverge from the great square at the northernmost gate.

We had to get around through the Piazza to the Via Babuino, running whatever gauntlet might be in the way.

There was a great, bustling crowd. A stoppage of vehicles; a murmur along the street. Some police checked us as we tried to pass.

"Needs to wait," — said our coachman, in Italian, " To wait — for the Princess Margherita ! "

Two or three open carriages swept round swiftly through the open space kept for them; in one sat the lovely daughter of Victor Emanuel with her young husband. The people are wild with enthusiasm for Marguerite of Savoy. Great cheers went up after her, and waving of hats and scarfs and handkerchiefs. We waved also ; General Rushleigh stood up in the carriage and lifted his hat high over his head with a quick salute.

" E buona cosa aspettare ! La bellissima principessa Margherita ! " said the proud cocher, as if he had presented us at court.

I wonder if the words rung afterwards in Paul Rushleigh's ears as they did in mine. " It is a good to wait for ! The most beautiful Princess Marguerite ! "

We all found letters at the banker's. On the other side of the world from home, people never apologize for opening their letters in each other's presence. We sat back in our separate corners, breaking envelope after envelope, glancing at contents, shuffling them together for full reading and re-reading at our leisure.

I was not surprised when General Rushleigh reached across to me a fresh, dainty note, in which was simply written, —

" If you come again, dear friend, I will see you."

"VIRGINIA REGIS."

CHAPTER XXVII.

IN MASK AND DOMINO.

. . . .

. . . . STEPHEN — wild boy! got them fairly into the Carnival that day, after all. They came back from the Villa Ludovisi, ate their lunch without waiting for me, and drove down to the Piazza di Spagna, to buy some of Anderson's fresco-photographs at Spithöver's, while it was fresh in their minds; and then he took them through Via Condotti, and all the way down the Corso to Piazza Colonna, under the fire of confetti that had just begun for the afternoon. Emery Ann and Edith had to cover their faces with their shawls to defend themselves; peeping out through telescopic folds at the funny maskers who crowded about the carriage with Italian jokes and shouts of laughter; for the laughter, — let Emery Ann say what she will about cosmopolitan language, — is as characteristically in their own tongue as the speech.

But they got their mood up for the fun; and the next day, nothing would do but they must arrange themselves properly and go again. I left them early in the forenoon basting up cambrics into dominos; masks they must have to save their faces; Emery Ann made a black cloak, and Stephen bought her a nice, respectable black velvet mask; Edith was to be all rose-color, — cambric and satin; and she pinned fresh roses into her white hat.

"You never saw such 'passing' in all your life, Emery Ann! Did you?" said the girl, gayly.

But she stopped to tie up a bunch of freshest violets from a basket Stephen had brought in, for me to carry with her love, to Margaret. "If she could only come, too!" said both the children.

But neither Carnival, nor Lent, nor Easter, comes with any self-same season, into different lives!

I drove down to Via Crociferi; taking the violets, and some of Emery Ann's cream toast in a pitcher for Mrs. Regis's breakfast.

I knew General Rushleigh would not present himself before twelve.

Mrs. Regis was up, upon the sofa in the salon, when I went in. Margaret had dressed and arranged her daintily. There was no cap upon her lovely hair; it was knotted loosely, high up on her head, in soft, looped twists, and an invisible silken net held it from rumpling. A blue silk blind was tied across her forehead, and shaded half her face; a gray cashmere wrapper with trimmings of black silk enveloped her figure, and a little gray slipper, bound and rosetted with black, showed beneath the fringe of the bright afghan that was thrown partly over her. Flowers, a fire, and sunshine, made the large room very pleasant.

But, seeing the general picture at one glance, I saw also that Margaret's face was gravely, anxiously tender as she met me, and led me in. When she said, "I am *glad* you are come!" she said it without a smile; only the same grave, tender look, and a sweetness in the voice; and it sounded as a gladness might that came of some welcome comfort to a trouble. It was not till I came close to Mrs. Regis, and she spoke, that I noticed something in her face, — strangely changed already by the affection of her eyes, — that startled me. A slight stiffness about the beautiful mouth, — a fixity of one corner, — like the cramp of some muscle. More than that, a kind of stillness, as if all the muscles did not play as usual. Was it merely the effect of the tension and swelling, — or could that be the way a worse thing might come on? A terrible word rushed suddenly into my thoughts.

"You see;" she said slowly, with an indescribable pathos. "I do not know what is happening to me. But I am to have a physician now. It seems to be more than we can manage with rose-water." And she smiled; that partial smile that frightened me.

" It is not much ?   It is the swelling coming down about the mouth ? "   Margaret spoke with an inflection modulated touchingly between assertion and question.   " It is less than it was at first, I am sure ; and it has only been since this morning."

It was very little ; but it made such a difference ; and such terrible names of things one knows so little about, flash into one's mind so !

" There has been a kind of — stiffness, — almost numbness, — with this swelling ; it has been in my fingers, too," said Mrs. Regis, lifting her hand and moving the fingers slightly.   They were a little swollen evidently ; the dinted knuckles had grown nearly smooth ; all the sparkling rings had been taken off.

" We have sent for Dr. G——," said Margaret.   " He is coming this morning.   And he will tell us it is nothing ; and then mamma will eat some breakfast."   She spoke with that tone of coaxing assurance with which one encourages at the same time one's self and another.

" She must eat something now," I said, uncovering my pitcher. " Will Gigia bring me a toast dish ? "

I made Mrs. Regis take a little of the nice cream toast, that had kept warm in the deep pitcher, pinned over with a thick napkin.   She had only had a cup of tea before, Margaret said. As she tasted it and we sat talking, she grew more cheerful. Margaret laid the bunch of violets on the delicate white handkerchief that was just shaken out of fold upon her gray, soft dress.

Just that little thing made it seem more impossible.   It could not be that to Mrs. Regis, — beautiful, dainty, fit only for all exquisite surrounding, — to whom flowers, and freshness, and every luxury of niceness and perfectness naturally belonged, — should come change, disease, wreck !   Oh, no ! one could not think of that terrible word with her !

We all grew cheerful in the subtle something that human companionship and sharing give to the meeting of whatever human anxiety or pain ; the inevitable lessening and wanting that come after the first surprise of any apprehension, brought their reaction. .

Our spirits rose even to something like gayety, as we talked.

I told them about the Carnival-going, and gave Edith's message.

"Dear child!" said Margaret. "Thank her,—ever so
much!"

How curiously the woman in her deepening experience looked
over at the child in Edith, across the scarcely three years between them!

There was only an hour; and then a ring of the corridor-
bell announced the coming of the physician.

Margaret met him in the ante-room. She looked suddenly
pale again, as she brought him in and introduced him. I felt
my heart tremble in my bosom; and Mrs. Regis said not a word
for three or four instants. From underneath all our cheerful
covering up, the thought we were afraid of sprang to its dread
and threat again, at the approach of the man who could decide
or dismiss it.

"Ach!" said the physician. He had drawn a chair to the
sofa, sat down and glanced keenly at his patient.

He proceeded at once to his business. He asked questions.
He lifted the silken shade, examined the eyes, the swelling,
made her look up and down, watched the movement of the lids,
pressed gently the flesh of forehead and cheek with his finger.
He examined tongue and pulse. He made her move limbs,
fingers; he placed his hand, his ear against her heart. At last
he sat back in his chair, again, regarding her.

"Ach!"

That was Dr. G——'s prologue and epilogue.

"It is not serious thing. It is heat,— cold. Too much of
travel; too much of Rome. *Fat*-igue. *De*-bility. And,— I
think,— some touch of poison to the system; maybe of malaria;
maybe — where you have been?" he asked suddenly.

Then Margaret told him of the days in the ruins; of the
gathering and bringing home the weeds and vines.

"Ach! — I thought! — You shall have Belladonna and
Rhus; then you shall have tonic; then, in two weeks,— ten
days, — you shall leave Rome!"

"You can make biff-tea?" he said to Margaret, in. the ante-
room. "She shall have plenty. She must be made strong. It

is more thing than one. You shall take great care. You shall
make her cheerful It is the nerves are worn; one cannot tell
what the nerves will do when they are like that. But *now?*
It is not serious thing."

The doctor was gone, to come again to-morrow. Margaret
came back to the sofa, knelt down beside it, and kissed her
mother. " You are just to be made bright and happy, and have
ever so much beef-tea ! " she said,— and then burst out crying,
gently..

" A very nice way to make me bright and happy ! " said
Mrs. Regis, lightly ; but her own voice trembled. She put her
arm around Margaret's shoulder, and held her for a second.
Then she made her get up. " There, — this must be all over,"
she said. " We have all been thinking of something terrible,
and it has been a long while since morning ! Now what I want
is that you should go out. Miss Patience, you are to take her
somewhere. She sees nothing ; she has nothing to come and
tell me of ; and I am to be made cheerful ! " The last words
were added before Margaret could speak, in answer to her rebellious gesture.

" Gigia can bring the beef first, if you like, and you can set
the tea brewing ; Mrs. Flitwick can wait upon me. The doctor's powders will come with directions ; I want to rest ; Miss
Euphrasia, or somebody, may come by and by ; I must get qui-
eted down by myself first. Miss Patience, she has never seen
St. Peter's. Take her there."

She was growing excited. I thought she ought to have quite
her own way. I knew how much of action and reaction in her
feeling must be straining, wearing her. " We will go a little
while," I said to Margaret, quietly. " There will be other days.
You will be quite enough needed. She will want us all sometimes."

I meant a promise in that " all," of days again like the old
days when we had been all together. And I think it touched
the secret faith of Margaret's patient waiting. She could wait
one more day. One at a time she had waited so many.

She went away to Mrs. Flitwick and Gigia. Mrs. Regis
turned to me instantly.

"If I had been going to have what you know you thought of, Miss Patience! If I had been going to die, perhaps, — it would not have been so much! But — in this plight,— to see Paul Rushleigh, — and get well after it! I have sent for him. And he will be sure to come to-day; I hope you feel the heroism of it!"

She was in a curious mood. She put real, vital things, in such a whimsical form. She set her sacrifice, — which made its crucial demand at last, as sacrifice so often does, of merest human weakness, laying its test-touch upon the quick at some small surface-nerve, — in the attitude of a frivolity.

"Are you sure it is not too much?" I asked. "Will it do for you, dear Mrs. Regis?"

"Nothing else will do," she answered, "but to let this thing right itself. It is this that has been too much for me. To have been a hindrance, — when I came with one clear, single purpose. We have met him, — and we have not met him. Margaret is an angel; but Paul Rushleigh, after all, is a man."

"Met and not met." Precisely his own words.

"You are so wise, and it is so good of you!" I did not dare say "noble," — "grand," with the emphasis I felt. But Mrs. Regis understood me.

"You think me generous," she said plainly and straightly. "I am not generous. For that very reason, I can just do the thing that is set me, — with a blind kind of heroism, as I said. It was set for me to come to Rome; it was set for me to stay. It is set for me to see Paul Rushleigh just as I am. These three plain things are possible to me to do; though I am not generous."

I suppose "generous" *is* "born-noble;" but is not "noblesse oblige" the pass-word all the way up? And how *much* born yet are we any of us, after all?

By the time Mrs. Flitwick had been given her instructions, and Gigia had brought the beef, and Margaret was ready, another half hour was gone.

"Never mind the book," said Mrs. Regis, hastily. Margaret was searching about for a library volume that was to be returned to Piale's.

"Here it is," she said, and tucked it under her arm as she stood drawing on her glove by the door. The bell rang just outside.

"Margaret!" Margaret turned.

"If that is General Rushleigh, tell Mrs. Flitwick to show him in."

Margaret opened the door, met Mrs. Flitwick crossing from the kitchen, and stopped her with her mother's message. Then she came back into the room, as if of course.

Paul Rushleigh entered. Margaret met him, gave him her hand, then moved to let him pass toward her mother. Mrs. Regis stretched out hers, putting the other, as she did so, to the edge of her silken shade; pushing it upward slightly that she might see from under it; her hand and the fine, laced handkerchief that she held in the bend of the smaller fingers, covering at the same time that changed corner of her mouth.

"In mask and domino," she said. "This is my 'Carnival.'" She lingered on the syllables; her Italian utterance of the word gave it back its meaning.

"Do not stay, Margaret." Margaret was drawing off her glove again. She looked at her mother with surprised eyes. Not stay? When he had come so often, and been sent away? Why was she to be sent away now?

"General Rushleigh will come again; he will excuse you now. I shall want you all sometimes, as Miss Patience says. But to-day,—I cannot see so many together, and you must have your drive."

It took all Margaret's new-found faith and love toward her mother; all her higher faith — grown to a habit — that the thing that happens to one, in one's duty, is the right thing; I could feel that. But her high certainty of Paul Rushleigh never thought of being tested! That he could misunderstand her for a moment,—*that* did not occur to or trouble her. Since her mother would have it so, she could wait one more day.

She went straight over to him with her hand reached out again. Her clear eyes looked into his. She said, with a simple, inexpressible grace, "I would not go, but that mamma wishes it. Do not let her talk too much."

He bowed gravely, kindly. His eyes were as steadfast as hers; but they had not her unquestioningness. In a brief, deep glance, they studied, searched her; it was a look intense, but not prolonged, — then he let go her hand, which he had scarcely detained, and she turned to her mother. She gave her a tiny hand-screen from the mantel. It had a long silk fringe about its small oval. Mrs. Regis's sofa was wheeled toward the fire. There was excuse for some graceful shielding of the poor, altered face; and the dropping fringe, as she slanted the screen before it, fell lightly against cheek and chin.

We left her so; General Rushleigh came to the door with us, with the half-purpose, apparently, to accompany us down-stairs; but Margaret said good-bye, and turned toward the kitchen for some last order to Mrs. Flitwick about the tea. He repeated her word with the same grave kindness, and returned to Mrs. Regis. Gigia ran down to the street before us, and called a carriage.

"San Pietro in Vaticano," I said to the driver, as we got in.

I remembered, with a kind of obligation, — though I did not know why, — that that was where we were to go.

CHAPTER XXVIII.

CONFESSION.

. . . .

. . . . I DO know what passed at that interview. I do feel, often and often, the unclosing of eyes that are not set in my forehead. Everybody does. Half our lives are made up of knowledges that come by imagination and influence only. We dramatize to ourselves continually, that which does or might take place concerning us, or the people and things we care for. We hear, internally, the words our friends — our enemies perhaps — do doubtless say of us. Our consciousness of what we are to them, of what they are, and will do, — takes this form. Else it would not be *con*sciousness. By these things we know that we are of the nature of those " living creatures " that praise before the Absolute Light, standing in the central vision.

" Hamlet with Hamlet left out ? " But what would the play be, if everything were left out *but* Hamlet ? That is what our life would be, if shadows and fragments and insights did not continually take form and place to us, and fill up the scenes in which we are not actually upon the boards.

I was in intense sympathy with Mrs. Regis. I was clairvoyante to the spirit of what was happening, at least, as I sat there again in the south transept of St. Peter's, while Margaret walked slowly to and fro among the chapels, and beneath the Dome.

If she had been well, — Mrs. Regis, I mean, — and they had been going and coming, — meeting daily, returning to their old, friendly habit and intercourse, — she might have let things adjust themselves. It might have been the only way. That was certainly what she had come to Rome for. She would have bided her time, at least, waiting if any direct word were needful. But now, I was sure, she had bent all circumstance to her will

36

to-day, that she might say some word, make some sign, call forth her own opportunity to convey to Paul Rushleigh that which his not knowing might prevent in some of these few remaining days all possibility of his coming to know; or of understanding what Margaret's way and manner, so high above the way and manner of any ordinary girl, was real expression of.

" You have been very kind, and I have wished to see you before. But I waited till I should be a less wretched object to be seen," I could hear her say; and she lays down the screen, with which she will not make a coquetry of disguise, and lifts again the silken shade a little, with that simpler defense of hand and handkerchief. " But now I know I shall have to leave Rome before very long; and I *have* been a little frightened. I could not have you kept away any longer, my friend."

She says those last words as they are only said when they hold one of the strongest meanings of a heart and a life-time. But she says them as any woman might say them to any man.

General Rushleigh looks pained and anxious at the change in her. He asks her with quick solicitude, if she has seen a physician.

" Doctor G—— has been here this morning. He says ' it is not serious thing.' " She quotes his accent, as well as his word, making light, so, of the matter, and then passes it quite by.

" I wrote two letters to you, when I supposed you were in the East. I sent them to Beyrout and Alexandria. Of course they have never come to you. If they ever should, will you return them to me? "

She would provide against those letters saying anything too plainly to him, by and by, — coming out of the by-gone with an asking, — if what she had to say to him to-day by any peradventure should fall useless and too late. She would mean that he should know clearly one simple fact; but she would be quite conscious that all this time might possibly have made a difference.

" I did not mean, you see, to give you up into the great haphazard of time and absence. I meant to hold something that I· thought I had gained. At my age," — she would put herself at once, into that clear, irrevocable attitude of elder years, — it was one of the things that in her " blind heroism " she could find herself "set to do," — " one does not make many new, real friends. But since you did not go, after all, to Egypt and the East, why have you not made any sign before, — yourself, — to us ? Why did you not let us know ? Why have we not sooner begun where we left off ? "

" Do you know where we *did* leave off ? But I beg your pardon. I will not ask. I will take the grace of your meaning. It answers something that I have felt a doubt of. Whether I might, — whether you would quite understand, — would trust me ? I could not bear to be outside of where I was before."

" I wonder," says Mrs. Regis, slowly, " if you know exactly *where* you are ? "

" I have been bewildered." I can think with what a smile Paul Rushleigh might say this. " But I think I see. You — and Margaret — offer me a heaven of friendship. At my age, also, one does not find that many times again. I must try if I can enter in."

" Margaret ? " There was much questioned, as there had been much spoken, in the mere utterance of the name.

" Yes, Margaret is as calm and sweet as Beatrice on the heavenly heights. I can see what that must mean."

" *Ask* Margaret why she is so calm and sweet ! "

" Mrs. Regis ! You know what I did ask her, once ? "

" Yes. You asked it one hour too soon."

" One hour ! "

" One hour. For in that hour she opened her letters. And she found — the faith she had been keeping, — with sacrifice, — flung back to her. She had known nothing about that before ! "

" My dear Mrs. Regis ! My dear friend ! " He had started to his feet.

" Ask Margaret what she said to me, coming home around the Punta, that night in Venice ? No — don't ask her that ! Ask her your own questions, and do not tell her that I have spoken to you ! "

" I must ask her what I can." His voice was deep with feeling. He came and took in both of his the hand that lay, unringed, upon the soft gray robe. "And how can I thank you?"

No change of feature could distort the smile he *felt* — and never forgot — in the faint parting of her lips.

"Margaret is at St. Peter's," she said, calmly. "And I am just a little tired. Will you please to ring for Mrs. Flitwick?"

She had done what she was set to do.

In substance it verily passed through my mind, — figured itself clear in my imagination. That is a meaning phrase that the French have, — "Figure to yourself." Only that is not the syntax of it. It figures itself to you. It makes itself a motion and a being. And I know that that was the substance of what passed.

By and by I found myself drifting into other thought. Whether this change that had come upon Mrs. Regis, heretofore so unscathed in her rich physical health, was to be the break of her splendid womanhood; whether her youth of full age was to pass away from her so. For, it occurred to me, there is so truly a youth to every period of life, and a decadence. And Mrs. Regis had just entered, as it were, into the early bloom of elderhood. Did you ever think of that, Rose? How we do have young days, over and over again? An old baby is an older thing, relatively, than a man or a woman of fifty. Its teeth are dropping, its growth is changing from the tender forms of infancy to the scrawniness and struggle of a muscle-and-bone development; then again when it is fully rounded and established to the springing beauty of a childish strength, comes the falling away from that into old-childhood, — the interval time before the bright youth of maturity, which we call youth by excellence, begins. And then the blossom of that shrivels for the fair fruit to set; and then succeeds a youth of ripeness. And just as surely, after the ingathering, comes the rich autumn flush, the youth of the last period of our days. There is a temperament, like a climate, in which its glory lingers long, and passes at last very softly into a winter whose evergreens, warm and rich in the sunshine, make color and fragrance like the leafage of a stronger spring.

It was only such a fulfilling of days that I could think of for a woman like Mrs. Regis. And how different a woman — yet how certainly an interpretation of the same — she had become to me now, from what she had seemed two years ago at Out-ledge, or in the early days of our companionship at sea, when I had wondered and half repented that we had become companions at all. Truly, it is He that "formed" who saith to every one of us, "Fear not: *I* have redeemed thee: *I* have called thee by thy name." And there is no name of separate being which shall not be redeemed into his glory!

I think that it must have been while these things replaced in my mind the clairvoyance of the moments before, that Paul Rushleigh was coming through the streets, over the bridge of the Angels, into the sunlit, fountain-musical square, up to the great platform and portico of the church where he had said yesterday that perhaps it would be better for him to go away, up the Nile. Where we waited now, — Margaret and I, — for we knew not what. For with all my clairvoyance I had not figured to myself that. Because, maybe, it was coming to the witness of my eyes.

She was standing by the marble balustrade, on which are hung the ever-burning lamps. She leaned there, looking over into the sunken space, at the statue of Napoleon's captive Pope, who in his imprisonment ordered the place and attitude of the sculpture, — kneeling forever before this door of Peter's tomb.

I came over to her from the pedestal-recess at which I had stopped before the statue of Saint Veronica holding the suda-rium; above, in the balcony, they say, is kept the precious relic, — the handkerchief with which she dried the sweat from the Saviour's suffering face, and received thereupon his likeness upon the napkin. Another story tells that she was the woman who had touched the hem of his garment, and who once after-ward brought Him water and a towel to wash; and the Image — the Vera Icon — was given back to her upon the linen. Either way, it was the *ministry*, — which may be offered Him always through "one of the least of these," — and the Face of the Healer, which shines back upon them who having been

healed would serve,—that they may go forth and manifest it
again for the restoring of souls.

"A dead thing; and a shut door; and one's life kneeling
before it. Do you see that there, Miss Patience? Must it
ever be like that?" Margaret said it to me, without turning;
still looking down upon the marble statue and the shrine, as I
came up beside her.

"It is the 'Confession of St. Peter,'" I said; remembering
again the word as I had thought of it and talked of it with her
mother; and I put one hand softly on her two, that rested
clasped upon the rail of the balustrade. "It is his life laid down
before the Lord; waiting his absolving. More than absolving;
justifying. For the *making right*—the *declaring right*—is in
it; it is con-fession; the having it all out, clear, *with* Him.—
You will think I am always digging among old roots," I said,
smiling. "But I have always been so glad of my little bit of
Latin. The roots of *things* are in the words.

"Everything is alive with you," said Margaret. "There is
no tomb for anything!"

"Except for mistakes, and wrongs, and things that we wish
dead. Yes; I do believe in just that gospel. Are you not
tired, dear? You have stood here so long."

I moved away with her toward the Tribune. We sat down,
near one end, on the upper of the two low, long steps that run
across before it, raising its floor from the rest of the chancel.
From that low seat behind, yet aside from, the great Altar and
its Baldacchino, we gazed up into the untiring grandeur of the
Dome. Before us stretched the long, solemn aisles; beyond
us, as we half turned ourselves toward it, was the Chair of the
Apostle of the Keys.

There was no one near us; the great space was comparatively
empty. All Rome, I suppose, was busy with the Carnival.
Some men had been cleaning the pavement; they were still
working their slow way through their long task, toward the
opposite transept. Here and there, down the distance and the
dimness, were groups of strangers, studying the sculptures. A
few praying figures about the Altar; one man, quite far at our
right, kneeled at the other corner of the Tribune.

I do not know what feeling, like being in the heart of the world, comes over one in a vast church like this, full of prayers that breathe up in it; full of stillness; with the common life astir and afloat all about it in a great city outside. It is the hidden quietness of the soul of humanity, large with its real hope, deep behind all the small rush and struggle of its nominal life. It is like what it had been in the heart of the mountain at Trient, — only without the terror; where the waters and the woods were leaping and waving in sunlight and winds overhead and out of sight, and we were hidden away in a deep centre of awful remoteness. I had felt it at Milan. I felt it here at St. Peter's.

I said awfulness; but it is an awfulness that one creeps into, and feels safe under.

And then, St. Peter's, with its "climate of its own," is so different from the churches that smite you with their chill; that are as if the heart of the world were dead and frozen.

"To get inside of something so great, rests one," said Margaret. "I think the tire of the world is the being so on the crust of it."

"A mighty shelter; the shadow of a great Rock in a weary land," I responded to her.

"I have such a waiting feeling; as if I could just let myself alone here, indefinitely, till something comes to me. As if I were blessedly buried, until some resurrection."

She was tired, I knew, heart and body, with her anxieties and efforts; with her waiting, — that was so much harder and more wearying, out on the crust, than in this stillness.

Away down in the far archway of the nave, I saw a figure coming. A figure and a movement that I knew. Small in the vast height and breadth and distance, and yet bringing a presence that was above the measurement of things; "the measure of a man; that is, of an angel."

I could not see feature nor outline, really; but I saw expression; the expression of Paul Rushleigh's noble, but reverent, carriage. His hat was in his hand; his bared head was lifted with some hope, some ardent expectation, as he came on; his step was firm, even, rapid.

He came, straight and steadily, toward us. I suppose his quick glance took in the few figures at either hand upon his way, and showed him that they were not those he looked for; but without seeming to look, until, passing around the Altar and the Confession, he came where he could recognize us as we did him, he kept on as if he had known just where we should be, or as if some unerring magnetism led him.

I do not know exactly when Margaret saw him first, whether as soon as I, or after. But she was standing upon her feet as he approached; and she moved forward some steps on the wide, silent pavement to meet him. I sat still where I was, and saw the two beautiful figures join each other with outreached hands, as two might meet upon some great pavement of the New Jerusalem.

" Margaret!"

His two hands held her two, now; his eyes looked down into hers uplifted.

" You belong to me?—you were waiting for me?"

" Yes: I was waiting for you."

" How long could you have let it be?"

" I could have let it be for all my life."

For all their life, they were betrothed; in that single moment; with those few words. Under the heaven-like Dome; in the shadow of the solemnly gorgeous canopy that roofs over the waiting Confession with its lamps of faith; more than all, with that kind Christ Face looking down upon them from the panel of the shut transept door. " Bound on earth; bound in heaven." The Word of the Master to him in whose name, under his Lord's, stands this typical church, seemed spoken to them here; but a blesseder Word was written above them in that promise of the Ascending Saviour,—" Lo, I am with you always, even unto the end!"

They moved down, as if from a marriage; I followed them along the nave.

When we got to the door they turned to me.

" Dear Miss Patience!" and " Dear Miss Patience!" they

said; and the tears aud smiles sprang into my face. And Margaret ·kissed me there.

Then we went out into the sunshine; into the grand square with its colonnades, and the saints walking together upon the roof of them. And the white plumes of the fountains flung their joy of pure waters up against the light of the sky.

CHAPTER XXIX.

"ICH."

. . . .

. . . . "Mamma! I never thought to ask you if you consented!"

"We have not been so separate as that, lately," said Mrs. Regis.

"We will never be separate any more, mamma! I feel as if I had found everything!"

"Margaret," I said, quietly, "when we first knew each other, your mother trusted me with something. It was a knowledge that belongs to you. I think the time has come for me to deliver up my trust. It was a discretionary one."

Mrs. Regis looked at me as I began so coolly and independently, with a surprise that was half curious, half vaguely alarmed. Then when I said "discretionary," she smiled, and the questioning apprehension in her face gave way to a quiet recollection. I would have stopped there, if she had bidden me, though I had so audaciously taken the bits between my teeth. But she allowed me to go on.

"Do you know, — did you ever guess, — that she never meant to have forbidden you at all?" And then I began to tell her what Mrs. Regis had told to me on our ride out to Versailles, that July morning that seemed so long ago.

"She put it all out of her power, — the penalty of those miserable conditions; she only kept her show of authority to hold you back while your own certainties might grow, — while *this* might happen to you!"

"Mamma!"

The girl half started from her seat; Mrs. Regis's breath came a little quickly, and her color rose. Her eyes grew soft, as she looked at Margaret. The silken shade had been laid by, and only a little heaviness of the lids remained now of the swelling of three days ago. "Belladonna and Rhus" had been doing their wonderful, neutralizing work; and into her face; with its return to its more natural contour, had crept also something that was not contour merely; that she had never had in it, so gently-prevailing, in its most radiant day.

But she did not move; and I hurried on, resolved that Margaret should hear the whole. I told her of the trust-deed; Mrs. Regis did not check me; I repeated, almost exactly, the words that had fixed themselves in my memory when I had received them with so great a wonder, and laid them by separately, as it were, from my other impressions of this woman, as something I could not quite make seem to fit her then, — but a garment of righteousness that she might grow to wear. It seemed a natural act, — a real soul-garment now.

" It was all made over to you, beyond recall; it was all made safe for you; principal or income, according as you might or might not marry with her unconditional approval. Her mere consent was another thing. It was easier to do things once for all. She had put a positive meanness out of her power." — I rehearsed the sentences slowly. The very character of the words told Margaret that I quoted.

She kept herself still, and listened. She waited, as a bird waits to take its flight. It seemed as if she, too, were resolved upon the whole. But when I had ended, the hands, half lifted, were stretched out; the parted, tremulous lips gave forth a heart-cry; she rushed toward her mother's side.

Mrs. Regis had only time to say, brokenly, hastily, — " I had not thought, — but it was better you should know now, than have it come when — perhaps — if" —

" Mamma! Mamma!" Margaret was crying at the same moment, " if this had come to me before I had begun to know you, *yourself*; it would have broken my heart!"

" Don't make your eyes red, Daisy," Mrs. Regis remonstrated, pushing her gently up from her, " Paul will be here presently."

" Paul would n't want hard eyes, that could n't cry! — But after all," she said, taking refuge in jest from too much earnest, as the Anglo-Saxon manner, even in the far-descended and transplanted generations, is, — " there has n't been a word *said*, even yet, about the 'unconditional approval!' And that is what I began with." She laughed, and dabbed with her handkerchief at the eyes that must not be red for Paul. Then she came down close to Mrs. Regis again, upon a little hassock at her side.

. " We only came and told you," she said. " I can scarcely remember how. I don't think there was much telling, that day. But now I just want you to say it, mamma! You *give* me to Paul Rushleigh?"

" Just as I have got you myself, Margaret?"

" Yes, mamma. That is why I want to hear it. Because now I am yours to give. Only there are some things that can't quite be given away!"

" You could have brought nobody into this relation," Mrs. Regis said, with calmest equipoise of word and manner, " who would ever have been so dear to me as Paul Rushleigh." She said it that way, plainly, fully, and with that careful steadiness, as if only so she could meet and bear the demand that was made of her. It is that way men and women meet and bear the knife or the fire. And it is with that strange embrace of mortal pain, that they pass through its climax, and from beyond it smile and sing.

" Yes, He was your friend first," said Margaret. " You have given us both. All we can do now, is both together to give ourselves back to you." And she leaned her face, all flushed and bright like a wet rose, over her mother's and kissed her. It was almost too much. Margaret was saying so much more than she knew. I was glad that the bell rang, and Paul Rushleigh came ; to take her away presently as had been arranged ; to see something, no matter what. Something that they were to see together. And I, as had also been arranged, settled myself for the morning, with Mrs. Regis.

I read to her a while, and then I took my crotchet-work and sat quietly by her. We did not talk a great deal ; there was reason enough on her side ; on mine it was partly because there was something I was wishing very much to say.

When the little cuckoo clock, that Mrs. Regis had brought from Switzerland, rang *one*, reminding me that Emery Ann would be in directly to pick me up on the way home with Edith and Stephen, the cuckoo sprang out of my heart in a hurry, also.

"Dear Mrs. Regis," I said, "I am always feeling that I should ask your forgiveness!"

"For what, possibly?" She turned her head toward me with surprise. Turned to me, also, I fancied, out of some far-wandered thought of her own.

"For the judgment I passed on you in my own mind at first, and for long. I thought you dainty, indolent, selfish. I told Rose Halliday so. Or I said as much to her, again and again, writing what I *thought* I saw of you."

"Rose Halliday is a myth,—a Mrs. Harris!" said Mrs. Regis, and she laughed. "You are always confessing about her. I don't care for her! But if you hadn't seen me so, — and if you hadn't thought me worth while canvassing with your Rose Halliday, who I tell you I know well enough is just your *alter ego*, you mightn't have done me all the good you have. I *am* dainty. So dainty that I can plunge both hands into a very disagreeable business, to *make* things dainty."

The door opened at that moment, and Emery Ann came in. But Mrs. Regis did not mind; she went straight on.

"So indolent that I can work hard to make a place and circumstances to be thoroughly and undisturbedly indolent in. So selfish that I must respect, satisfy *myself*, somehow, and cannot be comfortable until I have faced the uncomfortableness. But I am beginning to see a problem. I was just thinking of it. What does it matter about satisfying one's self, after all? It can't be, through and through, — till one gives it up, and leaves off caring. And then — what has become of the satisfaction? Is it anywhere?"

"Yes. 'I shall be satisfied when I awake in Thy likeness.' We wake just there, don't we, as we do out of bad dreams, at the point where we give up and leave off caring?"

Emery Ann stood still in the middle of the room, with a bowl of tapioca jelly in her hands. She had gone home first, and got that.

"We have to go through a good many sudses," she said, entering into the conversation in her own fashion as if she belonged there, "before we come out like that! One washing does n't git red of it."

"Get rid of what?" asked Mrs. Regis, looking for her certain amusement; perhaps her as certain help.

"What that North-Ireland woman, — Patience knows, — that washed our blankets, called the '*ick*' in the wool. The sticky grease of it."

"The *Ich!*" Mrs. Regis breathed it to me, with her soft rendering of the German rough aspirate.

But Emery Ann does n't know German from Gaelic, or how Gaelic, from the German, strikes its curious, significant parallels.

She carried her tapioca jelly across into the dining-room to Mrs. Flitwick. "She 's to have that, with sugar and *cream*," we heard her say, emphatically. "Creamer *montata*, finally, — if she likes it. Though *I* don't think there 's anything creamer than the real plain thing, unflummeried, riz slow and rich, of its own accord, and just skum!"

Mrs. Regis stopped herself in the middle of the irresistible laugh.

"You can't one of you keep clear of the morals!" she said, "and you just go about infecting everybody else — consciously and unconsciously. The real, plain thing — riz slow and rich — and just skum, — when the time is ripe! That 's living and motive; not forcing a thing because you know it has got to be, and you can't be comfortable till it is — and is over."

"I suppose that is the divine urgency though, in the lowest and the highest, is n't it? Water is restless till it finds its level; and the milk is n't *comfortable* till all its cream has come to the top!"

"If you let it alone and give it time," — put in Emery Ann, returning; — "but then you need n't whisk it up as soon as it does come into six times its own amount of froth and syllabub. I always did despise that, for *my* part."

"Thank you, Emery Ann," said Mrs. Regis. "Mrs. Flitwick, I'll take my cream plain, if you please."

We bade good-bye, and went down-stairs.

"That cream's risin'," said Emery Ann. "I've seen it for some time. But it ain't all up yet, and don't you go to stirrin' it too much beforehand."

CHAPTER XXX.

RIGHTNESS.

. . . .

. . . . We are carried through many a hard thing by the
very press and stimulus to our whole nature, summoned in
its integrity to act or to endure. It is like the fifteen pounds to
the square inch, which we *rest* in ; because we bear it on *all* the
square inches. Then there is a point beyond which nature
— bodily or spiritually — refuses pain. And there is also an
individual nature which reacts to the acceptance of a different or
contrary condition, because it cannot suffer the continual realization to itself of a condition that may not be.

Mrs. Regis is of this temperament. And in these early days
of Margaret's engagement, so much gathered around her and
made her its centre ; she was so far from being left out, lonely ;
such new, blessed relation in life opened to her, instead of what
she must reconcile herself now to the acknowledgment of having
missed, in one sole possibility of experience, all her life long ;
that her instinct of self-defense found plentiful refuge ; her
pain — her temptation — its pledged " way of escape."

How good it was for her that we were two old maids ! That
she could look upon us and think, — " Here are women who
have missed it too, each in her own way, as I in mine. And
yet we none of us have missed our living." I think that is the
blessing that we lonely women may be, and greatly what we are
made for. Everybody *sees* that we have missed — as the world
calls it — one whole, beautiful side of life ; other missings,
where outward relations seem all fulfilled, are secret to the
hearts that bear them. And everybody may see, if we stand up
to our witness to which we are called, that for all that, we are
not maimed creatures ; that life *is* whole in us, after all !

There are quantities of things I should like to tell you, Rose, of what went on in these days; of the life that I entered into and was conscious of, in this new, fulfilled aspect that all things were taking around one happy centre. There are things I should like to tell you, at which you would cry out, "But you must have *listened*, Patience!" Yes: as anybody may. There is a whispering gallery in which we may catch all secrets. It runs through hearts.

Shall I tell you little scraps, little signs, that everybody talks of who is just outside the thing that makes all its signs delightful? Would you like to know — as everybody does like — what ring Margaret wears, new and beautiful, on her left hand? It is not diamonds; *they* have been bought and sold too much. It is a fair circle of entire, pure pearls; large, lucent; lovely in their native forms, ridged slightly, or dimpled, or pear-curved; they are like the truth of her own nature, — like the truths that are between them, — not halvéd, or carefully matched, or set to a pattern; but real, individual, precious for exception.

And he has given her another such beautiful name-token, — gem-spelling of the name in which he delights! It is her marguerites that only one might ever give to her for wedding-wearing.

Not in the paltry, perishable filigree of the Genoese wire-workers, exquisite though that be: these are pearls also, set like daisy petals, starlike, around their tiny centres of pure gold, fretted to the likeness of the crowding golden stamens of the flower; linked delicately with slenderest possible catches, tip to tip; it is a throat circlet, which lies gently against the fair round of her neck, where the pulse from the heart comes up and throbs beneath it softly; it half hides itself among the edges of the light, fine lace she wears. Yes: he has read it through, and found both synonyms in it, — the pearl and daisy nature. Rare and pure and queenly as the jewel; simple and tender as the field blossom.

One other thing he has given her, — a lovely clasp, for collar or band, of two crossed fern-leaves, in emerald enamel. She never said anything about it; but she knows I read the token of that also; — the little fern-leaf of Rhigi, — the *two* fern-leaves afterward, that were like the old broken coin of pledge. Not ex-

37

changed ; kept separately, but with one faith that met in the separate keeping. Fern-leaves for *invisibility :* fern-leaves for the viewless, patient hope.

They go and come together ; I know how they stand, again and again, in the beauty of the Pantheon, under the one light from the blue heaven, and remember their coming back to each other there ; I know how they have stood silent under the moon-light, when the shining world that waits upon a world sails slow across that wondrous opening and pours its glory down to fill the place as glory pours into a soul open to heaven only. I know how they have wandered in the hushed galleries of the Coliseum in that same night-splendor, that is like the night-splendor of time, softening, hallowing all; I know how they have sauntered - deliciously in the blossoming Campagna, and gathered violets and anemones, and crocus-cups, and told each other, in every telling of their separate lives, the same beautiful story of their life-belonging ; I know how they have gone back through the last months, in which what always must have been was just born into the world, and have talked of the mystery of it, like the mystery of every mortal birth that is only a com-ing into form of what has been in the Father's love from the foundation. I know how high and dear he was to her for all that had had to be of deferring in his life ; and I know how high and dear she was to him, for her true waiting, — for that very refusing, which had been out of her inmost truth. I know it all, because of this old maiden that I am, in whom it is all fresh and true, and has not been overworn and confused, by the poor, partial living of it out, as it has in some who think they must know far better, and who may laugh at the old maiden's insight of that with which she has nothing to do — only to be-lieve in it all her days, and to wait for it in·heaven.

I know how sweet it was for him to tell, and for her to listen, the old, curious stories of the ruins and the sculptures and the inscriptions, and the massive remains of works men wrought those thousands of years ago. I know how they have walked through the dim vastness of the excavated palace-galleries, and come out into the smile of gardens. I know how they have

climbed the woody heights of Tivoli, and sat beside the glory of
its falling waters, and looked forth over the misty Campagna
spreading from nearer waves of foliage to a far, dim, horizon
sea, on which lie strangely motionless the great forms of wreck
that break its wild monotony. I know how up the beautiful
Pincio they went often, in morning hours before the crowd
went, to rest upon the margin of the exquisite Fountain of
Moses, where the child lies in his leafy ark on the little island-
centre, and the mother, — one hand lingering in the leaving of
him as she has laid him down, and the other held to the bosom
that is to miss him and he may moan for, — lifts her face upward in a prayer. To look down from this upon all Rome, —
upon St. Peter's and the Vatican, — and think between this and
that, and *beyond again*, what a history of God's dealing in the
world, — what a slow telling of Himself unto the nations. I
could think the very words that they would say; I could see the
care that he would take of her; I could feel her perfect, happy
peace and trust with him.

It was in their faces every time that they came back. It was
writing itself there, daily, the most beautiful idyl of the spring-
time. They were not living it for themselves only.

"It is one of the perfect marriages," said Miss Euphrasia,
once. "Of which there is so seldom one that seems concluded
here."

"And suppose this had missed, — as it came near doing?"

"It would still have been. Margaret had found that out.
To belong to such is really to be joined," I said.

"Nothing misses, that is," said Miss Euphrasia. "Though,
as I said, it may not ultimate here."

"That is very vague, very spiritual. It hardly has much
promise of the life that now is, that we have all got to live."

"Does that seem so to you? I think it has promise of all.
Since the hour that cometh — in any truth of love or worship,
— now is, always. And one such outward fulfillment is a fulfillment, inwardly, for many. It is part and type of what is prepared for all souls, when they shall come into the Great Marriage, and be conjoined to the Lord. When we shall all be
numbered with the Saints, in the glory everlasting."

"That is part Swedenborg, and part Prayer Book, is n't it?"

"Yes. The word that is the lightening from the one part unto the other part, and all one heaven."

I think you know where Mrs. Regis spoke in that talk, without my putting her name in.

"It is a righteousness," I said, myself, to her, another time, when she had referred to its inevitable fitness, of her own accord. I always waited for that own accord. I remembered Emery Ann's wise-homely word, and would not "stir the cream."

"It is a righteousness; you see it now."

"I saw it then; or I should not have done it. But righteousness is a hard thing, too! It bears cruelly upon that which has failed of it! Which must help it come, but only outside itself!"

"My dear Mrs. Regis, — what do we mean by a righteousness? Or what do we suppose the Lord meant? Is n't it the *rightness* and the blessedness that nothing is to be finally outside of? And if we help it, ever so little, anywhere, is n't that the very proof that it takes us in too? Is n't it what we are to seek first, that all may be surely added? Mus n't it spread by its own living-ness, till righteousness and peace have kissed each other everywhere? To do one rightness, is to enter into all. To touch the outmost hem of the garment, is to begin to be healed in the inmost of ourselves. Certainly as we are waiting souls, of His Kingdom and His righteousness there shall be no end. Certainly as it makes us hunger and thirst because it is outside of us, we shall receive it to ourselves and be filled. He will never make us to ask for bread, and give us finally a stone!"

"I should be glad to read it so," said Mrs. Regis.

"I can't help reading it so. Life is full of it. The Bible is full of it."

"Your Life. Your Bible."   •

"Yes. Because everybody's life and Bible are just made to go together. Because everybody's Bible is most full of what their lives seem most empty of, most shortened in. Sometimes I think God shows Himself in as many separate Scriptures as separate souls; or as a soul's separate questions. It *all* answers *everything*. My Bible is full of promises to people who have to wait ; to give up things ; to give them *away*. Margaret said so true ; there are some things, after all, that can't be given away. ' If any one forsaketh anything for my sake, he shall have a hundred fold more, in *this* life. And in the world to come life everlasting.' Everything in us is planted in the image of the resurrection. And ' as the earth bringeth forth her *bud*, and as the garden causeth that which is *sown in it* to spring forth ; so the Lord God will cause righteousness and praise to spring forth before all the nations.' "

I was almost crying ; I felt it so deep — so real. I went down so deep for it among my own secret aches and lonelinesses, and brought it forth for this, my friend.

For Mrs. Regis and I are friends now.

She took my face between her two hands when I had said it, and drew it down toward her, and looked into my eyes.

" You are — just Patience — Strong ! " she said. She did not kiss me. She let me go. But it did not need a kiss of lips to tell me then that our hearts touched each other.

They seemed to bring all Rome into that room for her. She did not drive out ; the air high up here, over the roofs, was better for her, she said, and Dr. G—— allowed, than the air of the streets and the Campagna, that had poisoned her. It may be that the inexplicable climate of Rome tests very directly the condition of spirit, through which the body resists, assimilates, succumbs.

Edith and Stephen got no harm from it ; the glow of their delight, their young eagerness, carried them hither and thither, unscathed.

Emery Ann found her antidote in her pleasure over them, — for one thing. She had altogether forgotten that jealousy of propriety, — that alarm for Edith's simple, unawakened girlhood, — in the first meeting of the two in the labyrinthine corridors of the Hotel du Parc. She had quite relegated to the limbo of outlived and outlawed speeches that alert protest and warning of hers against the mere " was " of Edith's story. " He *is* — if anything ; and he 'll continyer to be ! " would, I believe, now, have been a hearty indorsement of Stephen Holabird, as she had found him out and adopted him into the circle of her confident friendships.

For another thing, she was shielded by her housekeeping. The lassitude of Rome did not touch her, active among her saucepans, — though she rebelled against the charcoal craters and the "shiftless ventolo-ing," with a continual declaration of independence, — and supreme with her own special parlor broom and feather duster. Also, she really enjoyed the excursions, and the reading up about them. Her incomplete New England district school education had kept her among the beginnings; she knew more of Romulus, and Remus, and Servius Tullius, and Scipio and Marius and some of the Cæsars, than she did of the Hapsburghs or the Bourbons, or does now of William of Germany and Victor Emanuel, or the complicated and transitional politics of her own country under General Grant. "Just," she said, "as she knew more about Exodus and Leviticus and Numbers, than she did of the Chronicles and the Kings; because she was always beginning to read the Bible through in course, and never got much farther than Deuteronomy."

Margaret and Paul Rushleigh walked in a charmed air; a perpetual catholicon of sunshine wrapped them round about; moved with them as their pillar of pure fire, burning away plagues before them. They never seemed to stay long away; except when they made their one or two outside excursions, they were rarely gone three hours at once. They went and came as the bees flit; as though the hiving home were the end and joy of it; not the mere buzzing into the honey-cups abroad.

Mrs. Regis's tables were covered with photographs. A large megalithoscope stood in a window, for which General Rushleigh brought her daily some new view, as he and Margaret came fresh from the seeing of the original. Over these they talked one by one, following each detail. They would let her miss nothing; they would not crowd, either, the mass of things she could not see, in one great hurried heap upon her. They planned, continually, how she should share with them as they went along. Unconsciously, but divinely led, they disarmed all chance for her of any apprehensive onlooking into what life might be to her, now she had given them to each other and put herself aside, alone. She could not get put aside, if she would. Life was full for her, — of their life and joy.

Flowers, in profusion, — handfuls, basketfuls; vases dropping with roses, heavy-headed with their own fullness of beauty; mignonette, violets, in broad dishes like beds of summer growth; always some new device, some lovely surprise, some untiring freshness. Fruits, — oranges, citrons, pomegranates; delicate wines, strengthgiving, that Paul Rushleigh knew how to take the pains to come at for her; a hundred comforts, raining all about her, from the overflowing upon her of a happiness that like God's own, must give again; from a real, warm love for her very self, also, that in all her life she had never tasted the like of before, and that drove her*self* out before it, turning it to a generous love again, as light and warmth leap back upon their sources.

Not bodily ministering, only, either; but spirit-sharing. Talks with her, of so many things; hopes, visions, brought to her, as to one who could enter in with them; yes, — because she had held the door, that they might enter in! Verily, it was already her reward. All her nature, at once, was being answered; woman, friend, mother — little child; for there is the little child in everybody that craves some cherishing, — nestles gladly and sweetly to some tender petting; and I think she had never been a little child, before, in this way. It came late and sweet. "I hardly know what age I am," she said, "between the deference and the caretaking."

"You are all the ages that ever you were, mamma!" said Margaret. "And you are to have the good of it now."

The great upper room in the street of the Cross-bearers was full of a true passover festival, — the *joy* of the bitter herbs and the unleavened bread, — the gladness that comes somehow with or after every pain, — the eating, with thanksgiving, of the flesh of the lamb that has been offered up!

Society also, the choicest in Rome, she had; though only a little at a time, as she could receive it. It gathered about her through her own natural claim and association, and through the longer residence and especial opportunities of Paul Rushleigh.

The H——'s came constantly, and seemed to bring their own sweet, poetic *chimney - cornerness* with them always. The S——'s came, with rich conversation, into which a life-time of art and thoughtful culture had distilled itself. The wife of the Minister sent kind notes and books; an accomplished attaché of the Legation made many an evening delightful with his endless store of historic fact and deduction and prophecy, — his chat of the day that was living history, his wonderful Italian fervor over Italian restoration. His English was so musical, — perfect in all essentials; so delicious in its few little slips and rapidities, that betrayed it was not native. " We are all Cattholiques," he said one evening, when we met him in Mrs. Regis's salon — " we Italians! But we do not all be-lief in the inflibbelty of the Pope ! "

" Pius Ninth? He blessed Maxime*l*ian; and Maxime*l*ian lost his head. He blessed Carlotta, and next day Carlotta went *in*-sane. He blessed Nap-oleon, and Nap-oleon died in exile. He cursed Beesmarck and Kin' William, and Beesmarck conquered France, and Kin' William is the Emperor of all Germany. He sent the Golden Rose to Isabella of Spain, and Isabella is *de*-t'roned. He cursed Vittor Emanuele, and Vittor Emanuele is Kin', and his palace is the Quirinal. I think I would be afraid of his blessing, now ! "

That was not half he told us; but it was enough to make me decide not to send the pretty carved rosaries I had bought for Mrs. Shreve's Joanna, and Aunt Hetty Maria's Winnie, to get his Holiness' blessing. I kept them till I got to Paris, and one day in the lovely, quaint old church of St. Etienne du Mont, with its staircase and gallery that goes winding up through the central space and along the mid-height between floor and roof, and at its shadowed aisle and chapel where the tomb of St. Genevieve stands within a golden grating, — I got the old priest to lift the little lattice-door and drop the beads upon the marble, and say his Latin prayers, and return them to me consecrated by their contact with the white sarcophagus of the girl-saint of Paris, the holy little shepherd maiden of Nanterre.

" I see that fresh consolations are still pouring in at the Vatican," remarked General Rushleigh, smiling, and taking up the " Roman Times " from Mrs. Regis's table. " Did you notice this? 'The Pope has received Lady L——, of H——, accompanied by rectors of the English colleges. She read an address to his Holiness, and presented to him a sum of 90,000 francs, subscribed by the young girls of the poor in England. The Pope thanked her cordially, and said that consolations were continually arriving to him from England, either by conversions or by marks of affection.'"

"The good old gentleman seems to have little now to do," said Stephen, " but to sit placidly at that receipt of custom."

" Sick bear," said Emery Ann, in the tone of ordinary remark. There was a laugh, and everybody turned toward her.

"I did n't mean to call him anything very impolite," she explained, changing her knitting-needles, and looking up composedly. "Only it puts me in mind of my brother Penuel and I, when he was a little boy. We each had a piece of apple-pie; and when Penuel's was gone he curled himself up in a corner, and said, 'Less play sick bear.' I asked him how. 'Oh, I 'm the bear,' he says, 'and I 'm sick, and this is my den; and you can come and feed me with pieces of pie.' And so I did; and it never come across me what the play meant, till I 'd fed away every atom of my pie without tasting it." She came to the end of her needles again; and changed her strip of knitting round with a little whirl, and sat perfectly unmoved otherwise, while everybody else, the " Cattholique " attaché and all, broke into a shout of laughter.

Emery Ann, in her unique way, never thrusting herself, but inevitably *herself* when she did come forward, — striking some spark of her own where a keener polish brought its edge to her native roughness, — was no insignificant element of the social life in our little sodality.

"Plain Emery," Paul Rushleigh said of her one day; "but of a substance with the sapphire and the ruby!"

I never thought of it before, I don't know as I knew it, — about the stones, I mean; but how true I know it of Emery Ann!

CHAPTER XXXI.

EMERY ANN'S COUP D'ÉTAT.

. . . . The ten days, the two weeks went by so. In the last week I saw less of them.

I had been kept up by vivid sympathies, and the. little things that I could do; but the Roman air had touched me also. I had been tired all the time. I had never been really rested after that first long day in the ruins. I had been content to share with Mrs. Regis, in the talks and photographs, many things that I must turn from Rome without actually seeing. Our second month for which we had taken our apartment began to look long to me. The languor of the rapidly-advancing spring fastened upon me.

The things that remained to be done became a nightmare. The "Beatrice" of the Barberini Palace, — the Guido's "Michael" of the Church of the Capuchins, — which I had not seen because they were close by, — haunted me with a reproach. I could not climb any more stairs; I could not stand about any more upon cold church pavements. My very powers of wonder and delight seemed fairly drained away. Things did not astonish or impress me any longer. I was acclimatized to the marvelous — I was *not* acclimatized to the malarious — atmosphere about me.

I had not been among the underground palaces of the Palatine; the Golden House of Nero was but a name to me. I had not been in the Catacombs; I had not seen the Columbaria. I had a weary wish they were not there; to trouble me with the missing of an enjoyment I could not hold out to enjoy. I could not feel the augustness of the Cæsars; hardly the sanctity of the Saints. I was under an apathy; and it grew upon me. One thing only seemed quick in me; the sense that my friends were going away, and I must be left to wait that month out. It was like being left for the last boat-load from a sinking ship.

But the children were having such a good time still! That was all that comforted me; that, indeed, was quick in me; and I tried, for their pleasure, as well as for the overstrained conscience one gets about these things, to fancy that I could somehow finish up what I had come for.

Stephen was close by, at the Hotel della Pace; it was like living with us. He came in every day; he made no programme for himself without us. But now, day after day, I let them go without me, usually with Emery Ann's matronizing; sometimes calling for Miss Euphrasia; sometimes, I am afraid, I let them slip away together, in the most unconventional fashion, taking the mere chance — or excuse — of possibly joining themselves to an elder party.

I had to sit with Murray in my lap, and the map of Rome spread out upon the table; trying to think what I could rouse myself to do, — to gather that I might take home with me. What, at least, I could comprehend from plans and pictures, while the descriptions of those who had been among the realities were still fresh or available.

Emery Ann watched me narrowly.

I could not make out that Golden House of Nero. I could not disentangle or combine my mental notion and location of it from or with that Nero's Palace they had told me of, which could be seen of a Thursday. Things are always to be seen on the particular days when you cannot possibly go. Whether there were two Neros, or two palaces, I do not think was at all clear to my mind. I believe I did not care how many there had been, if I could only shake off all personal responsibility about it. I came round suddenly through my morbid mood to Emery Ann's sentiment; forgetting that she had spoken it.

"What *did* they dig them up for?" I exclaimed. "Has n't the world enough to do *to-day*? I am out of patience with this dead and gone Rome that won't stay buried, though the Lord has put it underground and piled up centuries upon it! It has no business among the living, and what should the living seek among the dead?"

Emery Ann stood still in the door-way to the kitchen, with a moderator lamp in her hand; she turned about and looked at me.

"You can't pick all the berries in the pasture. And if you could, you could n't make them all up into pies," she remarked.

I looked up, listlessly. "I suppose not," I answered her.

"Nor yet you can't eat, forever, off the bushes," she continued.

"No; and I'm tired of meeting the dead-carts,— the ashes from the excavations," I laughed, faintly;—"and of smelling old decays. But the children are having a good time," I brightened up to qualify with; and I shut the Murray, and pushed away the map.

Still Emery Ann stood motionless. A new sense of the position seemed to be dawning upon her. Rushing up into broad day, rather, and turning into one of her convictions, which have life in them.

"No; you shan't!" she pronounced briefly, and with decision after a moment, but spake no further.

"Shan't what?" I asked meekly.

"*Be!*"

"Do you mean that for the verb 'to exist,' or only as an auxiliary?" · It drawled itself feebly from me, as ideas drawl themselves in falling asleep; and my smile relaxed itself as limply, almost without my will.

"I mean a line of poetry that I picked up once, that comes back to me now, that you shan't be!"

But she would nòt quote the poetry. She walked off into the kitchen with her lamp.

I let her alone, partly from my own strange passivity, and partly from a dormant recollection that things "ran in her head," and popped absently out at her lips when she was off her guard, and nobody — apparently — listening. I was conscious of a slight, helpless curiosity, and that if like Bopeep I let her alone, she would come back to the subject and bring the whole tale behind her.

She came in, and set the lamp upon the table. Then she took the duster from the mantel corner, and went round whisking among knicknackery and books. She came to the pile of

Baedekers on the side table. As she lifted it, she glanced over her shoulder at me. "'Butchered to make a Roman holiday,'" I heard her mutter slowly to herself, as one who hums a scrap of tune to get rid of it.

And that very day Emery Ann made her coup d'état. The Regises and General Rushleigh had gone four days before.

Emery Ann put her bonnet on, brought me a cracker and a glass of milk, said to Eligia: "Restate qui!" one of her set Italian cabalisms which she had learned to pronounce for the mystic influence to certain definite effects, — the natural connection with which she could not in the least imagine, — and cut her straight line presently across the piazza, down through the knots of Italian loungers, the groups of beggars and fiacre-drivers, and past a slow line of solemn priest-students; — a Yankee flash as exceptional across a foreign firmament as an Aurora stream might be above the equator.

In half an hour she came back again.

"I've done it," she said. "But I've left it, so's you can *on*do it, if you like. Only I guess you ain't got spunk enough."

"What have you done, dear Emery Ann?"

"Well — it's roused you to more words than I mistrusted. I've been to Shea's."

"To the house-agent's?"

"Yes. And I've put him in mind that he said if we did n't want to keep the rooms the two months out, we might have the privilege of underletting. And I told him I did n't believe we should stay — *if* we could git red of the rent. 'Consider the apartment rented at any moment,' he said, right off short. I s'pose *he* don't care how many times it changes hands, if he gets his brokerage every time. That was why I said *if*. 'It's a very favorite one,' he says; 'there'll be no difficulty at all. How soon will you give them up?' And he took up his pen to write it down. But I stopped him there! 'I'll tell you tomorrow,' I said. 'But if anybody inquires, they might call and see.' I've done my first piece of real estate business, and I rather like it!"

"Oh, Emery Ann!" I ejaculated, half dismayed in my

supineness, at her hurry. "I don't know about this. We might as well have taken it easily."

"Yes," returned the indomitable woman, "I do, alwers. But there's two ways of takin' a thing easy. You can take and leave it alone, — or you can take and do it!"

It was taken and done. Stephen and Edith came in, Miss Euphrasia with them, and stayed to lunch. Miss Euphrasia had been looking at me anxiously every time she had seen me for a week past; and every time she had asked me some question, — such as "did n't I think that *well* was an objection, right in the middle of our building?" Or, "Did n't I dislike that mortar-dust from the new hotel going up on the opposite corner?— Mortar was made here in Rome of a good deal of old, dangerous stuff;" or, "For how long did I tell her we had taken the apartment, and was I quite sure Rome still agreed with me?" Questions which all pointed from and toward the same thing; her suspicions that I was under the malarious influence, and the more than doubtful prudence of my making Rome my "continuing city." And as usual when a thing is once done, everybody had been thinking that it ought to be — or would be — or something; and all spoke at once all their withheld opinions and their eager counsel.

Stephen was delighted; he could take care of us all the way to Genoa, — perhaps even to Paris; for his own allotted time for Rome was really out, and he could make two days do for Naples; he would be back by the time we were ready; he would get rooms for us at the Della Pace; we should want to rest after our break up here; and he could leave to-night for Naples.

While we talked, there was a ring at the bell; three ladies and a gentleman come already to look at the rooms. They walked through, and were charmed; I told them, persistently, about the well, and that I could n't quite approve of the new building opposite. "Oh, there was mortar-dust everywhere in Rome!" And, "In these sunny rooms they should not certainly be afraid." They evidently looked upon my pale face and languid, worn appearance as quite a matter of time rather than place. Edith was blooming; even Emery Ann was rugged and wiry; in short, *could* we leave to-morrow?

It was all like a little private kind of earthquake. I supposed we *could* be toppled over and out in a moment, by catastrophe. Emery Ann undertook the inventory, and the grocer and dairy and bakery books; Edith the trunks; Stephen could do anything for us for the next three hours; Miss Euphrasia would stay and help.

The next day at noon, we were driven across the Piazza and down the Via Felice, followed by our hastily packed trunks, and our half arranged catch-all baskets; they laid me down, exhausted, on my bed in a small odd-shaped bedroom in a kind of corner tower, with little balconies. Edith plunged into the inner darkness of a room lighted only from mine and from the passage; Emery Ann went I never knew exactly whither; the kind hostess came up to offer any and every service; Eligia, already transferred to a new fealty with pots and pans, linen and silver, but clinging kindly and regretfully to us,—appeared amidst all the first confusion and electrified us with her big bowl of " nocche," as a parting attention; and our episode of Roman housekeeping was over, as it it had begun, in a whiff and whirl that was like the smoke of an incantation, or the explosion of some demoniacal advent and disappearance.

I had found out at any rate that I was really getting ill. The struggle of the removal, the half-fainting bewilderment in which I seemed to blindly endure those next two and a half days, in which final, indispensable errands were done and business concluded and trunks properly settled and corded, were something that I looked back on afterward as one might look back upon a drowning, out of which one had been dragged when just drowned enough to feel the small, indifferent, personal consciousness slipping forth into a vast inextricable identity with the merging flood that was swallowing it up.

Somehow it was over. Somehow all was done; dear Miss Euphrasia who had sat with me nearly all the last day and kept the quiet of her peace about me, had said good-bye to us again; the third morning — Edith and Emery Ann waiting upon me, and wrapping me up, — we departed from the hotel; we were driven once more through that curious mingling of to-day and fifteen hundred years ago, — the Baths of Diocletian; we

met Stephen Holabird at the railway station; (he had come
late the night before, breakfasted earlier than we, and preceded
us with our luggage;—what should we have done without
Stephen?) we had passed the walls, swept round from among
the scattered villas into the Campagna, caught our last glimpses
of the lonely, majestic arches of the Aqueduct, — of the reced-
ing city, and its mighty Dome, — and wound away northward
into the wild, desert beauty of the volcanic hills.

CHAPTER XXXII.

AS THE SWALLOWS HOMEWARD FLY.

. . . .

. . . . Is there a Shylock in you, Rose, I wonder, that demands the whole of the bond, to the limit of the letter ?

Of course, yes ; and in everybody ; and in everything else, also ; otherwise Shakespeare would never have been either written or read.   Otherwise some stern theologies would never have been in the world, answering to the Shylock in the soul of man, that will not let even itself off without the uttermost farthing.   Thank God for the Portia also, that feels and finds the blessed way of escape !

To the Shylock in you, then, — to the Jew in myself which you know possesses me to a demoniacal thoroughness, — the Portia in me comes to the rescue with this : —

I did promise that you should "go with me, every step of the way ;" that I would not skip, nor jumble ; that I would keep back of my own tracks, and follow them up with you.   Very well.   Did I say anything about bringing you *back*, in like manner ?

Rome was the end.   From Rome we turned our faces, gladly, homeward.   So, as the swallows fly, you will have to speed with me, in the pleasant twilight of a story, whose mid hours had their heat, their burden, and their pain, as well as their bright shining and their busy joy.

Back over the rainbow hills outside of Rome ; in whose air, clean from the dry volcanic rock, swept pure by winds that course from sea to sea above the crests of Apennines, — I began instantly to breathe a life again that swept out the old death of the Imperial City.

I cannot tell you how beautiful they were, that spring morn-

38

ing; soft, in their manifold convolutions, with a misty light, that made them look, themselves, like piled-up vapors; every lovely color in them, — gray, blue, amber, rose, peach, — up to the pure white that crowned them and married them to the clouds. Once, — at one surpassing point and reach, — I saw real, rainbow hills; golden and green and red and purple. Beyond and over the rainbows, a single peak lifted itself with summit bare and glowing in the light, and sides asmoke with a thin, fleeting drift of snow; like a fine, clear flame, the misty breath of it showing upwards, burning behind the nearer outlines. As we had gone back, — down — into the Past, through the same wondrous avenues of approach, the shadows had been dropped, thicker and thicker, with the closing hours, upon them. Now, we came up, out of them, in the morning. *Day* was upon the mountains! And *with*, — not against the day, any more, — we were to move westward, to our own time and home again!

As the swallows fly. Small time or chance, by the way, to score, except in viewless airs of thought, our wingbeats. (Small strength, for me, to do more, in the pauses, than reckon up the flights that had been, and bring their story even with its pledge. Far on the homeward path, — very near to the face to face rejoining in which the poor old pen shall be flung away, as we shall fling speech away some time, maybe! are the last chapters written for you!)

As the swallows fly. Perching, — do swallows perch? at quaint, old Pisa, first; gathering there, again, as the birds gather, in our full flock, for companionship across the land and sea to be retraversed. We overtook the Regises and General Rushleigh here, after a week of rest, in our turn, at Florence. They were just going, but they gladly waited. We found them at the Hotel de Londres, recommended thither, as we had been by mine host of the Alleanza. We found "stone tombs" again, as Emery Ann reported, when sent up to reconnoitre, — to sleep in. "With pink hearses, this time, in the middle of them. But I *will* say the sun comes in!"

Truly it did, — the broadening, mounting sun of the springtime! It lay all out over the level, upon which our windows looked. It glowed along the Arno, — this new loop of it by which we had alighted; it touched the curious, charming old French Gothic towers of the little church of Santa Maria della Spina (named from its thorn — relic of the Saviour's Crown, — I say it without a scoff, for it perpetuates the thought if it do not keep the reality it believes in) that we passed by, with a new pleasure each time, in a quiet corner of the Quay, when we drove along toward the bridge on our way over to the buildings that are the glory of Pisa and the world, in the far opposite corner of the city. It poured into the Square of the Dome, — it bathed with mellow light the beautiful tawny marbles of the Tower that leans, — the Cathedral, — the exquisite round of the Baptistery; it lay warm under the line of wall that shuts in the Campo Santo.

The Tower that leans! Before I went to Europe I used to say — how foolishly! "There are things I do not care for; that I am tired to death of already, in all sorts of prints and models and in everybody's talk. And the Tower of Pisa is one." How it bent above my head its majestic reproach, — its biding adequacy of deathless beauty to the repeated expectation — the re-echoed eulogium — of the ages and the generations!

"What did they make it lean for, — and *did* they make it lean?" There was not, to us, any question at all in the old problem. It leans, as the highest does lean; bends with the tenderness of a might; it slopes to the earth as the earth's axis slopes to its path about the sun. It bent down out of heaven, that was so deep and blue beyond it. It stooped as if to whisper some great, loving secret out of those depths; to strike softly, — we almost waited to catch the tone, — some mystic note with its bell-voice, that no note of bells hung far in an inexorable uprightness could ring down into the heart of the world! That which leans toward the near, the least, is perpendicular to some grand planisphere of suns. Who shall guess or say, now, what dim sublimity of apprehension moved the soul of the builder who made it point so, — silently, mysteriously, forever?

The Cathedral, with its aisles full of sculpture and paintings; its high altar, sumptuous with precious marbles and glowing with lapis lazuli — surrounded with pictures, — angels, saints, Abraham's sacrifice, and the Sacrifice of the Cross; the Roman

sacrifice of the Mass going on before it when we were there, so
that we passed quietly away into the side aisles, whence we
glanced back at the moving glitter of the rich-robed priests going through their offices, and the kneeling congregation gathered
in the choir, — catching more and more faintly, as we walked on
under the long arches, the chanted intonations of the service that
seemed almost to follow us with a reproach into our profane
sight-seeing ; — the Bronze Lamp that we came back to afterward, in the upper end of the nave, and stood before in the silence of the ended prayers and litanies, recognizing reverently
in it, as Galileo the truth-searcher had done, one of the everlasting signs of God's own mighty silences, swinging there in the
wonderful poise in which all things hang or tend to the earth's
great heart, and patiently keep their holy secret of Law for
them who will seek for it with all their souls ; — these were
what we entered into first, that morning among the structures
of glory.

Grouped here, immortally, — in the grouping of these marbles
of time, — the thoughts that came and were proved by them.
The swaying Lamp that told the mystery of Gravitation, beside
the Leaning Tower from which the seer of Science dropped his
different weights to the ground, and saw with a solemn triumph
that the lesser came as swiftly and as instantaneously as the
greater ; type again of all tending, and that the least among the
thoughts and souls of men draws with as sure a speed as the
mightiest, by the law that takes no count of bulk and weight, to
the Heart and Centre of all.

Sign again, — this simple lamp, — of the simpleness of central
fact ; to which correspond alike the first clear, single flash of
inspiration and the last aphorism of great deduction, though between must be all the ponderousness of appliance and mechanism, built for research, measure, demonstration. Between, — in
Galileo's Tribune, at Florence, — the great mass of means ; his
tubes and wires and instruments, by which he elaborated his
thought ; — before and after, the instant-quickened apprehension,
and the four eternal, dauntless words ! The vision in the Dome,
and the defiant whisper ; the swinging Lamp, and the " *E pur
si muove !* "

Into the still, green, sacred shelter of the Campo Santo next.

General Rushleigh was our guide; he knew well in what order to take us. Over the pavement of tombstones, around the many-windowed corridor that looks into the quadrangle filled with earth from Mount Calvary, and fresh with grass, and is walled on the other hand with stories in painting, — lives of saints and hermits, visions of Death and the Last Judgment, — the Mosaic Recital, from the Creator with the world in his hands, just formed, to the history of Moses and Aaron; from these the continued record along to David and Solomon; scriptures in stone that the old sculptors were never tired of, and the old world of art never full enough of. Roman relics placed along the gallery and in the corners, everywhere; sarcophagi with mythological reliefs; columns, vases, busts; — on the wall, high up, the old chains of the city harbor; — Greek heads, statues, monuments; bronzes; Egyptian antiquities; everything dead and buried, and yet living in a long human interest, — stronger and more investigating the deeper the ages have rolled over them. Was this the fitness, I wondered, of such a museum-arcade around the Holy Field of burial?

Out into the sunshine again, and across to the last, most beautiful, of the Three Buildings. To find here something grander, sweeter than all, in the exquisite circle of the Baptistery! The *round* again, that always holds an inscrutable charm, — reaches about with an ineffable significance!

In the middle, the great, marble Font; octagonal, — its sides rose-sculptured in double panels; three low, broad, marble steps running their successive octagons around it.

The Pulpit, six-sided, resting on its six trefoiled arches and its seven columns, one at every angle, and one central beneath; each alternate pedestal upborne by a great, carved lion; statues over the capitals; beautiful clustered pillars again between the entablatures, — these masses of most wonderful reliefs, representations of scenes from the Annunciation and Nativity to the Crucifixion and the Last Judgment; between these final subjects the reading desk, supported upon the great spread wings of an eagle, whose feet plant themselves grandly upon the half-pillar at this angle.

Back of the Font, a low Altar, with its Crucifix and six tall candles.

Around and above these three the wide circumference, the lofty dome.

Gospel; Belief; Gift. — Lord; Faith; Baptism. — Father-hood; Sonship; Holy Spirit. — These three: and the deep, perfect Unity, — the House of the Lord, which is the Heaven, — overarching and including them forever!

On the topmost step of the Font, by the rim of the basin, General Rushleigh stood a moment, and beckoned us to come near. I knew nothing of what was coming, nor did Edith or Emery Ann; but Mrs. Regis and Margaret moved up beside him and waited; and we followed. Just three notes of a chord of music he uttered softly, in the rich, clear voice I remembered on the Lake of Lugano. I had a second to remember in. And then — what took them up, as they floated into that deep arch overhead? What repeated, and combined, and dropped again the lovely intervals of sound, mingling them into all untold, wonderful, manifold chords and harmonies?

Winding, and winding, — floating, soaring; finer, sweeter, in each remoter circle of echo; till they seemed to melt away at last into a silence that was made, — like white light from all the rainbow, — of all the infinitely divided and multiplied threads of a celestial and undying music.

"From down here, — three notes — made up there into all that heavenly chime!" I said, when I dared breathe and speak again.

"Yes," General Rushleigh said. "It only takes little, single, feeble tones, to be caught up and repeated into all harmonies."

"And the higher they go, the more they multiply," said Margaret.

"So that when it gets to the *highest*," he said to her, — to *her* in a separate voice, as she stood by his side; but we all hushed ourselves, and heard it; — "when it gets to the highest, it is interpreted into everything. A breath is enough, below; as it goes up, it declares itself. It changes, and grows, into the joy of the angels. Above all, it unfolds to the whole meaning, that is Divine. And there, it is silent."

" Do you remember the *opposite* echo?" I asked him, afterward, as we went out.

He looked around at me quickly. "Yes; the echo of the *depth*. We had that among the Alps; the reverberation of the stone, dropped down into the ice-chasm!"

As we walked away, I looked back, — as I looked many a time in our movings to and fro, those few, marked days of our stay; as I looked, last of all, when the train glided slowly northward with us from the city, bearing us along the coast and toward Spezzia, — upon the Three; — the Tower leaning down, out of the sky, — the Church with its Altar, — and the Place of the Font, — that stood there speaking in their joint and separate beauty the same three great words — the Lord, the Faith, the Baptism!

Chiselings; architectures; things beautiful and wonderful to look at and pass by? Are these what we travel for? No: but the great Meanings that have grown living in the earth, and that the earth was made for, that from it we might pass into the heavens!

After this day of great things, we had a morning of charming little every-day things. Every day in Pisa, that is; for there is no such every day to be had anywhere else.

A morning among the alabasters. A long, low shop, running in, basement-like, from the pavement, under an old building; its shelves and counters rough and clumsy; its stone-floor cold and damp; its far corners gloomy in shadow, and a dimness everywhere, out of which gleamed the pure white shapes, crowding shelf and table. The delicate, translucent, soft stone, — something between snow and crystal in its spotless half clearness, — carved into every semblance of the rarest things in art and architecture and nature. Greek and Roman vases, models of temple fragments, pillars, obelisks, statuettes; all exquisite forms of birds and animals; caskets, cups, lamps; globes that were for lamps, also, to hang in the air like great white moons; above all, over and over again, — singly, and grouped, — in every size, and varied in tint from the incomparable fairness of the natural stone to the tawny and time-beautiful hue

of the edifices themselves, — the three piles of marvelous fabric
and figure, — the Tower, the Dome, the Baptistery.

General Rushleigh and Mrs. Regis bought many things.
Mrs. Regis set aside this, that, and this again, till a space had
to be cleared for her selections, and one large table hardly held
all she coveted. The counting up and thinning out came afterward, for even her purse could not indulge her reasonably with
all. General Rushleigh and Margaret chose together. The
lovely Roman vase with the doves, that one is never tired of,
— some beautiful dove-figures with hovering wings, such as
we have at home in biscuit, to hang by invisible wires, — some
statuettes — an Ariadne, a Faun, a Ceres of the Vatican ; a
great basin in which a tiny fountain might play for the middle
of a summer-room; a moon-splendor, — a globe of more than
a yard circumference, — that they lighted us all into ecstasies
with, putting a three-socketed tin candlebranch into it and setting it aglow with three soft flames ; — a large group-model of
the Three Buildings, — and last of all, a charming casket
wreathed with rose-buds and leaves for Margaret's dressing-
table.

I bought, among other modest bargains, a little globe upon a
pedestal, — a lamp for a corner bracket ; and Edith chose for
her mother a small copy of the Cathedral group.

It was our last day in Pisa. That evening, over our pleasant
dinner table, in our own salon at the hotel, we rejoiced over our
purchases, which we had left to be packed, and to be sent home
by sea all together.

"There is a room at Lakeside," General Rushleigh said afterward to Margaret, when he came and stood in the window with
her by Mrs. Regis's easy-chair, — "that I mean to put them all
in, — if you like ; and we will call it *Pisa*. There is a whole
wing of rooms that my father added just before his death that
have never been used or furnished. They run out toward the
water-side ; a drawing-room with a little *salon*, we should call
it here, at either side ; all opening together, very prettily. In
one of these we will put the Roman things ; and in the other,
the alabasters, — the basin, with a little fountain in it, the
moon-globe overhead, and the Cathedral and Campanile models

upon some table or console; the doves in the bay-window, with
orange-trees and oleanders and ivies. In the large room, we
will have carvings from Switzerland, and bronzes that we will
get in Paris; and all the pictures in all the rooms shall be pictures of things that we have seen together in Europe. We will
make a little Old World of our own, — and yet, such a *new*
world ! "

I half guessed the words he ended with ; he spoke quietly all
through ; but the last were with a nearer leaning toward her,
and a dropping of his voice into that tone which is more beau-
iful than a whisper.

" And mamma," said Margaret, who never leaves her mother
out when she can draw her in or make her one, — " mamma
will have a whole suite of alabaster rooms, I think ! "

"*Mamma*," said General Rushleigh, quoting Margaret's word,
with an indescribable grace of tone and smile, " will find a
suite exactly over these I speak of, with real Swiss balconies
that open right out into the linden-trees upon the lake-bank.
They are just the rooms for Lady Virginia to make beautiful."

He has given her this name, — his own name for her; for he
would not ever seriously call her " mamma," and he will hold
her a great deal nearer than he ever could do as " Mrs. Regis."
She smiles when he speaks it; she feels she has her own place ;
that there is something for her now in the world in which for so
long she has been " step-everything," that is own, and dear, and
tender, in which the late crown of her life blossoms with flowers,
and is full of a fragrance of all springtimes. . . . . .

Flitting along, by rail, to Spezzia. Through a lovely mountain region, — the mountains that reach their slopes down toward the sea ; — past heights crowned by old castle towers ;
through tunnels that pierce the great rocky flanks to come out
into new openings and windings of beauty between, — with
glimpses, far off, as we near the journey's end, of the white
veins of Carrara laid open and shining to the sun, — while on
the other hand the blue of the Mediterranean flashes more and
more broadly on our sight, — we skim over the shore that begins to be called the Riviera di Levante, and touch suddenly, at

last, the head of the beautiful gulf lying in its deep fork of the Apennines, and fold our wings for a day and a night at the fortress-guarded arsenal station.

We were to have taken steamer here, for Genoa. But we found that it would be a night trip, on a most uncomfortable boat. Neither Mrs. Regis nor I was equal to such an endurance, and so by beautiful accident we fell upon the decision which gave us still another day like a day of dreams.

And of all the visions through which we had been borne in our travel, sighing for very ecstasy, thrilling with pulses of pleasure too deep for speaking, — this day of visions between La Spezia and Sestri was fit to be the very last!

We were in carriages again ; the Regises and Paul Rushleigh in one, and we four in the other. The weather was cloudless ; the sunlight rained golden streams upon us, — it did not merely shine, — we climbed into cool airs that tempered it ; we went up and down among vast rocks that threw cool shadow ; but above us always was the deep blue basin poured full of the warm splendor.

Winding up and down, hour after hour, among those enchanted, desolate hills, robed in color, like the hills out of Rome ; made radiant through their very desolation. Wild, torn, ragged ; but mellow and bright in the distance, and in the softening air, with every tint to which volcanic fires had burned their substance ; — crimson, gray, yellow, relieved against masses of black ; great slopes and piles of the last looking like actual, enormous coal-heaps, but really broken out-crops and débris of black marble ! All the way along, grand glimpses of the Maritime Alps, lifting dazzling white outlines up into the sky, above the soft, misty colors in which their lower declivities lay.

As the afternoon fell lower, and the shades deepened and the lights grew level from the sun, the mountain-range grew wilder and wilder ; took indescribably strange and startling groups and forms ; until at last, over some summits whose sheer edges beyond us seemed like the end of all things, — as if from them we must drop off the globe into blue space, — we came, along their giddy brinks, upon the broad, glorious view of the Mediterranean ; smooth as glass, shining with color, as if the mountain masses we had seen all day were melted in it; blue, green, purple, silvery; out under the sinking sun, pure golden.

From point to point, repeatedly, we came upon this surprise. Always a great, last rampart, beyond which was empty sky; the roadway winding along the precipices and under the threatening of immense bare cliffs, — until nearer and nearer, we approached the verge; and lo! instantly the beyond revealed itself in glory, — the shining, outspread sea, the golden dropping heavens!

We wound down, behind the fortress-like bulks of mountains that shut all away again; deeper and deeper into rocky defile and chasm; a silence and a deadness around us that seemed apart from any living, breathing, growing world; and then, — a sweep, a level, a curving shore, a gleaming bay, a little fisher-village; a queer, rambling, musty, old hotel built around a court-yard at the head of a beach; old, old rooms, far away from the entrance through winding corridors; vast in size and height, with great canopied beds that might once have been beds of state, but whose hangings were heaped gray with dust; wood fires kindled quickly, in deep, ancient chimneys. And Saturday night had fallen, and we were nestled, as if we had got into some old rookery, — we wandering swallows, — at Sestri.

Sunday upon the beach. All day until we had to go in for dinner; lunching upon cakes and fruits as we sat there upon our shawls and cushions thrown down on the warm slope of sand; writing pencil letters, — reading a little from our Sunday books, but a great deal more from the great, illuminated pages of sea and mountain and sky. All day in the wonderful stillness, as if we had got out of the world. As if, it seemed to me, looking on that blue, blue water, in color most like the Geneva lake, as that is most like a sapphire; — water, — hemmed in by the grand headlands on either side and margined westward by the soft curve of the world and the heavens, — that came softly swelling in and whispering at our feet; while the fisher-people were spreading their great nets to dry all along the pebbly ridges, and the women were laying out white garments from their washing upon the rocks; — with that tender, sun-filled azure of the air bending and wrapping us all round;—as if. we were back beside the sea of Galilee where Peter and Andrew and James and John came in from their fishing, and Jesus stood in the little boat, or on the still, warm shore, and told them a gospel, that was larger than the heavens about the earth, and deeper than the sea, and tenderer than the shining from the bosom of the sun.

I felt so happy, getting out of the dead old galleries, into this live, quick, beautiful picturing, — this to-day of God! For, after all, painted moments are little; painted faces and mere groupings are nothing. The Lord meant men and women and little children, and the lives of them, to be his picture-gallery; making in each act and expression revelation and beauty for Him and for each other. The world ought to be so full of this vital representation, so rich in lovely instants, and we so earnest in realities, that there should be small pause or need to paint over and over the Past. Its truth and love should re-paint themselves, continually. As this bay between the mountains, this morning on the Mediterranean, make over again, on the day of the Lord, the day of his spoken word beside the Sea of Gennesareth. Nothing real was meant to have been ever stopped, or isolated; but to be born again and again, illustrating and gathering the old in the presence and quickening of the new. " God does n't keep the sunset, does He ? " a little child said to me with child-wisdom once. " He tears it right up and makes another."

" I was so happy, too, seeing Margaret and Paul Rushleigh walk up and down in the light, arm in arm, between us and the shining water.

Mrs. Regis, resting beside me, followed them with eyes intent, yet quiet. I knew it was sure to be all right with her. There was no need to meddle with the process. One need not meddle with a healing ache, — a newly-rooting plant of peace. The ministries of beam and breeze, and subtile strengths and harmonies better than we can find out the secrets of, are all about it, to restore and vitalize. We leave it quietly with them.

But it shows them forth in new, spontaneous motions, — in fresh-born, unfamiliar fragrances.

"What a curious word *other* is!" said Mrs. Regis to me, as we sat upon the sand. "It is nothing without its presupposed correlative. I am getting analytical, like you." And she laughed gently at herself.

"Yes; it is only half. Of two that are not so much separate, as one. *One* — and an*other*. That must be always another *one*. 'The others' are the rest. The other parts; the completion. What this stops short of, these fulfill. That is the greatness and gladness of human nature and possibility. One's self — one's life — without the others, — it does not hold the half, and never can!"

"I used to want to be in the rainbow though, when I saw it shining down into the trees and grass."

"If you were there, it would be only trees and grass."

"With a great light upon them!"

"Yes. But the *rainbow* is only for those who look from farther off. To see it, clear, is to be out of the cloud and the crying, in the full, broad sun!"

"It would be a different kind of a planet, if people could take life like that."

"Oh, dear me! how many different kinds of a planet it is!" said Emery Ann. . . . .

Thirty miles more of delicious carriage-journey; all day long, again, doubling and winding, creeping along overhanging verges, passing through galleries that cut the solid tongues of cliff, conquering promontory after promontory that stood precipitous in the sea, — gaining wild heights, and descending delightful zigzags into deep ravines; everywhere, the blue sparkle of the Mediterranean breaking upon us from turn to turn; everywhere, as we gained our way northward, the mountain masses growing greener, — clothed and in right, gentle minds, again, after the old volcanic heats and frenzies; forests, turf-slopes, vineyards; by and by a parapeted road beside high walls of villas that hung in mid-air over the waters; ramparts and towers guarding the twenty-mile circumference of the city throned among the hills, — a rapid trot down into its narrowing thoroughfares, its crowd and hum; and at twilight a stop in a

wide square, before a tall building and open entrance; bowing
hotel clerks once more taking our dusty wraps and ushering us
in; and we were lighted, — as the birds might light among its
palace roofs to rest and to be off again, — in Genoa the Superb.

Just to hide our heads under our wings, we elder ones, still
invalid and easily wearied. I was so tired! So hungry, too, for
more of the beautiful, fresh, unbuilt-upon earth! So incapable
of beginning again, after those days of sea and mountain, on old
palaces and churches and galleries. Our drive into it had given
us the best the city could give us, — the grand, general glimpse
of its mediæval splendor, its august position, seated on its high
amphitheatre slope, behind its double fortifications. At the
Hotel de Gênes, it was like everywhere else, a wilderness of
big halls and staircases and salons; a glitter of chandeliers and
a pomp of service; delicious, late, feverish dinners, — two of
them; an unpacking to rest, and a packing to start again; a
studying of Bradshaw, and a choosing of trains; the third noon
we were away again on the rail; the third evening brought us
once more beneath the white presence of the Alps, and then
into the brilliant modern streets and squares of the Pied-
montese capital, — the six-years capital of Italy under Victor
Emanuel of Savoy.

Rooms in the Hotel de l'Europe, on the great arcaded square
of the Castello. Emery Ann and I took our little hops along
the pavement, beneath the arched shelter, from brilliant shop to
shop; quite descended, in our surfeit of sublimities, and our
physical fatigues, to the commonplaces just around us; the
pleasure of merely pretty things; the delight, even, of exquisite
and delicious confectionery, that we bought in new and tempting varieties. We only went out for half an hour at a time;
it was just stepping from the door, and straying along in a
gorgeous bazaar, that did not seem like a street. We went out
and in again, back and forth from our rooms, as we happened to
feel; then we would sit with books and sweetmeats, in the long,
broad gallery that was used like a reading-saloon, between the
" Bureau " and the dining-hall. " It is so nice to be *let down* a
little, and just nibble sugar-plums in peace," said Emery Ann.

Edith and Stephen thought very much as we did. It was the

AS THE SWALLOWS HOMEWARD FLY.   607

least foreign place we had been in for long. It was neither old nor strange, they said ; but just "gay ;" though they, with Margaret and General Rushleigh, went over the ancient " Madama " Palace ; the dowager-house of a duchess of the early eighteenth century ; a castle, with towers, of the Middle Ages. It is the only Middle-Age building in Turin. We were fast melting off from the grandeur of antiquity to the smoother shows and garnish of to-day. The Palazzo Madama and the Armory, — where they saw the arms, gifts, trophies of Napoleon, Prince Eugene, and the Sardinian Kings, — both buildings a part of this same splendid quadrangle of the Castello, — were all the sights they went to here.

"And I'm thankful," said Emery Ann, "that there don't seem to be much more, to speak of. It's a burden on my mind, the things other folks undertake, after I'm clear wore out!"

So, a day and a night later, we took flight again. Up, toward the great mountain-barrier of the Alps of Savoy; through the heart of it, — by a way the birds know not of, through the long, awesome Tunnel of Mont Cenis.

We were coming into France in the springtime; it was now just upon the first of April. We were making haste, for every reason ; because of our inability to endure the fatigue of any more city life and sight-seeing; because it was essential to Mrs. Regis and me, — to all of us, I think, indeed, — to escape from the lassitude of these airs of Italy, at least in the crowded places where alone now we could conveniently have paused; and because Mrs. Regis and Stephen Holabird were both anxious to reach Paris by the beginning of the month. Stephen had got letters in Florence from his sister; she was leaving Nice for Paris, where she hoped again to be met by her husband; and Stephen himself, it was now decided, was to begin his medical studies in that city during the summer. Mrs. Regis had business ; she also expected to meet friends.

We looked forward with a kind of half shuddering expectation to our passage of the great tunnel. To run under ground, — beneath a whole, great Alpine spur, — eight miles and a half; thirty-five minutes of burial ; as long as from Boston out to

Hilslowe Mills It may not sound much; but it *is* much, in experience.

The lantern in the roof was ready, with its pale glimmer, for the plunge into darkness. There was a French placard, framed, and hung at each end, above the doors, which Stephen and Edith chattered over, until Emery Ann begged for a translation; and Stephen rendered it with impressive literalness: — "My lords and my ladies the voyagers are prayed not to affright themselves of the petards that will make themselves to detonate from time to time on the rails in the gallery; these are to make warning of the approach of the train to the mechanicians of the gallery."

"We are to run over a lot of big torpedoes, at rapid intervals, I suppose. How they will thunder in the 'galérie'!"

"We shan't, really?" exclaimed Emery Ann. "Why, it's awful!"

"They won't quite dare to blow us up, of course," rejoined Stephen, comfortingly. "Don't you see my lords and ladies are entreated not to agitate themselves?"

"Oh, dear; that's what makes it awful!" ejaculated Emery Ann. "I can't bear to have my mind prepared for anything! And those lanterns are real ghostly, waiting in the daylight for the darkness we're coming to. I do think such things are a tempting of Providence!"

"How high is Mont Cenis?" inquired Mrs. Regis.

"Nearly seven thousand feet, Baedeker says," replied General Rushleigh. "About the same height as the St. Gotthard."

"And we're to go under all that!" cried Emery Ann, really dismayed. "What if those torpedoes should crack something!"

"Under all that is the very strength of it," replied General Rushleigh. "If men had built an arch of so much stone, — with miles of piers and buttresses, we should think it pretty firm. And of course, Miss Emery Ann, — if it is any consolation, — we don't go right under the very central mass, I suppose. *That* is the pier against which our arch is built."

"I suppose it is all right," she sighed, relaxing just that breath's worth and no more, of apprehension, — "but the world is getting dreadful venturesome!"

Creeping along the great laps and knees of the mountains,

climbing by gradual ascents from the plains into the fastnesses, shut in more and more by the rolling of the vast cliff-scenery about us, — we came to the low, black mouth at last, that, under its frame-work of finished masonry, shows where the bold shaft plunges, seemingly, into the very heart of the earth; and the little gliding train passed in. The daylight faded, faded, — till the small, spark-like opening far behind ceased to shoot ever so feeble a ray to overtake us, till the dim lantern overhead glowed into consequence, a lurid, yellow, smoky light, like a light of Tartarus; the solemn roll of the wheels in the solid rock sounded deeper and deeper; the minutes lengthened fearfully. Think how long the seconds seem, when one sits for a photograph; and then multiply that seeming by sixties, and those sixties over and over again till you have made your half hour of it; a half hour of a buried midnight with an Alp overhead!

I think Emery Ann was really crying; I felt her tremble; and I got hold of her hand to comfort her. "Think of the strength of the mountain." I whispered to her.

"I guess I do," she gasped. "And I'm thinking of them petards!" But all was deadly silent, except the thick, dead rumble of the wheels. A light flashed now and then, at long intervals outside. It was from large lanterns kept burning, like lanterns in a mine; so deep, so far we were, if anything happened! The oppression of it grew like the oppression in the Gorge du Trient.

"I'm afraid they've *forgotten* the petards!" exclaimed Emery Ann, at last.

Stephen laughed; we had all been very still, and the laugh and the exclamation were a strange kind of cheer, reminding us of each other as bodily presences. It was so dark, with that poor, high-up, smoky lamp, that we and our wraps beneath were scarcely more than undistinguishable shadows. We just sat there and felt each other's thoughts in the awesomeness, as if we had been spirits in prison.

Just then, a small, polite, deprecatory, easy-as-possible little explosion. A mere snap; a popgun under those smothering thousands of feet of rock.

39

"Messieurs et mesdames les voyageurs sont *priés* de ne pas s'effrayer des pétards ! " cried Stephen with most absurd emphasis. And we all laughed, and the sound lightened about us, spread, somehow, out of the depth of smother ; a faint glimmer stole in past our windows ; away on, there was a spark of daylight again.

The air freshened ; the light broadened ; we slid quietly forth as we had slid in ; a river ran by at our left ; the mountains sloped back from a wide valley to the sky ; felled timber lay along a sandy level under a hill-side ; the track we were to follow bent and wound and doubled beyond, in climbing curves that confuse themselves in my recollection ; Emery Ann hastily brushed and sniffed away her tears, and said, cheerily, in a voice that seemed to belong to quite the other side of the Atlantic, and to have been produced from her traveling-bag like a forgotten home-cordial, — " *That's* off our minds, anyhow ! And I will say it's a credit to somebody ! "

" And we are out of Italy ! " said I presently after, as we came into Modane, and stopped for the weary examination at the customs. " Good-bye to the land of beautiful, old dreams ; of sculptures and pictures and histories of thousands of years ! "

" And good-bye to tomb-houses, and pink hearses, and slow fevers, and fleas ! " said Emery Ann. " But Ittle-y's a beautiful place to look at, too ! " . . . .

Skimming along woody slopes, — dropping into widening valleys ; leaving behind us, more and more, the wild Alpine grandeurs. Sweeping our swift way from the Arc and the Isère to the Rhone, and the Saône ; reaching at night the old, wine-trading city of Macon.

A fascinating little " Hotel de l'Europe," an arched porte-cochère opening to a paved, sky-lighted salon green and gay with plants and blossoms, shining with gas-lights ; four French-women, — a mother and three daughters, — keeping the house, and meeting the new guests with bewitching grace of French smiles, and gestures, and politesse ; *dressed*, to the shaming of our dusty travel-wraps, in silks and velvet ; their little bureau-room, half shut from the entrance-hall by large slides of glass,

and daintily fresh with flowers; on the other side a large drawing-room open with long windows to the quay, and sleepy, slug-
gish, canal-like river; up-stairs, endless winding of corridors
and confusion of bedrooms; and we at length, after delicious
broiled chicken, biscuits, wine and tea, tucked away in our separate nests, to flutter out and find each other as we could in the
morning.

That was the wayside lighting. That was all we saw of
France between the Savoyard frontier and Paris.

CHAPTER XXXIII.

BUILDING UNDER THE EAVES IN PARIS.

. . . . Just as the swallows do. Bringing our sticks and straws, and building a nest, just for six weeks of the spring-time, under the eaves, in a strange city.

For it was a new place this time. Quite another Paris than the one we stayed in for five days last year. Then we were in the old Rue de St. Honoré; back of us, and all around, the ancient, narrow, crowded, crooked thoroughfares of the old Paris, in which we wandered and lost ourselves in very small circuits, and only brought ourselves up by the central landmark of the Place Vendôme, where we got our money and our letters, and wondered at the facile Parisians building up carefully the pillar in the midst, which they had torn down in a provident, prescient fury that took time to put away all the pieces!

Now, our daily ways lay along the grand, new boulevards, and through the gay, open squares. How alive it was! With the spring freshness, the green of the grass and trees, the sparkle of the sunny waters!

"It's as if we had come up from underground, through that old tunnel!" said Emery Ann.

Yes; this was the life of the upper earth; of the very peel and surface of it. This was the smooth cuticle of to-day that covers all; underneath, in Rome there, and all through sombre, beautiful Italy, — underneath here, also, as well, only with blithe decency *kept* under, — were the bones, the time-patched lesions, the inheritances of disintegration and decay.

Bringing our sticks and straws; which were first our big "bagages," that arrived after three weeks' meandering by "petite vitesse" from Florence; Edith's canvas-covered London basket with the lock wrenched off and carefully laid inside, — the cords replaced, and everything within in apparently untouched order after the unprotected transit from the frontier, — no lace or ribbon rumpled, no pin-box out of place, — but half-way down an Italian grammar — just where she herself had put it, — with a blank leaf doubled down, on which was politely penciled, "Ouverte á la Douâne." My fac-simile, — half full of photograph portfolios, a Roman lamp or two, and a bronze model of the Coliseum, — had passed without inspection beside it. Other straws — for plenishing and comfort — gathered here and there in the shops of the boulevard, around the corner we had chosen. But this was not till after a week at quite the other end of the great city; in which we had picked up crumbs and fluttered pleasantly enough in and out of a high-railed, cage-like little pavement-garden, that opened — and opened only — from our long windows on the ground-floor of the Hotel du Palais, away up on the Cours de la Reine.

We thought we never should get there, that after-midnight of our arrival; when we had been whirled along the endless quays, — across illuminated bridges, — up broad quays again and past great squares gorgeous with gas-light, — a perfect galaxy of out-stretching constellations unrolling their interminable mazes as we rushed on; until, as Edith said, "it was as if we had been let loose in the starry universe, to hunt up our own particular little world that had been put out."

We came to it, out in the far edge however; and we fell upon its utter darkness, as we might have supposed. The next day, or the dawn of that same morning, revealed to us our surroundings; a suite of pretty rooms, — except that one was a *dark* bedroom, — and the trellised veranda leading forth into the little ivied garden aforesaid.

But pleasant as it was, we could not make our nest there; because we soon found that the charming ground-floor apartments would not do. Rome will have her tax paid, sooner or later, within or without her own borders; Edith and Emery Ann both began to be ailing here; and nothing would be safe now but high, dry air, and sun-purified spaces. Also General S—— and Mr. C——, United States Ministers, were exchanging office and civilities; and the incoming dignitary had his rooms and his dinner parties here; and we had to live more like birds of the air than we fancied; bits here and there in odd corners, at odd times; the regular table d'hôte entirely boule-versé, and all system disregarded. We preferred to know when and where to find our modest, unofficial dinners; so Stephen and I scoured up and down, with a broker's list, all the way on the right bank of the Seine, from the Arch of Triumph to the Boulevard Sebastapol, for a sunny apartment of three or four pieces, and found it not, without some drawback that neutralized all answer to our requirements.

Mrs. Regis had rooms on the entresol, facing south upon the sunny "Cours" and the river. She bided patiently the blow-ing over of the diplomatic turmoil, and the recovery of the head-waiter, who was disastrously sick. Stephen had established himself in students' lodgings in the Latin Quarter, and was stren-uous with us to give up our prejudices, and go over to the left bank, where were plenty of rooms, he said, with twice the air and sunshine for half the money. At last one morning, when poor Edith had not risen to breakfast, and Emery Ann, after waiting upon her with some, had gone back to bed herself, Stephen came again, with a fiacre, and insisted that I should at least drive over to the Boulevard St. Michel, and see what he had found at a large, new Maison Meublée on the corner oppo-site the Square and the beautiful bronze Fountain.

St. Michael, and the sword, and the dragon, again, of course. Magnificently cast and grouped, at the top of the pile of mimic rock, down which rushed the clear-falling water. A great, open space, full of sunshine; a wide avenue running straight from the Pont St. Michel to the Place of the Observatory. On the first corner beyond, the tall, white hotel building; — its angle upon the street cut off, according to the recent law that leaves no sharp turns of building to shelter insurrectionary surprise, — its balconies, one above another for five stories, across this sec-tion, full to the southwest; blossoming plants, tier above tier, filling them up before the long, open windows; a cheery, "above-ground" look all around, that I knew Emery Ann would appreciate; and I climbed bravely the three long, double stair flights that led to the one unoccupied balcony suite.

Well, this became our nest. Here, that very evening, we brought our invalids, our sticks and straws ; here, within a wonderful circle of new delights, — Notre Dame and Sainte Chapelle close by upon their island over St. Michael's bridge, — the Pantheon, the Luxembourg, Saint Sulpice, St. Etienne du Mont, the flower markets, all within every-day walking, — if I took them one at a time, and once in a while, as I meant to do, — and dear, lovely, shady, solemn old Cluny on the very next square.

We were sorry to leave the Regises ; but then we went back to them every day, almost, or they came to us ; and it was delightful to be driving round almost every day, by that airy, sparkling, joyous Place of Concord, and the green Champs Elysées with their lily fountains.

Does everybody notice, I wonder, how perfectly the white spray curves into the tall flower-shape, with the denser central column shadowing forth the slender pistil in the midst ? Scattered up and down beside the wide, shaded avenues between the great, beautiful trees, — they open up their vases to the light, created new continually, alive with the gentle music of their growth ; the pure, colossal, softly-splendid water blooms.

There was always sure to be some errand, — to Galignani's or the bankers, — if not the particular plan of our day together, — to take us round by that turn ; and anyhow I do not think we should ever have come home contentedly without it.

The mystery of getting well is known to few physicians ; and those few know it by something independent of their art.   All medicine is but the flinging of a rope — either to body or spirit : something that it will take to, and cling to, and so be drawn back into its natural relations.   And the best rope — all doctors know — is that which is flung out to the spirit.

Emery Ann got well from the time she found out that the "rez de chaussée" of our hotel was a large, fine grocery ; whence, stepping down to it, without even the ceremony of a hat, one could order tempting little pound boxes of butter with cool green leaves laid over them ; fresh little brick shapes of Swiss cheese, white and tender, done up in tin foil ; fruits, fresh or deliciously preserved; biscuits; honey; what one pleased. When, also, she discovered that corresponding, at the opposite corner of Rue St. Severin, was a wonderful repository of every kind of housekeeping article; from delicate, odd china that you could pick out in single pieces, in charming variety, unbelievably cheap, to skillets and flat-irons; that half a dozen doors up the Boulevard, was a little bit of a confectioner's shop, where could be had meringues, ices, gâteaux à la crème; — which last means a kind of pudding-cake, delicate and spongy, covered with a froth custard, piled up high and beautiful and just brought with a touch of baking to a pale buff crust, and of an exquisite coffee flavor like its color; — that, in short, there was real housekeeping to do here up under the eaves, in all sorts of novel and convenient little French ways.

We ordered our dinners sometimes, in the house; sometimes Stephen came for us, and we walked up two squares to a restaurant, where for ten or twelve francs for the whole party, we could get a dinner of four courses and wine, from a delicious soup to a dessert of raspberries, strawberries, or a "petit pôt de crême;" which means a tiny custard, — through intermediate fried soles or salmon, green peas, chicken or turkey or beef, and cauliflower or artichoke or Brussels sprouts as a separate vegetable. Sometimes, again, we all went, or met together, — the Regises and our party, — in the Palais Royal, and ate a similar "déjeuner" there, sitting by windows that looked out into the green, lovely garden-court, full of trees and fountains. Our breakfasts and teas we partly ordered and partly made from our own stores, at home; and six o'clock, regular dinners we utterly abrogated.

Edith got well from the time that Stephen Holabird came, that second morning, springing up the long stair-ways, to herald a florist's cart that was at the door below, with plants for our corner balcony; fuchsias, dropping their coral rain of blossoms; roses nodding with bloom; great bushes of heliotrope, purple, perfumy; miniature beds of mignonette and violets, in boxes, to set upon the sills. How proud we were, setting forth our show, that said to our neighbors, We, too, have made up our home, and it is blossoming into your faces as yours into ours.

Edith brought a low stool and sat in the shadow of the tall full plants, and breathed their incense, that the sun, sifting through, warmed richly from them. She took them under her special charge, and for her special delight, from· that moment; and they ministered back life and strength to her.

I got well seeing the others better, and resolving to take just life as it came to me, and not count myself a traveler or a sightseer any more. I should have daily walks and drives: and I could not help the sights I should that way come to ; but I put Baedeker down under a pile of winter flannels in my trunk, and resolved not to look at him for a month if I could help it ; certainly not to give him the least of his old despotism over my movements here.

I watched an old pair who had built over opposite; above the eaves, as we were under. I looked up to their balcony which ran all along one side of the Mansard-roof, out from whose windows they used to come for their lofty promenade and airing. I doubt whether they ever came farther down into the world.

They were old people ; man and wife ; French, indisputably. There they lived, and chattered to each other. Past migrating; past new annual nest-buildings; content in their high perch, quiet and resting away up beyond all the din and rush of the busy streets. The old man, in his flowered dressing-gown and scarlet slippers, would emerge first of a morning ; he would walk up and down the narrow balcony floor of two planks, — (how I looked up from *under*, and realized with a half shiver the slight foothold that held him in his airy walk fifty feet above the crowded pavement!) hardly finding room behind the oleanders and orange-trees and laurestinus that made his hanging garden ; then Madame would come forth with her fresh face under her white curls, and hang her canary against the wall ; and a little dog would find space under their feet and among the flower pots to run a few irregular turns back and forth, and then put his black nose through the railing, looking abroad like a dog that perfectly understood his high position in the world.

I hardly know which I was most interested in ; the roof-dwellers or the orange-women, away down underneath, on the sidewalk corners; sorting their fruits, half peeling the most tempting ready for the consumer, chatting with their com- mères that came up and down.   Then there were the charity school processions, with the quiet, black-robed sisters marshal- ing them along; the bourgeoise women going to and from the markets; the bakers' carts with the six-foot rolls laid across the front, for sign; and every now and then, somebody half shoul- dering one of these amazing lengths of bread and carrying it home.   All these amused me, and enchanted me into rest and health again.

We drove out, — in the mornings mostly, — to the Bois de Boulogne.   We went once in the afternoon, and fell in with the interminable line of carriages on fashionable parade; we passed in review the fine toilettes, the made faces, the glitter of caparison; we delighted in the magnificent *horses* for a while; and then the dust choked us, and our eyes were weary, and our hearts and heads ached with so much humanity all in one poor external phase; and we said to our coachman, "Turn as soon as you well can:" and he wheeled us instantly about through the seemingly hopeless double line, and fell in with us to the returning stream.   Back by the Arch of Triumph, looking down the splendid slope of the Avenue des Champs Elysées, we saw the finest of it, the great mass; a sea of equipages, whose waves were tossing manes, proud heads, the sparkle of rings and buckles and all rich mountings of glittering harness, the roll and flash of countless wheels; — we came down our- selves through the midst into the cool shade again, and thought the common people had the best of it, sitting on the benches with their needle-work and knitting, — their children, — their chats with groups of friends, — while the wind lifted gently the foliaged branches and whispered over the bright growing grass, and blew aslant in vanishing white mist the broad corol- las of the lily fountains.

But the Bois was perfect in the mornings, when the world was not there.   Away out, beyond where the trees were ruth- lessly hewn down for the siege, — among the lakes and the châ- lets, the cascades and the grottoes, around the lofty sweep where the avenues command the valley views, and the heights of Fort

Valérien; and home through the arrondissement of Passy, by
he Bridge of Jena, and the Long Quays, past the Field of
Iars and the esplanade of the Invalides.

We shopped in the Palais Royal, — that bewildering place,
where everything so sets off and displays everything else,
nd all so entices and bewilders with the sense of absolute
novelty and improcurability elsewhere or forever, that you lose
ll comparative judgment and calculation, and buy blessedly
nd recklessly; where Emery Ann told me I was " wasting
my substance in riotous giving," when I bought a charming
little silver portable clock for Gertrude, and a fascinating Rus-
ia leather traveling-bag with the furniture of a whole dressing-
oom in it for Eliphalet, and trinkets of the loveliest crystal and
namel flowers for the girls — Gertrude's and everybody's, —
nd sleeve-buttons and belt clasps, and viniagrettes and châte-
aines for general distribution; in my happy fever of nearing
ome and wanting to bring all Europe bodily to you all.

We went after new hats, — that we all needed — with Margaret and her mother. We saw the new fashions, — the par-
erres and the aviaries, — yes, the Zoölogical gardens, — that
head-gears are growing into; we turned over heaps of distract-
ng French flowers, bending and trembling on limp, cool stems as
f just cut from the growing; lilies, hyacinths, May roses, carna-
ions, grapes, currants, cherries, bright little apples, berry sprays
nd clusters, defiant of seasons; birds, butterflies, ladybugs,
dragon-flies, green and gold lizards, — absolutely, tiny gray squir-
els with shining eyes, — only these last were for winter wear;
— *owls !*

" Why would it not be that a camel might be pretty?" suggested Edith, simply, to the modiste. "A camel, and a date-
palm?"

"Or a hippopotamus," suggested Emery Ann, when we
laughed and translated, — "among some big bulrushes? I presume we *shall* see the lion and the lamb lying down together,
before long, on the same bonnet! Won't it be beautiful?"

We drove up and down the boulevards at nine and ten o'clock
n the evenings, to see the gay gas-lighted world of out of door

Paris. And all Paris is out of doors. You know, without my
telling, how they sit on the broad sidewalks, at the little, round
tables, eating ices and cakes, drinking light wines and beers,
reading and chatting the news and gossip of the day in the clear
illumination of the countless lights. But you cannot imagine,
without going out into the midst of it as we did, after our prim-
itive, Dearwood and Hilslowe bed-times, — and finding the immense glitter and life and motion into which you plunge outside
your threshold, and to which there seems no end, from blaze to
blaze of avenue and square, along miles of splendid thoroughfares, — across the bridges, past the tall, dark tower of St.
Jâques, — down the Rue de Rivoli, parallel with the Quays and
the river, — around through the Place de la Concorde to the
Madeleine, back by the old gates of St. Denis and St. Martin,
midway in the grand semicircle of the Boulevards — the Ital-
iens, Montmartre, Poissonnière, and the rest, — that sweep
around four arrondissements to the Place of the Bastille and
the Quays again, as far up from your central starting point on
the Seine as the Place of Concord is down.

You cannot imagine the multitudes of human beings, that are
not *crowds*, or special gatherings, but just the great, continual,
effervescing *deep* of population that overflows into the city
spaces and foams up and down, a ceaseless airy dance of atoms,
— a seethe of yeasty bubbles. You cannot think what the light
is, that replaces the day with its gorgeous, lavish illumination, as
if for some feast or triumph. Every shop sign is a device of
flame-tips, spelling with flaring burners its advertisement.
Every shop window is an Aladdin's cave of some special, unlim-
ited treasure. Each kind of ware is made imposing by mass
and multitude ; one window is a mountain of straw hats, piled
up and up from pavement level to ceiling within ; another is a
silver grotto of teaspoons ; another a sea-cave of lovely, delicate sponges. And the windows of bronzes, and the windows
of jewels ! Rose, you would n't have believed it if you *had*
seen it !

We came to things as we went along. We meant to ; and we
could n't have helped it, either. We grew used — not *blunted* —

o the exquisite architecture of the Pantheon, as we caught sight of
; daily, up the side street that ascended to it from the boulevard
it. Michel ; to the grand double Gothic towers of Notre Dame
ising up out of the river-midst ; to the beautiful old galleried
ont and curious unmatching turrets of Saint Sulpice ; — we
new by heart the bridges and statues, and gardens, — the col-
mned glory of the Bourse, the solemn stretch of the Louvre,
ie shut-in square of the Carrousel that has earned its name by
opular tournaments, undevised by kings, since it got it first
om the gay joust of Louis the Fourteenth ; we passed to and
o the ruined buildings of the Ministries, the devastated west-
rn front of the Tuileries, the wild cinder heap that had been
ie Hôtel de Ville.   We " realized " our newspaper history of
iree years ago.

It all grew to belong to us ; the glory and the wreck, — the
ntouched, time-mellowed landmarks of the abiding centuries,
nd the landmarks of blank and destruction made by the fury
f the present-passing years.   I laid up these aspects, these fa-
iiliarities, for an old and new association and knowledge to
ather to and be illustrated by ; so much of Paris was becoming
piece of my own living, to which I could refer, and around
hich I could recognize, always, hereafter, the things of which
remembered, or might learn, that it was scene and centre.
Ieanwhile, I was sensible, sometimes, — waking, perhaps, of a
iorning, or when I had got lost in a quiet thinking of many
iings, sitting alone for a half hour in my room, — of a queer,
reamy feeling, — a confusion of places that I had got so many
uccessive impressions of in different sojournings, — out of which
had to shake myself to present consciousness, and *place* my-
elf with a quick mental running over of names ; Florence, Lon-
on, Milan, New York, Boston, Geneva, — ah, yes — *Paris!*
is we lose ourselves, sometimes, in different rooms of the house
re live in ; living over in a dream the things that have happened
ere and there — yes, — in the very spot where we are dreaming,
nd where we seem to have left and forgotten something of our
odily selves in the mere bodily surrounding, while the spirit
vas away in the spirit place it stands for.

· · · · · · ·

. . . . How can I tell you of what even *I* did and saw, more than this slight, glancing synopsis? If Paris had been at the beginning, instead of at the end, I could have done no more. It is such a world of things and life; — the present and recent, as Rome is of the old and gone. For even the old and gone seems fresh in Paris, somehow, as if of only yesterday; and so it crowds and rushes upon you the more. It does not wait to be dug up, and studied out; it flashes upon you at every turn. Because it is all history of a live people, not of a dead; it all reaches down by living threads into to-day, and pulls at the present, palpitating moment.

How can I possibly tell you, then, what these weeks were to Margaret and Paul, — to Edith and Stephen, the children — ah, children of *last year*, Rose! I began to find that out, before — well, it was not much; but I will tell you presently.

Their drives and saunterings, — their lovely, sunny days at the Trianon, at St. Cloud, at Fontainebleau! Their flittings in and out, their young, untired seeing of half a dozen things and places to our slow, elderly one; their absences, — I mean Paul's and Margaret's now, for it truly never entered my head to think of the boy and girl as of the man and woman; and I know, it did not really, definitely, enter theirs; their absences, that were not blanks but full of beautiful interest — that were poem-days — to me, in my sympathy and involuntary following of their happiness; their comings in, with the light upon their faces, and some new telling, of enjoyment, of discovery, of acquisition, on their lips; — these, rather than any of the sights or sounds of Paris, marked and made most living our living there. And these cannot be told. But the beauty of them and the gladness that such things are in the earth, comes without the telling, and is also a possession, a laying-by, for us even who are only with it for a little while, but to whom it is an interpretation of a reality that is as much ours as theirs forever.

Edith was a great deal now, with her great friend Barbara. Lieutenant Goldthwaite had got two months leave. The Katahdin had been ordered home, and he had come out in a

French packet to meet his wife here, and accompany her back.
They, with Stephen, — to say nothing of Bud, — quite monop-
olized my child. They were always coming up the river in
one of the little "mouches," — the tiny steamboats that ply up
and down continually with passengers, like river-omnibuses;
and were carrying her back with them, or away down and out
to St. Cloud, or even back and forth, through the whole city
between Bercy and Auteuil, — by the same gay little water-
flies; or calling for her of a bright morning, — and nearly all the
mornings were bright — in a nice open carriage, and taking her
off for a drive out to Vincennes or St. Denis, and keeping her
all day with them. It was all Holabird as well as holiday, with
her now, we told her. So Emery Ann and I had chances to
stay by ourselves sometimes, in the nest under the eaves, and
rest; or tidy up our walking and traveling suits, between the
wears and tears; or write, — as I did these long pages, hurrying to catch up with myself before I should get quite home.

Mrs. Regis, as she grew strong, made herself busy about the
trousseau. She seemed to put all her heart into the gathering
of lovely things to make lovely, and "comfortable," in the most
perfect sense, this life, this home, that were to have visible being
from the invisible blessedness between these two. No, it was
not all just between them, — even the positive tenure and enjoyment of it. The mother, — the friend, — the gracious,
queenly woman from whose open hand and deep heart ran
ministry and sympathy, — was throned, — was more than
throned beside it; was taken in and held dearly almost in the
heart of it. It was to be her life, henceforth; for they had
made her promise that she would not leave them. They came
to her with everything; and she found her pleasure in new
surprises of her bountiful care for them. She was growing to
be the woman of all womanhood in their joined esteem; this
that she would have been to Paul, alone, she was becoming to
Paul completed; what she would have seemed at a mere acci-
dental and uncertain tangent of his life, she was being made at
its permanent centre; she was rising to the greatness that was
offered her; partly, doubtless, from that very flaw in her nature, — if it were one, — that could not bear discomfiture and

unsatisfaction, — but none the less certainly. The Lord knows how to make stepping stones for us of our defects, even ; it is what He lets them be for. He remembereth — He remembered in the making, — that we are but dust ; the dust of earth, that He *chose* to make something little lower than the angels out of.

The generosity of this woman, that was generous because it could not be comfortable in anything less, — that defended itself by its own extreme from any possible or past meanness, — that chafed against any conscious half-readiness as a tide against a barrier, — ran over, overbore the thing it struggled against ; flowed wide into a new place ; grew tranquil as it spread ; became a sea of a new being over which a new morning dawned.

Just a little of the restless rush, doubtless, was in the first busyness ; a little of the determined not-recollecting that makes other thought a continuous will-cataract aside from it. But I look back now, to those eager rapids, and I can see, already, how all their hurrying was only toward the great, sure, shining calm.

I was waiting for them all one day in the great Egyptian Hall of the Louvre. We were to go up together into the gallery, and afterward to spend an hour in choosing some silks and laces at the Magasin du Louvre over opposite. They were belated, somehow, and I had a half hour to myself, among the sarcophagi and sphinxes. Emery Ann had gone with Edith and the Holabirds to buy cuckoo clocks.

I sat here thinking some of the thoughts that I have just been writing down ; gazing, also, at the great, strange forms about me ; and I wonder if the things in my mind had something to do with the meaning that seemed to grow to me out of the huge sphinx-shape that lies so prone, and yet erects itself so grandly, in carving of dark-red stone, there by the entrance.

For, all at once, the meaning of the Sphinx seemed to tell itself to me.

It is just the human nature, whose double attitude could in no other outward figuring be combined. Prone, — the animal form, — upon the earth; resting, upon the material, — since rest must have some basis; a mighty repose revealing itself so, that feels underneath it the everlasting, tangible facts; — erect, as to the head, with a life and power that are grand under the light of the broad heaven; one can think of it so, in that far desert space, waiting sublimely through the ages; — a combination of two postures that are incompatible together, in the mere animal, or the wholly human, — that is, godlike.

Is not that it, — the riddle and the allegory of man, — the natural and the spiritual, by which he leans upon the earth and lifts up his face unto the skies; *lays down*, also, his earthly, that his heavenly may be the more freely lifted up? So that by the very feebleness and mortality of the mortal, comes the forgetting of it all in the repose upon an eternal strength, and the calm upraising of his expectancy, which is divine, toward that eastern horizon, out of which, already, walks the morning?

"There are two things in that sculpture," said Mrs. Regis, standing beside it with Paul Rushleigh, afterward. " Rest — and hope."

Paul Rushleigh said it all — repeated it rather — in two sentences.

"It is the 'flesh, also, that resteth in hope;' 'the earnest expectation of the *creature* waiting for the manifestation of the sons of God.'"

"Thank you, Paul; you always *fulfill*, for me."

Something that had shone for an instant upon Virginia Regis's face when she had stood with him on the Wengern-Scheideck, and the Silberhorn had flashed out upon their vision from above, seemed to have descended to abide upon her, now. It was changed; it was growing into a more gentle peace. I thought it was the beginning of the peace of being *numbered with them* who dwell in the light everlasting.

We crossed over into the Assyrian Hall. There, again, were the gigantic, winged bulls with human faces, — looming up above us as we gazed at them, vast monoliths, miracles of stone.

"It came into the world, here and there," I said, "in the

40

same figures. The first, rude, magnificent speech of it was in these stones."

"Yes," said General Rushleigh, "the early building of ideas was Cyclopean, like the early walls. But it was not to remain. The truth was not to be hewn out in any rock. No hammer can be lifted on it, after all. Not one stone laid one upon another is ever left to stand for it continually. Because the work is *not* stone, but living bread."

"They carved wings for signs; but the sign-wings never lifted the sign-creature."

"Nor any more," said Paul, "can the *signs*, however grandly interpreted, lift us."

"Only," said Margaret, softly, "the living spirit in the creatures and in the wheels."

There was a still expression in Mrs. Regis's face. She listened. I listened more through her, than of myself. It was so certain to me that the Ephphatha had been spoken to her; that the ears to hear had begun to be inwardly opened. Once, a well-bred blank would have been in her face at such words. Once, she would have said, — as she had said not long since, — "I cannot enter into subtleties. I can only take life as I find it before me."

But she had found her life to be a subtlety. The sword of the spirit had touched her under the joints of the armor of it. She had been wounded into a new vitality; bruised into a blessed healing.

. . . .

. . . . How enchanted we were, at last, to pack our big trunks again, and to send them off to the Cunard Agency, to be shipped direct to Liverpool! How pleased we were to put " Steamer Sahara, June 10th; *Hold*," on the directions! And how lovely looked to us the printed certificates of state-rooms taken and advance paid, when Stephen brought them up to us from the office!

The Goldthwaites were to go in the Sahara also; that took off a slight shade of the regret with which we must say good-bye to Stephen. Edith was already promised for a visit to Westover, at Mrs. Holabird's, as soon as her mother could possibly let her go again ; she was to be introduced to Rosamundi, and made free of the Horse Shoe ; henceforth she was to be one of " we girls," as Barbara calls her family and special friends, ignoring the nobler sex included in the relations, — " as why should n't we assume the generic title now and then, as well as be taken in ourselves to the grand general order of ' mankind ? ' "

It did happen one afternoon, among the very last of our days in Paris, — with how much premeditation, I don't know, — that Stephen came up to the Bird's Nest, when Edith was away with his sister ; and said he had come on purpose to take a last walk through Cluny with me.

We asked Emery Ann to go, too, but Emery Ann was in the height of beatitude, putting new bindings to her flannel wrapper, "to be miserable in on board ship ; " the anticipation of that intermediate purgatory lighting her face, at the very mention of it, with a radiance of the home-paradise beyond.

" I 've had my roots in the air for a whole year," she would say ; " now just carry me back and set me out in the old door-yard again, — *water* me well, — and let me be ! "

Poor Emery Ann ! How she had hated, all through Europe, the " light wines of the country," and how she had missed the cold orchard spring at home !

We were never tired of the old Abbey House, now the Museum Hotel, with its paved court-yard inclosed between high walls and the towers and angles of the quaint, half-Gothic building ; the odd, irregular corner-entrances ; the stately-primitive rooms with their rafters and benches, their ancient cabinets and chimney pieces, — the long corridors hung with weapons, — the halls crowded with rich and curious relics ; ecclesiastical robes, — missals, — carvings, — ancient furniture ; — a whole suite of rooms full of precious porcelains, — a salon of carriages ; — relics ; the nine crowns of the Kings of Spain ; the Golden Rose of Bâle ; the gilded effigy-ship, with Charles V. and all his court ; the dusky room in which the large old state-bed of the time of Francis I. still stands, with its dim, brocaded hangings ; the deep, vaulted, Roman bath-hall, last and below all, its ruin open to the garden.

Least of anything could we tire, or get enough, of the delicious old garden itself, whose walks wind about in their ascents and descents, amidst heavy shades, and in the completest quiet, behind one of the busiest boulevards of Paris; where the ivies run richly over everything, the old-time fragments of disinterred sculptures that are set here and there, showing forth from among the darkly-shining foliage; the pleasant corners where we used to sit and rest, and say to each other how fascinating it was, how like a dream, and how we never should forget it; and from which, then, we would emerge, as we came down from our dreams to breakfast,— to cross over and get our dinner of turbot, and " cotelettes," and raspberries and cream, and ice, at our restaurant.

Stephen and I seated ourselves now, on a block of stone that lay in the grass down by the street wall, — once perhaps a part of a temple column, or a piece of a sacred beast, or a heathen altar, —and grew quite silent, thinking how it was really the last time; I, wondering a little why he had so particularly fancied to come here the last time especially with me; when, quite suddenly, and with a voice that sounded just a little difficult and embarrassed, —though I did not see from his first words why it need:—

" Miss Patience, — I want to ask — may n't I *write* to you? May n't I know something, now and then, from yourselves, of you all?"

And when I said, quite simply, " Surely, Stephen. It would be great pleasure," he lifted up his head quite manly fashion, and went straight on:—

" I am not much more than a boy; but I shall never forget this six months, of all the six months of my life! And I can't bear that — you — should forget it altogether!—Pretty soon, Miss Patience, the years will be making a man of me. I mean they shall. You'll stay my friend, Miss Patience?"

He repeated my name with a kind of earnest beseechingness. What could I say? Away from Eliphalet and Gertrude, with their child on my hands? Had I been doing — or leaving undone — anything imprudently? Had I been letting things happen, that could n't *un*happen any more, ever? What would Emery Ann say to me if she knew it?

The worst of it was, you see, there was nothing to say " no " to. And that, when I took another minute to think about it, became clearly the best of it. Because it was one of the things that are just marked out, plain enough, so far; that take us in hand and settle for us.

He had done just right, this boy, to come to me. No man could have done wiser, or would, perhaps, have done half so well. We were to keep on being friends : there was a little door to be held ajar into the years, — two or three certainly, — in which he would not be with us again. He had a right to that; they both had a right to it; it was a piece of their lives. And I don't think we older people — in our fears and notions for something that may happen too soon, or to the shutting out of a crowd of possibilities, that indeed are often far safer shut out and delivered from — have any right to cut out pieces of life-thread for these young creatures, and tie up the ends in our own hard, bungling knots, and say to ourselves that we have saved a tangle. What comes early, — in any right, natural, orderly way, — comes because it is sent early ; because, maybe, it may take much time to prove itself, and turn out the full, strong certainty, either way, that it is meant to be.

If there had not been everything likeable, trustable, about this Stephen Holabird, — proved and commended to us in him already, by all that had gradually gone along, he would not have been with me to ask me this question now. And that being so, he had now quite a right to ask it. Thinking of this, I repeated my simple answer with some added words, that the words he had added called from me.

" Surely, Stephen ; write to me. I think I should have asked it of you, if you had not asked it of me. We have known you so well, now, — we have grown such friends, — that we shall want to know what the years are making of you as they go along. And when you come home, — count us among the friends to come to."

I think there was as much answer in it as there had been question in his asking. As much as could be between him and me, anyway. My good thought of him ; my good word of him at home, — the link he wanted ; my own promise that I should stay his friend. I shall tell the whole to Gertrude; then it will be their business, by and by, if it comes to be any business then, at all. And I think there was in it, also, just the delicate taking for granted that he was quite delicate enough to understand — to have had no need, indeed, to understand from me, — that this was all in such direction, that could in any word or manner be suggested.

I would quite as willingly let him and Edith come together to-morrow and say good-bye to Cluny, as if to-day's talk had not been. With all the intimacy, with all the fun, and the freedom, and the liking, — there was in these Holabirds something so high and of such a really dignified refinement, — I could trust Edith, in her simple girlishness to it all and among them to the very last, and have no fear of glance or word or sign that should make her shy or conscious for an instant. I was so very sure, too, that if there ever could have been anything, it would have driven her right back to me. There is no safeguard like — there is no safeguard *but* — the simple, native, royal-innocent reserve that does not know itself to be reserve.

But I will tell you what Emery Ann did say, when I told her about it.

" Do you *suppose*, Patience Strong, that our common-sense was amongst the things in that bag we went and left at Dover?"

"No, Emery Ann," I answered her, calmly; "for I quite well recollect your having had yours about you the night we got to Lugano."

"Well," she returned, letting her tone subside from its first surprise to a certain reassurance, "I presume it's our consciences and our common-sense that's been settling things as they came along, finally. And I *don't* presume there's any need for a special rummage and judgment now."

Than which I think one cannot have a better method or reliance in any of the circumstances or responsibilities of this mortal life.

CHAPTER XXXIV.

THE CAPITAINE-MAJOR AND THE GRAND EMPEREUR.

. . . .

. . . . OUR very last sight-seeing in Paris, — our very last day there, — was a mixture of the magnificent, the absurd, and the ignominious.

Emery Ann and I had never seen Napoleon's tomb. We only knew the golden dome of the Invalides from the outside. Stephen Holabird and Edith insisted that we could not conscientiously or respectably leave Paris in that way. So they set forth with us, in the middle of the day, and we drove around, first to the Cours de la Reine, with an errand to the Regises, made our final arrangements with them for the morrow, and then across the Bridge of the Invalides to the Quai d'Orsay, and round the Esplanade to the great front.

As we went, we saw that grand movements were on foot. A splendid review had evidently been going forward. All over the esplanade was a glitter of arms and equipments, a rushing and wheeling and massing of bodies of cavalry, — lines of infantry marshaled in beautiful precision, — groups of commanders and state dignitaries mounted apart; — the whole Place swarming with a brilliant and imposing stir.

We passed unchecked around the side avenue, where carriages filled with lookers-on were pausing, and came to the front. We must have passed here at the last possible moment; at any rate we got round to the eastern avenue, and were driven to the side entrance where visitors to the Dome and the tomb are admitted.

But everything was closed and barred. Nobody appeared to to answer to our summons. And no one seemed moving in the quiet grounds. A placard by the gate announced that it was open on Mondays, Tuesdays, Thursdays, and Saturdays; but that " strangers with passports " might be admitted on the other days. This was Wednesday.

Another carriage drove up; with strangers and their passports, like ourselves. We all went and tried at an iron gateway farther back, within which was a little lodge. Here some one emerged at last to answer our inquiries. " Il faut chercher le gardien," we were told. " Le gardien du tombeau — à O'autre côté ; " and we were pointed, or thought we were pointed, toward the front again. But at the opening of the avenue into the square, we were stopped by mounted police, and the advancing column of cavalry. Already its head was appearing before the long, terraced entrance; carriages full of spectators were crowded back upon the curbs ; the wide way was cleared ; and, six abreast, they came on.

Grand horses, — splendid riders ; in companies of color, — black horses, bay horses, chestnut, iron-gray, white ; in compact line, even in size, trained in step ; a perfection of mounted display. From away around as far as we could look, their solid trample sounding steadily over the ground, they kept pouring into sight; up the avenue beyond, straight down toward us, past the gates of the Invalides, then curving around and streaming away into the distance again upon our left. It was by no means what we had come expecting to see, but it was a fine accident !

At last, all were by ; the wide frontage seemed clear ; carriages began to move slowly off, when three or four gentlemen rode rapidly past, on splendid chargers, — there was a lifting of hats among the crowd, — the rider in the middle bowed, as he swept by ; and then all really was over, and we were left to imagine whom we had caught glimpses of, — doubtless, the Marshal President and his staff.

Well, we alighted again before the great gates. A crowd of foot passengers still impeded the way ; among them limped along a few Invalides, proud of the day, proud of their disability, that told what *they* had been, in some other day that they were far more proud of. One came close to us, wheeling himself in a kind of chair. I stopped, and asked him, respectfully, if he could tell us to whom to go to get admission to the Dome and the Tomb.

"Il faut demander au Capitaine-Major, — là-dedans." And he waved his hand toward the pavilioned façade.

Up we passed, along the deep slope of terrace. We had to ask again and again, — " Whom can we seek who can permit us to enter to the tomb of Napoleon ? We are strangers with passports." And always the answer was, with increasing roll upon the final " r," — " Monsieur le Capitaine-Major-*r-r* ! "

It was like a pilgrimage to Mecca. We were in at last. But the vast court and endless corridors utterly bewildered us. The other carriage party who had met us at the first gate appeared. wandering, like ourselves. Everybody said, " Capitaine-Major-r-r !" but nobody told us where we could find the man.

At last, a door, — quite near the front, under the arcade, — to which we came round after useless explorations up and down the quadrangle and colonnades, — and upon it marked the talismanic title.

"CAPITAINE-MAJOR."

We knocked, as if at a gate of Paradise. It is so good to get *anywhere* at last, when one has found it nearly hopeless to arrive. And the greater the difficulty, the farther from our thoughts the simple solution of renouncing the endeavor and returning quietly home, where we did know both place and business.

A young woman opened the door. We asked for the " Major-r-r," with as much accent and roll as possible. He was not in. We should find him, here, some part ; and she leaned from the door-way and looked around with polite anxiety, and made a very vague, general gesture toward the shifting groups, with a most charming confidence. " You will demand of one with the white ribbon, ' comme ça,' " — and she crossed her hand over her breast from shoulder to waist. Then she shut the door, and we turned round and saw five men with white bands, talking together.

I was nearest, and I attacked the group. " Monsieur le Capitaine-Major ? " I said inquiringly, glancing at all five.

" Là-bas, madame, — celui qui porte les épaulettes d'or." An old Invalide with a wooden leg stepped forth from among

them. "Madame, je vous montrerai. Venez! Venez!" And
he stumped off before us down the dark corridor to the left beneath the building.

Down there, they were cleaning the pavement with buckets
full of water, which were poured like libations before us, as we
lifted our skirts and picked our way.

Only a knock and a question, after all, at another door; then
round, through the floods again, across the court-yard, down the
whole length of building.

Stephen walked forward quickly with the old Invalide, who
got on faster with his one leg than most of us felt able to with
our two. Now and then they would look back for us and halt;
then we would catch the rapid chatter they were keeping up in
French; or both together they would say something to us in the
two separate languages; we, meantime, explaining to each other
breathlessly, as we hurried on, in a misprinted kind of way, the
detached fragments as we got hold of them. It was a long explanation about the day, and the confusion, and the difficulty,—
which really had already explained themselves, — and the good
will of the white-strapped Invalide to do his possible for us.

" *Is* it admitto, or is it prohibito?" panted Emery Ann, much
bewildered, but contributing cheerfully her useful little Italian
terminations to the general effort at understanding.

"Or have you beguiled us into an enchanted castle, Stephen?" I asked him, as we turned at the far end to mount a
great stone staircase, of repeated flights, with deep landings.

"That might really be an object for me, Miss Patience," he
said, dropping back beside us. But he fell quite back behind
me with Edith, though he spoke my name; and I saw the two,
as I began the second ascent, lingering along the landing.
"The nice little betweens," I heard him say, "are only from
one climb to another. Everything has to keep on."

"And the niceness is, as Aunt Patience always says, that
everything *does* keep on," said Edith, brightly. Little woman
that she was, she would not let Stephen droop for a minute, this
last day. She knew how much harder it was for him to let us
all go and be left, than it was for us to leave, even. And she
said that so simply, — with the royal innocence of that free re-

serve, that is broken forever, as I said, the moment it discovers itself to be reserve! The moment it is reserve from *others* instead of from *one's self.*

A long corridor across the end, above; a turning into another, running lengthwise; at last a door, unmistakable we thought this time, with "Adjutant-Major" outside.

A knock by the Invalide, into whose hand, — with a delicate diffidence, in view of the white strap, — Stephen had taken opportunity to slip some silver, which was pocketed without any diffidence at all; the other party of people, who seeing we had got upon some track, had swelled our cortège from below, gathering up behind, and waiting with us; the whole group absurdly collected together, like cats — supposing cats to hunt in company — before a mouse-hole. I began to wish myself out of it, before the upshot came.

Back flew — not the door knocked upon, but one close to it; and out bounced, like a jack-in-the-box, a fierce little old officer, thin and gray, in full uniform. Stephen took off his cap.

"Would it be possible, sir," he said, deferentially, "that we should see the tomb of Napoleon to-day?"

"No, sir! No person is admitted to-day. To-morrow, sir."

"But we leave Paris, to-morrow; we are foreigners, with passports. And the placard" —

"Il n'y a *point* de passeport," thundered the irate Capitaine-Major, with an emphasis that could only have its point and twang in French, "qui puisse faire admettre qui que ce soit aujourd'hui!"

And without further courtesy, he whizzed off down the gallery like a shot from a mortar.

The poor old Invalide had taken the advance from the instant that door had sprung back from before our faces; he was well nigh beyond hearing by this time; but the Capitaine-Major overtook him as in a breath.

"Et VOUS!" he exploded upon him, as he seemed to sweep him along with his own swift motion; and then followed — the sound diminishing as they went — a hurtle of small, rapid objurgations, such as one might suppose the bombshell of his wrath would be filled with.

"Nails and slugs!" ejaculated Stephen, "what a discharge of canister!" And as the rain of it pattered away through the long stone distances, we meekly turned about, our train following, and descended, as we had come up, the grand staircase.

"No worse than the King of France himself," said Edith, laughing. "When he marched up the hill with fifty thousand men, and then — marched down again!"

"I'm glad I'm not that Invalid, though," said Stephen; "but that Invalid deserved it! He had got his francs, — the white-ribanded old humbug, — knowing better all the time! He was half way down the corridor when that knock was answered. As for ourselves" —

"What of it?" said I. "We haven't got in, to be sure; but neither did Napoleon! Who cares for seeing the tomb where he isn't buried?"

We found ourselves at the foot of the grand staircase, at the entrance from the Hotel to the church. We went in and up the aisle toward where, across it, was stretched a coarse gray curtain; before this a scaffolding; workmen busy; mortar falling about.

"Behind that gray curtain, if we could lift it and get in," said Edith, "is all we have come to see."

"Yes," I answered her. "Behind the Gray Curtain, also, is the Grand Empereur. Perhaps it is the fittest thing to look at, after all."

"And the rubbish," said Emery Ann. "They're always hanging up gray curtains, and doing things over, and making a clutter generally, in France. It's pretty suitable, I think, myself."

And the unawed descendant of the Forefathers walked as serenely out and down from the Invalides as if it had been down from the door yard of Old Farm.

But it was not Stephen's last day with us, notwithstanding. It occurred suddenly to Barbara and Lieutenant Goldthwaite, that there was no need that it should be. He had seen nothing of England; why shouldn't he run over and see a bit of it with us? So they invited him; as their little appendix,

Barbara said, to the birthday present the rest of them at home made up for him last winter; "a *bonne bouche*, that would n't have been *kept* over winter, if they had n't been bright enough not to think of it before."

And so, we were a merry enough party still, that went down out of Paris that next noon toward the sea-coast of Picardy, to take steamer at Boulogne for London by the Channel and the river.

CHAPTER XXXV.

OUR CHIMNEY CHINK IN LONDON.

. . . .

. . . . How happy we were steaming up the Thames, after our sea-passage round from Boulogne!

Coming into London by its great water-gate, past the docks and the shipping and the high, black, business-grimed wharves. Past the walls of old warehouses, that stand up from the dark water, — past piers and strands, and the dim city edges that dip drearily and dreggily to the brink; their very dreariness and uncleanness made classic and thrilling to us by the mysteries and pathos of Dickens's stories, that have brought us here in pictured scenes so often, and that have made themselves living presences forever in the land and the city where he wrought them out.

How beautiful it was to hear everybody talking English again, as if they could n't help it, — and yet how strange! " Kind of tremblesome somehow, almost," Emery Ann said, " You don't hardly know what to make of it all of a sudden, most as if they were so many Balaam's asses! But we 're fairly above ground now," she added, with a long breath. " We 're through with the Hivites and the Hittites and the Gergashites and the Jebusites, and have got back to our native fellow-creatures again! England *is* next door to America, finally, after all!"

Yes; England is next door; it is just the other side of the same human heart; and the great throbbing ocean, beating between the Old and the New, is no such separation, but the life-giving current bearing back and forth through a great round of quickening and use, the self-same elements of the best and happiest civilization the world has come to yet. Not the best it *shall* come to, thank the dear Lord, or the happiest this Anglo-Saxon right and left of hand and heart may help work out yet upon the struggling, distracted, half-blind, bettering earth!

We dropped right into a chimney chink of thorough English comfort. Some dear little *Swifts* took us right in; two sister-birds that had a big flue all to themselves in Euston Square; their long lease of it their sole property and their living.

Just as nice as wax, though, in the middle of what we have been accustomed to call sooty London. For the life of us, we have n't been able to find out its uncommon sootiness! Large rooms, comfortably fitted; windows opening generously into generous spaces; the green square, all leafed out and sweet with smell of the new grass and foliage; a stretch of garden with shady trees, down from the back.

. A long parlor with three front windows; Mrs. Regis's bed-room opening from that, by folding doors, behind. Up-stairs, a corresponding suite for Emery Ann, Edith, and me; Margaret sleeping in a little hall-room that led from her mother's. General Rushleigh came here with us, and had the "third floor front." We almost did not care so much to sail away in the Sahara in three weeks, after all. Only almost; in our hearts nothing could have stopped us longer from the home-going. But it is nice to have the last stitches set smoothly; to go the last mile through the pleasantest bit of the whole journey. Paris had been a great improvement upon Rome and Florence; we were not ungrateful to the memory of our home-making there. But it had been home-*making*; we had had to struggle and shift for it; here it was home-*made*.

The charming breakfasts that we came down to! The table laid in the parlor, with its fresh cloth, and its four dishes, home-fashion. Its tray of cups, and its big coffee-pot for Mrs. Regis to pour out for all from! Its rolls and muffins, its shrimps and soles, its steaks and chops and eggs! Not all together, of course; but as many of them as we wanted; with Miss Bessie, the younger of the two Swifts,— so sweet and ladylike that it seemed a shame to sit and let her wait upon us,— bringing in for us and carrying out. So interested, too, in our plans for the day; for the Tower, or the Gardens, or out to Hampton, or to

the Museum, or the Galleries. So proud of our dress and turn-
out, the day we went in livery barouches for our ride in the
Park, in the fashionable drive. So pleased to have us tell her
when we came back, that we had passed the Princess of Wales
close to, five times, and how pretty we thought her ; that we had
seen the Duchess. of Edinburgh also ; and so full of a proudly-
loyal familiar mention of " our" royal names !

It was really an experience, those five turns in the Ring Road.
Those carriages full of fair, high-born women, passing and re-
passing ; those grand-looking, courtly old English gentlemen,
whom we saw lift their hats to the Princess as she drove back
and forth, — a mounted, special policeman galloping on before
her up and down at a certain distance all the while, to keep
clear way, for the pace of her carriage ; — her pretty bows in return ; — her quietness in dress and bearing as she sat there,
representing the royalty of England to the people, and yet taking her daily airing with the simple composure of the least pre-
tentious lady in the land. " Just because," Edith said, " there
was nothing for her to pretend to."

We had talked a good deal about these things over the tea-
table. Nobody, I think, could possible have gone for the first
time into that full current of representative high refinement and
illustrative nobility of the most refined and proudest race of people on the globe, and *not* have thought and talked of it with an
interest something more than that of vulgar, gaping curiosity.
Nobody, at any rate, could hear our little Swift chatter of her
Queen and her Queen's family, and mention the grand names of
her country as if somehow, away off perhaps, but yet really,
they were names of her own blood that she had a right to be
proud of, — and not feel that underneath, or above, what is
called only curiosity, or a plebeian adulation, is something of the
highest claim and consciousness of grand human nature, that
chooses its kings and queens to wear for them the regalia that
they are too busy earning for the world to wear for themselves !
There are harms and falsities that come from it ; but I don't
know that they are so much less, as different, in our piece of
Anglo-Saxondom ; in our republic, as contrasted with the old
monarchy. Here are things that have outgrown their reality,

doubtless. But with us, on the other hand, we so fast *overgrow* our realities. Everybody on our side is in such a hurry to *wear* the regalia!

It was after that, when I had been sitting up-stairs a while in the twilight, by my window looking over into the green branches of the Square, and across to old St. Pancras's Church that made the corner close by, — that I heard General Rushleigh's voice, singing, in the parlor below. I had never heard it but three times before; once when we sang hymns on the deck of the steamship, — once on the Lake of Lugano, when he took up the refrain of the beautiful " Angelus," — and on the steps of the Font in the Baptistery of Pisa, when he had called down those echoes out of heaven.

I knew he and Margaret were alone in the room. Mrs. Regis was tired, and had gone to lie down.

He was touching the piano with simple chords of accompaniment; his splendid voice was sending forth with its full, rich tones, some words of that glorious song of all love songs, " My Queen!"

> "And she may be humble or proud, my Lady,
>   Or that sweet calm, which is just between;
> But, whenever she comes, she will find me ready
>   To do her homage, my Queen, my Queen!

> "But she must be courteous, she must be holy,
>   Pure in her spirit, that maiden I love;
> Whether her birth be noble or lowly
>   I care no more than the spirit above;
> And I 'll give my heart to my Lady's keeping,
>   And ever her strength on mine shall lean,
> And the stars shall fall, and the angels be weeping,
>   E'er I cease to love her, my Queen, my Queen!"

What need was there of any telling why he sang it; of any guessing of the happy, tender, humbly-blessèd look with which Margaret, crowned queen of better than a kingdom, would be listening? What need of prying — as one may pry with unbidden imagination — into the sacred pause that fell after the singing?

I took up my little Chapél Prayer Book, that had the mark in at the Collect for the week and read it over, that I might *not* pry. And it was the prayer of the Sunday after the Ascension:

41

the great upburst of gladness that the Only Son had been exalted into the heavens, — Type and Promise of all exaltation, — and the "beseeching" to "leave *us* not comfortless;" but "send to us thine Holy Spirit to comfort us, and to exalt us into the same place, where He liveth to make intercession for us at the right hand of God for ever and ever."

At that right hand, where "are pleasures for evermore." Where *all* is laid up, — for us also.

I did say to General Rushleigh, an hour after, — "It seems strange never to have heard you sing but two or three times in all this year; never *really* since the hymns on board the Nova Zembla, — before I heard your voice to-night?"

My tone questioned him; and he answered me, — "I think singing *should* be almost sacred-seldom; song is a higher — and ought to be even a truer — utterance than speech."

How alike these two were, in their most intimate perceptions! Margaret would not sing the Hymn of the Cross, because she "had not come to it."

Paul Rushleigh was singing to her the crown-song of her life.

The cross may yet lie upon the pathway of these two; but, I think, whatever it may be — even to what we call parting, — they will take it up together. For not height, nor depth, nor any other creature, can separate, or put them asunder, now!

That next Sunday was Whitsun Day. Stephen came over early, from the Goldthwaites' lodgings in Gower Street, to go to church with us.

Old St. Pancras was all alive. As we looked from our windows, after breakfast was over, we saw a little throng about the gateway. Poor, common people; people by no means in anything like Sunday clothes; people who looked, some of them, as if they had never seen the inside of a church. Women with shawls over their heads; women with babies on their arms; unkempt boys; little children. All hovering and waiting, as for something about to happen that touched even their degree, and gave them a share in it. Something with a sacredness in it, — for they waited at the church gates for it. Something that was to them what royalty was to Bessie Swift, — strange and apart, yet common and close.

We asked Bessie what was happening. Cabs were driving up, bringing couples and parties of the humbler class, — not very many grades above these lookers-on, in their every-day perhaps, but in this holiday lifted up by some separation and dignity of occasion. Just enough higher for the living sympathy to quicken and redeem the curiosity.

"They are the Whitsun weddings. They are married without any fee, to-day."

"Why should n't we go into the church and see?" said Edith.

"Certainly you can," said Miss Bessie. "But you 'll need to go at once. It will soon be over."

So we hurried on hats and gloves, and while cabs and flies were still rushing up to the gates, and brides in all degrees of bridal adornment, from the white muslin and lace veil to the plain pale gray stuff and a simple white ribbon, were flutteringly alighting, and bashfully going in, we crossed over, and entered.

Margaret was on General Rushleigh's arm, and Edith was hastening along beside Stephen; putting on her second glove as she came up.

"Them 's real quality!" a woman whispered. And another said, "Is n't she a sweet young thing? And she has n't got her glove on yet!"

Emery Ann and I hurried the child forward with us. She had not heard it, and I was glad; but I think Stephen did. No; she had n't got her glove on yet; she was by no means ready. But how long should we keep her unconscious? How long with that man's hope wakening up in Stephen's eyes? Well, — when it comes it will be the Whitsun gift, — the Lord's own Pentecost into her life. And He knows when.

It was a curious scene. A long row of them, before the chancel rail; a clergyman moving up and down before them, as if giving a communion; saying a part of the service in turn, to each pair. Until at last every response was made, every ring put on, and the men with common, working-world faces, and the girls, — some of them with something higher touching them with sweet solemnity, — some with only the ordinary brief importance of their bridehood, — came down the aisle. So many new life-beginnings made together in the world, this Whitsun Day morning. I wondered if they thought there would be special blessing with the day, or whether it was mostly with them the opportunity of matrimony as a free gift.

"I should hate to be married in scraps, like that," said Emery Ann. "It don't seem as if it would hardly hold together."

"My dear Miss Emery Ann," said General Rushleigh, "we are all married — we all live — we all die — in scraps. Nothing comes all at once to us, any more than rain comes solid."

"That's so," said Emery Ann. His "any more" was after her own heart. "And I suppose, finally," she added, "that that was the way that the Lord always fed the multitudes, and always will. He won't finish up anybody altogether separate. It's the best way, after all, forzino. More like living. But I don't think it's much consequence to me, particularly."

We went home and finished our street dress a little, and then we all went to service at Saint Paul's. I liked seeing the grand old Cathedral in the service time; sitting quietly with the congregation, instead of wandering about, merely *looking*. Taking into my thought its greatness, like the greatness of the thought of worship for which it was built. But we were left quite to our own individual visitings and impressions. Not a word could we, where we sat, receive, of the prayers or the discourse uttered. A solemn continuity of sound, — of leading and response, — and then of the preaching, — accompanied like a reminding undertone, the current of our thinking; that was all.

After lunch, we drove out to Lady Christian's. We knew what her Sundays were, and that we should break neither our own keeping of it nor hers.

We found her with all the children, and some friends, in the garden. We had afternoon tea with them, and shared their lovely little private twilight service. We made appointment to go next day with them to the Doré Gallery, and to see Holman Hunt's "Shadow of the Cross."

They gave us cordial welcome; but there was something in it that was less like a beginning again than a keeping on. It was as if we found our place still warm; not warmed up in a hurry to receive us.

OUR CHIMNEY CHINK IN LONDON.   645

There was not much need of telling news. The new relation between Margaret and Paul Rushleigh told itself. Mr.
Truesdaile shook a hand of each together as we came away,
with eyes that were full of a glad blessing ; and Lady Christian
kissed Margaret's forehead.

And Lady Christian, following Mrs. Regis with a look she
had never had for her a year ago, said to me, lingering last
upon the threshold, — "I think an angel has come down there,
and troubled the waters, to some life that had never stirred
them before."

"Every earth," I answered her, "waits with the darkness
upon its deep, until the spirit of the heavens passes upon it.
Then there is light, and all manner of new life, that it was full
of, but did not know."

. . . .

. . . . We went into a picture world again. We stood before
the marvelous painting, — the Dream of Pilate's Wife. Nothing
engraved from Doré ever showed me his power, or gave so
much meaning with it, as these visions in color. The revealing
light is the wonder of all his work. His angels shine out as
they must have been "suddenly with" the shepherds, that night
when the "glory of the Lord shone round about them" on the
hills outside of Bethlehem.

I have been sore wearied, distasted I thought, with the con-
tortions, the writhing, the serpent-swarmings, the hints of evil
shapes wriggling into life; the confusions, the horrors, the
massing of agonies and physical destructions, — in his pictures
from the Bible. But it is always this wonderful flash of *dis-
closure,* — the blazing out of the light that *is,* showing suddenly
all that is, *as* it is, in it. I think the key to all he does is a
lightning touch, quickening whole atmospheres to a laying open
of farthest secrets; the dimmest, most remote, made clear and
present as in a kind of Judgment Day. It is a strong shining
upon some single leaf of the books that shall all be opened under
an infinite, intolerable radiance, at the last.

Down the broad marble stair-way, in the picture, — from the
splendid room above, where the draperies of a luxurious couch
lie tumbled in the distant intense illumination, — comes the

Wife of Pilate, walking as in sleep. Above and beside her, with high, white, deep-drooping wings, hangs a great angel, impelling and accompanying her; the glory all about him; the woman-figure, in its loose robes, and all the . pathway downward, vivid in the streaming brightness; the slow step in which you feel the mysterious enforcing, — the troubled trance of the face, — the still straightness of the form and the falling garments, — all the grouping and detail of this left side of the painting full of the awe, the supernaturalness, the possession.

Down below, in a vast outspread, the main representation; of *what* possessed her, — what she saw.

The Life — that she knew of; that had been these three years known in the world; its work, its history. The foreground full of it, in faces, groups, actions. In the midst, beyond, the present awful Moment. The seething, riotous multitude; •the central Figure; the Roman officers; Pilate, the Governor; the demand, the hesitation, the showing of the Man; almost the cry, Crucify Him! Crucify Him! Far off, the path to Calvary; the Hill, the Cross.

There was so much, so crowded, that one could not disentangle and interpret instantly. The meaning came upon me only in a whole, at first; and afterwards I found it difficult to be sure just what I recollected in the particulars. I may fill it up and connect, somewhat, after my own understanding. But the understanding was certain to me. It was a great impression, though I strive in the recalling of details as one strives to define to one's self the eluding features of a face out of which an unforgetable look has shone.

We went from this, to *the* picture of the Exhibition, — the Christ descending from the Prætorium, — as from a fitting prelude — the preluding fact.

The *two* descents; the coming down, in her restless dream, of the vision-haunted woman ; the coming down from the small, blind, human condemnation, of " Him that condemneth ! "

The Judge of all the earth, passing forth, in the midst of petty mockeries, from the judgment hall of Pontius Pilate, bowing his might to a mortal anguish, — " suffering it," as he had suffered the baptism of John, " to be so now ! "

"I have power to lay it down, and I have power to take it again." That was in the whole meek majesty of the sublime, calm Figure, moving full toward you as you sat and looked, along that staircase that makes the midst and front of the great representation; at whose base seethes the persecuting crowd; from whose last step He will deliver Himself up into their grasp; between which and the Mountain of the Skull, lies the terrible pathway,—the crowd, the jeers, the fainting, the weeping of the disciples, the wailing of the women of Jerusalem.

He comes down alone; they touch Him not.

"No man taketh it from me. I lay it down of myself."

You feel that He might even now "pass through the midst of them and go his way." You have seen the mighty angel-shape that drove the terrified wife of the governor down from her troubled sleep to send Pilate warning. Are there not more than twelve legions of angels waiting for his word? But "He openeth not his mouth!"

Perhaps it was a pity that we went from this to see the picture of the Shadow.

I could not like that picture. I could not find the Christ in it. I do not think the Lord ever foreshadowed his Passion by any such weary, listless outflinging of those arms, tired with carpenter's work! He never tired of his building; He the Son of the Builder! He never prefigured his suffering so!

If I could paint a picture, and dared to try to paint that, I would make Him as He stood with loving arms outstretched over Jerusalem; a divine Face bending, yearning above it; *forward*, at the feet,—the way they were set to go,—the Shadow. And even that shadow should have tenderness, willingness, saving in it. The Shadow under which men shall hide, and trust, and abide, and rejoice; the Wings that are spread out for his people and his redeemed forever!

. . . . The Exhibition was open again, and of course we went there. And of course, from among the innumerable things to see, the many delights of the hour, only a confused remembrance comes away and remains, as always does to them who try, as Emery Ann says, to pick up beans by the bushel.

I never have stopped to write down things at the very time. I have been so wholly determined to write out only what outlived, — after the test of weeks or months. And sometimes I have been almost sorry, as I have turned back and tried to grasp again, precisely, for you, the things that gave me ever so definite and full result, in thought and apprehension. The little points of fact escape me; so that I find I hardly dare describe minutely that which seems to me must have been, but which I cannot quite see over again. I often turn to Emery Ann, and ask of her more literal memory, what I find I need. And sometimes she sets up the very type again, — or rather produces it stereotyped, — and prints it over for me. And sometimes she says, — " Don't ask me! There ain't any ' M ' before my name, you know."

" But indeed there is," I tell her. " A very capital ' M,' sometimes."

" That's all the satisfaction there is about it," she replies. "It's clear there, or it's clear gone. I remember distinctly, and I forget distinctly! But it's most generally forgetting."

Writing this, on the home voyage, I recollect two pictures there, that hung near each other.

Everybody recollects the one; the instantly-famous " Calling of the Roll," by a girl-artist, — her first exhibited picture. About which, day by day, pressed a packed throng; slowly moving, by individuals, past the painting; never moving, as a totality, from that corner of the second gallery, near the door into the Long Room; where policemen managed the approach and the departure, and kept people from monopolizing too long as they paused in turn at front. If you wanted a second look, you had to go around the outskirt of the crowd, fall into line and trickle slowly through with the mass again, like a sandgrain through a funnel.

It *was* wonderful; in its clearness; its individuality; its varied and intense and soul-touching expression; its technical skill; its marvelous correctness of figure and detail. They say it was a heart-inspiration; that she had a brother in the Crimean war. It goes *to* the hearts, inevitably, of thousands of the English people.

But over against it, at right angles, hangs another picture, large, central, in the end of the gallery. There is no crowd beneath that; there is no wonder, and no rush. I stopped outside the throng, and looked up at it; and I thought, — "That is a death-roll; a battle-register; — that is the way men look after their mortal strivings; — this is the way the world's Peace came down upon it; this is the beginning of the reading of the Lamb's Book of Life; the calling over of the great compassions of the Highest." And the one overbore, and blotted out in light, the other.

In the Catalogue, it says — "The Healing Mercies of Christ," . . . . for the Chapel of St. Thomas's Hospital. — "Unto you that fear My Name shall the Sun of Righteousness arise, with healing in his wings." — "Go and show John again those things which you do hear and see: the blind receive their sight, and the lame walk, the lepers are cleansed, and the deaf hear, the dead are raised up, and the poor have the Gospel preached to them."

And the Lord stands among them, and they gather round his feet, and reach out to touch his garments; the women bring their sick and their dead; the lame and the leper struggle toward Him; the blind grope to the sound of his voice; the blank face of the deaf is lifted to the speaking of his face. And his hands are held out to them all; His eyes shine down upon them, full of mercy; strength flows forth from Him and enters into them; and all around Him, they are rising up, they are seeing, hearing, living; glorifying the Father, and believing in the Son.

It is God's Roll Call over the battle field of the human. Yes; it is his *last judgment;* his restoration that shall be. *This,* and not the fearful work of Michael Angelo in the Chapel of the Vatican.

I do not care how great the picture may be as mere art. It is written only, modestly, against the title in the catalogue, — "This picture was *undertaken*" — at the request, and for the gift of Sir William Tite to St. Thomas's Hospital. But the thought of it glows through the color on the canvas, and transfigures it. The meaning makes you forget the means. And the Gospel in it is greater than Michael Angelo's.

CHAPTER XXXVI.

OVER MERRIE ENGLAND.

. . . .

. . . . Down into the rich-breathing, blossomy country !

We had had nothing like this before, for a whole year. We
had had mountains and sunny valleys ; wild, splendid Alps and
Apennines ; dreamy lakes ; forests, vineyards, rushing river
courses ; country scenery around Florence, Rome, Paris, where
the whole country is elegant pleasure-ground, or just greenly
beautiful by not being city, or some soft, blank waste, as the dim-
stretching Campagna ; but country like this, — all alive, and
aburst, and teeming ; triumphant with fullness, sweetly still with
very surcharge of utmost vitality and perfect utilization, — this,
I think, is nowhere but in England, and in June, as we saw it,
— plunged ourselves deep into its delight, — steaming down
along the rail through beautiful Oxfordshire and Warwickshire ;
landing in delicious old Warwick itself ; riding up from the station, past where the Castle walls stretch along by the river in
stately extent and lift up tall turrets and wide battlements from
the woods against the sky, like the outshowing ramparts of a
city, — through the quaint gateway arched under the tower of
an old, old, church, — past the esplanade of Leicester's Hospital, whose wall slopes up beside the roadway, evening the
grade of the hill for its upper level, whereon stands the row of
charming houses with their pointed gables, — their projecting
storys over columned porches, or just overhanging the pavement, — their tall, picturesque chimneys, their latticed case-
ments, and their open doors along the terrace, shaded with its
row of trees within the rail ; where the old pensioners sit in
their chairs, or walk up and down, enjoying the balm of the
air and the serene content of their safe shelter and provid-

ing ; — by and beside all this, to the quiet street right under the shadow of St. Mary's Church, and into the sound of the pleasant, ancient chimes.

"How much time," I used to think, as I lay and listened to the bells of a morning, ringing out the separate bits, "they must have had in the old days that they could stop to count all through in this fashion ! What slow leisure it is a sign of; what long minutes measured by long ways of doing !" First, the quarters, deliberately signaled; then the strokes, with a pause after each till the echo has died out ; then the chime, six times repeated for six o'clock, — twelve times for twelve ; the whole melody, of two strains, of " Bluebells of Scotland," or " Over the water to Charlie !" We should have got there and back, and brought Charlie with us, — or all the blue bonnets would have been over the border, in these days, while they were ringing to tell of it !

But it is delightful to one's conscience to lie and listen it all through, before one must fairly acknowledge that it is, truly and wholly, seven o'clock, and time to get up.

We had fluttered into a nice old Marten-box, here in the hill street that runs up to the church, — Church Street they call it, and it runs from the Main, or High, with its quiet, nice shops ; — do you wonder we felt ourselves more like happy, migrant birds than ever ?

They keep a shop, the Martens ; and they let lodgings above it, in a long range of rooms that overlooks the garden, with its brief, but pretty vista, its boxed edges and pebbled paths, its shells set up in heaps at the corners, and its little summer-house shady at the farther end.

Our lady-party was all accommodated here ; the gentlemen went, with the Goldthwaites, to the hotel.

It made little difference where we lodged, however ; we were together in continual, most charming excursions, all those long, summer days, every one of which dawned more perfect than yesterday, and set in rosy and golden promise of a yet fairer to-morrow. Such days as they were to remember England by, — to mark for us our last of Europe, putting the greenest leaf in at the closing page !

Every morning two baskets, packed in the shop below,—a pastry shop it was; every morning two carriages at the door, with nice, old drivers, full of the respectability of their established years, full of pride of their Castle and the shows of their old town; full of deference that touched its hat continually, and behaved in a general manner as if we were earls and countesses from somewhere, where we had Castles and Guy's Towers, and Porridge Pots of our own,—and so we have, have n't we? Every morning a fresh plan that would take all the lovely day; every day a large piece of unspendable delight in the anticipation, an unspent treasure of invested joy, to last us in dividends of memory years and years!

. . . .

. . . . One day to Stratford. Like the Tower of Pisa, a threadbare name; like that, when we had seen it, a name made into a reality that never could be threadbare any more; that could not join itself to the threadbare thing we had got miserably into our heads beforehand. .

The lovely drive upon the Avon side; the green glades of Charlecote, down which we peered as we rounded by the old stone gates; the old church, standing in almost as deep a glade, at the back of its long yard, thick shadowed by great trees, with its wide flagged walk beneath them, up and down which so many generations have passed, wearing the stones into thin, smooth hollows; the open, sunny town, with its real English High Street,—lined with cheerful shops, but quiet as a Sunday; the House itself, level with the pavement, its low rooms leading off directly from it, and its worn, clumsy stair-way winding up to the one where the Poet was born. The low-browed opening into the other chamber, through which you see upon the opposite wall, a picture that startles you with the familiar lineaments, —the high sweep of the brow, the deep glory of the eyes, the fine, tender, laughing curves of the mouth, the wavy-flowing hair and the shapely-trimmed beard,—looking forth upon you, the only abiding presence here within the swept and garnished walls that once saw common life enough, but are set apart now, a shrine for the world's pilgrims. A presence that seems to fill and make to-day of the vacancy and the long memory.

Two old-fashioned little ladies show you about, and tell you everything. They make you feel, on their part, as if they were gossips of the household ; — as if they had been by when the baby drew his first breath here where they tell you of it ; and had taken caudle-cup with Mrs. John, who made a far greater day in the world than she dreamed of; as if they had dropped in and out, neighborly, while the boy was a grammar-school boy of the town, coming home for his holiday times ; as if they had known all about his love-scrapes and his poaching-scrapes, and shaken heads in sympathetic counsel with the worthy glover and his wife after the escapades at Charlecotè ; and now, after what time you forget to reckon, had helped off the last burying or removal, and stayed by a while to recount in the straitly-tidied rooms, to whatever friendly comers, the stories of how it had all been, and the particular end it came to. You go out of the low door-way under the beetling timbers, into the warm street again, as if you had come out from the sixteen-hundreds, and hardly yet could find your place in the present chronology.

You do not find it while you stay in the quaint place, so slow of changes ; as you drive by its inn-yards and over the Avon Bridge, where the river and the meadows look like the stream and meadows of a poem ; as you go on through the lanes to Shottery, and stop at the old farm-cote and get admittance to that other yet more ancient-seeming hearthside, where the big oak settle stands, and they tell you William and Anne sat together. As you drink a cup of water from the Hathaway well, brought up by the old sweep and bucket, and receive some pinks and lad's love from what they still call Anne's garden.

And then you go back, — I mean we did, — through the town to the old church again, and read the names there in the chancel, and make sure that they were dead and buried long ago ; and sit in the carriage outside the church-yard wall, under the trees, and eat your cakes and sandwiches, and afterward go rolling deliciously through the fragrant hedgerowed highways and by-ways back to your Warwick lodgings, and hear St. Mary's chime out six Bluebells or six Charlies, and find yourselves hungry for the muffins and strawberries and tea, in the dark wainscoted little garden parlor.

. . . .

. . . . One day around to Stoneleigh Abbey and back in time for Warwick Castle.

Away off, in a country road, among the farms and hills, we stopped before stone gateways. A woman came out from a pretty lodge standing in an ample shaded space among magnificent trees, and opened to us, — courtseying to our acknowledgment as we passed through.

We entered a woodland avenue, that stretched into distances of beautiful shadow, — emerged to cross wide sunniness of open turf, — wound gently down into large dips and hollows, — climbed easily long, gradual swells. From this road we looked forth everywhere upon expanses of unsurpassable beauty ; pretty copses, — pretty open ; — groups of trees, multiplied into scattered forest ; their majestic, graceful lines of trunk sweeping upward clean and perfect from the clean, unblemished sward ; soft spreads and slopes of grass land, smooth as any bit of daintily dressed lawn ; vista after vista widening to us graciously, and sweetly closing in ; all these reaching to and gathered under an horizon of their own, — a sea of beauty. No bound or margin anywhere ; no highway visible, no village roofs ; no sound breaking upon the summer music of the soft wind in the leaves ; a separate world of exquisite seclusion.

Stephen drew a long breath. " I thought we had got *in*," said he. " But it seems rather to be *out!* Is there any end — or even any middle to it ? "

An end came that was but a fresh beginning. Another gate, — another lodge ; children running out to open : another park, through which still swept the beautiful roadway ; deer feeding and roaming away off under the shades, lovely in their tender fawn and spotted coats ; still only the horizon, apparently, for bound. At last a fair white building, standing in a smooth, clear extense of lawn ; a gateway, aside at the left, opened once more to us ; and we stopped under grand old trees, between which we looked through, along the abbey-façade ; many windowed, beautifully pilastered ; — a long, rectangular pile, balustraded evenly around its roofs, low-chimneyed ; a perfect bask of sunshine lying over it ; set on its even, broad foundation and lifting up its *placid* architecture with a very comfort of absolute repose; a *smile* of luxurious beatitude.

And this was one of the noble homes of England.

Emery Ann counted the windows. "Fifteen in a row, and three rows," she said; "forty-five front windows! And twelve in the end. That *is* a house to keep!"

"Lord Leigh's daughter was married just a little while since; it was a great wedding!" said our driver, with the invariable touch of his hat. "The family is not here at the present."

Margaret and General Rushleigh had alighted; so had Stephen and Edith and the Goldthwaites. They walked in through the side shrubberies, to the front of the mansion; when they came back, they stood about the carriages, while the horses rested.

"It is wonderful how the little island holds out, is n't it?" said Stephen.

"Holds out, — how?" asked Edith.

"To help round; in such slices as this."

"Ah, but it does n't help round, you see!" said Margaret.

"No. We don't see. We can't see anything here but the Stoneleigh estate. We don't know where the rest of England is. And there are scores of estates after the same fashion. I say it's wonderful how the island holds out."

"It seems to me it is beautiful for everybody," said Edith, as she had done last year, "I think I'd rather be poor in England, — in the country, I mean, — than anywhere."

"It's very well for these nice farm counties, and for those who get work and live on the great estates," said Stephen; "but you have n't seen the mills, and the mines! and you don't think how the poor get hustled out of the way in heaps in cities, to keep room for country like this!"

"So they do at home," said Margaret. "Partly because they *will* hustle, instead of taking country and working it up. But it is beautiful to see it worked up. If it only could be done so that everybody should have the pleasure of it. I think the whole earth ought to be made clean and beautiful, and every inch fit for people to be as blesséd as this in!" said the girl, enthusiastically, her face lighting with the thought of the "new earth" that can only be as the heavens come new into it.

" When men all work for *man*, it will be," said Paul Rush-leigh. " When there is one pleasure in all doing, and all delight in every having."

" Yes," said Harry Goldthwaite, — " When instead of ' every man for himself' — it 's ' every man for every *other* — and God for us all !' In the mean while, as Barbie will tell you, we must all make horseshoes."

" The world 's a smithy," said Barbara Goldthwaite, standing in the glad sunlight with Rosebud by the hand. " We may hammer in silver and gold if we can ; there 's no harm in that, — only iron is stronger ; but we *must* make horseshoes ! "

" What do you mean by your horseshoes ? " asked Emery Ann.

" Something, perhaps, like what the freemason means by his square and his compass. It 's a sign : it 's the shape of a mag-net. A thing whose two ends come around toward each other : and make one power out of opposites. Power that could lift the world up if it was made big enough, and anybody could hold it over the world that was strong enough."

Somebody does. Somebody who wants all his human parti-cles to make his magnet with, for the lifting. Some One who held his hand out once over a sea, and drew together the creatures in it for his followers to gather in great multitude ; and who bade them leave their nets upon the shore and come away with him to the gathering of men.

" We have got to be *in* the horseshoes, I guess," said Emery Ann, and touched the secret spring of the matter, and the un-spoken perception that was with us all.

On again, — not back ; more gates, more park ; multitudes of deer ; as long a drive, I think, almost, as we had on entering ; out, at length, — quite at another part of the country-side, — upon a shady road, along which we drove ever so far, still under the Stoneleigh walls ; then round, returning by Guy's Cliff and Mill, that we did not have time to stop for, only to glance in at ; the beautiful old house up at the end of its superb avenue of beeches, opening away from the high-road, behind its low, even line of stone wall ; and the mill, in its heavy sequestered shade, deep down by the river. Then home to a luncheon-dinner,—and the long, late summer afternoon for the Castle.

. . . . Mrs. Marten told us she had a friend who was house-maid at the Castle, and showed over visitors. She told us we might use her name. But we did n't. We went in the most unpretending manner, as mere strangers; asking only ordinary public favor.

Indeed, it was not the rooms of present occupancy, nor even the picture-gallery, nor any of the small inside part that visitors are shown through, that made the charm of Warwick to us. It began as we walked up the long stone slope of the approach, cut through the solid rock, whose dark faces are mantled with richest ivy, to the huge barbican, its archway opening beneath and between two towers,—"gloriously grim," Barbara said,—through to the main gateway of the double wall; whose thickness gives space for the square chamber on the left, where we saw the arms of Guy of Warwick, the gigantic Earl; his lance, his staff, the pieces of his mail; most notably of all, the huge iron basin that they call his Porridge-Pot, that holds a hundred-and-something gallons, and in which, to this day, punch is brewed on the coming of age of the eldest sons.

Afterward, in a long, open greenhouse beyond the shrubbery and pleasure gardens, they showed us the famous Warwick Vase, of sculptured marble, vast in size also, and of curious antique beauty, that was dug up at Tivoli. But with all its unknown and *broken-off* antiquity, it could not interest us as Guy's Porridge-Pot did. When we explained about it to Emery Ann, she said,—

"Don't tell me of dug-up things. I like that old iron bowl that has *stayed* up."

That was precisely the difference again, that I had felt before; between things of the altogether Past, and those that have had live association,—that have been warm with human touches,—all the way down.

But we had not got in. I must step back for you. I must come in with you through that second gateway, and say, Look round you, Rose! Look at that lovely sweep,—that great

42

circle of lawn and shrubbery, with the little daisies thick upon the turf, — shut in behind these long, embattled fortress walls and their huge turrets. See how the Castle-dwelling reaches away beside you at the left, from " Cæsar's Tower " that guards the lower front, with pleasant, spacious rooms looking from low, ample windows out upon the grass and flowers, contrasting their safe, cheerful homelikeness with the stern, loop-holed defenses of the ancient time. Battlemented, — their long roofs; in keeping with the rest; and on the river side reaching deep, solid walls down to the water that washes past their rock foundation ; but this way, with their sunny aspect, and their drapery of vines, and their pleasant door-ways leading forth into the fair garden court, hardly minding you of the dark rock avenue, and the disused moat, and the arch where the old draw-bridge was, and the frowning towers.

You look back and you see them reaching around you, their sides thick-grown with ivy, the great trees lifting their nodding topmost boughs above the ramparts, and you feel yourself, — I, that is, taking you in with me, — as you have done many a time in this old-world hemisphere, inside a dream. — Think what it is to live here, Rose ! To come out from these pleasant door-ways into the June morning sunlight, and walk among your roses, and look up at these dusky outworks built five and seven hundred years ago; rebuilt, then, in the place of what stood here, first, three centuries longer ago than any stone was here that now remains ! I suppose you would think it something to be descended from old Earl Guy !

I turned round and said something like that to Emery Ann.

" Well, I don't know," she answered me. " I was thinking. I don't know whether I should feel most like Methusalah or a day-fly. Most as if I 'd got something, or was only put in a row of people to pass something along. You see, the *Earl of War-wick*," she pronounced both Ws carefully, — " if you count all the way back, without minding stops and new beginnings, — might be, according to what they tell, eight hundred years old. But *Guy*, and *John* and *George*, — they just take turns standing under the name of it for a while, and then they 're done with. And the porridge-pot is brewed up for George, before it 's fairly cold after John. — Of course we 're all like that, one way and another; but I think I should feel it more if I was somewhere in the middle of one long name, than as if I was just Emery Ann Tudor, that never was before and is n't expected to be ever just so again."

You laugh at that — don't you? and you keep on with us, then, following the others, through the shrubbery, into the farther pleasure-grounds; where park and garden open out about you, as they did at Stoneleigh; where you wonder what has become of the town, and where the rest of England is. You see the tree that Queen Victoria planted, and the place beside it where another was, which the old servitor — " here, forty years," he says, — tells you with reverent, significant pathos, " Prince Albert planted; but it died."

Last of all you go up the long stair-ways through Guy's Tower; you step forth of a corner loop-hole, upon the parapet, and sit down there and rest, looking over into the green, warm, ivied court-yard, and off beyond it to the meadows and the river; you reënter, and climb on to the very top (if you like; we did n't, all of us, but took the top on the fresh hearsay of the young ones), where the guide tells you to look away and see Edge-hill, and where the Avon rises; (Barbara told me he said it " took its horridgin; " but neither she nor I believed that of the Avon!) You read the prisoner's names carven in the guard-room, in the old war-times; you come down upon the parapet again; and you see the light is slanting from the west, and you all feel tired, and some one says to you, " Kenilworth to-morrow!" And so you all go away under the barbican again, and over the dry moat, and down the channeled causeway in the rock, and into Warwick Street again; and never in all your life, most likely, will you see old Warwick Castle any more.

Though if ever I do cross the great water again, Rose, it will be to put all my holiday into one delicious summer in this old, beautiful, time-perfected mother-land, and try to see this over, and the rest of it.

Mrs. Regis and Margaret and Paul had had their own day I guessed, inside the day we had all had together. In the long, de-

licious morning drive, — in the beauty of Stoneleigh, — out here
in these great pleasure-grounds among the young plantations,
where they walked slowly, all together, a little apart; when
afterward Paul and Mrs. Regis sat upon a garden-bench ·be-
neath the shrubbery, while Margaret climbed the tower with
the other young people, and I sat on the parapet, at the half
height.   Margaret is not a girl who cannot take her happiness,
and walk away with it sometimes, among other people; and
Paul Rushleigh knows truly how to be both friend and lover.

I looked down over the old battlements, and saw the two sitting there facing the long, southward-looking range of the splendid, sunny-cheerful habited building of the Castle, — still under
process of restoration from the fire-ravages of a dozen years
since, but showing no incompleteness to the observation; — and
I fancied something of what their pleasant talk might be, suggested by this princely home, that is after all, at the heart of it,
home, and can be nothing better or more.

I think nothing that they three, especially, — perhaps nothing
that any of us, — saw in those enchanted days, but borrowed its
enchantment and translated it to them — and us, — by our simple human appropriation of what in it might gather just as
really round our own centres of living, though in smaller and
less grand circumference.   What *spreads*, truly, from those centres, in every possible dream and hope, that widens our borders
out from mere bare fact, into some beautiful growth, some future
fulfilling.   Is n't it a common phrase that we "build castles?"
And we all build them up from our own little, actual foundations.   And who knows how far we *do* build, what we come to
live in by certain, slow degrees?   We are building when we are
taking in, as we were taking in to-day.   Life is fuller and
sweeter, from that point on, for every fullness and sweetness
that we take knowledge of.   And to him that hath, cannot help
being given, from everything.

General Rushleigh, I know, did much of his home castle-
building with Mrs. Regis.   Her grace of taste and appreciation,
— her at-homeness in all ideas and appliances for beautiful, har-
moniously-arranged living, — her delight in his reference to her,
— her wealth of elder experience and large acquaintance with

the world of gentle ways and elegant means, — from which she drew continual suggestions for him and Margaret, adaptable to quiet scales and orderings of things, but full of charming hints of the more in the doing of the little, — made her a real architect in the ideal for them. Her instinct for comfort is surely an inherent law of harmony in her nature; for bringing those things together that should be "strong-together," in the literal meaning of the word. And so she puts back from herself with that strong-together impulse of the rest of her against a weakness or a discord, all that would have jarred, or broken, and could never have done anything else; she will not be conscious, — she is a woman of power enough to will that, — of anything that could not have full life in her, and completed relation. It has not been done in a moment, — it has not been without suffering; but I believe she will never own to herself, now, that which she has done. She is Margaret's mother; she is Paul Rushleigh's friend. Life is larger for her than it ever was before. She is large enough to be capable of her life.

She told me, afterward, things that they had talked about to-day.

CHAPTER XXXVII.

KENILWORTH IVIES.

. . . .

. . . . For that third day, we sat, for hours, in the same sweet sunlight, in the breathing pleasure of the same rich summer air, upon the slopes and under the old, silent walls of Kenilworth.

Up the hill, over swells of quiet pasture, from the ivied walls whose gateway let us in from the high-road, we walked, — as we might have walked over any remote, still, browsing-fields, in a dreamy country-side where the dumb creatures and the beautiful morning had the world to themselves, — to where, scattered brokenly along the crown, lie the lovely, desolate walls, and rise up the tall-windowed towers that crumble into the air at their tops with such vision-like softness, — of Robert Dudley's palace.

We climbed the turret stair-ways to the galleries open to the sky; we looked down into the spaces of great, vanished pleasure halls, and fancied at what window it had been that Walter Raleigh wrote his couplet, and the Queen finished it with hers; we peeped from narrow Gothic arches, that had been bower-casements, into the large, old "pleasaunce," run to a green wildness, now, of turf and shrub and tangled vine, among which lie blocks and fragments of the wide ruin; where once, we said to each other, — in her unpermitted, surreptitious stay, in the days of the great feasting, — poor Countess Amy ventured forth, and met Elizabeth, — woman-rival and royal enemy; — we passed along high platforms that were parts of old stone floors, and that looked off now, unwalled, upon the pleasant country-stretch; we gazed curiously through the shattered openings of towers that could not be ascended; we found our way forth and down, by different windings, and met each other, unexpectedly, beneath the heavy, many-angled walls; we crept into vault-like passages

and chambers ; we rested, at last, upon shaded seats, and opened
our baskets, and ate our lunch there, hardly knowing what most
made our pleasure, the old, stately, exquisite ruin and its romance, or the present glory of this most beautiful to-day.

In a cool turret corner of the front wall, looking down the
sunny slope, Mrs. Regis and I sat together a long while, and
fell into a talk.

" I thought," I said, " that England was foggy, and that London was all smoke. But what weeks we have had here ! And
how near home it makes us feel ! "

" Home is more a feeling with me than a locality," said Mrs.
Regis. " I have lived such a wandering, unanchored life. With
Colonel Regis, it was almost always army-quarters ; and since,
— I have changed about. One gets a habit of restlessness.
And I never cared to set up a mere ' place.' — But it is curious
how the home-feeling always comes with pleasantness."

" That is just what I had been saying to myself yesterday
Stoneleigh Abbey and Warwick Castle did nothing so much for
me as carry me back to Old Farm."

" They carried us to the home that is to be," said Mrs. Regis.
" Paul is full of plans. And they will have it that I shall try
that old mother-in-law experiment over again ! That I have
always said I never would try ! "

She looked at me as if she would see whether I really
thought that it would do.

" I think you are already a part of it," I said. " They can
never detach you from their story. It has grown with and about
you. You belong to it. It is life-relation, not law."

" Thank you, Patience." She had never called me by my
simple name before.

" They are to live at Lakeside," she went on. " The country-
place that was Mr. Rushleigh's. It has been let for years ; ever
since his death. The Kinnicutt Mills, you know, are Rushleigh
property. They were burned down, once ; since they were rebuilt, they have been under the management of an overseer.
Paul means to take it himself, now. The time is just expiring
in which, by the will, the business was to be carried on for the
benefit of the widow ; now, he is either to take it, or it will be

sold. He began there, long ago; but then the fire came, and the war, and — other things; and his plans were broken up. He says that his work and himself fit together again, as he had not thought they ever would. And so — you see we are all castle-building. The home is beginning to grow, already."

"You will all carry into it every lovely thing this year — all years — have given to you!" I exclaimed, warm with admiring sympathy, and sharing pleasure. "It will all make expression for itself there. Yes — I knew you were castle-building."

"I believe you know pretty nearly everything," said Mrs. Regis, smiling.

"Because everybody's castle somehow seems just as if it were a piece of mine. I can't help it; it puzzles me, sometimes, — like the resurrection of the body, — what will really belong to me, and how it will come together, by and by. But I know it will!"

"You say that as I have heard it sung," said Mrs. Regis, thoughtfully, "in the Oratorio of the Messiah."

"I say it as I think Job sung it. Even upon the *earth*, — among the human things, — shall stand the Redeemer. Even in the flesh — the real body — though 'after the skin' this body seem to be destroyed, — we shall see God, and we shall have all!"

That night when we had got back to Church Street, I was walking up and down the little garden in the twilight. General Rushleigh and Stephen were away somewhere together, upon some errand. Margaret and Edith were at their open bedroom window, above. A telegram was brought in to me, from Liverpool. I had been writing to the Cunard agents about our trunks.

"Edith! Margaret!" I cried to them as I tore the envelope open and glanced along the printed line. "We are transferred to the Nova Zembla. We are to go back in the dear old ship! The Sahara is taken off, and the Nova Zembla sails the ninth. — But, after all, they had no business to!" I added, with a righteousness of resentment at what had accidentally made me so glad. "What if we could not possibly have got there, that day earlier?"

"It's outrageous; but ain't it complete!" cried Emery Ann, leaning out her head between them. "Ain't you *pleased?*— But it's no thanks to them! I don't half think we ought to put up with it, finally!"

"They always do," said Margaret. "They change people about anyhow, going home. But they do get them there! Suppose, though, they haven't changed us all?" she suggested, suddenly.

"Oh, they would! We wrote together. We are all one party. That *would* be too bad, and we would n't have it."

General Rushleigh came through the house at this moment. He, too, had his telegram.

"We are assigned to the steamer of the ninth; we ought to leave by the day after to-morrow," he said to me. And then he looked up and saw them at the window.

"We are to sail in the Nova Zembla, Margaret!" he said, gayly. *That* way of the telling belonged to her. And Margaret nodded, vanished, and came down. "I think she was put on purposely to take us home again," he said, as he met her at the door. "Where is Lady Virginia?"

Mrs. Regis came out from the little parlor. Stephen rushed in from the street; we all held council; it was a mingled excitement of delight and disappointment. We were sorry to have one day less with Stephen; and he must return from here to Paris. But home was made to seem so suddenly near to us, — we could not otherwise but be glad. And the ship we came in, — why that almost bridged the ocean for us; made it but a step across her decks, from Prince's Landing to the East Boston pier!

An hour later, I came down from my room into the garden again to find Edith.

I found Stephen with her; they had been putting carefully into little bottles, — cutting places in the edges of the corks to fit the stems through, — some bits of ivy that they had brought from Kenilworth, — that they had run all the way up to the castle for, after we had got down to the outer gates. The short, stout little jars with their phial-mouths, were partly what Stephen had been away into the town for now.

" Yours is nicer than mine, Edith," he said, with a joking manner, but with a tone that suited rather the look in his eyes, as he
watched her press a scrap of wax softly around the stem, and tie
the bottle neck with a loop of ribbon. " Play I 'm a sick bear
and change with me ! "

She reached out her ivy to him instantly. " Only you know
better," she said, looking at the two, as she held hers near. He
was busy, now, fixing something about the rim.

" Only I know just as well — ! " he answered her, and went
on with his work. It was a bit of chain with a trinket, — a
Roman amphora — that he had worn fastened to his watch.
There was a split ring, by which it had been appended. He had
wound the chain around the phial-neck, and managed to run the
ring through the larger link when it parted in two to hold the
two handles of the little vase.

" You can hang it up by that," he said. " I have n't got any
blue ribbon."

It was a kind way of giving her the best, perhaps she
thought ; and with it that little Roman keepsake, without any
fuss of presentation. And perhaps — she did not examine what
she thought ; but was only pleased, and touched, and happy, as
her eyes and color showed, when she looked up at him, and
took it with frank, modest thanks.

" I am sure it ought to grow," she said. " And I shall always
keep the little vase ! "

And — perhaps — it was just as well that old Aunt Patience
came along, and saw it all and took no notice ; and that the three
said their last good-night together, in the long nine o'clock twilight, in the pretty little, still, box-scented English garden.

Early the next morning, when all the lanes and ways were
dewy-fresh, and the sun came up slowly and tenderly to his day-
height, we drove off with Stephen to Leamington, for his London train. And Edith was very quiet coming back, and old
Aunt Patience sat very loving-quiet for the most part by her
side, and Emery Ann wrinkled her nose and fidgeted, and
looked restlessly and apprehensively responsible for something,
and remarked after a wise interval, that " life was a tug ; there

was always something taking the seasoning out of things ; " and
when we got home it was a blessed provision that we all had to
be busy packing, and settling bills, and laying out what we
wanted for the morning ; and that we were glad to go to bed
before the twilight was over, and while the chimes were playing " Life let us cherish," for the ninth time, to fall fast and
quietly asleep.   As Edith did ; for I watched her.

And the green little Kenilworth ivy, in the bottle with the
golden chain and tiny vase, stood on the round stand by her bed-
side ; and I knew it was the last thing that she looked at before
she shut her eyes, and went away into pure, sweet dreams of all
the pleasantness it stood for.   The pleasantness of months that
had made a strong young friendship, and of years to come in
which it surely should grow old.

CHAPTER XXXVIII.

OVER THE BROAD, BLUE SEA.

. . . .

. . . . WE got letters from Stephen Holabird in Liverpool. He wrote to his sister, and also to me. You know I keep always a separate little box for separate real correspondents. I put Stephen's letter into a pretty little French one that he had given me full of bonbons. I wrote his name on the cover, in the corner, under a rose-leaf. Edith saw me do it. She had read the letter, of course; she knew by the way I put it by, that it was the beginning of regular news, that would come to *us*.

I shall let that box stand on a table in my room, where I keep books and note baskets, and such things, that Edith is always poking into and arranging for me, when she comes out to Old Farm. She will always find the last ones there; and she can read the old ones over. I think the little box will be big enough. I think it will only be for a while that Aunt Patience will be minister of foreign affairs.

The two families will come to know each other; Edith will be under the final countenance and authority; that can be asked of her then which could not be asked of her here, traveling with only me. A letter will come some day, petitioning for a letter; I know how Gertrude will do; she is a fairly wise woman. And then — oh, I shall get one once in a while after that, even; but the little violet-gray box with the roses and the golden butterflies on the cover won't be the whole United States mail any more !

We all wrote Stephen a round robin from Queenstown.

I don't know why it seemed strange, just because it was the nicest thing, almost, that could be. I don't know why she should n't have happened to be there, just as we were. A hundred other people, nearly, were; all going back to America by the best way people can go. Everybody likes June for a voyage; and of that June's steamers, everybody was pretty sure to try for the Sahara. Only, this hundred of us had got billeted over to the Nova Zembla.

And why should n't it have happened, as it did, that Miss Euphrasia Kirkbright should write to Liverpool from Brussels, to engage a state-room, the best available in the steamer of the tenth, and be sitting on her luggage upon the landing, when we came down among the porters, and the boxes, and the bustle, and the strange crowd at the wharf-edge, beside which the red chimney of the Nova Zembla stood up like the blessed pillar of fire and smoke that was to lead us children of the land of promise over?

Why should we be astonished and half-believing, when things fit and fall in, — we who are astonished and not believing at all, when they mismatch and fall out? Yet, truly, it is to me always one of the miracles of the inscrutable order, so far more wonderful than disorder, when the sum-total reappears at the foot of two columns of differently broken figures representing the same amount; and I *can't* see why the little flying needles of the sewing-machine should always catch up the loops of all its stitches. So, if I can't take the marvel of two and two, and of sure mechanics, I must expect to go on being surprised when I meet my friend at the street corner, where neither of us would be but just for that precise instant in whole months perhaps; or when I find that the same ship, in the same eleven days of all the year, is to carry us across the sea together. And that was pretty much what we said to each other, then. And then, directly, it was just as if it could n't have been otherwise; we were used to it, and took the gift " for granted."

But you are not to be eleven days getting over with us, Rose. One or two things, only, that pointed and specialized the voyage, and you will have arrived.

It was twelve hours out from Queenstown, at three in the morning, that I was roused suddenly from my sleep; from a sleep so deep that I hardly knew what kind of noise or jar it was that waked me. But I knew what finished waking me. It was Emery Ann's voice calling out in dismay from above,— as if I were accountable, —

"What *was* that, Patience Strong?"

"Thunder," I answered her at random, habitually accepting at first demand, the responsibility, and meeting it with the first available answer.

"Cat's foot!" she interjected, contemptuously. "It left off square. Thunder don't. Besides, it bumped. We 've struck something!"

"Struck something? Out in the open ocean, in clear weather, and sailing right along?"

"Of course. They always sail right along. They never take any kind of notice, unless they begin to go down."

"Well, we are n't going down, at any rate. Maybe something is loose in the hold. Something shifted."

"That sounds more reasonable." The word "shifted" was evidently a happy inspiration. Things do shift, in vessels' holds. The right term, of common use, was comforting. "But I should like to know why it does n't keep on bumping."

"I guess we won't trouble about what things don't do," said I. "We won't get nervous at the very beginning. It is only just past six bells. I 'm going to sleep again."

We both slept again for an hour. Then we were waked by that most startling thing that happens, in any ordinary voyage, at sea.

The engines stopped.

The ship lay like a dead thing in the deep. Worse than *still; dropping*, to and fro. Cradled, in that helpless way, in the water, that makes you feel as if each faint roll were a sinking.

"My soul!" gasped Emery Ann, leaping straight up in her berth, and bumping her head dreadfully, and taking no manner of notice of it. "This is awful! It 's like being dead, and lying thinking about it. What *is* the matter?"

I got up. It was fearful, that silence of the great heart of the vessel; that stop of all its strong, tireless urging.

I began to put on my boots.

There seemed to be no alarm; no movement, more than common, about us. There was not quite as much movement as common. Was that the way, I wondered, when things happened? Was there a little pause of dreadful waiting, before people dared to find out?

"I did n't expect we should get safe over; but I did n't think it would come so soon!" said Emery Ann, getting out of her berth with the strange calmness of assured trouble that is recognized and must be met. That chilled deeper through me than her outcry had done.

As I fastened my boots, and belted my wrapper about me, it all went through my mind in a strange way, like things I had read of in the newspapers. The Ville du Havre, — the Europe, — the Amérique, — all these were recent in memory. Now it would be the "ill-fated Nova Zembla.'" It had happened again, and we were in it. There would be the "list of passengers," and we — our this moment breathing selves — were the people! I tell you, Rose, one can feel all through a thing like that, in one terrible apprehensive minute, on board ship! It *had* seemed too good, too beautiful, to be sailing, certainly, home again!

General Rushleigh's state-room was next to ours. I stepped out into the passage, and gave one tap upon his door. I heard him moving within.

"Can you think why we are stopping?" I asked him.

"I am going up to see," he answered me. "But everything seems quiet. I think there can be nothing wrong."

All continued quiet. Emery Ann and I went on dressing. It was quite daylight now, and we would go on deck also. Still that deadness of the ship in the midst of the yielding waters. Still that passive sinking, to and fro.

Only just as we ascended the companion way, the throb of the engines began again; the ship thrilled with motion and pressed on. "She 's alive again, anyway! Thank goodness for that!" said Emery Ann.

We were the only women on deck. It was early, beautiful morning. The first officer was on the bridge; the captain was walking back and forth. A few gentlemen had come up; Gen-

eral Rushleigh among them; that was all. And of course nobody was seemingly aware that there was anything to explain.
They never are on shipboard. I wondered who had satisfied
everybody. For, certainly, there had been a shock, and a stop.

General Rushleigh helped us to get our chairs, and went and
brought our wraps to us. He told us when he came back, that
Mrs. Regis and Margaret would soon be up. "Had they been
frightened, — and what was it?" No; they knew he would
come, if it was anything. And what it was, precisely, did not
seem to transpire. One couldn't catechize these ship's people.
Some floating timber, it was conjectured, — something we had
just struck as we passed; and the engineer had thought it best
to stop, and look after the screw. That was what Captain
K—— said.

"The motion has been different," I said to General Rushleigh, "ever since. There is a jerk, and a jar. We have got
some damage to the propeller. I believe there is a blade
broken."

Now that was perfectly ridiculous of me, who had the dimmest possible notion of what the propeller really is like. And
yet in that instant, it flashed, like an intuition. I believe, before, I had actually thought of the "screw" as a great spiral,
twisting in the water, — and I had never heard of the "blades."
But it came to me, what it was, and what had befallen it; and
five minutes after, General Rushleigh stopped beside me again,
to say, "You guessed right. We have broken a blade. But it
will make no difference. There will be the same power, but
quicker revolution. That is all."

Only this difference. That the day was brighter, gladder,
because we were saved from worse disaster, so far. That the
night would be more solemn, more anxious, to us, after this.
That every morning would be something to be separately and
more heartily thankful for. Because, you know, in the great
sea there might be other floating wreck; there might be ice-
fields; how easily we might break another blade!

And the home-shore felt farther in a possible uncertainty, —
seemed dimmer and more tremulous to our great desire, in its
distant mists, beyond its great white surges!

; Our pleasant ship-life settled itself again ; went on. We had day after day of sunny weather ; day after day we walked the breezy, springy deck. Evening after evening, we sat in the broad stern, and watched the flash and glory of the waters ; night after night we saw the stars come out and sail across the heaven.

It was good, after all, and notwithstanding the uncertainty, to have this ocean distance to go over ; this long, grand waiting-time between shore and shore.

Between what had happened to them in their year in Europe, and the life they were going to begin together in their New England home, Paul Rushleigh and Margaret Regis had this beautiful drifting over, — this happy rest of anticipation and forecasting. Between the rush of enjoyment, the hurried grasping of things abroad, and the quiet life-long realities at home, this pause and possession of each other in a perfect leisure. There had been two wonderful tides ; that which carried them forth, all uncertain, unbelonging, separate, — this which bore them back, joined hand with hand and hope with hope, so as no breaker of rough waves, — no storm-wind out of the north or south, could divide and lose them from each other ever, — ever !

We did the same things we had done before ; there were the same walks and talks, and games ; the same groupings under the old boat-shelter, — the same hymn-singing out by the wheel-house, — the same counting of days, — the same wishings of good-nights ; and they were things, as truly, that we had *never* done before ; for the life in them was new ; we were all more and different to each other. Into, and behind the circumstance, we had gone together ; we had found each other in a sphere that is neither east nor west ; neither of the summer or the winter leaning of the latitudes ; not of that world, or of this, even, but of the Kingdom in which all worlds lie, and in which the things that are for each other never fail of their finding.

One day, as often, there was a game of chess. Mrs. Regis and General Rushleigh were the players. It was a long, careful contest of keen ability. As it ended, — I really don't know which checkmated, — Mrs. Regis swept the pieces into the middle of the board, and looked up with a smile. " Strange," she said,

43

" that the only game there can be contrived for human amusement is some strife to prove which can get the victory of the other. I wonder what games a better order of beings would invent? I think there would have to be the development of something that would make possible a mutual relation altogether unknown to us here. A new faculty of nature."

" You can play give away," said Emery Ann ; " at least, you can in checkers."

" That only changes the point of the contention," said Mrs. Regis. " It is still to overcome each other."

" Not exactly each other ; " said General Rushleigh ; " but some difficulty that each represents to the other. Did you never play both sides of a game ? "

Something strong and quick showed itself in a passing expression of Mrs. Regis's face. Something that never would have been in its comfortable calm a year ago. And yet, as it passed it left a deep light shining.

" I think life itself sets us at that game ! " she answered him.

" Yes. The only *life* that can be contrived for human beings is to overcome," said he. " But — ' each other.' Each other, is really, *each's other*. Or else, there could be no humanity."

" Perhaps the new faculty of nature comes with the finding of that out," said Mrs. Regis.

General Rushleigh met her word with a smile that might have satisfied anybody. It said so plainly, " You are one of them to whom comes the revealing ! " But they talked no more ; for he shut the little board for her, and rose to go and meet Margaret.

As they were walking up and down the deck together, Mrs. Regis's look followed them.

" Each's other," she repeated to me. " That is the rest of what you and I were beginning to say one day, Miss Patience. It helps a little to understand the *step*-relation. I used to think one only married, or came by marriage into that ; but I believe we are born into it. I fancy one must be thankful if one can but come to be ' step-everything ' at last ; since otherwise one must *stand still*, in a very poor little unsatisfied centre ! "

" Yes," said Miss Euphrasia, who was with us ; and she

turned to her with a full rejoicing fellowship in her eyes ; — "because, after all, you know, this is only a step-world ! "

. . . . "Land in sight ! Cape Cod upon the weatherbow ! "

A cheery voice said that coming in upon our little party in the upper saloon. It was cold and wet on deck. A drizzling fog had hung about us for days, and was barely lifting now. We knew we were nearing shore ; but we had had but slow work of it, since before we came off Newfoundland. There had been one day of storm that had driven all below, except a few persistent ones who had their chairs lashed to the decks, and stayed it through. The ship had lurched from side to side, with great struggling flings that had sent everything crashing. The stewards *slanted* in and out, and waited upon us with approaches and retreats like insane ballet-dancing. The dinner slid into heaps across the tables, and the cabin floors. The swinging lamps hung horizontal, this way, that way. We were in shrieks of irresistible laughter, above a smothered dread that was always praying it might not grow worse ; that the fog might not last into the night-time ; that the few more mornings might surely rise upon us.

That afternoon, as the wind and rain abated, we had gone on deck to see the magnificence of the waves. Clinging to the stern-rail, — holding by each other, — we had stood in the midst of a commotion of glory that no words can make you comprehend. Mountain ridges heaved along our contracted horizon ; moving mountains, black with their massed waters, white crested with their bursting foam, swept down their towering bulks upon us. The little ship leaning away till her guards touched the water, drifted up the impending wall, rode for an instant the great peak, the sea circle widening to us as she hovered there, then slowly leaned herself the other way, and drifted down.

The slippery decks were almost perpendicular. And the great shrouding fog brooded about us, changing continually the round of sky and ocean ; now gathering in as if to shut us into invisibility, — extinguishment ; then pulsing out again, the low sun struggling through it, making it softly golden ; — at last dropping gray and heavy, in yet hopeless rain, and the unstaying sun . gone down. Night, — and great waves, — and the laboring vessel toiling on ; the hoarse fog-whistle calling into the gloom, and admonishing us from hour to hour how it still hung over us. Day and night and day and night again ; that was how they had passed, as we came down under the chills of Labrador, — across the Banks and around the threatening capes of Newfoundland.

The sea calmed, but the fog continued. We occupied ourselves with our books and writing, our packing, making out our declarations for the Customs. It seemed hardly like a real approach to port, still feeling our slow way through blinding mists.

Into this weariness of waiting, this monotony of endurance thrilled suddenly that jubilant call. How proud we were of old Cape Cod ! *Our* headland, — outwork of our Continent ! How proud and glad we were, sailing up Massachusetts Bay ! If Massachusetts had sailed out to meet us, we could not have felt more the grandeur and importance of our coming in across the seas.

Saturday afternoon. — Word has gone on, by signal and telegraph, — " The Nova Zembla will be up by three o'clock."

Already they have got the news in Summit Street. Already they are driving down to the wharf, toward the ferry ; they will be at the old pier where we waved good-bye last year ; we shall see them standing there as we come steaming up.

We are all on deck. The sun shines out. The air is soft and clear. We see the blue line of Milton Hills.

That is Fort Warren, drifting by. There come the islands ; there, behind us, safely passed, at last, is dear old Boston Light.

Margaret and Paul stand together, quite forward, beyond the bridge. Margaret leans on Paul's arm ; but her hand is in her mother's.

Barbara and her husband are near us, with little Rosebud dancing up and down between them. She chatters over all the happy story of the home-coming that you can guess the mother has overflowed with, the voyage through, in sweet talks to her child, until the baby knows it now by heart, and says it back to them, who are too full of its sudden glad reality to speak.

Miss Euphrasia is comforting a poor little woman who has made the voyage in charge of the stewardess, — a sort of second cabin passenger; she is coming out to her husband, a young mechanic; and he will meet her on the wharf; and their little child died at sea and was buried in the water in the storm.

Edith waits with me, almost shivering with the joy of her instant expectation. She holds carefully the little ivy-plant, green and fresh in its bottle, which she has tended all the way; bringing it up on deck in sunny weather, and into the saloon in wet, — out of the close, mildewy sea-damp in the state-rooms below.

Emery Ann is counting packages; looking to see if everybody has got their umbrellas; wondering with a certain hystericky hitch in her voice, if we shall get in to catch the last Hilslowe train. Her eyes are misty with more than the sea air; it is the air of the hills that has got into them,

Gathered together, as we belong; nearest and dearest close beside each other; yet one dear human sympathy more alive than ever between group and group. As we should be if it were that other arrival; if instead of sailing up our harbor here, we were dropping into the deep, to find ourselves, presently, at that Other Land, with those other faces waiting!

I *would* write just these words, Rose, at the very last; though I tack them afterward to what must be finished out between.

Now, the penciled scrap goes hurriedly into my satchel.

Now, you will not have another syllable, till you come and get it at Old Farm.

www.ingramcontent.com/pod-product-compliance
Lightning Source LLC
Chambersburg PA
CBHW031145120726
47905CB00006B/1827